ORDINARY
JEWS

הושע פּערלע

(צייכענונג פֿון פֿעליקס פֿריידמאַן)
(Drawing by Felix Freedman)

ORDINARY
JEWS

Yehoshue Perle

Translated and with an introduction by
Shirley Kumove

excelsior editions
State University of New York Press
Albany, New York

Words Like Arrows: A Collection of Yiddish Folk Sayings, University of Toronto Press, 1984, Shocken Books, 1985

More Words, More Arrows: A Further Collection of Yiddish Folk Sayings, Wayne State University Press, Detroit, 1999

Drunk From the Bitter Truth: The Poetry of Anna Margolin, State University of New York Press, Albany, 2005

Published by State University of New York Press, Albany

For information, contact State University of New York Press, Albany, NY
www.sunypress.edu

Excelsior Editions is an imprint of State University of New York Press

Production by Kelli W. LeRoux
Marketing by Fran Keneston

Library of Congress Cataloging-in-Publication Data

Perle, Iehoshua, 1888–1943.
   [Yidn fun a gants yor. English]
   Ordinary Jews / Yehoshue Perle ; translated by Shirley Kumove.
     p. cm.
   Includes bibliographical references.
   ISBN 978-1-4384-3550-3 (pbk. : alk. paper)
   1. Jewish fiction.   I. Kumove, Shirley, 1931–   II. Title.

PJ5129.P4—dc22   2010031859

10 9 8 7 6 5 4 3 2 1

The translation of this book is dedicated to the millions of Polish Jews—Yiddish-speaking men, women, and children, who went to untimely deaths and whose graves are unmarked and unknown, annihilated in the Shoah simply because they were Jews.

May the translation of this novel stand as a monument and redeem their memories from eternal oblivion.

Contents

Preface

It has been said that the past is a foreign country but it's one in which I have always felt at home. The expression, *in der heym*, by which my parents meant Jewish life in Lodz, Poland, where they came from and to which they often referred and told stories about, was in many respects as familiar to me as many aspects of the Jewish world of Toronto in which I spent my formative years.

What is left of the Jews of Poland today? Of a population of some three million Jews on the eve of World War II, several thousand people remain. Buildings that once housed a Jewish community dot the landscape here and there but the communities themselves and the particular culture and unique way of life of the Jews of Poland are no more.

Obliterated, vanished from the face of the earth. What are left are echoes, shadows, traces, vestiges—and a remarkable novel that was first brought to my attention in conversation with Professor Dan Miron of Columbia University when he lectured at the University of Toronto several years ago.

He spoke very highly of the author, Yehoshue Perle, and of the achievement of this novel. It piqued my interest and led me on the journey that culminates with this translation that arrives among us like a star that is visible light years after its creation.

I want to acknowledge here the contributions of Professors Benjamin Harshav, Dovid Katz, Dan Miron, and Ruth Wisse. Their bodies of work have been especially helpful to me in understanding the world this novel is based on and I recommend their books as excellent resources for those interested in pursuing in greater depth, the subject of Jewish life in Eastern Europe and in immigrant North America.

Acknowledgments

I am indebted to the following for their assistance:

Arn and Fania Fainer: Arn was acquainted with Yehoshue Perle in his youth in Warsaw where he was active in Bundist circles and is thoroughly familiar with the vernacular Perle employs. He was able to clarify many of the regional variations in speech while Fania helped with the Russian derivative words and expressions.

Henya and Nokhem Reinhartz: Henya, noted Yiddish teacher, a graduate of the remarkable Vilna Teachers Seminary and Nokhem, Yiddish typesetter. Nokhem was especially helpful with the translations of Polish and Russian expletives.

I was able to discuss troubling questions with all four of them and they generously shared their knowledge with me about the historical, literary, political and social scene in Warsaw and in eastern Europe generally, in the years between the two World Wars.

Poet and translator Roger Greenwald for his close reading of the text and his inspired suggestions. I was helped immeasurably by his critical eye, and his impressive judgment. Kalman Weiser, Silber Professor of Modern Jewish Studies, York University, who read the text carefully, for his painstaking attention to historical accuracy and vernacular consistency.

Michael Rosenbush and Marian Schwartz for locating the original Russian poetry citations from Pushkin and Lermontov contained in Chapter 29. Danuta Borchardt and Marian Schwartz for verification of the Polish and Russian expressions cited throughout the text. Shoshana Disenhouse Morag and Eileen Garber for suggestions on improvements to the text.

My husband Aryeh who undertook careful readings of the text in their various stages of evolution offering suggestions of both style and content. His depth of Jewish knowledge, reading of Hebrew source material, intuitive appreciation of the novel and of the context in which it was set, his critical judgment and his steadfast advice and encouragement are as always, invaluable to me.

I wish to express my deep appreciation to my publisher, James Peltz of SUNY Press who championed this work and shepherded it through the various stages of publication.

I am grateful to the National Yiddish Book Center in Amherst, Massachusetts for providing me with a copy of the original second edition of *Yidn fun a gants yor*, published in Argentina in 1951.

The bible states: "*Hakol kol yakov v'hayadayim yedey eysov.* The voice is the voice of Jacob but the hands are the hands of Esau." As it is written: The errors are mine alone.

Yehoshua Perle taken with a group of Yiddish writers in Lemberg in spring 1941.

The photograph appears in a Yiddish book of memoirs, Wandering in Occupied Territories, by Tanya Fuks, published in Buenos Aires in 1947.

Sitting from right to left: Tanya Fuks, Nyusha Imber, Peretz Markish, Alter Kacyzne, Yehoshua Perle and Nokhem Bomze.

Standing: Hersh Veber, Shmuel Yankev Imber, M Herzog, Sanye Friedman, Ber Shnaper and Yisroyel Ashendorf.

(Of these, only Peretz Markish, Tanya Fuks, Nokhem Bomze and Yisroyel Ashendorf survived the Holocaust.)

A group of writers in Warsaw in the 1920s

1. I. M. Weissenberg   2. Dr. I. B. Zipper   3. Yoel Mastboym
4. S. I. Landinski   5. Yisroyl Shtern   6. Fishl Bimko
7. Avrum Zak   8. Yehoshue Perle

Introduction

The novel *Ordinary Jews* by Yehoshue Perle was originally published
in Yiddish in 1935 in Warsaw, Poland. Literally, the title means "Jews
of a whole year." This novel stands as one of the finest achievements
of Polish-Yiddish literature.

Ordinary Jews is an autobiographical coming-of-age novel. It is
the story of a pre-Bar Mitzvah boy, Mendl Shonash, who grows up
in squalid poverty in the provincial city of Radom at the end of the
nineteenth century. Radom—or Rudem as it is pronounced in the Yiddish dialect of Central Poland—is where Yehoshue Perle was born and
spent his early years.

The novel scrupulously recreates a complex society at the end
of the nineteenth century. We meet beggars, porters, tailors, doctors,
maidservants, tavern keepers, teachers, gravediggers, rabbinical students,
mental defectives, and a whole range of people living close to the bottom of the social scale.

The economic, social, and occasional ideological conflicts depicted
in *Ordinary Jews* are now long gone, but the social hierarchies, intrigues,
and shady dealings, the pretensions, grotesqueries, and superstitions
still engage us, because Perle has invested his characters with a deep
humanity that brings them to life before us.

The Economic and Political Status of the Jews

Ordinary Jews is set in the period before World War I, when most of
Poland was still under Russian rule. Jews had lived in Poland for more
than nine hundred years. They had privileges and obligations and some
rights. Among their obligations was that of paying an arbitrary and
disproportionate amount of taxes. Because they received no services in
return for their taxes, Jews had to provide their own.

Over the preceding centuries, a whole range of community institutions and charitable organizations had been created and refined, including

1

bathhouses, cemeteries, and a network of mutual aid societies, such as free loan societies, orphan and old-age homes, and societies for the burial of the dead, for the provision of dowries for impoverished brides, and for visiting the sick. Later times saw the establishment of separate religious and secular schools, sports and exercise clubs, scouting and youth groups of all kinds, libraries, summer camps, theaters, newspapers, books and publishing houses that issued books in several languages.

By the late nineteenth century, most of the world's Jews lived in Eastern Europe, mainly in Poland. By Russian law, they were permitted to live in a geographically defined area known as The Pale of Settlement, in distinct areas but they were not separated from their Gentile surroundings. Often they lived side by side with the local population. Among themselves they spoke their own language—Yiddish. But by the 1880s, cracks began appearing in this enclosed world that had, until then, been resistant to external influences.

By the 1880s, Jewish life was undergoing drastic changes because of several factors. The birth rate among Jews had risen significantly, contributing to greater poverty for increasing numbers of Jews. A decree in 1882 further restricted the areas in which Jews were permitted to live. Rapid urbanization and industrialization uprooted large numbers of Jewish tradesmen and artisans from their tradition-bound villages and small towns and thrust them into the larger and more overcrowded towns and cities.

Social and cultural changes occurred as well. A significant minority had already become modernized and politically active; they gravitated to the larger centres from the outlying provinces. Political forces had a deeply unsettling effect. On the one hand—anarchism, Polish nationalism, Jewish socialism, Zionism, the push for civil rights to be granted to Jews; and on the other hand, the imposition of harsher legal restrictions. Some Jews turned to assimilation and conversion as a way out of the turmoil. Hundreds of thousands fled to safer havens in North America and other parts of the world.

Although a few Jews became renowned as professionals and intellectuals and were admired for their roles in business, the vast majority of the Jews in Poland were mired in poverty, suffering hardship and restrictions. They remained for the most part simple, pious Jews; plain people who prayed three times a day, observed the traditional customs of Jewish life, spoke Yiddish, and knew enough Polish, Russian, or other local languages, sufficient to conduct transactions with the non-Jews among whom they lived.

By the turn of the twentieth century, there were a substantial number of Jews who had moved from the villages and small towns into the cities. They were mainly shopkeepers, workers in small factories, and craftsmen. Although some became urban or even cosmopolitan types, most, like the people depicted in *Ordinary Jews*, remained provincial, uncomprehending of the ideological ferment swirling around them. They were consumed by the daily struggle for survival, and they carried on as they had always done. But Jewish life was crumbling.

To the Jews the Poles were a given, they were simply "the goyim," the Gentiles, the unavoidable circumstance of their lives, as pointed out by Ruth Wisse.[1] Even though the two groups remained apart socially, their daily habits and their cultures—including languages, foods, and music—inevitably intermingled, and these had a considerable mutual influence. Jews and Poles lived in similar dwellings, sometimes side by side. The Yiddish language was infused with Polish terminology, and Goyim who had dealings with Jews learned to speak a rudimentary Yiddish. Jewish musicians and klezmer bands played at Polish festivities, and Polish and Gypsy musicians played at Jewish weddings.

Radom, where *Ordinary Jews* is set (the city is not named, but its landmarks and the neighboring towns are identified), was a fair-sized city for its time, a railway junction and an industrial center. It manufactured chemicals, glass, leather goods, metal, textiles, and tobacco products. It was located in the geographical heartland of Yiddish-speaking Eastern Europe and had connections to a network of similar towns. About 30 percent of its inhabitants were Jews. They were mainly self-employed as merchants and craftsmen; they dealt in agricultural products and were the carpenters, furriers, shoemakers, tailors, house painters, peddlers, blacksmiths, and wagon drivers of the area.

In the aftermath of World War I, the Poland where Yehoshue Perle came of age as a writer was transformed from a territory under Russian rule to the newly independent republic. This change had a harsh effect on its more than three million Jews. International treaties aimed at protecting national minorities in Eastern Europe offered Polish Jews the expectation of equality in their native land, but these treaties were more often ignored than observed. Jews faced officially sanctioned discrimination, including boycotts and quotas for university entrance, as well as frequent outbursts of unrestrained anti-Semitism. Polish nationalists portrayed Jews as obstacles to their own aspirations.

At the same time, the political situation in interwar Poland created a fertile ground for Jewish intellectuals and artists, who responded to these new challenges with energy and enthusiasm. The main influences on them were the Jewish Labour Bund, which advocated social and cultural autonomy for the Jews in Poland in the Yiddish language; the Zionist movement, which advocated a Jewish homeland in Palestine and favored Hebrew as a language for Jews; the Jewish section of the Communist movement, which was invigorated by the Russian Revolution next door; large Jewish religious groupings, which championed a whole range of views from traditional to modern orthodox; and a movement toward Polonizing the Jews of Poland. All of these groups except for the Communists were represented in the Polish Sejm (parliament).

Although most Jews continued to speak Yiddish, the use of Polish was growing. According to Celia Heller,[2] in the census of 1931, almost 80 percent of Poland's Jews declared Yiddish their mother tongue; by 1939, an increasing number of Jewish high school students were reporting Polish as their mother tongue. By the late 1930s, most Jews spoke Polish as well as Yiddish, and they were attending Polish gymnasia (state secondary schools and Polish-language Jewish schools) in greater numbers than ever before.

By the 1930s, Poland was crumbling economically, politically, and socially, and conditions for the Jews were deteriorating rapidly. Poland, at odds with neighboring Germany, the USSR, Lithuania, and Czechoslovakia because of territorial disputes, harassed its Jewish population; traditional anti-Semitism was the prod. The Austrian-Jewish writer Joseph Roth, traveling through Poland and observing the unsettled situation of his fellow Jews in the 1930s, wrote: "They managed to refute the proverb that says when two quarrel, the third is the winner. The Jews were always the third party and they always lost."[3] On the eve of World War II, Jewish life in Poland was divided between the old ways and the challenging promise of the new. Yet even though life was exceptionally difficult and Jews were no longer able to emigrate either to America or to the recently created Soviet Union, the barriers to their political and economic progress in the interwar period were strong enough to present a resurgence and flourishing of Jewish culture, most of it in Yiddish.

The Yiddish Language and Its Literature

The Yiddish language and its culture formed one of the major achievements of Jewish life in Eastern Europe. Almost one thousand years old, Yiddish came of age in the past five hundred years. As a literary language its major achievements occurred from the mid-nineteenth century until the advent of World War II.

Yiddish is characterized as a fusion language. It had its origins in the Rhineland when Jews migrating from northern France began speaking a Germanic vernacular laced with Hebrew, Aramaic, Old French, and Old Italian. With the movement into Poland, Slavic elements were introduced. Written phonetically, with the letters of the Hebrew alphabet, Yiddish became an authentically Jewish language that by the end of the eighteenth century was spoken in Jewish communities from Holland to the Ukraine.

Yiddish and Hebrew-Aramaic complemented one another, Hebrew, the language of the Bible and Aramaic, the language of the Talmud. Together, they form the sacred language known as loshn-koydesh, used for prayer, for study of the Bible and the Talmud, and as well, for scholarship, official documents, community records, and formal correspondence. Jews functioned in three languages. Yiddish was used for everyday concerns—family life, trade, education in the schools, community meetings, storytelling, and all forms of oral communication. Additionally, Jews had at least a smattering of the various languages of their non-Jewish surroundings. An entire way of life sustained the Yiddish language and also provided a barrier against the pressures of assimilation. Even though speech patterns and pronunciation varied from region to region, Yiddish was understood throughout the Yiddish-speaking world.

Until the late nineteenth century, Yiddish literature consisted mainly of folk tales, popular rhymes, and religious tracts for people with limited education. Benjamin Harshav points out that "Yiddish had no tradition of a high-style literary language . . . Yiddish . . . was colloquial, 'juicy,' expressive and powerful."[4] Toward the beginning of the twentieth century, however, under the influence of German, Russian, and Polish literature, Yiddish became a vehicle for significant cultural expression. In an explosion of creativity Yiddish poets, novelists, essayists, and dramatists began to explore and examine the social and political challenges of modern life. This development not only enriched modern Yiddish literature but Hebrew literature as well.

Yiddish literature had an impact on modern Hebrew literature because most of the modern Hebrew writers had Yiddish as their mother tongue. Remarkably, the earliest modern Yiddish writers, Mendele Mokher Sforim, Sholem Aleichem, I. L. Peretz, as well as later Hebrew writers like Chaim Nachmen Bialik and Yehoash, produced much of their work in both languages, sometimes starting in Hebrew and then switching to Yiddish to reach a wider audience. Most scholars describe Mendele as the "father" of both modern Hebrew and modern Yiddish literature. Mendele called this bilingual creativity "breathing through both nostrils." According to Benjamin Harshav, the interaction between Yiddish and Hebrew literatures "within one hundred years created the most powerful contribution to Jewish culture since the Bible."[5]

Modern Yiddish literature reflected the decline of religious faith, the disintegration of cohesive communities, and the weakening of ethnic ties.

The critic Reuven Brainin describes Mendele Mokher Sforim as having
evoked a world that was coming to an end—ghetto schools, teachers
and their helpers . . . abandoned women; widows and orphans; victims
of fires; bankrupts; beggars (especially on the days before Shabbes and
holidays); natural and unnatural disasters; charity boxes; the feeling of
being cramped and confined; and weird ways of trying to make a living.[6]

      This is the world in which Yehoshue Perle grew up, and which
his novel mirrors.

Perle's Life and Times

Yehoshue Perle was born in Radom, Poland in 1888, into the family
of an impoverished hay dealer. He studied in a cheder until the age
of twelve and later studied with a tutor. He was a diligent student
and mastered the curriculum of a Polish gymnasium. Like Mendl, the
hero of *Ordinary Jews*, Perle came from a complicated family. He was
the only child of his parents, but had several half brothers and half
sisters. According to Rokhl Oyerbakh[7] who knew him in Warsaw, his
early life was difficult and he left home at age fourteen, found work
as a manual laborer, and later worked for a manufacturer and then
for a locksmith. In 1905, after a romantic disappointment, he went to
Warsaw where he first became a bookkeeper in a bank and later in a
large mill. He remained in Warsaw until the onset of World War II.
Perle didn't find bookkeeping especially appealing but he wasn't ready
to forego a steady income for the uncertainties of an author's earn-
ings, so he chose to hone his growing literary skills in his spare time.

      Aspiring young Jewish writers were streaming into Warsaw from
the smaller cities and towns, and Perle quickly became acquainted with
members of the existing literary circles. The most influential figure of
the era was the Yiddish writer I. L. Peretz. According to Ruth Wisse,[8]
Peretz charted a course that would lead Jews away from religion to
a secular Jewish existence; he strove for a natural transition from the
religious, small-town, communal life of the past to the individual and
secular life that young Jews aspired to. He encouraged his followers
to gather folk material—the stories, songs and sayings of ordinary
Jews that he argued were as important to the creative life of a people
as the more formal works of their writers. Influenced by the Polish
ethnographers, Peretz wanted to shift attention away from the Jewish
intellectual aristocracy of rabbis and Talmudic scholars to the common
people and he sought to strengthen the claim that Jewish culture was
distinct. He believed that folk material would supply fresh inspiration
for Jewish creativity.

From the mid-1880s until his death in 1915, Peretz was a mentor and guide to young writers. More than any other Hebrew or Yiddish writer, he shaped Yiddish literature and he influenced modern Hebrew literature also. He viewed Yiddish as an instrument of national cohesion and tried to fashion a modern Jewish culture that would be rich enough to compensate for the decline of religious tradition, the absence of political power and the steadily rising waves of hatred, social ostracism, and violence directed at the Jews. His vision energized Jewish institutions—choirs, drama groups, literary circles, musical societies, open universities, and theater companies, all of which involved ordinary Jews in the creation of culture rather than handing it to them ready-made.

Perle was influenced by Peretz's modern treatment of traditional life and by his narrative style. He also was influenced by Sholem Aleichem and Sholem Asch. Perle's early work reflects his admiration for Asch's delicate Polish romanticism, his gritty lyricism, and his sober view of Jewish family life. Later, Perle adopted a more realistic approach, influenced by the Russian writer Maxim Gorky.

By the time Perle entered the Yiddish literary world of Warsaw in 1905, it was already a vibrant center of journalistic and literary activity and a unique phenomenon in the context of Jewish cultural life. Perle immediately immersed himself in reading, in attending literary gatherings and in the Polish theater. In the pre-World War I period from 1905 to 1915, there were three major literary salons that were presided over by I. L. Peretz, Hillel Tsaytlin, and Noyekh Prilutski. Perle preferred the salon of Noyekh Prilutski (1882–1941). Prilutski was a multifaceted personality: a lawyer, politician, linguist and journalist, and the associate editor of the Yiddishist daily newspaper *Moment,* which had been founded by his father, Zvi-Hirsh Prilutski. The younger Prilutski played host to young people who were interested in theater and folklore, as well as in good literature. Because he also was an ethnographer, he recruited volunteers to reach out among Warsaw's underworld and collect examples of the speech patterns—of the vernacular spoken by the extortionists, hustlers, thieves, pimps, and prostitutes of that city. Through his exposure to Prilutzki, Perle refined his interest in and respect for ordinary Jewish life.

Despite holding down a full-time job, Perle was nevertheless very productive. He began writing at age sixteen and his early literary activity consisted in translating Russian and Polish works into Yiddish and writing poetry in Russian, but when he turned exclusively to Yiddish, his writing expanded to include novels, short stories, literary sketches, criticism, and articles. He published work in most of the Yiddish literary journals and publications in Warsaw. Perle found a following among those readers who were prepared to accept literary coarseness and grittiness on the grounds of honesty. He took Tolstoy's words to heart: "The more we devote ourselves to beauty, the further we get from truth."

In the 1920s, Perle began hosting literary gatherings of his own, attracting and encouraging the younger Yiddish writers. Perle was well liked in the Warsaw literary family. He was affable, charming, a good friend always ready to lend a hand. He insisted on speaking the particular regional Yiddish vernacular he grew up with, sometimes to the chagrin of his literary colleagues who spoke a more deliberately cultivated language, but his honesty, sincerity and easy laughter were contagious. His friends called him by the affectionate diminutive, Shi'ele (literally, little Yehoshue).

Despite the regard in which Perle was held, his writings evoked criticism. Isaac Meir Weissenberg, a harsh critic, would jab Perle from time to time, calling him: "a watchmaker of a writer." By that he meant that the little wheels turn, the hands move, the bells sound, but there is no soul in the writing. Perle was not a man to carry a grudge. When Weissenberg died, Perle wrote a heartfelt article about him, praising his work.

When Perle arrived in Warsaw, it was the largest Jewish community of Yiddish-speaking Jews in all of Europe (Warsaw boasted 260,000 Jews in 1906). After the Russian Revolution of 1917, Jewish Warsaw became more important as Jewish creativity in such centers as Kiev and Odessa in the USSR came under increasingly harsh political restrictions. By contrast, Warsaw in the 1920s presented abundance and variety. Clubs, parties, and organizations covered the political spectrum.

Warsaw also was a vibrant center of Yiddish publishing. It boasted a number of Yiddish daily newspapers, literary journals, and popular magazines. More than 1,500 Yiddish newspapers, periodicals, and miscellanies were published in Poland between the two world wars, 650 in Warsaw alone. There were dailies in all of the major cities in Poland. The two largest newspapers were the Zionist *Haynt* (Today) and the Jewish nationalist *Moment* (Moment), both founded before World War I. The Yiddish press in Warsaw provided an important forum for Yiddish literature in all its forms, ranging from trash to highly sophisticated and experimental writing.

Aspiring artists and writers gathered in cafes, meeting rooms, and literary salons to exchange ideas and debate literary and political ideologies. Theater groups and cabarets played to full houses. A Yiddish film industry flourished and news-vendors sold Yiddish dailies, Hebrew periodicals, and cheap, paperbound romances.

Perle became a member of the Association of Jewish Writers and Journalists that began operating in Warsaw in September 1918. It later merged with the Yiddish PEN Club, which was affiliated with the International PEN Association. The Yiddish PEN Club became a major cultural institution for Eastern European Jews in the interwar period and it stimulated translation into Yiddish of all the major western European works from fiction to philosophy. It also promoted good writing by publishing annually the most promising first book by a local author.

Wanting to improve his material circumstances, Perle wrote several lurid romances that were serialized in the Yiddish newspapers. This type of work paid well, but Perle did not want to put his own name to it so instead he signed it with three asterisks. Perle was hardly unique in dealing with this type of material. Although I. L. Peretz had complained as far back as 1888 that, "Yiddish has no words for sex appeal and for the things that lovers feel,"[9] later Yiddish writers were able to find the vocabulary to describe erotic and romantic feelings. Perle's mentor Prilutski published an anthology of erotic verse in 1908. Members of the PEN Club in Warsaw were producing similar works, but it seems they were more circumspect. Perle was attacked on all sides and *dray shterndlekh* (three little stars) became a term of contempt.

At a literary conference sponsored by YIVO in Vilna, Perle was not allowed to read from one of his novels. Although this distressed him, it did not deter him. "Everyone writes, so I can too. I don't want to be more saintly than anyone else." Sometime later, Yiddish writer Joseph Opatashu complained, "We have talented writers who have become rich, but they breed nothing more than literary trash."[10] Perle took these words to heart and abandoned sensational material. His dedication to his craft steadily increased, and the creation of an individual, supple prose style, more naturalistic and hardened by life, became the moving ambition of his life.

In Warsaw, Perle was also exposed to the half-assimilated Jewish bourgeoisie. He ridiculed the entrenched snobbish belief in the "higher culture of better education," a slogan of the times. He showed up the ludicrous habits, the callousness and the lack of spiritual values of this stratum of Jewish society. His sympathy for the plain, simple people incited him to rebel against the "congealed intelligentsia," who boasted of their lack of engagement with the world around them. He depicted as a horror the yawning life of petty ambition, weakness, and worthlessness.

Yiddish literature began to concern itself not only with the comic and sentimental, but also with the dark, underground forces that impel great literature. Perle belonged to that generation of writers who stood at the crossroads between the old and the new eras. Before he began writing *Yidn fun a gants yor*, Perle talked about the powerful impression made on him by Maxim Gorky's autobiographical trilogy, *Childhood*, *In the World* and *My Universities*, which depicted the wretchedness of the lower depths of Russian society:

> I understand that he has unclothed himself and stands before the world Adam-naked, writing about everything honestly and openly; he didn't even spare his own parents. That's a great writer![11]

Perle viewed Yiddish literature as a bridge between a stagnant past and an uncertain future. He asks us to consider the most ordinary circumstances in the lives of his characters as an extraordinary achievement.

Perle's first successful writing venture was the romantic, sentimental portrait, "Shabbes" (1908), which appeared in Noyekh Prilutski's journal, *The New Spirit*. In the following years his literary output included the following: *Under the Sun* (1920), a novel about the big city; *In the Land of the Vistula*, (1921) a prose poem about Jewish life in Poland; the novel, *Sins* (1923), and *Nine O'clock in the Morning*. His short story "An Honourable Woman" received an award in 1927 from the newspaper *der tog* (The Day) in New York. The novel *Mirl* (1920) was dedicated to his wife, Sarah, then translated into Hebrew. (*Sins*, "An Honourable Woman" and *Mirl* contained lurid elements.) The novel, *naye mentshn* (New People), was also published originally in the newspaper and then reworked into a three-act play called, *mentshn* (People), which was staged by Ida Kaminska at the Novotshni Theatre in 1936. Many of Perle's stories, including *hintergasn* ("Back Streets") and *di goldene paveh* ("The Golden Peacock"), were published in the Yiddish newspapers. The latter story appeared in *folktsaytung*, (the People's Newspaper) in Warsaw in 1937–1938 and won an award from the Yiddish PEN Club of Poland and also the Prize for Literature from the Jewish Labour Bund. His literary and critical essays appeared in *Literarishe bleter* (Literary Pages) and in *Di tsukunft* (The Future) published in New York.

Initially, Perle wrote lyrical poetry and prose pieces, later, romantic stories. He was quite prolific, achieving his literary zenith with naturalistic descriptions of the petit bourgeoisie, big-city types, office workers, officials, and the impoverished masses. In writing about love, he emphasized the erotic.

Yidn fun a gants yor (Ordinary Jews) was widely read and received prizes from both the Jewish Labour Bund and the Yiddish PEN Club.

Additionally, this novel received the prestigious Peretz Prize awarded by the Jewish PEN Club of Poland.

In *Ordinary Jews*, Perle wrote honestly about his own childhood and early youth. He did not gloss over the fact that his father was unlettered or that his mother was flawed and weak. Perle disclosed everything unsentimentally, refusing to exploit either quaintness or charm. Of these plain people with worried faces, bent backs, and threadbare clothes, Perle said: "These are my people."

Unlike most Yiddish writers of his generation, Perle ignored politics, even though he was surrounded by a world in turmoil. In the world outside, Marxists, Socialists, Communists, Fascists, and Hitlerites battled for control, but Perle the writer remained aloof from every ideological impulse. He did not interest himself in national or social issues and exhibited distaste for Zionism. He used to say:

> I'm Luzeh Shonash's son. In my native city, the Zionists were all well-fed Jews wearing holiday top hats on their heads. They avoided my father's poor house, so I avoid them today.[12]

Perle was a sympathizer of the socialist Jewish Labour Bund, and in the late 1930s, he joined this party.

Most Yiddish writers of the time were indifferent if not actually hostile to religion. Even though many of them no longer lived in religious communities, they were nevertheless, surrounded by religion, and they often responded to it contemptuously. Perle, on the contrary, had respect for Talmudic scholars and felt an especial affection for traditional Judaism. He loved to sing religious songs and enjoyed spending Saturday evenings at rabbinical gatherings, listening to Hassidic teachings. When the Yiddish essayist and short story writer Hersh-Doved Nomberg died, a deathwatch was held with most of the people bareheaded; Perle however stood with his head covered. "This is the Jewish way of honouring the dead," he said.

Perle married. It is believed that I. L. Peretz brought the pair together. Perle's wife Sarah, the daughter of a gravedigger, had long braids and was considered a beauty. She was active in a drama group. She and Perle lived together amiably and had one son, but according to the Yiddish writer Meylekh Ravitch, their neighbor and close friend, something more than sadness emanated from Sarah's eyes. Ravitch goes on to say:

> One evening in 1926, as Perle and I were walking home together, Sarah greeted us and began asking me about youthful

exploits of a sexual nature. . . . The next day, at noon, the whole literary family ran to Perle's house alarmed. He lay on the floor, prostrate with grief.[13]

Sarah had hanged herself. She left no word to explain her action. Their son Lolek was then seven years old. After the tragedy, according to Rokhl Oyerbakh,[14] Perle lived in dread that misfortune would threaten his son and he kept a close watch over him to the end of their lives. The son became an engineer and when he married a fellow engineer, Perle took the young couple into his home. Perle formed no other romantic attachments, devoting himself entirely to his family and his literary pursuits.

When World War II broke out, Perle fled with his family from Warsaw to Soviet controlled Lemberg, where until 1941 he was the chairman of the Writer's Union. Some time later, he went to Kiev, where part of his work about the plight of refugees was published. He returned to Lemberg, but when that city fell to the Nazis, he went back to Warsaw illegally, working until 1942 in a ghetto shop and actively participating in literary circles.

Leo Finklestein says that Perle felt a glimmer of hope when he obtained forged U.S. citizenship papers, because this promised to allow him and his son to go abroad and to receive better treatment in Warsaw while they waited. But Rokhl Oyerbakh[15] says that Perle fell victim to a scam that pretended to provide him and his son with papers enabling them to escape to South America. (His daughter-in-law Yiddehs had already been picked up by the Nazis in the first round-up of Jews in Warsaw.) In fact, Perle and his son were sent to the infamous 'Hotel Polski,' ostensibly to await transport to Switzerland, but in reality they were sent to Bergen-Belsen. Even here, he was active in literary circles. On Simkhat-Torah of that year, Oct. 21, 1942, separated from his son, he was sent to Auschwitz-Birkenau to the ovens. Perle was fifty-five years old. Leo Finklestein, in paying tribute to his friend and colleague, states that Perle went into the ovens together with "his" Jews and adds:

> Allow me to shed a tear publicly on the grave of my kindly, amiable comrade and fellow townsman, Yehoshue bar Elieyze, z.l. (of blessed memory), a tear that soars off into the empty void, because just as one says after all martyrs, one can also say of Perle in the words of the Bible in describing the death of Moses: "*v'loy yado ish kevoroysoy*," and no one knows where he is buried.[16]

Part of Perle's literary output from the Warsaw Ghetto years was found after the war in the Emmanuel Ringelblum *Oyneg Shabbes* archives, a secret buried repository whose name reflects that its materials were collected during the weekly celebration of the Sabbath. Some of this work by Perle was published in anthologies in 1951 and 1955.

Rokhl Oyerbakh[17] relates that in 1939, Perle had completed the manuscript that was to be a sequel to *Yidn fun a gants yor*. It takes up the story of the hero Mendl, and his transition from the provincial town in which he grew up to the big city of Warsaw. Perle envisioned this as the second in a series of three volumes that would complete his autobiographical novel. This manuscript was to be published in autumn 1939 but with the outbreak of the war that plan had to be abandoned. Upon departing for Lemberg, Perle left this manuscript with friends and when he returned, he retrieved it. In 1940, he asked Oyerbakh to read the manuscript but before she could finish reading it, the second roundup of the Jews of Warsaw took place from Jan. 18 to Jan. 21, 1940. In the ensuing turmoil, Perle's manuscript was placed amid some bed linen to be spirited out of the ghetto for safekeeping. But a robbery took place at the ghetto gates and the bed linen with the manuscript hidden inside it, disappeared. Efforts to retrieve it by bribing the ghetto police and the city constabulary failed and the manuscript was never found. Disheartened, Perle accepted this blow with stoicism.

Perle perished in his prime with his creative talent fully matured. It is fair to speculate that he probably had great works of literature still to impart. There remains the hope, however slim, that the lost manuscript, a sequel to his masterwork *Yidn fun a gants yor* may yet be found.

The Novel

Yehoshue Perle sets *Ordinary Jews* in the period around 1900. He makes his narrator, the twelve-year-old Mendl, roughly the same age that Perle himself was in that year. In deceptively simple prose, in the language of a child, the autobiographical line pulls us into the novel. Perle captures the worldview of a preadolescent boy who lives, as children do, in the present, and he succeeds in fleshing out this boy on the threshold of manhood. Mendl devours the facts and the experiences of life around him; he revels in them and assimilates them but he is not yet capable of evaluating them.

Perle portrays the broad canvas of Jewish poverty and the peculiar style of life of ashen-faced Jews—the dreary life rhythm of an impoverished layer of Jewish society that was always waiting for a miracle and believing that fate would finally deliver good fortune. This varied grouping of figures lived out their lives in faith and superstition, wrestling with continual worry while constantly polishing their poverty to make it look festive. Poverty bred the unrealized longing and the unlived possibilities.

Perle describes his setting in gritty detail; on the opening page, Mendl wakes up and smells his father's sweaty body while cats yowl outside. Perle's characters speak in the unvarnished vernacular of the streets, but he often hints at the raw and the ribald rather than presenting it directly. The book's strong realism supports Perle's identification with the suffering masses of demoralized Polish Jews. Although Perle's insights into individual character are often striking, the strength of the novel comes at least as much from the portrayal of a particular segment of Polish Jewry as it stood on the cusp of crisis.

Perle avoids ornamental language. He is not given to moaning, wailing, or gnashing of teeth. His language is colloquial, expressive, juicy, and powerful, full of regional expressions and usages, Hebrew allusions and scraps of Polish and Russian. He uses understatement, naming each experience and emotion plainly, accurately, without varnish, and without pretense or embellishment.

Several powerful themes emerge: the harsh daily struggle with unremitting poverty and the fatalistic attitude toward life on the part of many of the characters; the dislocation of most of the adults who long to be somewhere else; and the yearning for education by the young narrator, Mendl, who is the center of the novel and obviously speaks for the author in expressing quiet pride in the life of his people.

We meet the Jewish boy Mendl, who lives with his parents in squalid circumstances in the slums of Radom where the author himself spent his early years. Through Mendl's eyes, we see both ugliness and beauty, the terrors of poverty and the power of sexual awakening. We are spared nothing of the crudeness of life under these crowded conditions. Despite the wretchedness and hopelessness of his life, Mendl absorbs two of the deepest values of Jewish religious culture: a passionate hunger for learning and the intense devotion to family life. Although Mendl is the novel's center of consciousness and the book is written from his point of view, Perle never steps outside Mendl's angle of vision, using Mendl's observations to describe the other characters. Perle establishes the emotional pattern that dominates Mendl's life. His family's warmth and love, however flawed these may be, conveys a sense of worth and meaning that is never entirely eradicated by the degrading and all encompassing poverty.

Several Yiddish writers have lashed out at the demoralization with which types such as Mendl's father confront the world. In his story *Bontshe Shvayg*, (Bontshe Meek) for example, I. L. Peretz rails against the grotesqueness of suffering in dumb silence. Perle chooses to depict the suffering of Mendl's father in more measured and sympathetic tones. Perle is not critical of this burdened man. He has Mendl describe his father, during an idyllic summer interlude in the village of Leniveh, as follows:

> Here my father was not just Reb Luzeh with the . . . absent-minded grey eyes that never demanded anything more than what was destined. . . . Here, Tatteh was one of God's Jews, one of those who together with Moyshe Rabeynu went out from ancient Egypt and stood at Mount Sinai.

Perle's treatment of women also exhibits empathy. Mendl's mother, Frimmet, is a woman who has come down in the world, yet she maintains the pretensions of a rich woman. Perle sees her weaknesses, her constant waffling between unrealized hope and wretched reality, but he also is sympathetic to her. She is a doomed, tragic figure, toiling for the sake of her daughter Tsippeh, Mendl's half-sister, who is unworthy of her mother's self-denial. Yet she uncomplainingly takes on the burden of marrying off her husband's four daughters. Perle describes the social contrasts in class-conscious terms, for instance, the wrongs, injustices, and insults Mendl's half-sister Toybeh endured as a servant in a wealthy household.

Perle depicts the envy and hostility of disgruntled, rag-tag cheder boys of the smartly dressed, Jewish gymnasium students in their uniforms—short jackets with shiny silver or brass buttons, and caps with visors and insignia. Uncle Ben-Tsion, the sedate and self-satisfied community official and scribe, is one of a class of various characters—pious, well-to-do Jews living comfortably but insensitively amid the squalor. In depicting these characters, Perle allows himself, however modestly, to criticize the well-to-do members of society for their callousness.

Perle depicts remarkable characters, for example, the feverish speculator, Mordkheh-Mendl, the *luftmentsh*, the dreamer undaunted by the daily experience of misery and frustration, who lives his whole life pursuing get-rich-quick schemes. His poverty and lack of real opportunity are matched only by his complete faith in his own abilities. Sholem Aleichem's Menachem-Mendl is a similar type who is subjected to humourous and gentle criticism, but Perle draws his character more sympathetically and does not chastise his luftmentsh for living on air. Mordechai Richler's Duddy Kravitz seems like a direct descendant of Perle's Mordkheh-Mendl.

Throughout *Ordinary Jews*, these characters move to the rhythms of the Jewish calendar. The novel powerfully evokes the various holidays, particularly Pesach, as well as the weekly observance of Shabbes. To a lesser extent, the novel also spans the Christian holidays and we are shown how these two sets of holidays intersect.

Perle describes the credulity and insularity of these Jews who are mired in old traditions and folklore, and are unable to see beyond their legends and superstitions. For example, the primitive rite that Mendl's mother Frimmet uses to chase away evil demons from her roomer Hodel, and the key that is placed under the head of Toybeh's husband to minimize, if not avert, the seizures he is subject to. Benjamin Harshav describes such characters as "inhabitants who lived in an imaginary universe, a mishmash of folklore and snippets of learning."[18]

The various teachers, from the cheder teacher through the teachers in the later "modern" school, are by turns irascible, petty tyrants, and sadists, characters acting out what appears to be an almost Dickensian parody of a religious education. Yet these people are neither caricatures nor grotesques. Mendl's teachers manage on rare occasions to rise above themselves and instill in at least one pupil, Mendl, the sense of the heroic Jewish past, as well as giving a lyrical description of the Exodus from Egypt, and praise of the nascent Zionist movement.

Perle depicts the town Mendl grows up in as harboring a number of modernized, secularized Jews, like Reb Menakhem the bookkeeper and his wife Rayzeleh the wine dealer. They read modern books, refuse to wear traditional garb, neglect religious observance, and seek escape from confining and stultifying religious belief and practice. Their children attend secular schools wearing smart new uniforms, and boys and girls associate openly with each other. Oyzeh, an older boy, the son of these enlightened parents, is rebellious and cynical. He whispers subversive thoughts to Mendl, questioning the truth of the Bible stories. Mendl, whose life until now, was circumscribed by traditional Jewish faith and religious observance struggles to resist. By the novel's end, one is left with the feeling that little by little and in time, ideas and images of a freer Jewish world would seep into Mendl's consciousness and feelings of rebelliousness and romantic yearnings would begin to throb. A curious boy such as Mendl will probably adopt modern ideas of worldly knowledge, romantic love, and sexual desire. More than likely, his hunger for learning will take a secular form; but the novel ends just as Mendl begins to prepare for his Bar Mitzvah by learning the laws pertaining to the donning of tfiln, the act signifying his acceptance of the role of a Jewish man. We are left with the sense that life continues beyond the confines of this story.

Perle's social criticism in this novel is both unsparing and implicit. But Perle looks at the lives of his people without condescending or flinching; he is not repelled by what he sees and remains fascinated by his inexhaustible, sometimes tawdry, often depressing, and always unique characters. Leo Finklestein, Perle's close friend, considers *Yidn fun a gants yor* to be Perle's most mature work, distilled from his intimate knowledge of his world, but he offers this criticism of the novel:

> The main characteristic of Perle's writing: he's too peaceful, too restful, too idyllic, too friendly with everyone and through it all, with the good as well as the bad, he is calm and his heroes are also calm. He doesn't rouse them, and he doesn't demand anything of them. Of course, he sees the social contrasts—the struggle for more air and more bread; the wrongs, injustices and insults that the servant girls, for instance, had to withstand from their wealthy householders. He depicts it all, but he is not involved ideologically.[19]

The family that Mendl grows up in appears unaware of the great social and political upheaval taking place around it. There is no reference to the mass migration of Jews then in full swing. The great 'isms'— Anarchism, Socialism, Zionism; or the modern religious ideas and the ultra-orthodox reaction to them—that affected Jewish lives are barely if at all remarked upon by any of the characters in the novel. Most of them are people whose vision is dominated by what the Yiddish novelist Doved Bergelson called: "*al kidesh hakopekeh*, the sanctification of the penny"—the worship of the penny in the incessant struggle for daily existence.

Perle does not mask or veil his people. His method of narrative is open and extremely realistic. He describes a distinct way of life and complex relationships in a naturalistic style, avoiding the extreme of brutish frankness. The critic Shloime Bickel has said that the uncovering of both the soul and the body of his characters in *Yidn fun a gants yor* "works in the same way as the bare nakedness of children at play on a hot, summer day,"[20] that is to say, unselfconsciously and unrestrainedly. Perle's language, while simple, is richly playful, with dialogue that is acutely authentic, reflecting Polish-Yiddish speech patterns. This vernacular expressiveness and ability to craft conversational sentences with which he mines the irridiscent, often comic, surface of things, are also used to plumb its ominous depths.

The way of life portrayed in *Ordinary Jews* is now frozen in time, irretrievably lost to us except in historical accounts and in literature. The critic I. I. Trunk remarks of *Ordinary Jews* that:

> This epic of a vanished generation now stands in the shadowy darkness of the past, but [Perle's] depiction of these . . . [Jews] still stands in the warm, bright light of the present.[21]

Time and circumstance render us distant from Mendl's world and yet, there are bonds that connect us to it. Perle has made it possible for us to see his characters as people: "in whose living blood and seed we ourselves lay dormant and waiting," to borrow Faulkner's formulation.

Perle's novel opens for us a window on a vanished world and the achievement is all the more remarkable for its modesty. Perle is an honest witness to time and place. He shows us the conflicts that lie under the surface of seemingly ordinary lives and takes mundane events and invests them with vivid human life. He has processed memory into art and embodied that art in simple but powerful language. In doing so, Perle demonstrates that even the most ordinary of lives is worthy of consideration.

Translator's Notes to the Reader

Because every language and every author has its own characteristics, the translator must constantly weigh both texture and nuance, seeking to convey equivalent effects in English from the original Yiddish text. Good writing resonates with echoes but also with silences. It is difficult to fathom everything that a writer had in mind, or at least what he intuitively grasped, but when the writer is no longer alive, the translator does not have the option of consulting the source. In the case of Yehoshue Perle, the problem is compounded; not only is the author gone, the whole world he portrayed is destroyed irrevocably. That is one reason his book is so valuable to readers and it is one of the reasons it poses so many challenges to the translator.

Ordinary Jews is told by a pre-Bar Mitzvah cheder boy who uses plain, every day Yiddish, not an elevated literary language. I have tried to convey this in the English translation. In addition, Mendl, a diligent student, absorbs words, phrases, and attitudes derived from a religious and cultural tradition that expresses itself in a language heavily influenced by Hebrew-Aramaic sources.

I believe that my primary obligation as a literary translator is to recreate for the reader in English the experience the reader had in the original Yiddish. This raises several issues in dealing with *Ordinary Jews*. These are: whether to foreignize or domesticate a text and to what degree this should be done; the pronunciation and spelling of both Yiddish and Hebrew-Aramaic terms; the use of Polish and Russian words; how to deal with diminutives; what if anything should be done about the author's short paragraphs; and how to retain the musicality of the language.

A frequently debated issue of translation is that of foreignizing or domesticating a text. Does one make a translation read as if it had never been written in anything but English or should it give a hint of the original language like a whiff of floral scent in the air? If translations always read as if they'd been written in the language into which they are translated, they would never expand the resources and repertoire of that language and its literature. So what is the translator to do? Should one simplify the meaning of the original in order to make the translation more comprehensible? Should one relinquish the connotations of certain words or phrases to make the work more accessible in English? This is the problem I faced when confronted with particular words that were familiar in the original but were difficult to translate because of the distance between the two cultures.

I responded to this work with my senses, drawing on my imagination and on as much knowledge of the writer and his times as I could acquire—of his cultural, personal, political, and social milieus and of the traditions he draws on. I have paid considerable attention to preserving culture specific features even though doing so presented an additional obstacle after the language gap itself. Both challenges were formidable, but I felt, not insurmountable.

I have opted to translate into English those terms that created no difficulty because they were easily translatable without explanation: thus *beysmedresh* became "study house," and *siddur* became "prayer book." But I have opted to leave other terms, that don't lend themselves to easy translation, in their original Yiddish. They are explained in a glossary. For instance, the word *tfiln* is usually translated as "phylacteries." However, "phylacteries," although accurate, is not a term in the ordinary vocabulary of English speakers. Trying to convey the intimacy and immediacy with which this item is viewed without using the original word would make for an awkward text.

A similar problem involves the term *Shabbes*. Although Sabbath would be a correct translation, I have chosen to retain the Yiddish word because it denotes a degree of homey intimacy.

The term, *l'havdil* literally means to make a distinction. It is a term frequently used by Yiddish speakers to separate the sacred from the profane. It is used when a comparison might seem an indecent denigration of one of the items referred to. Similarly, *may he/she be separated from the living* is a common linguistic formula in Yiddish used as a mark of separation between the living and the dead.

To assist the English reader with the Polish-Yiddish pronunciation of names, places and concepts, I have departed somewhat from the Yiddish standard advocated by YIVO. For instance, the father's name is spelled Leyzer but he is called Luzeh throughout because that is how his name is pronounced in the Yiddish of Central Poland. Similarly, one of the female characters names is spelled Edzheh but is actually pronounced Yadzheh. The "ay" in the names of various characters such as Zaydeh and Rayzl, is pronounced "i" as in iron.

I believe the reader would find it difficult to pronounce many of these names using the YIVO standard. For instance, according to this standard the feminine name Toba would be spelled Toybe. This would most probably be seen as a one-syllable word when in fact, the final "e" is pronounced. By adding an "h" to the ending rendering it Toybeh, I believe the reader will more easily recognize this as a two-syllable word. This accords with the reader's familiarity with such terms as Rosh Hashanah, Bar Mitzvah, Torah, kapoteh, shivah, and the like, which also use this configuration.

Other names are treated similarly unless the spelling and pronunciation do not differ markedly, such as Ben-Tsion. In such cases, I have left them in their usual form.

Today, most people who know Hebrew, usually know modern Hebrew pronunciation. But in this novel, people pronounce Hebrew-Aramaic words with the accent of Ashkenazi Jews who lived in Central Poland and I have carried that accent over into the translation. For instance, the modern Hebrew word for the autumn festival is *Succoth* but here it is *Sikkes*, because that is how the characters in this novel pronounced it.

An exception is made in the case of Chapter 19, which tells the bible story of The Selling of Joseph. Biblical names in the text are rendered in the familiar English translation and pronunciation, but in conversation and in declamation, standard Ashkenazic Polish-Hebrew pronunciation is used. For instance, Our Father Jacob becomes Yankev Avini, Joseph the Saint becomes Yoysef Hatsadik and Mother Rachel becomes Mammeh Rukhl.

The familiar spelling of the word Torah is used in the narrative but in conversation, Toyreh is the preferred locution, again reflecting the speech pattern of Polish Jews. Other words, for instance cheder, a primary school room, should be pronounced *khaydeh* but is left in the former spelling because that is more familar to English readers.

Hebrew words are transliterated and if more than one word in length, are italicized. As an aid to the reader, the glossary points out that Ashkenazic pronunciation generally accents the first syllable as in *Sha*bbes and *Toy*reh.

Polish and Russian words are transcribed as they are spoken by the characters of this novel and not according to Polish or Russian standards of speech or spelling. These words and phrases are retained in the original and italicized with glosses provided in the text. This is because most of the characters in *Ordinary Jews* have a rudimentary command of Polish and Russian, sufficient to converse with their non-Jewish neighbors. However, certain geographical references are spelled in the Polish way to make it easier for curious readers to identify the locations.

Yiddish is full of diminutives and other word endings that convey nuances of relationships and shades of meaning. For instance, proper names: Luze(shi), Mendl(shi), Frimmet(l); the names of family members: Mamme(shi) (Mommy), Bubbe(shi) (Granny), Meeme(shi) (Auntie); even the name of the Deity: Gott(enyu) (Dear God) are very often modified in this way. Just one male name—Layb (Leo) gives us such variations as Laybl, Laybtsheh, Laybkeh and Laybish. An equivalent for Tsippeh gives us Tsippeleh and Tsippeshi. In Yiddish, these word endings reflect not only the person's age, but also the degree of intimacy between the speaker and the person being addressed, and emotional shadings ranging from affection to contempt.

Often these diminutives convey an ironic attitude. For instance, take the word *mamzer*, which means bastard, but if you refer to a *mamzerl* or a *mamzeyresl*, you're not talking about a bastard at all, but about a clever, mischievous child. The term *mamzeyres* used in one of the last chapters of this novel by the teahouse owner about her grown daughter, emphasizes feelings of betrayal and the contemptuous tone in which they are expressed.

For the most part, I have retained Perle's short paragraph breaks except where the flow of the English translation allows for an easy combination.

To ensure the musicality of the language, I read the translation out loud several times. Everything I translate is put to this test—folk sayings, poems, short stories, novel, because sound is an integral part of translation for me. It has everything to do with melody, resonance, rhythm, and tone—the image together with the sound. Beyond questions of accuracy and faithfulness, my focus is always on the cadence. Is the dialogue idiomatic and persuasive? Because what the tongue does with consonants and vowels is every bit as important as what the mind does with the words. The precise order of the words may have to be changed, and some words might even be lost in translation from one language to another, but the question I ask myself is this: Will the loss be compensated for by a different kind of music that manages to capture the original?

If it becomes necessary to depart somewhat from the literal meaning, to add, cut, or even transform it, will one arrive at a transposition of the melody that, although different from the original, still occupies the same register and oddly enough, produces a similar effect? If so, I'm willing to consider it. A sequence of words may be harmonious in the original, but the words that correspond to them in the translation may not have the sparkle, the verve or the wit. One may succeed in translating insights correctly yet fail to convey their luster, the stylistic pitch of the sentences, and the sense of difficulties overcome. I return to the original again and again to ensure that I have not deviated from the intent of the author.

The characteristic lilt of Yiddish speech, as well as its spoken idiom, convey a colloquialism that should not be neutralized in English. Images, allusions, and rhythms of speech must be respected. But I am sometimes forced to replace a Yiddish colloquialism or idiom with an English equivalent. There are phrases common to Yiddish that just don't work in English so that I've had to do something different to still capture the spirit and the music of Perle's intentions as best I could to bridge the cultural and language divide. For example, the expression *skotsl kimt* is an idiom literally meaning that someone by the name of Skotsl has arrived but actually it's an ironic statement meaning "look who's here" or "look what the cat dragged in." The latter is the term I've chosen to use.

Take the case of the expletive *Pshakrev, cholera*! This translates literally as *dog's blood, cholera*!—an extremely strong and powerful expression in Polish. Rendering it literally would make it incomprehensible to English readers. I have chosen to translate it as: *Son of a bitch! A cholera take you!* This stays reasonably close to the word dog and retains cholera but makes sense of the strong expletive.

I have tried to recreate in English the atmosphere, the sense, and the impact of the original. If the reader is able to forget that this rendition is a translation and can allow the illusion to take hold that this is an original work, then I can consider it a successful translation. Yet I must concede that certain nuances will inevitably be lost. I can only hope that the losses are offset by the pleasure of gaining access to an important writer.

Mordechai Richler, the Canadian novelist who has familiarized us with the gritty characteristics of Jewish life in Montreal, once said that there would come a time when the place he described would no longer exist and that he wanted to be an honest witness to it, he wanted "to get it right." As a translator of Yehoshue Perle's great work, *Yidn fun a gants yor*, I feel the same impulse. I hope that this translation does justice to the author, and will give the reader some sense of the worth of his ordinary Jews.

א בוך פון א פֿאַרגאַנגען לעבן

A book about a life that was . . .

Warszawa   Omnibus z prowincji

Scenes from Jewish life in Poland in the early years of
the twentieth century.

Chapter 1

Cats yowling under the window jolted me out of my sleep. I lay facing my father's back, breathing in the sour smell of his heavy, hairy body. He was snoring loudly, with a rattling sound as if gargling phlegm. I raised myself up and looked over his shoulder. A small kerosene lamp was burning on the dresser that stood between the beds of my father and my mother. The glass shade of the lamp cast a flickering reddish glow through the ragged shreds of darkness up onto the overhanging beam.

The two brass hands of the clock had stopped during the night, one hand pointing down to the dresser, the second hand hanging like a sawed-off foot.

By the crowing of the cock that cut into the cat's yowling, you could figure that it was busy dawning outdoors.

I saw that the other bed where Mammeh should have been sleeping was already made up. Tossed into the middle of it was a big black splotch, a hint of clothing hastily thrown off. Mammeh had not yet come back from the hospital.

She left last night right after Tatteh finished eating supper and was wearily mumbling his prayers. I had just come in from cheder, overdressed and bundled up. Mammeh had already set out my supper. Wrapped in her grey woolen shawl, she had run to the hospital to see Moysheh, the youngest and brightest son by her first husband.

Moysheh was certainly bright. Fathers of daughters looked him over from afar and sent marriage brokers to him. Moysheh had a round face like the full moon, dimples, ruddy cheeks, and an elegant penmanship. He was already eighteen years old and working at Israel Aynbinder's bookbinding shop, where he rolled up long strips of paper patterned with birds and flowers for the customers.

The walls of our plain humble house with the four-paned window were also supposed to be covered with this same paper.

But instead Moysheh went out strolling with the girls. He went off in a coat whipped by the wind and came home late at night. Yuzheh the barrel maker's daughter, who lived in our kitchen and helped Mammeh with the housework, opened the door for Moysheh.

The next morning Moysheh couldn't get up. He moaned quietly and muttered that something was stabbing him in the side.

"Who could know? Who'd have thought!"

Strangers wearing spectacles began coming by. Yuzheh scrubbed the threshold every other day and helped the strangers to take off their overcoats and then put them back on again.

The strangers told Moysheh to breathe deeply, tapped him on the ribs and left small pieces of paper with writing on them to be taken to the pharmacist who would send back little medicine bottles filled with oddly colored liquids.

The frosted windowpanes in the house were etched with white-needled trees. Sometimes these trees hinted of a ship at sea and sometimes of an old night-capped Jew with a pointed beard.

Moysheh, teary-eyed, looked at the windowpanes. His skin, which had a green cast, was stretched tight now with brown wrinkles around the eyes.

The sweet-sour smell of Moysheh's medicines and of his sweat settled in the house. Mammeh forgot to comb her wig. Her chin got more pointed and the veins in her hands were swollen. Yuzheh, the barrel maker's daughter, black hair messy, shuffled around barefoot, praying at her iron cot in the kitchen.

Coming home at night, Tatteh looked with absent-minded eyes and asked, more with his nose than with his mouth,

"Nu, how's Moysheh doing?"

Nothing more could be done for Moysheh at home and he had to be rushed to the hospital. Just like that! Suddenly in the middle of the week, between a yes and a no, they rushed him off!

Tatteh stood in the corner, enveloped in shadow, reciting the late afternoon prayers. A confining, chilly blueness settled on the four frosted windowpanes, a reminder of ships gone down.

Moysheh was propped up on a cushion, wrapped in Mammeh's big woolen shawl and covered with his own overcoat, the same one in which he had caught cold.

Mammeh and Yuzheh together with a strange goy in a yellowed sheepskin coat, moved him out of the house. They moved him carefully, step by step, the way you sometimes inch out a wardrobe.

Everything was blue outside: the snow, the houses and the roofs. Moysheh was laid out like a thin dead fish onto a low wide sleigh, his wrapped-up face to the sky.

Mammeh sat at his feet facing him, her feet dangling in the snow. Women with frosty noses gathered alongside, wailing:

"*A refi'eh shleymeh*! A speedy recovery!"

The sleigh began gliding over the soft blue snow leaving behind two wide furrows. The farther the sleigh traveled, the smaller it got in the deepening blue of the night.

The crumpled bedding on Moisheh's iron cot was still warm. On the floor lay tangled pieces of damp straw. The medicine bottles on the windowsills were crammed together brotherly fashion, necks bent toward each other. Moysheh's mother-of-pearl cuff link glinted from under the table like a dead white eyeball.

At the hospital they tapped fluid from Moysheh's side and took out two of his ribs. He lay in a separate room with two tall white windows. A tree with twisted branches stretching upward, as naked as its mother bore it, looked into his room through clear blue-tinged windowpanes.

Mammeh stayed at the hospital night after night keeping vigil.

At home, Yuzheh who had chopped firewood earlier was now blowing right into the open flames with puffed-up cheeks. A stiff, dark cold still clung to the walls. When Mammeh returned from the hospital, Tatteh was reciting psalms by the light of the small flame of the kerosene lamp. She came in silently, eyes red, unslept, and right away stuck her head under the tin roof that hung like a peasant's cap over the cooking section of the kitchen. This is where she cooked breakfast for Tatteh, and this is where she secretly wept into the unwashed and blackened pots from the day before.

Tatteh dunked a bit of bread into some salt and asked from the table: "Nu, Frimmet?"

Mammeh, her head hunched between her shoulders, answered into the well-worn pots: "He needs God's mercy now."

Mammeh was no longer standing under the tin roof in the kitchen and the cats had gotten tired of yowling under the window. The sharp, non-stop scratching of a mouse was heard somewhere in the empty darkness of the house. The cot in the kitchen where Yuzheh slept creaked but the mouse didn't stop. Yuzheh grabbed something and threw it into the darkness.

The crack of an earthenware pot was heard. I drew my feet in and moved closer to Tatteh's sweaty back.

Suddenly there was a pounding at the door. Yuzheh ran to open it. The house began echoing with a drawn-out gasping that sounded like a cork popping out of a barrel.

"Luzehshi, Luzeh dear!"

Tatteh's gurgled snoring stopped mid-way. I sat up quickly and saw Mammeh standing in the middle of the room, swaying sideways, both hands to her head. She let them drop, heavy and hard as if from a pain from which there's no escape.

"Such a young tree, such a refined person . . . !" Mammeh rocked back and forth, sobbing.

Tatteh sat up abruptly in his bed. "Heh, what's up?" His sleepy hoarse voice rang out deafeningly in the house.

"He's gone!" Mammeh stretched out her arms as if crucified. "Luzehshi, he's been taken from me!"

Yuzheh was standing near Mammeh, shirt rumpled, looking like a black sheep. She was kneading her cheeks with both hands as if she wanted to tear pieces out of them.

She turned up the kerosene lamp. The quivering glow of the red knob fanned out onto the beam looking like a weirdly exploded eyeball. The wind blew through the house. I got out of bed and began to dress quickly. Tatteh put a pair of blue feet down onto the cold floor and searched around for his leggings.

The four small windowpanes were turning blue. Suddenly in all this blueness, strange faces appeared; a stooped old woman in a red feathered sleeping-cap who slowly, softly, head bent like a half-asleep baby chick, shuffled toward Mammeh, staring into her face. A shrill woman, a neighbor from the first floor came running in a pair of unlaced shoes, soles flapping.

Later, fair-haired Fayvl came with his dented tin can, the very same Fayvl who every morning poured out a dipperful of milk straight from the cow for us. Today nobody with pots came near him. Two more women shuffled in with him, complete strangers. One woman, a hunchback, looked our house over as if she had misplaced something here. The other one in a pair of tin-framed spectacles fastened behind her ears with two white strips of ribbon, looking like a rebbetsin who taught girls, shuffled around the house like she owned it. Her small, sunken lips muttered something to Tatteh's absent-minded eyes.

Tatteh glanced sideways at the woman, his great black beard slowly rising:

"Yeh, yeh, "the beard said. "Frimmet's son, Moysheh, my step-son."

It was already broad daylight. No one had yet turned off the lamp on the dresser. The strange woman in the spectacles pointed her finger at the clock on the wall and said: "The clock stopped."

At that moment, the door burst open and Aunt Miriam almost fell in, her lips pressed together in tiny wrinkles, her thin nose sharp and red.

Her manner surprised me. Aunt Miriam was soft-spoken all her life, she talked more with a wink than with words. She held that loud talk was a habit of the goyim. Jewish children, she said, should speak softly and act properly. She took it as a sign that biblical Mother Rachel had also acted properly and probably hadn't talked loud either.

Now this same aunt barged into our house alarmed and upset. The noise, the screaming that should have surfaced at once, lay unsaid in her round-eyed appearance.

Mammeh sat huddled and crushed on the low footstool, her head buried in her hands. She sensed that someone familiar had come into the house but she didn't rightly see Aunt Miriam. She pulled herself up, stretched out her arms stiffly and with head lowered, she wailed: "Dear sister, save my child!"

At that moment, as if waiting for Mammeh's cue, Aunt Miriam let out a wail that reached right up to the seventh heaven.

Tatteh stood facing the window. Mammeh's weeping seemed to come not just from her throat but also from her heavy, frozen garments. Suddenly she stopped in the middle of the floor as if struck dumb. It got quiet. She looked around with hot tearful eyes. Aunt Miriam, wrought up, ran to her sister. "Frimmet, Frimmet!"

But it seemed Mammeh didn't hear. She rose up tall, unrecognizable that this was really the same Mammeh who earlier had sat so crushed.

The crowd pressed together. A quiet restrained shudder hummed over their heads. Mammeh hurled herself at the wardrobe, threw open both doors as one does, lehavdil, the Holy Ark, and began wailing once again: "What use is all this to me now? My child is gone! Take, kind people!" And she began throwing Moysheh's leftover clothing out of the wardrobe. "Pray for my poor child! May the Master-of-the-Universe tear up this dark decree!"

Tatteh bent his head even closer into the frosty windowpane. The "kind" people took and the wardrobe was quickly emptied. Mammeh, arms stretched out in front of her as if she was carrying an infant to the circumcision, ran out of the room.

Empty blackness gaped out of the open wardrobe. Tatteh retreated from the window and lowered the flame of the lamp. Suddenly, Yuzheh came up to me, embraced me with big warm hands and quietly said to me in Polish:

"Bi'edni, bi'edni, khlopatshku! Poor, poor little boy!"

One by one the strangers shuffled out. Left behind in the house was the sour smell of empty bellies. As he did every morning, Tatteh sat down to recite psalms.

He swayed quickly today, with his whole head, repeated each word several times, buzzing like a fly on a windowpane. The shadow of Tatteh's head bobbed up and down over the low beam like the big, smeared stain of some weird creature.

But the Master-of-the-Universe did not tear up the dark decree. Moysheh, it shouldn't happen to anyone, was dead.

The black gate was locked when I came running to the hospital. Two lanky Jews with thick beards were arguing with a goy while a scruffy dog was sniffing around the hems of their kapotehs. Several women were stamping their feet in the snow.

Uncle Shmiel, Aunt Miriam's husband, came a little later. Hands flailing, he fell upon the two lanky Jews, and in a loud, drunken voice, exclaimed:

"Died! Neh! What d'ya know?"

The two Jews turned up their beards and looked at Uncle Shmiel strangely, surprised. I wanted to kick the scruffy dog. Uncle Shmiel saw me, smacked his thick, slobbering lips together and exclaimed:

"You're here too? Who sent for you? Who?"

And who sent for him? Who needed him here at all with his drunken voice? He ran back and forth in front of the black gate, spat into the snow, stopped the peasants' carts as they passed, poked around in their sacks of grain, asked the price, never having dealt with and never knowing whether grain grew in the field or on trees in the forest.

Meanwhile, Tatteh arrived with his heavy, slow tread. Right behind him came Aunt Nemmi and Uncle Ben-Tsion in a horse-cab. Uncle Ben-Tsion, small and round like a stuffed pillowcase, couldn't climb out of the cab all by himself so Aunt Nemmi, she with the refined lips and the knowing air, gave him her shoulder. Uncle Ben-Tsion allowed himself to be supported and in this way, he managed to get down.

He remained standing a while, belly puffed out, panting, looked around and out of his fleshy red lips he at last burst out:

"Cold! What do you say to such a frost? What's the temperature today?"

Nobody answered him. The scruffy dog lowered its chin to Uncle Ben-Tsion's galoshes, and Uncle Ben-Tsion backed off and screeched in Polish. "A pudzhes! Get lost!"

The dog hung its head obediently and wandered over to me. He looked at me with warm moist eyes, wagging his tail sorrowfully. Maybe, if he could talk, he would ask me: "Your brother really died? So what's the matter with your Uncle Ben-Tsion? Why's he so cold?"

No one noticed that night was quickly falling. A flock of crows flew across the clouds. The snow lay in strips on both sides of the highway in some places black, in some places blue, and in some places reddish-white. Across from the hospital on the porch of an inn stood two broad fur-coated girls, talking loudly with two bent-over, shadowy men.

Only then did the black gate of the hospital open and the heads of two weary and quivering horses with black ears appeared. Behind their long and untended tails wobbled a narrow black cart. Suddenly, a crowd of swaying men, black kapotehs flapping, moved swiftly like birds awakened from sleep. Women rushed about, disorderly, shoving and constantly adjusting the big woolen shawls on their shoulders. Mammeh and Aunt Miriam, distraught, pale as death, mouths wide open, were right behind the men, Uncle Ben-Tsion and Aunt Nemmi in the horse-drawn cab in the rear.

The dog followed me watching his own steps. From time to time he gave a kind of angry grunt from his damp nostrils.

A strange woman bent down to me and in a well-meaning voice, said that boys who have living parents, until a hundred and twenty years old, shouldn't go to the cemetery. So I followed no further than halfway to the three trees. The hearse with the crowd following melted together into the darkness as it swayed along toward that "good place."

Nobody accompanied me home except for the strange scruffy dog rocking at my feet, grunting at his own footsteps.

At our door he stopped ahead of me. Did he know that I lived here? Why'd he prick up his ears?

I stopped also, and shouted into the dog's alert ears:

"What's your name? Burek?"

The dog wagged his head from side to side looking as if it was shaking off so common a name as Burek.

So I called out other dog names: "Lapa? Buket?"

No. He still wagged his head sideways.

I was cold; the heavy overcoat weighed my shoulders down. So for the last time, I yelled into the dog's ear: "Good night, dog."

He grunted at his own footsteps and lay down on the snow with paws stretched out toward the door of our house.

৵৽

I went inside. Yuzheh was sitting alone at the small table in the kitchen where the kerosene lamp stood, chin cupped in both hands, staring distractedly into the bluish-red flame. She quickly dropped her hands when I came in and stood up hastily.

"It's already after the funeral?"

"No, not yet."

"You didn't go with them?"

"Only to the three trees."

"You're hungry, yeh?"

"No, I'm not hungry."

"And you're cold, yeh? Come here. Sit down."

She took charge of me the way you take charge of a sack of cotton padding or feathers. She sat me down beside her and embraced me with big warm hands talking right into my mouth:

"Warm yourself. Warm yourself good."

She blew onto my stiffened fingers, took them into her mouth, then rubbed them between her hands.

"Maybe you'll lie down, yeh?"

I don't know whether I answered her or not, but she left me sitting at the table and went into the other room to get Tatteh's bed ready. Then she undressed me, led me into the big room and tucked me in with the bedding up to my chin. She sat at my feet as my mother had once done when I was sick with scarlet fever.

"They'll come soon, don't you think?" Yuzheh suddenly asked me.

"They'll probably come after the funeral."

"When after the funeral?"

"I dunno."

Yuzheh got up and went into the kitchen. I heard her fumbling with the lock on the door.

It was good and dark in the house now; only a thin strip of light showed from the kitchen doorway.

She came back, sat back down on my bed but this time, not at my feet. She gave off a sweaty, sultry smell, sweet to the taste and the nose. I'd never smelled anything like it from a human being before.

"Ar'ya warm now?" She bent her big face to me.

"A little," I answered. I felt Yuzheh's smell in my throat, and somewhere deep in my insides.

"Soon you'll be warm all over."

I heard two deafening thuds on the floor. Yuzheh had thrown off first one shoe, then the other.

"Soon, soon," she breathed hoarsely, trembling.

Chilled, tired, half in dream, I saw how she took off the red caftan and unlaced the coarse cotton tunic; it must be that the laces had knotted somehow because her breathing became short-winded, panting. She threw out in Polish into the dark:

"*Pshakrev, cholera* . . . ! Son of a bitch! A cholera take it . . . !"

But that didn't last long. The bedding suddenly heaved and I soon felt the big warm body of Yuzheh beside me.

My throat tightened. It must be from fear or surprise, so I moved quickly over to the wall.

"C'mere, closer," she pulled me toward her.

"You'll be warm right here. Give me your hands, Nu? Warm?"

"Warm."

"Bend your head closer. Like that . . . Nu? Warm?"

"Warm."

"Your mouth is so cold, my little man. Your poor mouth is frozen."

I pulled in my legs. The bed had become crowded, but I didn't understand why. I always slept here with Tatteh. How come it was never crowded with him? How come his body was never on fire? And why was I now so different? Could it be because her lips didn't stop warming my frozen mouth?

I don't know how I managed to fall asleep. I didn't hear Yuzheh leave and I didn't hear Tatteh and Mammeh come back.

When I opened my eyes again, Tatteh was sitting on the bed, his legs toward the door, pulling at his boots. Mammeh, her head wrapped in a little shawl, sat huddled on a small stool like a child, rocking herself from side to side. Yuzheh was chopping firewood in the kitchen with quick spare strokes as if she was mad at somebody.

Yeh, Yuzheh! What was the matter with her? Why was she chopping wood? How long was it since she had warmed my mouth? Tatteh was already sitting on the bed beside me, his back turned to me. Yuzheh was in the kitchen. It was daylight. On the grey walls, long in need of lime, a sleepy greenish light played.

A small blue flame of oil emanated from a thick glass on the windowsill. Tatteh finished pulling off his boots. His big, yellowed tallis-kotn lay wrinkled on his back like a worn out page from an old bible. He turned his beard toward me in the bed and said:

"Get up, we'll soon be davening."

He put his arms into the sleeves of his old robe and went outside.

He quickly came back with two small surprised Jews who looked around the house strangely. Tatteh left them standing and went out again. He did this several times, until our house was full of unkempt, bearded strangers wearing chilly, everyday kapotehs.

A quick, dry murmur carried from the window to the wall and back again. Flattened and broken shadows played on the dresser and on the wardrobe right up to the beam, as if the very house itself had become too crowded.

Mammeh moved away toward the stove with her footstool. Yuzheh stood from time to time at the open door with a piece of kindling in her hand. I huddled among the chilly kapotehs of these strange Jews and was afraid to look over to where Yuzheh was standing.

The fringes of the prayer shawls were dragging on the floor like white worms. A Jew with hunger in his voice, swallowing his words loudly, swayed from side to side over the table.

Tatteh who was standing opposite me, placed his hand firmly on my shoulder and with his face showed me in the prayer book:

"Nu, here."

After the davening, Jews began shuffling out. Their heavily caked boots scraped uncomfortably on the floor. They passed Mammeh's low stool and muttered something to her.

A damp smell of old cotton padding and worn clothes hung in the air. Two prayer shawls with yellowed fringes lay scattered on the table. Tatteh was carefully unwinding the hard greasy leather straps of the tfilin from his cold and blue-tinged hands.

This is how it went the whole week of sitting shiveh. Mammeh almost never got up from her footstool. Yuzheh, when she finished chopping firewood and the fire was already banked, also sat herself down on a footstool and just like Mammeh, rocked herself from side to side.

The aunts who came in the evening to comfort the mourners brought with them the silence of the snow outside. They sat with us a while, eyes downcast, half-dozing, didn't take off their outer clothing, didn't speak to anyone, not even a single word. They sat, left without saying good-bye, shrugged their shoulders and went off to their own homes where no one had died and no one had to sit shivah.

Only the two uncles let themselves be heard from. One of them, Uncle Shmiel, he with the flailing hands, couldn't forgive Moysheh for dying. The second one, Uncle Ben-Tsion, kept rubbing his fleshy little hands together and constantly complained to the Master-of-the-Universe: "What d'ya say to that? What a winter we've got! Why, coal is worth as much as gold! So I said to my wife . . ."

At this, Aunt Nemmi half-closed her placid eyes and with something of the rich woman's lilt, hinted, "Ben-Tsion, maybe we'll leave now . . . Eh, Ben-Tsion?"

Chapter 2

People didn't come into our house to comfort the mourners anymore. A photograph of Moysheh that Mammeh had framed, appeared on the dresser. Moysheh didn't have a round face or ruddy cheeks in this photograph. Instead, a thin young man with a pale frightened face stood on the lifeless paper, one hand white, the other black looking like it was covered in a rubber glove. He looked stiffly to one side as if he didn't recognize anyone in the house.

Another photograph arrived soon after, all the way from Yekaterinoslav where Laybkeh, Tatteh's son by his first wife, was serving in the Russian army.

He was a different type altogether from Moysheh with a different look and a different kind of figure. Laybkeh was tall, had a trimly pointed mustache, epaulettes and buttons, wore a round cap without a peak, and he sat sprawled at a table, grim-faced. He had a sharp-eyed expression on his face as though he saw the enemy coming at him with rifles and swords.

Tatteh moved the kerosene lamp closer in order to better study Laybkeh's photograph. At the same time, his big black beard looked as if it was parted in two, one part light, the other dark. Tatteh stuck his tongue out in great concentration and slowly ran the point of it from one corner of his mouth to the other, from the light side to the dark side.

"What d'ya say to my Laybkeh?" He said into the photograph. He moved it a bit farther away, then brought it closer and continued studying his son's portrait.

"He's gotten to be quite the officer in their army!" He meant these words for Mammeh so that she would answer agreeing with him that Laybkeh had really become a somebody. But Mammeh had seen this photograph earlier. She had already cried lots of tears staring at her own son's portrait. Blowing her nose and sighing deeply, with her head to one side, she muttered:

"And my poor Moysheh lies in the ground . . ."

Now that Tatteh was talking, her head drooped to one side. Her nose sniffled but she didn't answer.

Tatteh wasn't a big talker. Absent-mindedness always lay in his half-dreamy eyes. He looked at a person, not into their eyes but at their mouth, as if he didn't have too much trust in their talk. Mammeh actually believed that he was hard of hearing and she spoke to him louder than usual. Tatteh liked to wander around the house in a warm quilted jacket, fixing a stool, rewinding the clock, cutting up pieces of toilet paper, so that if Mammeh spoke to him louder than usual, he would stop in the middle, raise his big, black-overgrown face, and stare at her dreamily:

"Why're you yelling at me? What am I? Deaf?"

"What then, you can hear?" Mammeh gave her judgment on him once and for all and on no account would she give in that he wasn't deaf.

Tatteh turned away from the table with Laybkeh's photograph, toward the bed where Mammeh was sitting. In his look was the uncertainty of meeting a person and not knowing if you really knew him or not.

"You're talking so quietly today," he observed.

"I'm not saying anything. Who says I'm talking?"

"So what did'ya say?"

"I didn't say anything. Leave me alone!"

Tatteh looked at Mammeh's mouth, the deafening silence shadowed in his eyes. She looked like a stranger now, someone not from these parts. Tatteh turned, looked at me and raised one eyebrow:

"We have to write Laybkeh . . . to Yekaterinoslav. . . . We have to write."

What he meant was that if he could, he would write such a letter himself, right now, today, but because he had to depend on Mammeh for writing, he had no other choice but to wait until she'd be in a better mood.

Meanwhile, he put Laybkeh's photograph into a dresser drawer among the clean laundry. From time to time, mostly on Shabbes evening after Havdoleh, he'd open the drawer, take out Laybkeh's photograph, look at it again and remember that he needed to write him a letter to Yekaterinoslav. But Mammeh was still not in a good mood and still didn't have a head for him or for his son Laybkeh.

It was a long and hard winter that year. Swollen icicles hung on the pump in the courtyard as if heavy pieces of glass were poured out of it. The contents of the slop pails, that had been poured out earlier, congealed overnight in the gutters. The lock on the outside of the door was icy and glinted silvery. At night, the walls of the kitchen where Yuzheh slept glistened with blue-green dampness. This same dampness also settled on the wall where Tatteh's bed stood. The iron stove with its half-rusted, tin pipes under the low beam in the middle of the house didn't help; the lime used to seal the cracks near the window didn't help; nor did the cotton padding between the double windows frozen in ice all winter long—that didn't help either. Tatteh didn't mind. He slept dead tired but around four o'clock in the morning, he began to stir, ready to get up.

He got up early because that winter he'd become a partner with another Jew named Mottl Shtroy. This Mottl was tall and lanky, with an Adam's apple bobbing in his throat, a pointed wispy, beard and long, thin hands that couldn't find a place for themselves.

All his life, Mottl Shtroy wheeled and dealed among peasants' wagons, chewing a straw between his teeth and poking into strangers' sacks of grain. From time to time, he ran into Mordkheh Gorkikher's soup kitchen to grab a piece of yesterday's goose and at the same time, to stash the accumulated banknotes into a long leather pouch. He did this for so long until he came up with a proposition that Tatteh should become his partner.

"It's possible," he said, "to buy up a large store of hay, good quality." Mottl would put up the money and Tatteh would provide the "expert judgment."

More than expert judgment Tatteh didn't have. In the village of New Mill, where Tatteh came from, there were great tracts of fields surrounded by dark blue forests. The little houses of New Mill were simple, made of rough lumber with thatched roofs and earthen floors. There they ate sour milk in big earthenware bowls and baked flat loaves of bread. Summertime they bathed in the river, slept under haystacks, and stared out at the fields. Tatteh must have brought his expert judgment about hay with him from that village.

So now after Moisheh's death, life took on a new look.

When Tatteh finally began stirring, night still lay sleepy on the frosted windowpanes. From time to time, his long drawn out yawns cut into the cold dark house. I turned my face to the bluish wall and waited impatiently for Tatteh to put down a foot already, so I could inherit the whole bed. But Tatteh was waiting for a sign, a signal that would make him get out of such a warm bed.

The signal came. Every dawn almost at the same time, there was a rapping of fingers on the windowpane and a clear, shivering voice called out:

"Pan Merchant! Pan Merchant!"

It was old Matshey the peasant, with the horse and cart with whom Tatteh traveled to the villages to buy hay from the landowners.

Tatteh groaned heavily and stuck his feet out into the chilly room. He turned up the kerosene lamp that blinked like an awakened eye. Tatteh busied himself with one of his legs by the red glare of the flame. For many years, he had been bothered by festering pus on one of his shins. There was a blue-red burned spot around a small open sore that Tatteh treated with green onion leaves that grew in an earthenware pot on our windowsill.

Finished looking after his leg, he yawned, groaned, remembered that old Matshey was waiting for him outside and opened the door to let him in. The tall peasant came in blue with cold, wearing a smelly and yellowed sheepskin coat, whip in hand and stood like a scarecrow, waiting for "Pan Merchant" to finish getting ready.

"Pan Merchant" was busy scrubbing himself over the slop pail and davening more vigorously than usual. Mammeh squirmed in her bed like a worm, groaning into the pillows:

"A depressing livelihood this is! You can't even close an eye!"

But Tatteh didn't hear. Yuzheh, the barrel maker's daughter, stuck out her black sheeplike head from under the coverlet, stretched out her bare hands and in a lazy, well-rested voice asked:

"Little Father, d'ya have a son?"

"Sure I do," the peasant answered, turning toward Yuzheh's bed.

"A young one, your son?"

"A young one, of course a young one."

"So send him here, little father, send him here."

"He's already got a wife, he doesn't need another one."

"He does? So what? I can also be a wife."

Tatteh was davening loudly as he wandered around the house. The conversation between Yuzheh and the peasant became tangled up in his prayers. Mammeh's bed began scraping vigorously.

"Luzeh!" she called out, "Luzeh, maybe a little quieter?"

But this too, Tatteh didn't hear. By the time he closed the door, Mammeh had tossed and turned in bed more than once, and had occasion a few times to remember her deceased first husband, may he be separated from the living, with whom she had the luxury of living in a house with brass handles on every door.

After Tatteh left, a restful stillness descended like after the passing of a wagon over rutted stones. The lamp was still burning. Mammeh groaned with relief. In my dreamy state, I still heard:

"A young one? Bring him here, little father."

I understood what Yuzheh meant. I quickly remembered that evening when Yuzheh had warmed me up but some time had passed since then and it seemed that she had forgotten about me altogether. Many times, I came home frozen stiff and found no Tatteh, no Mammeh in the house, only Yuzheh sitting all alone at one end of the kitchen table, wide-eyed, staring at the flickering red flame ringed with blue. I had to undress, take off the grey overcoat, look in the pots for something to eat, all by myself, and I even had to make my own bed. Yuzheh didn't see me.

But once, actually for the last time, she called out to me,

"Come here, little one," she said, taking her fixed eyes away from the lamp and pressed me against her coarse cotton vest. She bent her face to mine, rubbed her nose against mine, and in a hoarse voice, asked:

"Did'ya tell your mother?"

I froze. "No," I said. "I didn't tell."

"Are'ya sure?"

"I'm sure."

"Swear!"

"I should live so long!"

My face found itself between her two hands.

"D'ya want a kiss? Yeh?"

I couldn't answer. As the last time, everything tightened in me.

"You want like the last time? Yeh?"

Yuzheh didn't wait for an answer but suddenly turned the lamp down. She quickly removed my clothes in the dim light. I understood that I should stay quiet.

"Here, by me." Yuzheh's voice became hoarser and her hands warmer.

"Come here, little one. Now! For the last time! I'm leaving here. You didn't tell?"

"No," I gasped, my face buried in her flesh.

"Your mother told me to go. You're sure you didn't tell?"

"I'm sure."

"So why's she telling me to go?"

"I dunno."

I couldn't say more. My body was burning. I was in pain from my head right down to my toes.

"Don't bite!" Yuzheh breathed, laughing right into my face: "Heh-heh, you're already a big boy, really big."

I couldn't account for what was happening but I wanted the pain to last as long as possible.

Suddenly, I had a feeling of emptiness, hollowness. Something came away from me. Something was taken from me. My heart was burning. It seemed to me that a piece of my body had been cut out of me.

"Why're you crying, you foolish calf?" Yuzheh's voice rolled out in the dark. "Such a big boy doesn't cry anymore. Nu, come here, you dog you."

But I gritted my teeth, tore myself out of her arms, rolled off the bed onto the floor and there on the floor, I began to cry loudly.

Yuzheh quickly turned up the lamp. Her round and messy sheep-like head was twice as large as ever. She stood over me, pulled on her vest, tied the laces, and threw out into the dark:

"I won't play with you anymore. You're a fool! A snot-nose! Come on now!"

She pulled me up. "If y'ever tell!" she warned me stiffly with a fist in front of my nose.

I shook my head, sniveling. I wouldn't tell.

Mammeh came home late. She seemed preoccupied. I couldn't eat supper and she didn't ask me why. It was as if she didn't see me. The chimney grates were cold, empty, and black.

Tatteh came home even later than she. He brought the bitter cold into the house with him in the very fabric of his clothes. Sighing deeply he pulled off his boots. My heart wept. Mammeh must have noticed something after all. She sat next to me on the bed. In a half-dream that stabbed at my eyelids, I heard her say to Tatteh: "It seems to me that Mendl has a bit of fever."

"Fever?" Tatteh somewhat deaf, repeated, all the while busy with his own leg, and replied: "If he's got fever it must be itching. Give me the onions."

I didn't hear the rest but later when he got into bed, I woke up and turned over to face the wall, as if I was afraid that he'd sense the change that had taken place in my red-hot flesh.

Chapter 3

There was a reason why Mammeh didn't notice anything unusual about me that evening and why she didn't even bother asking me why I wasn't eating. As I realized later, she was wrapped up in her own thoughts. You could see it in her pursed lips and in her anxious uneasy eyes that stared at everything and everybody.

I wasn't fooled and a week later, her worries surfaced like oil on water.

It was snowing that evening and Tatteh came home earlier than usual covered in white fluff like a featherbed. His beard, his mustache, the folds of his plush cap and his shoulders were covered with snow.

Mammeh wasn't at home. Moysheh's death chased her out of the house. She sat day and evening at the neighbor's or at Aunt Miriam's, talking about the wonders of her son Moysheh.

Tatte came home that evening and found empty pots, a cold clean chimney grate, and me, newly arrived from cheder, still bundled up in my overcoat. Glancing around, his weary absent-minded eyes took in the damp and dreary walls, the sight of Yuzheh the barrel maker's daughter kneeling at an open trunk, and in a dry, hollow voice, he asked:

"Where's my wife?"

"Pani Frimmet's not here," Yuzheh answered, talking into the trunk.

"That she isn't here, I can see for myself. But where'd she go?"

"She didn't tell me."

"Maybe she's inside?"

"No, she left this morning."

"This morning? Where'd she go?"

"I told you, I dunno." Yuzheh answered, almost angrily.

"Neh!" Tatteh shook his head, and moving heavily, began to take off his outer clothing.

"And you, Mendl, you just now came from cheder?"

"Yeh."

43

"Did'ya eat yet?"

"No, not yet."

"Are'ya hungry?"

"No, not much."

"So where's your Mother?"

"She must be at Aunt Miriam's."

"Maybe you'll take a run over there?"

No small distance! Aunt Miriam lived at the other end of town, among the kosher butcher shops. You had to go through the Central Market, Shoemakers' Lane, the whole length of Warsaw Street and at last, near the goyish hospital, there was Aunt Miriam's place. I was always glad to go.

Aunt Miriam lived in a separate wooden hut surrounded on all sides by wind and sky. The floor was yellowed from scrubbings three times a week. Gleaming copper frying pans with their backs shiny like mirrors hung from the walls. The white-glassed cabinet was always full of four-pound loaves of bread, dried farfl, and aged cheese from Pinczow—ready for everybody who came.

So was it any wonder that I put on my overcoat again and went out to Aunt Miriam's to look for Mammeh?

The snow was soft and deep. I walked quietly as if afraid of waking up those who were really sick.

I had to go through Shoemakers' Lane, with its narrow and crooked sidewalk. On one side, hunched low roofs over shabby huts; on the other side, a peeling building with crumbling chunks of mortar.

In this building there was a room with a red door where the kosher, milky-faced Dobreleh lived. She had come back from Buenos Aires wearing a broad-brimmed black hat. It was said of this Dobreleh that she came back a pious woman. Why she even washed her hands and made a blessing over thunder! The landed gentry drove up to her door in coaches and even though she slept with them, nevertheless, she loudly recited the bedtime prayer. Dobreleh had taken a fancy to the cheder boys. When evening came and coaches didn't come, red-faced Dobreleh would appear at her door and grab the cheder boys with whom she also recited the bedtime prayer.

So, it was better for me to avoid Shoemakers' Lane altogether and go by way of the boulevard. The snow fell bluer and softer here than in the Central Market. At the narrow, pointed German church that stood right here among the small parks and gardens, a bent figure now knelt crossing itself, having fallen into the downy snow.

It was still far to Aunt Miriam's. The jail rose up before me with its yellow, high-walled fence. A fur-covered sentry paced back and forth, rifle on his shoulder. You weren't allowed to go past him, so you had to cross to the other side. From there you went to Jailhouse Alley and after that, onto Warsaw Street itself. The way to Aunt Miriam's was as familiar to me as my own ten fingers.

I went confidently. Right here was Shimshen-Shloymeh's tavern. Further along was the big Russian-Orthodox church. Right here should be a red wooden stall where the guards warmed their frozen fingers.

But I didn't see any stall. Could it be because now the snow whipped my face on both sides? I saw as if it was right on top of me, something tall and overgrown, singing. It was a wonder to me! How could you sing when the snow was whipping your face? It turned out that there was no one there, no one was singing. I was actually standing at a long crumbling building. Nothing else but I had wandered into Shoemakers' Lane and was sidling along the building where the kosher, milky-faced Dobreleh lived.

But it wasn't that building either, it was actually the fence of the goyish hospital. So not far from here must be where Aunt Miriam lived. It seemed to me that over there was that little hut—yeh, right there, the two lit-up windows. But I couldn't find the wooden vestibule that stood attached to the building like a child to its mother's apron. I couldn't see the low, round pump either.

I heard a bell ringing; a sleigh gliding past in front of my eyes and I heard the refrain:

> "Little boy, little boy, where are you going?
> Little boy, little boy, where are you standing?"

I didn't know where the sound came from, whether from the sleigh passing by or from Aunt Miriam's hut. Maybe I was reminded of crazy Mordkheh Hokkeh, the Hook. He had a habit of boxing your ears to that refrain.

I was standing . . . no, it must be that I was actually lying . . . it was soft . . . warm . . . it tickled my nose . . . my eyes got heavy. . . . Yeh, I was lying with my face to Tatteh's back but I didn't smell the familiar odor of his hairy body. It was another odor I smelled. You smelled such an odor on Fridays in the kosher butcher shops but it wasn't Friday today. Yeh, I remembered now. I knew . . . ! Tatteh was hungry . . . it was really a wonder to me about him. He was already asleep, so how could he be hungry in the middle of sleeping?

I couldn't figure it out anymore. All around me it was blue and hot and I was choking, lying on a high bed wrapped in a featherbed and pillows. A burning smell of press irons hung in the room. A shrunken old face in a red nightcap bent over me.

"Swallow!" said the red nightcap, and shoved a big wooden spoon into my mouth.

"Swallow, my dear Mendelshi . . . it's magnesia with almond milk. It'll bring down the fever."

At the foot of the bed, like a cross, stood a thin, straight Jew with a small white beard, in an unbuttoned vest, buckles hanging loose. He held a piece of white thread that wriggled like a skinny worm in his mouth and a tailor's tape measure hung from one shoulder, green with black markings like a snake crawling down out of the other side of his sleeve. He kept moving the piece of thread between his lips, bit off pieces with his teeth, spit them out and kept on shaking his head.

"Swallow . . . swallow! Neh! What do you think of that? Sending a child out in such a blizzard!"

So, I had fallen not into Aunt Miriam's house, but into Bubbeh-Zaydeh's. That sunken old face shoving the wooden spoon into my mouth was actually Bubbeh Rakhl herself, the same Bubbeh who was always heaping curses on my mother because she didn't take any responsibility for her own children. This was Bubbeh Rakhl who day and night sat on a small wooden trunk, staring through wire-rimmed glasses that had only one lens, sewing stiff white muslin caps for pious old women. That lanky Jew over there, the one standing at the foot of my bed was actually Zaydeh—Duvid-Froykeh's the Tailor, in a long, black cape and a hard yellowed hat. He loved his liquor and when Shabbes ended, he would go off to one of his cronies for a game of cards till all hours of the night.

Nu, so what? He was a good Zaydeh and it was a great pleasure to visit him. He was indeed a tailor but different from the other ones. He didn't take on customers for kapotehs, jackets or pants, but only accepted orders to sew garments for the students of the Russian gymnasium. Short navy-blue uniforms with a slit up the back, silvery white buttons, each and every one of which Zaydeh himself sewed on with his own ten fingers.

Zaydeh pulled the pieces of thread through a yellow veined piece of wax. Sitting on a backless high stool, one leg bent over the other, he drew the needle quickly up and down, all the while singing:

"Success lies in the plow
That's a good life now."

When he got tired of 'the plow,' he took his right foot down from his left one, threaded the needle with a fresh piece of thread, drew it through the wax and began to sing another tune with different words:

> "You're pretty my darling, like pure gold
> Others I got rid of but you're the one I hold . . ."

Bubbeh Rakhl sitting on her little trunk, raised her small, shrunken face, looked over her wire-rimmed spectacles and in an angry and disagreeable voice, she threw out:

"Maybe, you'd stop with your tunes already?"

"Why's my kosher little wife so jealous?"

"Nu, stop already, you moron."

But Zaydeh didn't stop. He only shook himself off, pushed the needle even faster, and began to sing a melody from the Gemorah,

"So," he rocked his head sideways. "If I'm a moron, what kind of an idiot is an old woman like you?"

And in order for Zaydeh not to be able to answer quickly, he began rocking himself even harder, wrinkling up his whole face, and went off into a cantorial wail from the Yom Kippur liturgy:

"*U'nesaneh toykef, k'dushes hayom.* . . . We will observe the mighty holiness of this day."

&

Bubbeh's and Zaydeh's hut was white and still now. Dark pieces of cotton padding lay like dirty fluff between the two windows that were hammered shut. From over the top of the small workbench, Tsar Alexander III looked right into my bed—a goy with a big yellow beard sprinkled with black fly drops. Zaydeh was sitting on his high stool, bent over, not singing and not making jokes. He was stubbornly sewing silver buttons today and from time to time, he threw out arrogantly:

"Maybe we should call Dr. Pomper?"

"How'll Dr. Pomper help?"

"How do I know? They say he's an expert."

"Leave me alone with your experts. I sent out for pig fat and more herbs. With God's help, he'll get better."

But it seemed that not the pig fat that Bubbeh smeared on my belly, nor the essence of bitter herbs that they poured into me helped. Dr. Pomper had to be sent for.

He came, stomped his cane and yelled at Bubbeh. They burned my flesh with boiling water, drew blood from behind my ears and from

my back, poured medicines into me, bitter, sweet, salty, until finally
redemption came and I opened clear eyes for the first time. I saw how
the wrinkles on Zaydeh's face smoothed out and his beard quivered.

But Mammeh wasn't there. That evening when I had gone looking
for her to Aunt Miriam's, it seemed I had fallen asleep in the snow.
That's what Zaydeh said. The janitor at the goyish hospital saw a
snowy parcel lying in the street. He raised an alarm and people came
running. Meanwhile, an old woman whose caps were made by Bubbeh,
recognized me and told them to take me to my Bubbeh Rakhl's. Where
else should she tell them to take me? Mammeh wasn't at home and
she wasn't at Aunt Miriam's either. She'd actually gone off, nowhere
else but straight to Warsaw! She was called away by telegram and she
had to go because her only daughter Tsippeleh, by her first husband,
was about to become engaged in Warsaw.

For many years now, Mammeh used to send Tsippeleh parcels of
yellow pears as big as bells, bars of chocolate, and braided and rolled
butter pastries. From time to time she even sent her a single ruble
note. Because of these delicacies, Tsippeleh developed rosy red cheeks,
a beautiful figure, and got herself a bridegroom without having to put
up even a penny in dowry. So why shouldn't her mother have gone? Ay,
she didn't even say goodbye to anybody? Where'd she have the time?

So what was the matter with Tatteh that he hated Mammeh,
Bubbeh Rakhl, and even me?

He knew that I was lying sick at Zaydeh's but he didn't even
come to visit. He sent an errand boy to find out how I was.

Bubbeh was so mad that she slammed the door shut on him.
"What does he think?" she yelled after the boy. "That his son's a
bastard? He can't come by himself? It's not fitting for him?"

Zaydeh burrowed his head into his shoulders, and in a high-
pitched voice murmured into the uniforms that my father was right.
"You don't go off without even a 'be well.' "

"And if the other one is about to become engaged?"

"So you put off the engagement," Zaydeh issued his verdict.

"You're a moron"

"And you're an idiot!"

Chapter 4

Mammeh stayed in Warsaw for one reason or other. The frost continued. Bubbeh's soft, high bed, where every few days Dr. Pomper thumped me between the shoulder blades, was now made up.

I shuffled around the house, small, shrunken, with a drawn yellow face, and drank goat's milk that Bubbeh brought twice a day all the way from the Mariatzke part of town.

While I was sick, Zaydeh's hair got whiter, his cheeks ruddier, and his nose sharper. Every morning when I drank my goat's milk, he'd pull out a small bottle that he kept hidden in a dark corner. He threw his head back like a goy, opened his mouth wide and gulped it right down to the last drop.

It bothered me that Zaydeh was drinking straight from the bottle. What was the point of having drinking glasses sitting on the shelf?

But Zaydeh explained to me that drawing from the bottle was the same as going out to a field in a heat wave and suddenly coming upon a spring of water. Where would you go in search of a dipper to draw water? You get down at once and you drink up like a goat. "On the contrary," he said, "show me which blade of grass, which flower, or for that matter, which animal needs a dipper for drinking? And what d'ya think a human being is, if not an animal?"

Well, maybe he had a point. It really is good to drink right from the well, but one thing was hard for me to understand. Zaydeh said that after gulping down such a bottle he got clearheaded. He became altogether different, he said. He'd been given a sign: if Moyshe Rabeynu, the biblical Moses, hadn't enjoyed a proper drink of liquor, he'd never have been able to lead the Jews out of ancient Egypt.

He gave this same reason to my teacher, Rabbi Simmeh-Yoysef, who came to pay me a sick call.

Simmeh-Yoysef was a short, stocky Jew with an overgrown beard and small, black, searching eyes. Listening to Zaydeh's account of Moysheh Rabeynu, he made a wry face; the explanation didn't appeal to him. This rabbi of mine explained to Zaydeh that in Moysheh Rabeynu's times there wasn't any liquor at all, not anywhere in the world.

"What d'ya mean, there wasn't any liquor?" Zaydeh plucked at his beard. "How can that be? So how did the Jews actually get out of ancient Egypt without a drink of liquor?"

"I'm telling you, Reb Duvid, that there wasn't any!" Simmeh-Yoysef issued his verdict.

"What was there then?"

"How do I know? Maybe there was wine."

"And wine isn't liquor?" Zaydeh replied gleefully. "May I and my wife Rakhl have as good a year as this wine tastes!"

"Oh, stop your babbling already," Bubbeh Rakhl put in from her seat on the little trunk. "You're talking a blue streak!"

"God forbid, Rakhl dear. As I'm a Jew . . . if not . . . you know . . ." Zaydeh turned his wispy, white beard toward the rabbi's overgrown face, "She, my wife Rakhl—she should live and be well—she also likes to soothe her heart with a glass of liquor now and then."

"Let your enemies talk! Look how's he's going on and on. Don't listen to him, Reb Simmeh-Yoysef. He's crazy!" But she said this quietly, so Zaydeh pretended that he didn't hear her.

"She treats herself in the middle of the night . . . Never mind, it's not a sin. An old person . . . why not?"

So this Zaydeh of mine became an entirely new person once I got up from the warm, high bed and Dr. Pomper stopped coming to thump me between the shoulder blades.

The tidy little house was full of gabbing and singing all day long.

Bubbeh sat sewing the muslin caps, and from time to time she stuck her head into the small pots bubbling away cozily on the grate. With every stab of the needle, Zaydeh nodded sideways and in a high-pitched voice sang out:

> "When God grants me success,
> I'll also wiggle my ass . . ."

Bubbeh took off her wire-framed spectacles, laid aside the muslin cap, and shook her head scornfully: "An old Jew like him and he isn't even ashamed of himself . . . !"

But this female contempt didn't bother Zaydeh. He finished his tune to the end and began a second one with a warm and weepy moan:

> "I love you, please believe me
> A moment without you I can't be

You're as dear to me as my own l-i-f-e . . .
But I can't make you my wife."

"Of course," Bubbeh nodded her head into the caps. "He loves her, but he can't marry her. Go to all the black years! Who needs you to love me anyway?"

"Silly Rakhl," Zaydeh rested one side of his beard on his lapel, "its just a song, a kind of story."

"We know your stories already!"

Many times, Zaydeh stood in the middle of the room at the big, bare table marked with black and brown spots from the pressing iron and began to cut out a uniform. The house got very quiet at such times. You could clearly hear the bubbling of the pots and the swaying of the clock pendulum.

Zaydeh stood in his unbuttoned vest, the tape measure around his shoulders. He looked at the piece of fabric covering the whole table, pulled at it, marked it with chalk, rubbed out the chalk marks, rubbed chalk in another place and quietly, from somewhere quite different, he began to hum under his breath, some kind of murmur that spun out slowly and sadly. Bit by bit this murmur became louder and began to reach higher until this little white-haired tailor who was my Zaydeh began moaning from the Rosh Hashanah liturgy:

"Oy . . . oy . . . oy . . . *Hineyni* . . . Here I stand . . ."

He tossed his head, his beard stuck out. The piece of chalk as if all on its own, smeared across the fabric. The moan became high and weepy:

"*Honi m'mas* . . . oy . . . oy . . . God in heaven . . ."

Zaydeh began to translate into Yiddish: "I, poor man that I am, who bows to the dust at Your feet, have come to plead for Your suffering people Israel . . ."

Bubbeh bent her head like a hen and the needle came to rest, the white piece of muslin hanging lifeless between her fingers. It seemed to me that the bubbling of the pots also got quieter. The pendulum stood still as if gaping in the air. Only Bubbeh's head was nodding, her nose sniffled, and a weak, womanly little moan escaped as if right from her heart:

"Oy, dear Father in heaven, take pity on your unfortunate orphans."

Who Bubbeh was counting among the unfortunate orphans wasn't clear to me. But when Zaydeh got going with his *hineyni*, Bubbeh began telling a story, right in the middle:

"So my mother, may she rest in peace, went into childbirth with Rivkeh and there was no water in the house, so my father, may he rest in peace, took the water can . . ."

"I've heard this story maybe a thousand times already," Zaydeh interrupted and cut into the cloth with his scissors.

"Take a look how he doesn't let you say a word, this Humen!"

"How many times already has your mother gone into childbirth with Rivkeh?"

"May your mouth grow out of your rear end!"

"Tra-la-la, tri-li-li-li," Zaydeh began a new tune.

Bubbeh couldn't forgive Zaydeh for not letting her tell her story from beginning to end. She looked for a chance to get even with him. And the chance came because Zaydeh had a weakness for arguing with witless Vladek, who was not only like a member of Zaydeh's household but also slept there.

In the evening around nine o'clock, when Zaydeh was already putting away his work for the day, the door would quietly open and in would come a short, overgrown person with an unkempt yellow beard and a pair of swollen, ruminating lips—Vladek.

His feet were bound in old pieces of sacking, and he wore a torn jacket full of holes, that had dirty tufts of cotton padding hanging out of it and was belted with a rope. Vladek gave off a smell of kerosene and chicken droppings. He had a long, heavy sack slung over one shoulder, just like the ones hanging from the sides of wayfarers.

He always came in softly, quietly, took off his wayfarer's sack, put it away carefully in a corner and then, taking the two empty water cans, he went out to the Bernardine church and brought back fresh water. He emptied the two cans and took them out again until Bubbeh's barrel was full.

Only when he came back did Zaydeh, not turning from his workbench, ask:

"Vladek's here already?"

"Mm . . . mm . . ." Vladek mumbled, nodding his head like a horse in span between two wagon shafts.

"So what's new, Vladek? You poured a lot of water into rich people's barrels?"

Vladek sat down on the floor not far from the warm kitchen, folded his legs underneath him like a Turk, opened up his sack, and out of that dark hole began putting into his mouth half-rounds of bread, no more than hollowed-out pieces of soft dough, like horseshoes. Along with this bread he sucked on big, twisted bones that here and there still had bits of gnawed meat attached to them. Sometimes Vladek added an old onion, half an apple, and a soft sour pickle to his supper. He ate slowly and took his time, like a cow chewing its cud.

Bubbeh already knew Vladek's habits. She knew that as long as Vladek hadn't finished emptying his sack, you could talk to him from today till tomorrow.

So she waited until the sack lay flattened out and Vladek had caught his breath. Only then did she ask: "D'ya want some tea, Vladek?"

"Mm . . . mm . . ." he muttered in his way, with a mouthful of food.

Bubbeh handed him his tea in a dingy little pot. He held it between his hands, sipping loudly. The drops that settled on his mustache he licked off with his tongue, and the rest he smeared over his beard.

"So, Vladek, what's new in the world after all?" Zaydeh let himself be heard from again. "They guzzle a lot of water, those scabby rich people?"

"Oho, oho," Vladek began to mumble quite differently now. "Pan Tailor makes jokes. Pan Tailor likes to laugh."

"But I'm not laughing. God forbid! I'm just curious to know how much water you poured into the barrels of the rich."

"Aha, lots of water, Pan Tailor. A lot, lots of water."

"So you must have a pouch full of money."

"From where should I have, if they pay only a two-kopek coin for a whole barrelful?"

"No more than a coin?"

"For sure not. And at Danzigerova's it's a big barrel—this big!" He showed just how big it was on the wide brown dresser that stood between Bubbeh-Zaydeh's beds.

"Ovah! So what else is new?"

"A big barrel at Danzigerova's—so big . . ." Vladek hadn't heard Zaydeh's second question.

"I already know that she's got a big barrel."

"Such a big barrel!"

Danzigerova's barrel was a sore point with Vladek. This barrel didn't let him get any sleep at night. Even when he dozed off after supper, he still didn't stop muttering in Polish:

"Danzigerova, *betska duza! Betska duza* . . . ! A big barrel! A big barrel!"

It took half the day to pour dozens of cans of water into it. Up and down the flight of stairs he went, up and down and all he got for these cans of water was no more than two copper kopeks.

"Let them burn, those rich people! Isn't that right, Vladek?" Zaydeh slammed the pressing iron into the hem of a uniform.

"Mm . . . mm . . ."

"Don't worry, Vladek, the time will come when they'll pour the water into your barrels."

"Oho . . . ! Oho . . . !"

"Get yourself a big barrel, even bigger than Danzigerova's."

At this, Bubbeh said her piece. Now was the time to take her revenge on Zaydeh:

"Maybe you'd stop with your complaints to the goy right now?"

"What's the matter, a goy isn't a human being?"

"A goy is indeed a human being, but you with your jokes, you're worse than a goy."

"And if you tell me your foolish stories . . . ?"

"So I tell. Whoever doesn't like it can plug his ears."

Vladek was still chewing his cud. He looked right at Bubbeh, nodding his head. "Yeh . . . Yeh . . . Danzigerova, *betska duza* . . . ! A big barrel!"

"Stop already with that Danzigerova!" Bubbeh took off her wire-framed spectacles. "Go to sleep, you stupid goy."

"Don't rush him. What's it to you if we talk a little?"

"Just look who he sits down with to talk!"

"If you have a wife who's an idiot then you have to talk with a Vladek."

Bubbeh made a motion with her hands as if to say: "Oh, you're hopeless!" Zaydeh fell silent.

The house got quiet. Bubbeh was softly shuffling between the beds. She took the pillows off the beds and put them on the stools. A cricket chirped behind the kitchen.

"Tell me now, dear Vladekshi," Zaydeh couldn't remain silent for too long. "What's the matter with you? What d'ya want from the girls?"

Vladek who a minute earlier had been yawning loudly, blinked his eyes and stared at Zaydeh like a calf.

"Is it really true what they say, that you lift up girls' dresses in the street?"

A thin rivulet of drool slobbered down from one side of Vladek's mouth. "Its good, Pan Tailor," he grumbled hollowly.

"It's that good?"

"Pan Tailor," the overgrown goyish face scowled: "They, the girls . . ."

"Stop that babbling!" Bubbeh turned away hastily from the bed. "I'll throw you right down the flight of stairs, together with that stupid husband of mine!"

"Pani Rakhlina, what can I do if they . . . the girls . . . ?"

"Is that so, the girls . . . ! Zaydeh raised his face from the cutting table. "And you like it this way? Ovah!"

"Yeh, Pan Tailor, I like it. I like to sleep with girls."

"Will you stop?" Bubbeh Rakhl leapt forward with a small fist upraised. "Get out of here this minute, you're disgusting! And you, you poor excuse for a tailor . . ." She looked at Zaydeh with fury. "Stop!"

Vladek got up heavily, lamely, from the floor, took his empty sack, and muttering under his breath, went into the cubicle where he spent the rest of the night.

"You had to talk . . . !" Bubbeh angrily beat the pillows.

"I just wanted to know if it's really true," Zaydeh answered, as if he had already been judged guilty.

"That's all that's on your mind. Are you any better than him? And you, do you let a girl pass by in the street?"

"If you have such a wife . . ."

"You don't like it? Then play that song backward!"

Zaydeh didn't answer. Bubbeh was angrily muttering that if only it wasn't still winter, she'd run away from here, wherever her eyes would take her, and except for the fact that witless Vladek brought water from the Bernardine church, she would throw him right down the whole flight of stairs.

The cubicle Vladek had gone into was now closed. I couldn't take my eyes off the low, yellow-painted door that now held behind it a great mystery. I had an overwhelming desire to go in there and ask Vladek if he'd also lifted up the dress of Yuzheh the barrel maker's daughter.

Chapter 5

The red Bernardine church with its long dark windows and tall arched doors surrounded by black iron railings stood beyond Bubbeh-Zaydeh's house. Broadly branched chestnut trees leaned over its high walls, guarding with cool stillness the face of the Holy Mother and Child.

It was wintertime and the branches of the trees were covered with snow that looked like powdered salt. The gates in the cold walls stood open and the dark face of the Holy Mother was bent down to her half-open breast as if in shame in front of the surrounding emptiness.

Sitting by the window one evening, I saw a really huge sun, like a flat golden plate, setting on the other side of the cross. A bright flare darted and flickered on the windows of the dark houses above the roofs and the cross across the way.

The lamp was not yet lit in the house. Bubbeh had dozed off on her little trunk in the stillness, Zaydeh had gone off to the study house to say kaddish, and I sat looking out sadly at the fiery cross thinking that tomorrow I had to go back to cheder. So my mood was heavy. I imagined what Simmeh-Yoysef's cheder looked like.

It was a large and disorganized house where the beams were so low they almost touched your shoulders. The ancient walls were dark green, showing the marks of furniture and clocks that had been removed. Along the walls, stood long greasy benches, rickety from propped up feet. My friends and I would shout all day, blow our noses into our hands, and wipe our fingers on the lapels of our gaberdines.

Simmeh-Yoysef was a Jew who wanted to pass himself off as a not mean teacher. He didn't yell and he didn't beat the students. When he wanted to yell, he would start coughing and ended up instead with a mouthful of phlegm. He had such a weird, broad backside that when he wanted to get up to beat someone, it dragged him down so that he couldn't whack the boys on the head. Nothing less, he was a rabbi after all, but on the table in front of him lay a dotted red kerchief, a snuff box made of horn, and a hairy sheep's foot with a split hoof from which dangled fleshy, round leather thongs, the kind that bore witness that lashes could sometimes fall over heads, hands and naked backsides that you yourself had to unbutton.

These punishments didn't take place every Monday and Thursday, that is to say, often, because Simmeh-Yoysef had another habit. He liked to sniff up a full nose of snuff, call out a pupil from some corner of the room and honour him with a pinch in his lower parts. At the same time, he had another habit, this Rabbi Simmeh-Yoysef, he would open his mouth, flare his nostrils at the same time and give out a deep sigh: "Oy, oy, oy, oy. . . ."

So tomorrow I would have to go back to that house. Simmeh-Yoysef's scrawny rebbetsin would probably be sitting by the door as usual, beside the full slop pail and the dilapidated broom with its mangy bristles. She'd be peeling potatoes lickety-spit, into a worn-out and dented tin pot, and calling out: "Simmeh-Yoysef, Simmeh-Yoysef!"

The rabbi would give a start and grab the red-dotted kerchief.

"Heh? Did'ya say something?"

"I'm saying, may you fall into an eternal sleep, my dear Simmeh-Yoysef!"

When I come in, she'll drop a peeled potato onto the floor and in her shrill sing-song, let out: "Look what the cat dragged in! He's here already, the jewel!"

She wouldn't let me take off my coat or unwind my shawl but just as I was, I'd have to go out to the pump and bring back two, three cans of water.

But all of this won't happen tomorrow. Until then there was still a lot of hours. If you wanted to count it up, it was hours without end.

Meanwhile, I was sitting at Bubbeh-Zaydeh's window. The church was getting bluer and darker and the sky was still red around the cross. Nothing else, but on this very spot they used to burn and roast evildoers!

Now as I sat here, it seemed to me that I heard Zaydeh's voice but it sounded somewhat muffled as if it was coming from the other side of the door. A moment later, the door burst open and a strange voice, not from these parts, was heard:

"How come it's so dark?"

I tore myself away from the window. I'd swear it was my mother's voice! I heard Zaydeh's voice in the dark: "You've just come?"

"I just got off the omnibus, but why's it so dark in here?"

Bubbeh woke up from her dozing: "Heh? Its Frimmet?" She asked with warm sleepiness.

"Yeh, its Frimmet," answered Zaydeh, "turn on some light. You could lose an eye in the dark."

"And where's my Mendl?" Mammeh asked.

"Here I am, Mameshi!" I sprang down from Zaydeh's workbench and ran right to the door where the shadowy figure of my newly arrived mother stood.

A frosty odor drifted from her clothes as if from a stall.

"Mendelshi?" she searched my face with her cold hand. "Come closer! Let me see you!"

I raised my face up to her and she bent down to me. It was dark. Bubbeh was fumbling at the lamp that was in no hurry to light up. Nevertheless, Mammeh sensed in the dark how I looked.

"My poor child! You've gotten so thin! Oy! Vey'z mir!"

"Thank God for that!" Bubbeh called out.

"Why didn't you write me that he was so sick?" Mammeh complained to Bubbeh.

"First of all, I did write you."

"Only that he was a little bit not well."

"What else did'ya want?"

"I'd have come running."

"You'd have made him better? Don't worry, Bubbeh also knew what she had to do, eh, Mendel?"

A reddish glow now lay over the house from the lit lamp. Zaydeh hung up on the door his winter coat with the split in the back and the two buttons at the sides. Bubbeh called this particular garment "the goyish coat." She didn't like it but Zaydeh gave a toss of his hand over the yellowed and tattered sheepskin as if he was patting the head of a beloved grandchild and exclaimed arrogantly:

"It's not a goyish coat, it's a *zhupan*, a long, man's coat like the Poles wear."

"A zhupan, a dupan . . ." Bubbeh ridiculed. "A Jew should want to wear only goyish clothes . . . ?"

Mammeh stood like a stranger. She had come from Warsaw wearing a long, black overcoat with an even blacker fur collar. Maybe it was the length, or the blackness of it, that made her seem bigger than before she went away. Now by the reddish glow, she kissed me and embraced me over and over again:

"My poor child, you were so sick? "

"Sick, shmick . . . !" Zaydeh called out as he was preparing to sit down at his workbench.

"Take off your coat, why are you standing?"

Mammeh unwound the shawl from her head, took off the long black overcoat and threw it onto the bed. Bubbeh picked it up carefully and hung it alongside Zaydeh's goyish coat.

"You had a new overcoat made for yourself?" Bubbeh patted the black collar.

"Gittl-Hoddehs gave it to me."

"Izzat so? Hm . . . What's new with them?"

"May no evil eye befall them! It should only happen to us!"

"And how is Hirsh-Wolf?"

"Like himself."

"And how's his hand? Can he move his hand already?"

"Yes, thanks to the Almighty."

I now took a good look at my mother. Without the overcoat she looked like she used to before she left. Not only that, but a new wig sat on her head, black and shiny with a thick twisted braid in the front like a bird.

It must be because of the wig that her face now looked fuller, smoother, maybe younger too.

"And how're Gitl-Hoddehs's children? May they be well!" Bubbeh asked again.

"Everything's good. Pinyek is already working in a pharmacy."

"And Pola?"

"She finished already."

"And Shlamekl?"

"He's getting married, with mazel."

I knew that Mammeh was now talking about her rich sister in Warsaw, my aunt Gittl-Hoddehs, who lived in a house with lots of rooms and balconies. The names of her children were not the Yiddish Mendl, but the Polonized Pinyek and Pola. There should also be a Yadzheh and a small boy who didn't have a name yet, but was called Malli, "little one." I haven't seen any of these children. I only know that from time to time I wear short pants with brass buttons at the sides that came from this same Malli.

"And how's Malli?" I quickly ask.

Mammeh smiled. "Oh, he's not called Malli anymore. May no evil eye befall him! He's all grown up and goes to the gymnasium."

Zaydeh, who was already sitting at his workbench shoulders hunched, turned round.

"Eh, What did'ya say?" And his wispy white beard pointed upward.

"He's already in the third grade."

"Really? In the gymnasium?"

"Yes, in the gymnasium."

"And he wears a uniform?"

"Of course, just like the one you're sewing."

"Ovah!" Zaydeh couldn't stop wondering. "Its too bad you didn't bring back one of his old uniforms."

"What do you need it for?"

"Oh, just to take a look, to see how they sew uniforms in Warsaw."

"Not any better than you, Tatteh."

"Also navy blue with silver buttons?"

"Yes, just like the ones here."

"Hmm . . . its one world everywhere."

Zaydeh was very pleased that in Warsaw they wore exactly the same uniforms as they wore here.

He laid down his piece of work and readied himself for the new ideas from Warsaw.

"And who sews his uniforms?"

"Who should sew? Why, a tailor, of course."

"So does that mean that there's a Duvid-Froykeh's in Warsaw too?"

"He thinks he's 'the only male in Moscow,' " Bubbeh now interjected.

"Stop it, old woman! We're talking about something."

I was standing leaning against Mammeh's knee. She didn't stop patting me, caressing my face and sighing quietly.

"And what else is new?" Bubbeh interrupted. "You actually wrote out the engagement contract for Tsippeleh?"

"Yes Mammeh, you can now wish me Mazeltov!"

"Let it really be with mazel! Is he a decent person?"

"A broom maker."

"A broom maker?" Zaydeh wrinkled his brow. "How come a broom maker? Why not a tailor?"

"Why? A tailor is more respectable than a broom maker?"

"A tailor is a human being, and a broom maker is . . . nothing more than a broom maker."

"It's not good enough for you?" Bubbeh raised her wire-rimmed spectacles.

"Naturally, it's not good enough."

"In case you didn't know . . . his pedigree isn't good enough for Duvid-Froykeh's."

"He took her without a cent." Mammeh threw in quietly.

"Some favour he's doing me! Give him more money!"

"Don't listen to what the fool says," Bubbeh thrust her face forward angrily. "And where was the engagement held?"

"At Avrum-Ayzik's."

"Why not at Gittl-Hoddehs's?"

"I don't know . . . rich people. . . . Maybe it didn't suit them."

"Naturally, go let in a broom maker . . ." Zaydeh took his revenge. Bubbeh quietly lowered her head. Zaydeh's needle flew swiftly.

"Poor Avrum-Ayzik, still doesn't make a living, eh?"

"He's struggling. He's in debt."

"And Simmeh-Layeh?"

"Beautiful, like gold!"

"How come they're not arranging a marriage for her?"

"It's just not happening."

Bubbeh let out a deep sigh. The house got very quiet. Three people sat with sunken heads, as if nodding.

"It's sad about Avrum-Ayzik, it's very sad . . ."

Uncle Avrum-Ayzik was a full brother of my mother, Aunt Miriam, and rich Gitl-Hoddes in Warsaw.

I knew my Uncle Avrum-Ayzik. He was at our place last year on Rosh Hashanah. He had a big but sparse blond beard, wore spectacles, and a raised eight-sided, pointed cap that no one had ever worn before or would ever wear again. He spoke in an expansive, drawling voice. During Rosh Hashanah and Yom Kippur he stayed with us in town and davened the additional service in the tailor's little shul. It was said of his davening that you could kiss every word he uttered. But what was the use if he couldn't earn a living and Simmeh-Layeh his beautiful daughter needed to be married off. The son in London was supposed to send money for a dowry, but . . . he didn't send it.

So it was very sad at Avrum-Ayzik's.

That's the story Mammeh told. While doing this, she unwrapped the parcel that Aunt Gittl-Hoddehs had given her. A pair of shoes with laces fell out, a man's jacket with sleeves that were too long, a cap with a goyish peak, trousers, and vests.

A whole treasure!

But this time, it didn't please me. Most of all, I was bothered by the cap with the goyish peak.

"I won't wear it!" I said and wouldn't go near it.

"Why not? Its such a nice little cap."

"Nobody wears a cap like this in our cheder."

"But you will."

"No! I won't!"

The clock began to chime hoarsely. I counted altogether ten chimes, but actually the hands showed no more than nine.

"Have you seen Luzeh yet?" Zaydeh suddenly called out.

"No," Mammeh replied angrily.

"I really wondered why you didn't go straight home?"

"I'll never go there again!"

The mute, pouting faces of Bubbeh-Zaydeh were raised together toward Mammeh. I also didn't understand what she'd said.

"You won't go back to your own home?"

"No, I've had enough of him, that burden of mine."

The two old faces looked like doves.

"What now, Frimmet?"

"What should be now? Its nothing, but the terrible curses that he wishes on me, should . . ."

"Sha! Sha! Don't curse." Bubbeh stood up from her seat.

"A Jew should be ashamed. Even a goy doesn't curse out his wife like he curses me."

"When did he have time to curse you? You weren't even here."

"In a letter he cursed me. So what if I went off. I have a one and only daughter, so why shouldn't I go to her celebration?"

"At least let someone know that you're going," Zaydeh mixed in.

"Who should I have told? Is he ever at home?"

"What did'ya want? That he should sit at home playing lovey-dovey with you?"

"Who's talking about playing? But he can't stop me from going to my own child's engagement."

"Not a single living soul knew where you'd got to. How did'ya have a nerve to just go and leave husband and child like that?"

"Ovah! Wouldn't you know! He didn't have who to cook his grub."

"What did'ya want? That he should do his own cooking?"

"Let him cook . . . let him not cook. . . . I've had enough of him!"

"You've got someone else in his place?" Zaydeh narrowed his eyes. "What do you think? That you're still a young bride?"

"Nu, stop already, you old fool," Bubbeh trembled. "And you, Frimmet, quit your fooling around and go home."

"Are you throwing me out, Mammeh?"

"I'm not throwing you out, God forbid, but a wife should go home to her husband."

"I don't want to know him anymore. What have I had from him? I wasted, my beautiful young years. He promised me that he was a good provider, that he had a farm. . . . Woe to his farm!"

Mammeh's eyes got small and red, not beautiful at all. Her nose also got red and more pointed.

"Nu, enough already!" Bubbeh wanted to smooth over Tatteh's sins. "Did'ya think he didn't ask about you?"

"He did me some favor!"

"A few times a day he came here to the courtyard."

"To the courtyard? It was beneath his dignity to come right up?" Bubbeh whispered as if it was a secret: "Y'know we don't get along."

"With whom does he get along?"

"Nu, never mind! He's not the worst. . . . It's really late now, but tomorrow, God willing, you'll go home."

"No, Mammeh, even if I knew I had to wash floors, I won't live with him anymore."

"What happened to you in Warsaw?" Zaydeh could no longer contain himself.

"In Warsaw, people live like human beings. Gittl-Hoddehs is a proper madame, a German frau. And look what happened to me? My first husband Berl, may he rest in peace, with him I lived in big rooms. I even had brass handles on every door!"

"Well . . . at Berl's . . ." Bubbeh sighed. "Do things ever turn out the way you imagine?"

That's how they carried on into the dead of night.

They forgot all about me. I listened but I couldn't understand any of it. Why did Mammeh come back from Warsaw so angry at Tatteh? It should be the opposite. It seemed reasonable to me that Tatteh should be the one to be angry with Mammeh. She's the one who took off and didn't even tell anyone where.

To tell the truth, I wasn't angry with Mammeh but it bothered me that she now remembered her first husband with whom she'd lived in big rooms with brass handles on every door. What kind of comparison was that? Her first husband was an old-time healer in Konskewola and my father dealt only in hay. How did big rooms and brass door handles get here?

Chapter 6

The next day I got ready to go to cheder. I got up early, washed carefully, put on a new pair of pants that Mammeh had brought from Warsaw, and took the two bagels Bubbeh buttered for me.

But I didn't feel like leaving the warm house with Zaydeh's tunes and my newly returned Mammeh. She finally realized this and as I was putting on my winter coat, she called out from her bed:

"Don't let him go yet. He won't miss any of his studies."

I looked out the window with new eyes. It was bright and blue outside. Zaydeh had already warmed himself up with some Acquavit. He went around the house self-confidently now, letting himself be heard from with his daily and festival melodies.

Bubbeh in her red nightcap, small, bent over like a lopsided shrub, shuffled quietly around the house lighting the fire and preparing the meal.

Mammeh was the last to get up. In the blue-white light of the windowpanes, her face looked younger and fresher. Until this morning I hadn't noticed that Mammeh had such a soft and warm double chin and such pale blue eyes.

She moved around the house in a thin, black skirt with lace at the hem that rustled like rough silk when she moved.

"Did'ya buy it?" Bubbeh bent down to feel the skirt.

"How do I come to such things?" Mammeh answered with quiet bitterness that didn't match her smooth face. "Gittl-Hoddehs gave it to me."

"Its silk?"

"What then, flannel?"

Bubbeh wiped the corners of her mouth with two fingers. Zaydeh looked off to one side and asked for no real reason: "How much, for instance, can such a skirt be worth?"

No one answered him.

Mammeh sat down, her back facing the room and began combing her wig.

I don't know why but I didn't like this black silk skirt that came from Gitl-Hoddehs in Warsaw. It seemed to me that Mammeh acted differently in this skirt. Not the same Mammeh who sometimes in the morning would spread her hands out pleadingly: "Moysheh's gone!"

I never saw Mammeh like this in our house. Her arms were never bare like now, she didn't wash with scented soap or stand fixing herself up at the mirror the way she did here.

"What's taking so long, Frimmet?" Bubbeh called out: "The food's already on the table."

"Never mind . . ." Mammeh patted a curl on her wig. "This is how it's done in Warsaw."

"But this isn't Warsaw."

It took long enough until Mammeh finished and finally came to the table. She walked stiffly, puffed up like a peacock.

Everyone was already sitting. She sat down opposite me, her soft and warm double chin quivering slightly. Only now did I see that Mammeh had brought back with her from Warsaw two dimples on either side of her face. She took small bites, drank her coffee as if with half a mouth, and in the middle of everything, she called out to me:

"Mendelshi, look how you're eating!"

"How should he be eating?" Zaydeh mixed in.

"In Warsaw they eat differently."

"Oh, leave me alone with your Warsaw! Look at that! She doesn't like the way he eats. Do I eat any better?"

"You also don't eat right, Tatteh."

"Rakhl, listen to this! Listen to what your daughter's saying! I've lived sixty-two years already and I never knew that I don't eat right. Ovah! And how do you eat right?"

"You don't grab. You take small bites."

"That's some impressive piece of Toyreh learning!"

Mammeh didn't answer. I tried to bite small pieces and not grab but my throat got tight and my eyes started to water. Suddenly Bubbeh put down her little pot of coffee, and called out loudly:

"Mendl, you're crying?"

Mammeh also put down her coffee. Her double chin lopsided now, wobbled a bit.

"Nu, quiet, Mendelshi, don't cry," and she began patting me. "I was only joking . . . nu, stop already. . . . You eat very nicely."

Zaydeh was muttering angrily: "Warsaw! Wouldn't you know . . . ? Neh!"

In the end, Mammeh quieted me down but I was still heavy hearted.

"What a beautiful day its outside!" Zaydeh observed, sitting again at his workbench. "Maybe Mendl should go outside? He should get used to fresh air again."

"I don't know. I'm still afraid," Mammeh hesitated.

"It wouldn't hurt." Bubbeh mixed in. "He really should go, as long as the sun is out."

They bundled me up, and I went out into the street like someone who comes up for air after being under water for too long.

"Watch out for the sleighs!" Bubbeh yelled after me, "and don't stay out too long. You hear, Mendl?"

"I hear, Bubbeshi, I hear."

In the street it was so white and still that I had to keep my eyes closed a while. I felt I had fallen into some strange city. Everyone seemed deaf and went about with quiet steps.

The snow lay between the iron railings around the church, on the ledges over the windows, and high and soft in the middle of the street. A sleigh went by with a thin ringing and arrogant sound. Students were already coming back from the gymnasium throwing snowballs, running and shouting.

How different the city got since I was forced to lie in bed. Tall, snow-covered posts stood on Lublin Street supported by smaller ones like outstretched legs. The street itself went far uphill and then it widened out. The Polish sentry with the blue nose was no longer standing at the booth. On Warsaw Street where Mottl Shtroy's wife had a shop, they no longer put pieces of coarse flannel outside or straw baskets. Everywhere it was white and silent.

I stared at the snow-covered cross of the German church on the boulevard. I remembered that it was somewhere around here that I had gone looking for Mammeh all the way out to Aunt Miriam's. It was very quiet now, not a living person to be seen. Suddenly a Jew appeared wearing a high plush cap.

"Mendl, where are'ya going?" I heard a warm and familiar voice.

"Tatteh!" I was scared for a minute and my throat got tight.

"Where are'ya going? You're better already, eh?"

"Yeh Tatteh, I'm all better."

This Jew in the tall plush cap really was my father. He had gone grey and his eyes were absent-minded . . . quiet.

"I went to see your rabbi today, to find out . . ." he said.

"I was supposed to go back to cheder today."

"Izzat so? So why didn't you go?"

"Mammeh came back."

"Eh?" Tatteh lifted up half a face, the absent-minded eyes squinted. "Mammeh, you say?"

"Yeh, Mammeh came back."

"When'd she come back?"

"Last night."

"Last night yet? So why haven't we seen her?"

"She's upstairs, at Bubbeh's."

"Izzat so? At Bubbeh's?"

Silence. Tatteh's eyes opened wide. He had such a big greenish-yellow mustache now.

"I didn't go up," Tatteh wasn't talking to me but to the German church, " 'cause I don't like her, that Bubbeh of yours. But don't think . . . don't think I didn't know about you, I knew everything. Who d'ya think sent for Dr. Pomper?"

His voice got quieter by the minute and more abrupt.

"So she came back!" Tatteh remembered all over again, and sighed. "She went to them. How does she look, your mother?"

"Good. Pretty good."

Silence. We walked together. The soldier with the rifle who guarded the jail appeared in front of us.

"Did'ya eat yet?" Tatteh broke the silence.

"Yeh, I ate already."

"Maybe you're cold? Come inside into Mordkheh's soup kitchen and you'll warm up."

"No Tatteh, its fine here."

"What're you doing in the street?"

"I came out for some fresh air."

"Izzat so? Good! Come, I'll walk you back."

He took my hand. I'd never walked with my father like this before. I didn't know whether to be embarrassed or glad. I only knew that it felt good.

"I went to see your rabbi today," he started once again. "Your rabbi tells me . . ."

He stopped in the middle, got lost in thought, and looked off into the distance. His big, fleshy nose looked as if it would separate from the rest of his face. Slowly, he began unbuttoning his old winter coat, let one hand drop into a deep pocket of his pants, took out a soft, flattened leather pouch and put something into my hand.

"Here," he said, "Here y'are. Buy something for yourself."

Tatteh was giving me money for the first time. What use was it to me? What could I buy for so much money?

"And buy something for your mother," he added quietly and led me to Bubbeh-Zaydeh's house. "Nu, go already. You could, God forbid, get a chill." Also for the first time, I wanted to kiss my father's hand but he grabbed it away and began stammering:

"Nu, enough already. Finished . . . go, go!"

In the middle of leaving, he called back to me.

"Mendl, what'd I want to say? Yeh . . . don't tell anyone there. I don't like your Bubbeh. I don't like her."

⌒

That same evening, Vladek the witless Goy, came home earlier than usual. He was red all over, his yellow beard damp and rumpled.

"What's your hurry today, Vladek?"

The goy muttered with a full mouth chewing into his crumpled beard:

"A cholera take her, that Magda. May she croak this very night, that cursed girl!"

"Who's this Magda? Why are you cursing her?"

"Why shouldn't he curse her? She slapped his face with a fish!"

Zaydeh burst out with a shrill laugh. Bubbeh raised her spectacles from the nightcaps she was sewing. "You're as useless as a beautiful, pure sacrifice!" She shook her head disapprovingly. "Who tells you to pester the girls? Who?"

"I pestered her? Convulsions take her!"

"We know that already . . . we know already. . . ." Bubbeh swallowed her words, and Zaydeh couldn't stop gasping.

"With a fish you say? Oh, I don't have sides left from laughing so hard. Nu, so tell us how'd it happen?"

"Never mind! Never mind!" Bubbeh mixed in. "Some news he wants to hear!"

Vladek seemed angry. He chewed, mouth closed. Mammeh didn't mix into this discussion at all. She sat at Zaydeh's workbench wearing her pair of gold-rimmed spectacles, looking into a book.

Vladek sat down at his usual place near the kitchen. Sighing, he pulled off his shoes, unwound his leggings and began pulling out big bunches of straw from his sack where he always kept his hoard of food.

The house was quiet; everyone was busy. The lamp burning at Zaydeh's workbench lit up the corner where he worked and where Mammeh was now reading. The rest of the room was enveloped in deep shadow. Zaydeh was hurrying to finish off a piece of work. From time to time his shoulders heaved as if he was bothered by hiccoughs. Nobody paid attention to what Vladek was doing in the corner near the kitchen. We all knew that he hoarded and chewed over the bread he managed to get from all the houses.

But actually, Vladek was not hoarding now but piling up a big bunch of straw at his feet.

He began poking around in his pockets; he poked so long until a packet of matches could be seen in the light. I watched Vladek thinking he wanted to light his pipe. No, Vladek wasn't smoking. He struck a match and put the small, flickering flame to the pile of straw that he'd bunched up around himself. A thin wisp of smoke began curling upwards and Vladek stretched out his feet to it. Nothing less, the goy was going to set himself on fire! I couldn't watch calmly anymore and yelled out:

"Bubbeh, look what Vladek's doing!"

Everyone's heads reared up from their work. Zaydeh turned his shoulder and squinted. Mammeh tore the gold-rimmed spectacles away from her book. Bubbeh was the first to spring up.

"Vey'z mir! It should never happen! What've you done? You crazy goy!" She screamed and started turning like a top.

The lit straw blazed.

"Duvid," Bubbeh wrung her hands, "We'll all die from smoke! Look what he's doing here! Help . . . people . . . !" She shrieked.

Zaydeh threw down his piece of work, his spectacles fell down to his mouth, the peak of his cap leaned on his ears. He quickly tried pushing the needle into a lapel and couldn't find the right spot so he flung needle and thread onto the worktable, sprang up onto the lit straw and began dancing around. It looked like Zaydeh had gone crazy. And Bubbeh too, because why else did she grab a pillow from the bed and throw it at Zaydeh's dancing feet?

"Are you crazy? What're you doing?" Zaydeh screamed at her, and kicked away the pillow. Mammeh quickly grabbed Bubbeh's shawl and ran to the door. Only Vladek stayed seated at his usual place, the soles of his feet red and frozen. He chewed, shaking his nose and his chin.

"You horse's head! What've you done?" Zaydeh didn't stop dancing on the straw.

"What've I done?" Vladek sniffled with a full nose. "Why are you screaming, Pan Tailor? Its winter! I just wanted to warm my feet. Convusions take her, that Magda! Why wouldn't she let me into her bed? Why not?"

"Go break your head together with that Magda!" Bubbeh blessed him with both hands. "Why did'ya come here to burn us all up?"

"I didn't want to burn anybody up. What ar'ya saying, Pani Tailor?"

"May you talk from fever, you idiot! This is how you warm your feet?" Zaydeh had actually danced out the fire but he was gasping like a consumptive.

They opened the window and the smoke wafted out in a blue, wispy cloud. Mammeh wrapped in a shawl protected me from the open window. Bubbeh wrapped herself up in one of Mammeh's kerchiefs. Only Zaydeh stood in his vest, patting his lapels. "Where'd I put the needle?"

At that moment while everyone was distracted, the door slowly opened and there on the threshold stood my father.

"Tatteh's here!" I was the first to see him and moved toward the door.

"Good evening," Tatteh said and looked in wonder over the unsettled house.

"Good evening! Good year!" Zaydeh went up to him and greeted him. "Shulem aleykhem, how ar'ya?"

Bubbeh closed the window. Mammeh's gold-rimmed spectacles fell to the floor.

"Get this garbage out of here!" Bubbeh bent over Vladek," Y'hear? Get lost this minute! Y'hear me? You dog catcher, you!"

Vladek stood up, heavily and silently, picked up the half-burnt pack of straw and carried it out, groaning.

"Why're you standing? Sit down." Zaydeh invited Tatteh.

"What happened here?" Tatteh finally asked, and looked over to where Mammeh had taken off her woolen shawl.

"Nothing, an idiot of a goy . . . he had an idea to warm his feet on a lit bundle of straw."

"Who keeps such a goy in the house?"

"I dunno. Sometimes he brings a can of water, sweeps up the rubbish. . . ." Mammeh found her spectacles. In the corner where Tatteh was staring, it must have been so dark that she sat down on the opposite side of Zaydeh's worktable and began once again to look into her book.

Didn't she notice the way Tatteh stared towards Zaydeh's workbench with pensive, absent-minded eyes?

She sat holding her head somewhat arrogantly, like a rich woman, her beautiful face withdrawn. Her soft and warm double chin quivered slightly.

"It seems Warsaw did a world of good. . . ." Tatteh's mustache barely smiled.

No one answered him. Bubbeh stabbed her needle quickly into
the white muslin. Zaydeh pulled a thread between his lips. I stood
leaning against my father looking up into his face.

"Ar'ya better already, Mendl?"

"Yeh, I'm all better already."

"When're you going back to cheder?"

"Tomorrow, God willing."

Silence hung heavily in the room. Tatteh slowly drummed two
fingers on the table. My throat tightened, even my clothes felt tight.
The gold-rimmed spectacles on Mammeh's nose glinted from afar so
hard that it actually stabbed my eyes but Mammeh's whole face shone.

"And how're you doing, Luzeh?" Zaydeh interrupted the heavy
silence.

"Thanks to the Almighty."

"And what about livelihood?"

"Not bad. No complaint."

Silence once more. Behind the stove a cricket chirped angrily and
stubbornly.

Vladek had already thrown out all the burnt heaps of straw. Now
he sat calmly at his usual place drawing on his pipe.

"You're not glad to see your wife?" Zaydeh began again.

"Eh?" Father repeated, looking right into Zaydeh's mouth.

"Your wife. . . . Aren't you glad at all?"

"Yeh, but she doesn't even see me."

At that, Mammeh raised her book higher over her face. The
gold-rimmed spectacles stopped glinting.

"Frimmet!" Zaydeh put down his piece of work. "Frimmet!
Luzeh's here."

"So he's here."

"Stop reading your book! Stop it!" Zaydeh's voice got hoarse.
"At your age you don't need to read books any more."

"I'm so old already? People older than me read books in Warsaw."

"Everything's Warsaw . . . but you don't live in Warsaw. You
have a husband and a child here. . . ."

"Some husband he is! He's a burden, not a husband!"

Tears rose in my eyes. Tatteh sat, his face closed, the fingers with
which he had earlier drummed on the table now stood half-raised,
deadened.

"What'd I do? I stole the vegetables in the field out from under
her?" he said at last.

"And the deadly curses he sent me all the way to Warsaw, that's
nothing?" Mammeh now took the book away from her face. "What's

the matter? I shouldn't have gone to my daughter's celebration? How many daughters do I have altogether?"

"Nu, enough! So he acted foolish. But how long's enough to be so mad?"

"I'm mad?"

"What then are you, my friend? You sit yourself down reading . . . what will you have from your reading? What?"

"And what will I have from him?"

"What d'ya mean, what'll you have? Is he your husband, or isn't he?"

"No, he's not my husband."

"Oh, stop already, you fool."

"What do you want from me, Tatteh?"

I want you not to make a fool of yourself. You have a home . . . a house. What kind of life is there for you here?"

"Don't worry, Tatteh. I won't be a burden to you. I'll always earn my bit of bread."

"What exactly will she do?" Tatteh interjected.

"He doesn't need to worry his head."

"What'll you do, really?" Zaydeh spiked his beard upwards.

"I'll do all right. Don't worry. I can always hold a pen in my hand. I can read. I can write. If I want to, I can even give lessons. I'll be able to earn my bit of bread."

"You want to become a rebbetsin of girls?"

"So what if I become a rebbetsin of girls?"

Bubbeh who was silent the whole time, now stood up.

"I didn't want to mix in," she began, "but if you're really going to talk nonsense, then I have to tell you, Frimmet, you're not right." This time, Bubbeh spoke quietly, shaking her head.

It seemed Tatteh heard Bubbeh's words by the shaking of her head and was encouraged.

"The house is heated," he said, "and the table's ready. I asked for milk, cheese and butter to be got ready."

"Go thank him for it! You see how he indulges himself?" And if sometimes I need more money, then the heavens open up!"

"You're worried about money?" Tatteh hunched a shoulder.

"I'm worried about everything. I'm worried that he should treat me right. With Berl, may he rest in peace, I had brass handles on every door! What do I have here?"

"If God will favour me, I'll have brass handles made for you."

"First of all, he found a place to live," Mammeh spoke as if to Vladek. "Dark! Cold . . . !"

"Who's to blame? You yourself wanted this place."

"I wanted it? How could I want it, when my poor unfortunate Moysheh got sick there?"

"It was the will of heaven, probably. But if you're worried about the place, then with the help of the Almighty, you can rent another one for Pesach."

"No small thing! 'Tshekoy babka latka' " . . . She quoted in Polish. "Wait like granny waited. . . . Wait till the cows come home!"

"How long is it to Pesach?" Zaydeh mixed in. "You see, Frimmet, he came to make up with you. What more d'ya want?"

"A nice way to make up with me!"

"If that's what matters," Tatteh wrung his hands helplessly, "What d'ya want me to do to make up with you? Never mind. So that's what I'm doing."

Silence fell again. Vladek was breathing dreamily, his pipe in his mouth. Zaydeh raised his needle to the lamp and threaded it quickly. Mammeh interrupted the silence. "Who turned on the heat?"

"I asked for it to be heated. There's milk, there's butter. Meat I didn't want to get ready . . . I didn't know. . . ."

"And the bed linen has been changed, at least?"

"Yeh, I asked for that too. Its warm, clean. . . ."Tatteh's voice became warmer. He stood up from the table and went closer to Zaydeh's worktable where Mammeh sat.

"D'ya have any parcels?" he asked. I'll get a horse and cab."

"Where'll you find a cab now?"

"We'll get."

Mammeh put down her book. I don't know whether she showed Tatteh where her things were, but he went straight to the parcel from Warsaw and picked it up.

"Maybe a drink of brandy, Luzeh?" Zaydeh put down his piece of work and was already rummaging around in the kitchen cupboard where he kept his liquor.

Tatteh's smile spread out over his beard and his yellow-grey mustache got bigger and thicker.

"L'khayim! To life!"

"L'khayim toyvim uleshulem! To a good life, and to peace!" May we drink only at celebrations! Neh!"

Vladek woke up from his dreaming, took the pipe out of his mouth and stood up. He smiled at Zaydeh's bottle, danced around and shook his ragged beard.

"Hayim! Hayim! Life! Life! Pan Tailor!"

"You wanna drink, Vladek?"

"Mm! Mm!"

"Here, have some," Zaydeh handed him half a glass full. "And drink to the health of Magda who slapped you with a fish!"

"No! Convulsions take her, that girl! To Pan Merchant, health! Hayim! Hayim!" Mammeh also sipped from a glass. I myself could now have drunk up a whole bottle.

"Nu, its getting late."

"Good night."

"Good night! Good year! To good times!"

Tatteh led the way, carrying Mammeh's parcel in both hands, Mammeh and I behind him. Vladek was dancing around. Bubbeh-Zaydeh stood in the open doorway, Bubbeh with the kerosene lamp held high over her head and Zaydeh with a thread hanging down from his lip, singing the refrain:

> "Let's make up, let's make up,
> Now treat me to some oranges."

Chapter 7

It was either a custom or maybe even some kind of law in our town that when you moved from one place to another, it could only be done on the goyish "*Shventi Yan*," St. John holiday, which this year fell on the week of Shabbes Nakhmu, the Shabbes of Consolation that falls in mid-summer. At such times, tufts of straw would roll around under the beds even though nobody was sleeping there. Doors and windows stood wide open and abandoned. Boys ran in and out, dogs crawled around in the freshly strewn rubbish and, in the middle of an ordinary Wednesday, proper respectable Jews went by on wagons loaded up with all their belongings.

But Mammeh didn't want to wait that long. She couldn't look at the old place anymore. The wind blew from every corner. So as soon as we left Bubbeh-Zaydeh's house she began looking, asking everyone until finally she rented a place to live, unique in the whole city—a palace, not just any place!

We waited until after Shabbes and on the next Tuesday, since it's a lucky day, we moved.

The goy who came every day to wake Tatteh up didn't know anything about it. At dawn he stood as usual under the window and rapped on the pane.

"Pan Merchant! Pan Merchant!"

But "Pan Merchant," that is to say my father, was already dressed. He let the goy in right away and told him that they weren't going to the village today because we were moving to a new place, and he should stay and help us with our belongings.

I didn't go to cheder that day either. We davened earlier, quickly ate something warm and right after Tatteh finished making the blessing, we set to work. Tatteh and the peasant, both groaning, moved the wardrobe away from the wall. A big, dark stain, spider webs, and dust were left behind. Cigarette butts, bent tin spoons, a wooden mold used to make Channukah dreydls, and a pair of dirty and stiff shirt cuffs from the deceased Moysheh lay scattered all over the cold and grimy house.

When the mirror was taken down from above the dresser, a large, flustered spider began running up the wall to the beam, stopped in the middle and looked down at the mess we'd created.

Tatteh took the beds apart by himself. The peasant wanted to help him but Tatteh made a face, showing two rows of healthy, white teeth, and said to him in Yiddish: "Don't touch! I'll do it myself."

Beds were always Tatteh's weakness. He held that a bed was like a wife: If a stranger came near, he'd spoil it.

Mammeh had gotten up earlier and was already dressed for work. Nothing of the Warsaw look was left to her. She was busy pouring boiling pots of water over the dismantled beds.

We stepped on damp half rotten pieces of straw that dragged stubbornly behind our feet. There was a smell of rags and unaired bed linen lay piled up under the cot that had once been for Yuzheh, the barrel maker's daughter. From behind the dresser we found some bent little sardine boxes that nobody knew how they got there.

All this was left behind including the echo that ran from corner to corner in the dark loneliness that stays in a house when people move out.

Our things lay thrown together on the sleigh without order.

The four braided legs of our big table pointed up to the sky like a tied-up calf and the red featherbeds that had been stripped from the beds were stuffed into the overturned table. The slop pail and the black, dented pots went into the drawers of the dresser.

All of this glided and creaked over the soft, deep snow.

Tatteh walked on one side, carrying the wall clock in his arms just like, l'havdil, you carry a scroll of the Torah at Succoth time. Mammeh walked on the other side holding the big lamp that used to burn from one holiday to the other in the old house.

I sat on the back of the sleigh with my face to the street, my hands holding the tarnished brass candlesticks. The pestle and the old pressing iron that Zaydeh had given us as a get well present, lay at my feet.

In this way we came to our new place.

Among a row of straight wooden houses on the street, one yellowed house stood forward from the rest. It had a wall and a steep, tin roof.

A white cat, whiter even then the snow, looked down at us from the roof, whiskers quivering. It stretched its head out, it must have been in great surprise because it suddenly opened its whiskers wide and yawned.

The sleigh with our things on it had to stay in the street because the gate was narrow and the courtyard even narrower. No pump could be seen. It smelled of pigs and from the old damp stalls that hung off the wooden balcony.

Under this very balcony was our new home. This place was smaller than our old one; the kitchen was blue, with crooked beams and thin, crumbling walls. It was four-cornered, with two windows looking out into the small courtyard. It wasn't bright, but for all that, the new place had a floor painted red. This had to be the only reason why Mammeh rented it.

"All the floors are painted red in Warsaw," she said.

Tatteh wrinkled up his nose. "Its so dark!" His eyes took in the walls.

"That's because its winter," Mammeh explained. "Summer, God willing, it'll be brighter."

I liked the new place. It was empty and clean, no spots on the walls, no damp straw scattered around. There wouldn't be any mice because a floor painted red discourages them, Moysheh wouldn't die here, and there wouldn't be a Yuzheh, the barrel maker's daughter, whom I couldn't stop dreaming about.

A grey and smoky evening looked in from the outside. On the balcony where the stalls hung, someone was running, making a noise under the eaves as if throwing blocks of wood.

Mammeh had lit the big holiday lamp and it was now warm and bright in the house.

Tatteh in his quilted jacket was putting the wardrobe together. He gritted his strong, white teeth and groaned a little while I held the small kerosene lamp up to give him light. Every time Tatteh groaned, I groaned too.

It was altogether different here from the old place. A fire was already lit in the stove and the black and dented pots with their empty, open mouths were sitting on the grate. It was warm and bubbling just like at Bubbeh's. One side of Mammeh's face was red and the sleeves of her blouse were rolled up to her elbows like bagel.

Every few minutes she stood on the threshold and in a warm, worry-free voice she reminded:

"Luzeh? Maybe you'll go wash yourself? Luzeh? The food's getting cold."

But Tatteh was still busy with the wardrobe. He was on the point of setting the cornice into place, hunching up one shoulder, bending his head a little, his tall broad-shouldered figure squatted, feet apart.

Suddenly he released his shoulder, bent forward and the cornice slid easily into place.

In the kitchen Mammeh was getting the table ready.

White hot steam drifted up from the bowls of grits. A big and spongy bread sprinkled with poppy seeds lay ready. Mammeh cut big slices from which Tatteh made small pieces, dipped them into the salt, and this is how he ate them.

Flies flew down from the bread and settled on the rims of the bowls. Every few minutes Tatteh put down his spoon, searched with long slow glances where it was that the flies intended to land next. Mammeh chased them off with her spoon, with her hand, meanwhile hurrying Tatteh:

"Nu, eat already. The food's getting cold."

I knew why she was rushing him.

There was no bigger aggravation in our house than when Tatteh, God forbid, found a fly on his food. When this happened, the dish could be the biggest delicacy and no matter how hungry he was, he wouldn't touch it.

But this time the flies got tired. Mammeh killed one of them with her dishtowel. The rest stuck themselves to the beams and from there looked down at the emptying bowls and the bread being cleaned off the table.

◦§

In the new place Mammeh saw to it that we should eat in the kitchen during the week except for Shabbes and the holidays. She had cleaned up the house nicely, placed the table in the middle of the room, not at the window like in the old place. On the table there was always a colorful tablecloth patterned with boxes, birds without heads, and large embroidered flowers.

Around the tarnished mirror above the dresser, Mammeh hung up the photographs of her sons and her only daughter Tsippeleh, who had gotten engaged in Warsaw.

She also spread out on the dresser a thick, grey, knitted cotton cloth with fringes. Added also was a smoothly polished, etched glass vase that looked like a small boat. Into this you could throw mother-of-pearl buttons, thimbles, pins, and most important, here lay the white jabot that Mammeh wore under her double chin every Shabbes since coming back from Warsaw.

But nothing was more decorative than the two greeting cards standing on the dresser that Mammeh got from her two sons far away.

These cards gleaming with gold and silver, had small round walls with gates and shiny gold letters in the German style on them that said:

"Heartfelt good wishes for the New Year."

The little doors in the walls of these cards had two white doves standing like the Guardians of Paradise with sealed letters in their beaks.

Tatteh knew nothing about this new decoration. He never saw these greeting cards in the old place. He noticed them for the first time now that they had suddenly appeared on the dresser. He wrinkled his brow, took the cards into his large hands stiff with cold, as if handling a delicate piece of glass.

"What could this be?"

"Greeting cards," Mammeh replied.

"Greeting cards? From whom?"

"From Yoyneh and Avrumkeh."

Tatteh's beard leaned into his lapel. With one hand he took off his spectacles, with the other he put the cards back on the dresser. He didn't look at them any more. His pensive, absent-minded eyes began searching for something around the mirror where the photographs of Mammeh's children hung.

It seemed that Tatteh was looking for the photograph of his son Laybkeh who was serving in the Russian army in Yekaterinoslav. He found it but it was hanging apart, together with a picture of an elongated woman's figure that no one in the house had any idea who it was.

Tatteh didn't have any complaints about why his Laybkeh was hanging apart but later when we were sitting in the kitchen eating supper, he looked at me with a pair of big, blue eyes and called out:

"He doesn't write anything, Laybkeh?"

Nobody answered him. Slowly, he cut little pieces of bread, sipped from his spoon and called out again:

"In Yekaterinoslav . . . among goyim . . . in such a place you can't even find greeting cards!"

❧

The order of our life went on in the same way here in our new place as in the old one. Every morning the peasant came again and called into the windowpanes:

"Pan Merchant! Pan Merchant!"

Tatteh left housekeeping money for Mammeh under the knitted cloth on the dresser before he went out. She tried to bargain with him, said that she wouldn't make any more meals but we still ate the same as always. The house was warm and clean.

But still, in spite of all this golden goodness, sadness lay on this house. Maybe it came from being too clean. Or maybe it was because the windows under the wooden balcony didn't let in any sunlight. Or then again, maybe it was just a sad house.

Mammeh was the first to feel it. She was like the swallow that senses right from the first rain that summer is ending. She began to get uneasy. From day to day, she was less strict about keeping the house clean and she forgot to make the soup ready in time.

But no one could have a complaint to her. What was she supposed to do? There were hardly any neighbors around. I sat all day in Simmeh-Yoysef's cheder, while Tatteh was busy traveling to the villages to buy hay. So she left the house and went off to see Aunt Miriam or sat sometimes with Bubbeh Rakhl. The pots on the hearth again began looking out on the house with empty and dark mouths.

Only when Tatteh came home did Mammeh start kneading dough and getting supper ready. Tatteh, who was hungry, got mad. Sometimes he cursed, and sometimes he even went to sleep without supper. So it was sad in the house, very sad.

Until once in the wintertime, the door angrily burst open and a tall unkempt youth in a quilted jacket pushed himself in. He carried a folded iron cot on his shoulders and a pack of bed linen in his hand.

"Where should I put it?" He grumbled, his voice raw.

"Right here, please." Mammeh showed him between the cupboard for dishes and the water barrel.

He put the things down, panting. A few minutes later, he threw the door open again and wheeled in a big blue upholstered trunk bound with iron hoops and fastened with two locks.

"Where's Hodel?" Mammeh looked at the youth.

"She's coming."

He was mistaken. She didn't come in as much as she hopped in. She actually bounced in. She was roundly padded and said loudly:

"Good evening, Frimmet!"

"Good evening! Good year! How come so late, Hodelshi?"

"What'd I miss?" Hodel in a brown fur coat with a tattered collar, looked uneasily over our kitchen, put down a mannish looking umbrella by the door and took a deep breath.

"Neh, can you beat that? That's some distance!"

"How far is it?"

"It's far." Hodel began to unwind her shawl wheezing all the while, and lifted up a shiny chin streaked from sweets to the tall youth.

"How much do I owe you, eh?"

"Two gilden, Auntie," the youth replied wiping his brow with his sleeve.

"What kind of an Auntie am I to you?" Hodel frowned with her small, pointed nose that reminded me of a little boot. "How come two gilden? How come? I agreed to pay only forty."

"For such a long distance? Only forty?"

"You don't like it? So take me to court!"

"Auntie, don't play the big shot with me and pay up as agreed."

"What kind of an Auntie am I to you, you lout of a peasant, you?"

"What's the matter? I'm not good enough for you?"

"Naturally, you're not."

"Well, if I'm not good enough for you, you can do me a favor . . ."

"You'll get such a smack in the kisser, that you'll see your great grandmother in front of your eyes!" Hodel sprang at the youth.

"Sure! Let's see what an old hag like you can do!"

Hodel was a greedy woman and she also liked to scream. If my mother hadn't interfered, she whose hands always shook when people started arguing, if she hadn't smoothed out the bargaining with another ten-spot, a fight would have broken out between Hodel and the youth.

The youth left, wishing a cholera on Hodel and she, in turn, wished him a second cholera. Afterward, she angrily began to unbutton her tight-fitting, brown fur coat that hung down to her ankles.

"Help me take off this coat, Frimmet," she called out, sighing.

Mammeh placed the fur coat on a bench, but Hodel made a face.

"How come on a bench? How come not in your wardrobe? How come?"

"It's a little crowded in the wardrobe," Mammeh all but apologized.

"If it's so crowded in the wardrobe, then you don't take in a boarder. What's the matter? My coat isn't a coat?"

"Who says so? God forbid! Second of all, I'll take another look. Maybe yes."

"No maybes! My coat has to hang in the wardrobe!" Her coat hung in our wardrobe.

Hodel also took off a knitted kaftan, a padded shirt and was left in nothing more than a flannel shift. Only then did she begin looking over the kitchen again.

"Here's where it'll be?"

"Right here, Hodelshi."

"It's really as warm as you said?"

"As warm as an oven."

"And where's the bathroom?"

"Outside, two steps from the door."

Mammeh spoke meekly to Hodel, with a fixed smile as if she owed Hodel something.

"And where's that husband of yours?"

"He'll probably come soon."

"Who's going to put up my cot? Who?"

"It'll be put up."

"And do you have a night pot?"

"How can you think there's no night pot?"

Hodel suddenly turned her big, catlike eyes on me. "This is your boy?" She grinned with her big, wet mouth.

"Yes, this is my youngest, Mendl, may he live and be well."

"You didn't have any more with your husband?"

"Another girl and him, may he have long years," Mammeh bent her head sadly.

"May no Evil Eye befall him! A young lad like a light! C'm'ere, you!" She motioned to me with her head but I didn't like this strange woman and I didn't go to her.

"Where're you studying?"

"At Simmeh-Yoysef's," Mammeh answered for me.

"D'ya pee with foam yet?"

I saw how Mammeh's face reddened.

Hodel grinned from ear to ear. I myself didn't know where to turn. This old hag had torn into our place like a cold wind. Neither my discomfort nor my mother's flaming face bothered her. She grinned right into my eyes, sniffled, pulled some sweets out of her shift and sucking noisily, she asked again:

"And when does your husband get up in the morning, eh, Frimmet?"

"At dawn."

"So he won't let me close an eye?"

"God forbid! He doesn't even wake me up and I'm a light sleeper, like a chicken."

I assumed from this whole talk that Hodel had attached herself to us and would stay in the kitchen. Mammeh would no longer be sad, there'd be another person living here the same way Yuzheh had lived with us in our old home.

Still, I fell asleep late that night. I kept seeing under my closed eyelids, this strange woman wandering around our house, fleshy and roly-poly like a featherbed. I kept hearing the scraping of her iron cot, her sniffling, the noisy mouth sucking and several times I even heard her relieving herself into a tin pot.

Chapter 8

Hodel, may she live to a hundred and twenty, was maybe forty years old but she believed that she couldn't be more than thirty. Her bitter life and hard livelihood had made her old and grey before her time.

Hodel had once had a man, a weakling and a failure, so she got rid of him and married somebody else. She wanted children with either husband, so she consulted holy men and doctors, drank all kinds of medicines but these husbands, the second one as well as the first, were both a bit deaf and didn't know what Hodel wanted from them.

In the large courtyard behind the shul where Hodel used to live, women and girls would stand around open-mouthed at the bleak curses that Hodel rained down on the heads of both her husbands. She screamed that she was as sound as a nut. All the doctors and all the holy men in the whole Kingdom of Poland had assured her of that! Nothing less than the men. . . . May a rage from heaven carry them off!

Hodel's second husband was a quiet, decent man. He could read a chapter of the Mishnah, sometimes come out with a clever saying, and his presence enhanced a celebration, but Hodel tormented him for so long that he finally got sick in the guts, went to bed, suffered a while, and never got up again.

Hodel didn't want to marry for a third time. If men were worth no more than death, what was the point in risking her life? So at age thirty something, round, ruddy, with a face smeared from sweets, she stayed a poor and desolate widow for the rest of her life.

It was sad to be a widow, all alone in the world, even for someone like Hodel. So she drew near to strangers and wherever she went, her ragged, green trunk on wheels went with her. From day to day it got heavier from the Shabbes candlesticks, the pillows and the clothing that poor people pawned with her and later didn't have anything to redeem them with.

It seemed that this time, Mammeh had arranged for Hodel and her trunk to stray right into our kitchen.

Mammeh said that first of all, it would help with the rent and it would be cozier too. Tatteh wasn't pleased with the new neighbor. He could manage the rent now and as far as cozy was concerned, he didn't understand why Mammeh didn't feel comfortable.

He took a dim view of Hodel, silently noted the ragged trunk, then turned his eyes to Mammeh.

"What's the use of it, Frimmet?" his eyes asked her frankly.

Hodel understood Tatteh's glance, and with her swollen, damp mouth she asked:

"Why're you looking like that, Reb Luzeh?"

"Why shouldn't I look? It pays to look at a good-looking woman." Tatteh joked.

"Ha-ha-ha." Hodel's face got even more crinkled. "But isn't it true, Reb Luzeh, that I've got nothing to be ashamed of?"

"Nu, stop already, Hodel," Mammeh mixed in quickly.

"Why should I stop? Why? Ar'ya jealous?"

"I'm not jealous, but I don't like this kind of joking."

"He doesn't hear anything you say to him anyway," Hodel belittled the whole discussion.

Its possible that Tatteh really didn't hear what was said but I did hear and I heard every word right from the beginning.

It hurt me that Hodel sneered at my father's deafness. Her loud and frivolous talk stabbed me in every limb and I hated this overfed woman like I hated spiders.

She brought screaming and clutter into our house. Her ragged trunk stayed in the kitchen for a few days and then, in the middle of an ordinary Wednesday, it suddenly rolled into our big room. From day to day, Hodel got fatter and her lips got more sugary.

During this time, Mammeh lost the beautiful double chin she'd brought back from Warsaw. Her face got drawn and even more pointed. In the morning, she didn't wear the black silk slip from Aunt Gitl-Hoddehs anymore but a plain flannel shift. She looked taller and thinner.

Hodel on the other hand, wagged her sides like a cow. She went around the house with her fleshy arms uncovered, combed her blonde wig with a thick paste that irritated the nose and settled on the tongue. She didn't stop chewing pieces of fruitcake, nibbling on rich, yellow halvah and smacking her lips like Vladek with his bits of pauper's bread.

Hodel ate with her face to the wall, never offering anything to anyone. If anyone found her eating, she'd wipe her lips, and with a mouthful of food as if she was hiding a theft inside, wait for the other person to leave.

Hodel was afraid of the Evil Eye. Every Monday and Thursday, Mammeh had to pour out a glass of water, put a hot, burning piece of charcoal into it, dip her fingers into this water and rinse Hodel's face with it several times, uttering the incantation: "To all the barren forests! To all the vacant fields!" In this way, my mother cast out the Evil Eye from Hodel.

The smell of marmalade that Hodel stashed under her cot and nibbled on, teased me. Even though I didn't like Hodel, still from time to time, I'd steal a look at where she was smacking her lips.

One time, she called me to her, looked me right in the face, and handed me a piece of fruitcake.

"Here you are, brat!" she said. "Take it! Be a fine fellow and you'll get more."

I don't know whether I was a fine fellow or not, but several days later she called me to her again, looked me over from all sides and gave me a piece of halvah.

"Eat, little brother, you're worth it . . ." She winked mischievously and pinched my arm. "It's good, eh?"

The halvah really did taste good but why did I deserve to be pinched? It hurt. My arm had a swollen blue mark that turned black after a while. I was afraid Mammeh would see it. I could do without the halvah and the fruitcake but I wanted Hodel to stop pinching me.

One Shabbes morning the house still wasn't tidied up. The damp yellow sand that was spread out the evening before now lay dry and faded. Cold plates with even colder fish stood on the windowsill. Mammeh had run off to Aunt Miriam's because someone was sick. There was no tea in the house and old Pavlova, who came to heat the kitchen stove on Shabbes, was late today. Tatteh had already read the weekly portion of the Torah and he wanted a warm glass of tea. Maybe because he was very thirsty, every few minutes he tried to get me up.

"It's time to go daven!"

It was warm under the featherbed and drafty in the house. Why would I want to get up? So I dawdled.

"Soon, Tatteh, just a little bit more."

But Tatteh couldn't wait, not for me and not for Pavlova to come, so he threw his tallis over his kapoteh, put on his overcoat on top of the tallis and, after warning me that for the sake of heaven, I should get up right away and come to the study house, he went off by himself.

Still I didn't want to get up.

So I started counting to one hundred and made a bet with myself that when I got to a hundred and one, I'd jump right out of bed. So I counted until two hundred and . . . still I lay in bed.

Counting in this way, I heard the door being locked in the kitchen. Why was the door being locked all of a sudden? What was Hodel up to?

It didn't take long and Hodel came into the room. It must be that she herself didn't know how she looked. She didn't even have a flannel shift on but stood there in a pair of wide, white pants with points like those worn by magicians who show black magic in Tshappeleh's shed. Hodel was also not wearing a nightcap and I noticed only now that she had a thin head of hair, grey too. What was the matter with her? She glanced stealthily around the room, went to the window and pulled the curtains shut.

This was very surprising to me. Why did it bother her that the curtains were open?

It seemed Hodel had her own ideas. Before I even had time to think it through, Hodel sidled over to my bed and sat herself down.

I broke out in a hot and cold sweat. I felt that it was shameful to have this strange woman sitting on my bed.

I didn't know yet what she had in mind but I quickly pulled the featherbed over my head and hid myself in its sweaty warmth.

"Why're you hiding yourself like this?" Hodel pulled back the featherbed, "Here! Here's some candy!"

"I don't want your candy! Lemme get up!"

"Stop yelling like this! D'ya know that I once choked a boy who screamed like this?"

Her voice suddenly got hoarse.

At that moment, I actually felt that I was that boy and that Hodel had already choked me.

I couldn't figure it out any other way. My tongue curdled, I was ice cold and it stabbed me all the way down to my toes.

"You fool!" Hodel loomed over me. "I've got oranges for you, and grapes and walnuts! What d'ya think I want from you?"

She didn't say what she wanted but unexpectedly, she grabbed my mouth between her two thick, swollen lips.

I lost my breath; I was choking. I tore my mouth away from hers, but Hodel was stronger than me. Her hands were like two pliers holding my head in a vise. Another second and I felt her overfed, forty-year-old body against me.

"Dear," she didn't as much say it as she wheezed it. "I'll give you money. I've got lots'a money. . . . And you'll also get a pocket watch. You're already a young man . . . so you should have a watch of your own!"

I remembered like in a fever how Yuzheh, the barrel maker's daughter, who also spoke hoarsely, had held me close when I came home chilled after the funeral. What did this Hodel want of me? I felt sick to the pit of my stomach. I was like some piece of trash in her hands now.

She lifted me up. I couldn't do anything.

"If I want . . . then you must!" She ground her teeth and tried to lift me onto herself.

But now a miracle happened. I suddenly felt my own strength and I didn't fall where Hodel wanted me to, but slid myself further over to the edge and with one twist, I was on the floor.

"People! Save me!" I panted, crawling on all fours.

"Will you stop screaming?" Hodel also twisted herself off the bed and sprang up as I was dragging myself along the floor. She put her heavy foot on my neck.

Nothing less, but Hodel was going to choke me for sure, the same way she choked that other boy!

I don't know how the plan came to me, God Himself must have helped me turn my face and with all my strength, I bit Hodel in the leg.

"Thief! Murderer!" She screamed sharply, springing back.

I let go of her leg and she jumped onto her other foot like a tethered goose.

"May you burn in hell, you vile son of a bitch!" she screamed. "Wait, I'll fix you! Such a little bastard, and already crawling into women! A cholera take you!"

She grabbed a candlestick off the table and threw it where I was standing, while with hurrying hands she hitched up her pants.

The candlestick fell into the soft featherbed and stayed there like a corpse. Hodel hopped into the kitchen on one foot. I must have looked like a corpse too.

I got dressed in the wink of an eye. I couldn't leave through the kitchen because Hodel was sitting there, so I unlatched the window and jumped out over the cold fish and the jellied broth.

"May you burn, hands and feet, life and limb!" I heard Hodel's blessing behind me.

I bumped into people in the street. I'm sure I lost my way. How could I go to the study house looking like this? Vey'z mir! I've wandered all the way to the old garden! What will Tatteh say and what will I tell him?

It took longer than usual to get to the study house. They were already in the middle of davening. Tatteh, covered in his tallis over his head, kept looking sideways at me with angry, heavy eyes but he didn't say anything. He only put his large hand on my shoulder and in a gloomy voice showed me where we were in the prayer book.

"Nu, aah . . ."

I dug my eyes into the torn, yellowed pages but I couldn't see the letters. Tatteh's harsh look burned into my shoulder. Hodel lay between every line. I didn't know when it was time to turn the page and I didn't

hear where Moshkeh the khazn was at. Every few minutes, Tatteh
turned his head toward me from under his tallis and muttered loudly:
    "Nu, aah."
    He didn't dare speak, but in that mutter that issued more from
his nose than from his mouth, I heard his stubborn question:
    "Where were you so long? Why aren't you davening? Why? And
how come you're so distracted? What?"
    It was hard to suffer this davening. It was pain! Hell! I begged
God I should be able to endure it, to be on our way home already.
But going home was even harder.
    "What'sa matter with you, Mendl?" Tatteh's voice drilled into
my brain like an awl.
    "Nothin, what should be the matter?"
    "Why didn't you come to the study house right away?"
    "I didn't have a clean shirt." I lied immediately.
    "What d'ya mean, you didn't have a clean shirt? It was laying
ready on the stool."
    "I couldn't find it."
    "Neh . . . ! And Mammeh didn't come back yet?"
    "No."
    "You're altogether absent-minded, Mendl. What's the matter with
you? Maybe you're not feeling well?"
    "My head aches a little." I wasn't telling a lie. My head really was
aching, my temples pounding. I felt sick to the pit of my empty stomach.
    Tatteh looked down at me, long and slow. It was hard to know
whether he believed me or not, but he didn't torture me anymore with
questions.
    We walked home in silence. The snow crunched familiarly under
our feet. Any other time, I would have enjoyed sliding in the frozen
gutters. I would have stolen away from Tatteh's measured Shabbes
gait and joined the group of boys making a snowman but today, the
white Shabbes-looking street looked black in my eyes. I was cold. The
crunching snow shrieked out my sin. I was ashamed to walk beside my
father, afraid I would dirty his Shabbes kapoteh with my unclean self.
    When we came home, the grates on the stove were white-hot and
the covered pots were already warming. There was a smell of goose,
of sweet cabbage, and of wood burning.
    Mammeh had already come back from Aunt Miriam's. She told
us that Uncle Shmiel didn't feel good during the night and, it shouldn't
happen to anyone, he'd collapsed. Toivyeh, the old-time healer, came
and put leeches on him. Mammeh was shuffling slowly, from one
headboard to the other, straightening out the bedding. It seemed to

me that she spent a minute longer at Tatteh's bed. My heart fell. Did she sense something? Did she see something there?

But she only turned the featherbed over, folded it and quietly smoothed it out.

Hodel was standing in our room with her face to the window. She wore a black dress with a long gold chain around her neck. Round and well padded, she was swaying over a prayer book into the windowpanes.

I glanced at her sideways, certain that any minute she would turn around and scream out the reason why I was so late for the davening. I got ready to answer. I also had something to say.

But Hodel didn't speak. She went around sullen, glum, wouldn't pick her head up, wouldn't look anyone in the face.

"Hodel," Mammeh tried asking, "Are you aggravated over something, God forbid, that you're going around like that?"

Hodel didn't answer. She left right after eating and stayed away that whole Shabbes, coming back late at night, when Tatteh was already sitting on his bed taking off his boots.

I decided to keep as far away from Hodel as possible. I already understood what she meant with the pieces of halvah and the fruitcake. Shabbes morning I no longer stayed in bed. Just the opposite. Lots of times, I got up even earlier than Tatteh.

Hodel stopped talking from that Shabbes on, not only to me but to everyone else in the house. She was furious. She didn't pay attention to anyone and didn't ask about anyone. She went around most of the day free as a bird, in a low-necked shift with bare elbows. She locked and unlocked her trunk seven times a day, loudly closed the lid, cooked in Mammeh's pots and broke our drinking glasses. Nothing less but the woman had gone crazy! Mammeh looked and kept quiet.

Tatteh never saw Hodel this way because he left at dawn. When he closed the door, she turned over on the other side and when he came back at night she was already worn out from dragging her female fury around.

Once, it shouldn't happen to anybody, Mammeh was sick in bed. Tatteh had to stay home and he saw Hodel. She wandered around in her low-necked shift, from the kitchen to the big room, from the room back to the kitchen. She had a lot to do at her trunk that day. She put in, she took out, locked it up, then unlocked it again. Tatteh was standing davening in tallis and tfiln. It was hard to know if his eyes lingered on Hoddl longer but all of a sudden, he began reciting faster and louder. Mammeh was lying sick in bed and couldn't talk but with God's help, she finally got up and said to Hodel who was wandering around in her low-necked shift:

"Hodel, aren't you cold, dressed like that?"

Hodel stuck her big face into a small pot cooking on the stove and answered into it:

"Why should I be cold? Isn't there a fire under the grate?"

"But how can you go around dressed like that the whole day?"

"How am I going around? How?"

"I don't know. Maybe you should put something over yourself? Its not right."

"Look at that! It's not right . . . ? What've I got to be ashamed of? Isn't it all mine?"

"But Hodelshi, at your age . . . I don't know . . . there's a young boy in the house."

"Look at that, look how she's afraid for the boy!" Hodel pointed her face around the room. "Never mind. That boy of yours, that sissy, knows more than both of us."

My blood froze. The moment had arrived. Hodedl was going to tell everything. Where do I turn? What should I say?

"Nu, quiet! Quiet!" Mammeh was stunned and began chasing Hodel's bitter talk away from herself with both hands. "May your enemies talk better!"

"I ask you plain, Frimmet," Hodel placed herself in the middle of the room, hands on her hips, "When'd you become such a pious guardian?"

At that moment, Mammeh's face looked twice as big as it usually did, bewildered, led away from the straight path.

"I haven't become a guardian," she began explaining herself, "but in a house with menfolk . . ."

"Menfolk! What d'ya know? I should have such a year as your Luzeh doesn't dislike what others do like! Ha . . . ha . . . !"

The woman said it with such a triumphant, secretive grin, with such vile arrogance that Mammeh's lips closed at once. It was noticeable that Mammeh was swallowing down not just a mouthful of air, but of blood.

My head was splitting. I would have swallowed my own grievance but Mammeh's grief tore strips off me. If I could jump Hodel and give her a kick in the stomach, it would add a hundred years to my life.

Mammeh must have noticed something. She stared at me with her light-blue and sad, half-dreamy eyes. It seemed to me that her look demanded a reckoning from me, that I should say something. Yeh, I wanted to. I wanted to tell everything. But maybe it would only make things worse?

For a few days afterward, Mammeh went around shrunken, not speaking, as if Hodel had thrown stones at her, not words.

The evenings were dark grey, oddly heavy. Mammeh darned, patched, mended, while Hodel continued to cook in her pots, turning to the wall to gulp down her soup with the chicken wings.

In those days our family didn't eat meat during the week. In the morning, Mammeh cooked grits and in the evening, borsht with fried potatoes.

The smell of Hodel's chicken soup settled in the mouth with a sweet hunger. Before going to sleep, Hodel chewed on pieces of orange with her mouth closed.

How was it possible to like such a person as Hodel? Never mind that we had to go to bed on a stomach full of potatoes while she savored oranges. But what did she want from me? And what did she have against Tatteh? What?

Mammeh stayed silent for a time, a long, painful silence. Finally, late one night, when Tatteh was already calmly slicing his grated potatoes, Mammeh who was in the middle of patching a shirt, moved closer to him, and in a quiet and restrained voice, said:

"Luzeh . . ."

The door to the kitchen was closed. I was ready to fall asleep but behind my closed eyes I felt that Mammeh was on the point of talking to Tatteh about something I shouldn't hear.

Maybe it was the tone of her voice, maybe the whole time of her bitter silence had made me prick up my ears and listen in on what they were talking about.

"Luzeh." Mammeh repeated and bent her head even closer to her husband.

"Eh?" Tatteh's spoon stayed put on his plate.

"Tell me the truth, Luzeh."

Tatteh turned his beard, his face registering blind curiosity. "Wha-a-t?" he asked.

"You see, Luzeh . . ." Mammeh choked on every word, "Hodel . . ."

"What about her?"

"Hodel says . . . that is to say . . . she doesn't say so openly . . ."

Mammeh put her hand on Tatteh's shoulder.

He was now bothered, pushed his plate of food away and stared at Mammeh with a half-open mouth.

"I don't understand anything you're saying, Frimmet! What are you saying?"

"I'm saying . . ." Mammeh's voice became deep and low, "I'm only asking, tell me the truth . . . you and Hodel . . . Eh?"

"Wha-a-at?"

Both of them were sitting facing the bed where I lay. They stared at each other but stayed silent. It was a tearful plea that rang out in Mammeh's voice. Tatteh paled.

"Frimmet!" He broke the silence with a tight voice. "Where'd you get such an idea?"

"She herself . . . Hodel . . ."

"What d'ya mean, she herself?"

"She said that you and she . . ."

It took only a split second, a moment of deliberation. Tatteh suddenly stood up, hastily pushed the stool aside and took a step toward the closed door to the kitchen.

"Luzeh!" Mammeh rose at once and stood in his way. "What are you going to do?"

"Lemme at her!"

"Luzeh!" Mammeh threw her arms around Tatteh's shoulders. "I beg you, listen to me! If not . . . May I not live to . . ."

"Stop it, Frimmet! Don't beg . . . I have to teach this witch a lesson once and for all!"

"You're not to go in there!" Mammeh clung to her husband's neck. "I believe you. If I didn't believe you, I wouldn't stay here another minute, so stop it. Come here, sit back down at the table!"

"No Frimmet, let her disappear from here this minute! Such a vile piece! Such a snake!"

"Luzeh, you can't go in there!" No! You won't give her such an honor! Nu, sit down already, I'm asking you."

She drew Tatteh back to the table. Every few minutes, he glanced toward the closed door but in the end, Mammeh got her way. But he wouldn't eat.

I was shaking. For the first and last time in my life, I saw my mother's fluttering hands around my father's neck.

They talked a while longer but their talk went round in circles like two drunken flies. Finally, sleep stopped up my ears. I nodded off with the sight in my imagination, of my mother's fluttering hands looking like two pure white birds.

Something woke me up in the middle of the night. My mouth felt like something was drilling away in there with an awl. My head was splitting. The bed was empty beside me. Tatteh must have gotten up already and left with the peasant for the village.

But what was drilling into me like this? What was causing such pain? Could it be a tooth? No, not just one tooth but my whole mouth was on fire. The pain went from my brain to my back and from there all the way to the very tips of my toes.

I was afraid to scream out. I didn't want to wake anybody. I tossed and turned, moaned and hid my face under the featherbed, but Mammeh became aware that I wasn't sleeping anyway.

"Mendelshi?" she suddenly called out, awake. "Why are you moaning? You're not feeling well, God forbid?"

"Oy!" I now groaned loudly, "My teeth, Mama!"

"Oy! Vey'z mir! How did you get a toothache?"

She got out of bed and in the dark felt with her hands over the tables and the stools "Where are the matches? Where?"

The house was darker than usual today. It was so thick you could cut pieces from it.

The pain got worse with the darkness. It stabbed me in the back and crawled deep inside my guts and into my brain. Mammeh finally found the matches and lit the lamp. Now I started to really toss and turn like a snake.

"Show me, dear Medelshi!" Mammeh bent over me, "Where is it? Just show me."

With her forefinger, she poked around in my mouth. I was choking, slobbering all over. I sat up. I lay down. I rocked back and forth, but the pain was stronger than I was.

Mammeh searched for alcohol, garlic. and pepper. She ran to prepare hot sand. The whole house together with the wardrobe, the dresser, the clock, everything was going round and round. Only Hodel snored loudly, in abandon, until the noise finally woke her up.

"What's going on in there? What's all the yelling about?" A confused voice suddenly called out from the kitchen.

"Oy, Hodelshi," Mammeh forgot for a minute that she was not on speaking terms with the witch. "A tooth, unfortunately . . . terrible pains and I don't even know if there's any alcohol in the house. Maybe you've got some alcohol, Hodel?"

"I don't have any alcohol. Where'd I get alcohol?"

"What can I do then?" Mammeh ran about the house like a frightened bird.

"What you can do?" Hodel shrieked. "Look what she's asking! You can choke him and good riddance! A grown boy and he won't let you close an eye!"

Mammeh didn't ask anything more of Hodel. She searched until she finally found some alcohol. She gave me some to hold against my tooth, put hot sand to my cheek, enveloped me with warm, trembling hands and in this way, she relieved my suffering.

But Hodel didn't sleep anymore. Her voice grated like rust.

"They don't let you close an eye! Spends half the night whispering sweet talk with her husband. If you want to bill and coo, don't take in a boarder! Now it's that little bastard with his teeth! Who told him to have teeth? Who? I'd have choked him, as big as he is!"

"Dear God in heaven! May you choke and croak yourself!" Mammeh prayed with her whole heart and caressed my pain-riddled head with even greater warmth.

Chapter 9

Tatteh didn't want Hodel around any more. Even if he knew he had
to live on the street, he said, he wouldn't stay under one roof with
this accursed woman.

But Hodel was unmoved. She screamed that she was an unfortunate widow, that they just wanted to make her miserable, that they
wanted to do away with her but Tatteh was firm. No! And no! Until
shamed, she finally moved out.

The sun glinted silvery in the gutters, on the dusty windowsills,
and on the damp roofs that day. Girls with disheveled heads, underclothes rolled up, stood at the open windows, polishing shop windows
and cleaning the sills, all the while singing songs of love and loneliness.

Pesach was coming, that beautiful holiday of which Mammeh
sang this song:

> "The Pesach holiday
> is so lovely and gay
> You eat till you're full.
> The wife is Queen
> The husband is King,
> and on the padded seat,
> poverty is able
> to dance at the Seder table."

All winter long, our little courtyard smelled of pigs and sour
pickles. Scattered under the headboards lay fluff and lint from the
beds, broken off feet from the wardrobes and torn out leaves from a
crumbled Yiddish version of the bible.

Dusty, smudged with soot, her head wrapped in a piece of grey
linen, Mammeh roamed around with a feather duster over all those
empty places where dressers and beds were pushed away from the wall.
She dusted the walls, wiped off the spider webs from the beams, and
cleaned the baseboards.

On a day when everyone was absorbed in preparations, the same tall peasant youth in the quilted jacket who had helped Hodel move in, came to the house grinning, and in a loud voice, asked into the half-emptied house:

"You're moving again, Hodelshi?"

"None of your business!" She spat out. "Take my things and get going."

The youth hitched in his belt, spread his feet apart like a scissors, and took himself to Hodel's trunk with the ragged hoops.

All through the time that Hodel lived with us, her trunk had gotten heavier. The youth was grunting and sweating. He pulled his belt even tighter and began talking to the trunk as if it was a sensible but stubborn creature.

"Nu, lets go! A black life to you! Look how overstuffed you've gotten! Nu, my proud fellow, give yourself up, damn you!"

"Who're you talking to like that, you lunatic?" Hodel asked in surprise.

"Understand me, Hodelshi," the youth winked. "Your trunk, may no evil befall it, is fattened up. . . . Its gotten a rich person's belly. So . . . such a belly you have to coddle."

"Go coddle your own stupid head, you ox!" Hodel unloaded her heavy heart on him. "Get a move on, you straw hotshot!"

In the end, he managed to get the trunk out. He placed it on a handcart, tied it with rope, then tried to lift Hodel's pack of bedding, but the bedding it seemed, had also gotten heavier with time. The youth grunted, strained, and asked heavily:

"It got pregnant, or what?"

"Stop gabbing, you clay dummy!"

Trading barbs with Hodel and with her belongings, he slowly emptied our house of Hodel's bit of goods.

Hodel didn't say goodbye. She didn't even turn to look at the house, but when she was already on the other side of the door and after the youth had finished loading everything up on top of the handcart, she ran over to the open window and shrieked inside:

"You should burn like Cain! You, with your husband, that lecher, and that bastard son of yours!"

Mammeh was busying herself inside and didn't answer. This enraged Hodel even more. She bent herself halfway into the house and began shrieking in a high-pitched voice: "Who doesn't know her, that 'tainted saint'? You think I don't know that you ran off to Warsaw to your lover. A black year take you! Don't think that this will be forgiven! Just take a look at her, this trinket!"

Mammeh's hands were trembling. She was restlessly looking for something. The grey piece of linen now hung down from the back of her head like a split bladder. Hodel kept looking for fresh curses, new sins to heap on Mammeh's head until Mammeh finally grabbed a dipper of water and poured it over Hodel's shrieking face with full force.

Hodel sprang back and Mammeh hurriedly slammed the window shut. The youth stood beside the handcart loaded with Hodel's things, laughing.

The sound of breaking glass was heard suddenly. A stone cut into the window and landed on the opposite wall where the photographs of Mammeh's children hung. It landed on the photograph of Avrumkeh, staining his nose with mud.

Nothing more was heard from Hodel. It seemed she had finally worn herself out.

The house got quiet. Mammeh's hands shook for the rest of the day. She dipped them into cold water and put a compress of grated horseradish on her forehead, but she told Tatteh nothing. When he came home at night and saw the empty spaces where Hodel's cot and trunk had once stood, he grinned: "She moved out, the witch?"

"She moved out."

"*Borekh shepatranu*! Good riddance!"

Our kitchen stood empty several days. When you talked loud, your voice echoed around the walls, strangely hollow. Something was missing but better for it to be missing than to have to look at Hodel's greasy mug.

We were supposed to be without a neighbor in the kitchen for Pesach. Tatteh was pleased. Where was it written that you had to have a hanger-on in the kitchen? But you couldn't see any satisfaction in Mammeh. She went around all the time now with compresses of grated horseradish on her forehead. She sighed quietly and said that God willing, she would consult a doctor on the holiday. The holiday came but she didn't go. She probably forgot all about it. When the holiday came, we got an unexpected but welcome guest, a member of the family.

Instead of Hodel's cot, we set up a different cot, also an iron one, in the same place. Instead of Hodel's bedding that was never changed, the new cot was covered with brand new bedding straight from the needle.

All of this came by way of Yitta, Tatteh's youngest daughter from his first wife, may she be separated from the living.

Yitta came from Warsaw, dark and big bosomed, with a pair of large and sparkling eyes, a short, stocky figure and broad hips. She came to us with a pair of cracked, work-worn hands over which she couldn't pull on the chamois gloves she had brought with her from Warsaw.

Tatteh's youngest daughter had spent the whole winter in Warsaw, cooking in wealthy, enamel-tiled kitchens with polished brass hoops. There, in the empty white pots and copper frying pans, she cooked and baked for pot-bellied Jews in silk skullcaps and for their refined big-bosomed wives.

"In Warsaw," Yitta said, "there are only 'Herrs' and 'Madames.' Sometimes you also find a '*Starsha Pani*,' an Old Lady or a '*M'lodi Pan*,' a Young Man, but other kinds of people you don't find in Warsaw."

In Warsaw, Yitta slept in the kitchen but it was a big and tidy one. She drew water out of the wall and had a bathroom right off this same tidy kitchen where she slept. She didn't have to burn kerosene in the lamps but had a kind of blue-green fuel that was called "gas."

I couldn't understand how you can light lamps without kerosene but Yitta explained to me that in Warsaw there was a factory that ran on coal. Thousands of piles of coal were burned there. From this coal came out a kind of gas that was sent through underground pipes into all the houses and this gave fuel. Mammeh said that Yitta wasn't lying. Gittl-Hoddehs had the same kind of gas but it still didn't make sense to me. Tatteh said that it must be a little different because it wasn't possible to understand how coal burned in a factory could give enough light for so many houses.

Yitta kept her own record book from her baking and cooking and this was kept in a safe. She wore ironed shirts with embroidered white lace. Every Saturday evening she went to the Yiddish theater to see "Bubbeh Yakhneh" and a lot of other moralistic pieces acted out in that not quite respectable place.

Yitta spent a lot of winters and summers in Warsaw. At holiday times, she yearned to come home to see Tatteh, look around and enjoy herself because in Warsaw she was alone like a stone. She pined for this town, for Aunt Frimmet and for me. She hadn't seen me for such a long time! She looked at me now with big, blazing eyes, her whole face creased from grinning.

"Look how you've grown, may no Evil Eye befall you!" she said. "I didn't even recognize you! Here, I've brought you a pocketknife and a little prayer book, and here's a pair of tfilin from Warsaw for your Bar Mitzvah. Enjoy them in good health, God willing."

Right the next morning, Yitta began helping Mammeh with the cleaning since there was a lot to do to get ready for Pesach.

She stood at the open window, solid as a door, her sleeves rolled up to the elbows, cleaning the windowpanes, rubbing the sills back and forth with damp chalk. Disheveled, she worked with fierce zest. In the small courtyard that still smelled of pigs could be heard a Jewish song, a kind of tune that Yitta had brought back with her from Warsaw:

"Once I loved a young man
Vienna was his home.
Once I loved a young man
Vienna was his home.
And he went home
to see his parents
to see how they were doing.
And he went home
to see his parents
to see how they were doing."

Mammah stood in the middle of the room, grimy, her face covered in soot, and spoke to Yitta's rolled up petticoat: "It was good to be in Warsaw, eh Yitta?"

"Good for somebody." Yitta gave a smear over the windowsill as if with the foam from soap, "but if you've got nobody in Warsaw, you pine for home."

"Who've you got to pine for?"

"What d'ya mean, who? You pine . . ."

Yitta wouldn't say for whom she pined. She turned to a far corner of the window, with one foot suspended in the air and took up her song again:
"And he went home
to see his parents
to see how they were doing."

Maybe that's why Yitta came home to her parents? But here, she only had a father. My mother was hardly an aunt to her.

But Yitta, whether she wiped the windowsills or washed the floor, didn't stop singing the tune about the young man who went off to Vienna.

Sometimes she got so dreamy in the middle of an unfinished line of the song that the young man was left dangling on a smeared windowsill or a half-washed floor. When Mammeh went into the kitchen, Yitta asked me whether I could write Yiddish and whether I'd be willing to write a letter for her to Warsaw.

Yeh, I could write Yiddish. If Yitta would dictate it to me, I'd write a letter to Warsaw for her.

But Yitta suddenly forgot all about it. She even forgot to sing her song about the young man who went off to Vienna.

It was the morning of the eve of Pesach. On the opposite roof, two doves had landed, a white one with an overfed double chin just like a rich man, the other a blue one with golden eyes. The blue one was screeching angrily. The white one moved away.

Yitta was standing with reddened feet spread apart, stirring a barrel of water into which Mammeh had earlier thrown a red-hot, glowing stone from a tin pan and then poured a pot of boiling water over it.

The water sizzled on the hot stone and white steam rose up, right into Yitta's sweaty face.

She panted, wiped the sweat from the corners of her mouth and left the barrel standing while she stared thoughtfully at the doves, smiling broadly up at the roof and pointed with her finger:

"See the blue one, that's a 'he,' the white one, that's a 'she.' He says 'darling' to her but she keeps her distance."

"Yitta," Mammeh scowled: "The barrel will burn! Don't you have anything better to talk about? Don't you?"

Yitta's soft and yeasty face turned red. She began rolling the suffering stone around on the bottom of the barrel even more forcefully.

I had no time to waste. I couldn't even grab a good look at the doves on the roof. It was the eve of Pesach, after all. Tatteh had swept up the bit of khamets with a goose feather from every corner of the house and put it on the wooden spoon that lay all night on the tin roof above the kitchen. I was supposed to take this bandaged wooden spoon that reminded me of an old slipper and run over to the study house to burn it, and come back in time for the lunch meal, the last of the khamets that could still be eaten before the start of the holiday.

I never liked this whole business of burning the khamets. I felt it was not a worthy undertaking.

I don't know whether I was ashamed of the poor spoon or whether I didn't want to leave such a tidy house but the whole business was upsetting to me.

Because of that, I didn't go to the study house and I didn't burn the khamets.

I ran through the side streets to the Circular Market where on one side stood the City Hall with the town clock and on the other side, the Polish castle with its round, old-fashioned windows.

There, in the middle of the market, between the City Hall and the castle, lay a small garden with sparsely growing grass.

Jews tossed prune pits, servant girls got rid of old bowls and pots riddled with holes into this garden. Sometimes a stray dog spent the night here.

So who would it bother if my wooden spoon also found refuge there? True, I didn't do this with a light heart. I knew that I was committing a sin. It wasn't allowed. Still I didn't burn the khamets.

This Passover eve I came early. The clock on the City Hall tower still looked blue and so did the old-fashioned round windows of the Polish castle. A peasant, just gotten up, came into the Circular Market with a cartful of straw that also looked blue.

I looked around on all sides. The sentry was standing at the City Hall. Surely he could see what I was going to do? Never mind, a sentry just like any other sentry. I'm not stealing but what will the Jews and the women hurrying by from time to time have to say?

Pasty-faced Berl with his foolish yellow beard now came straight toward me.

I waited until he passed, my heart beating wildly, until the janitor was momentarily blinded, and the peasant with the cart of straw had disappeared. When finally at long last, I didn't see anyone anymore, I carefully took the spoon out of my sleeve, turned my face to City Hall, ostensibly to look at the town clock and stealthily threw the offending spoon behind me over the iron railing into the little garden.

I didn't run off wildly but walked slowly and stiffly as if I would have swallowed that very same spoon. No doubt, any moment now someone would grab me by the back of the collar and demand:

"Stand still a minute, my young man! Whose son are you? Eh? What did you throw away? What was it?"

But God is merciful. No one had yet caught me in the act. Even so, all through Pesach it seemed to me that everything in the house was still khamets. I kept quiet but it bothered me. I promised myself that next year, God willing, I would burn the khamets, but when next year came, the promise went out the window.

I hurried home. Who knew whether I'd arrive in time for the khamets meal? Mammeh would complain: "You shouldn't be able to depend on a boy, not from here to there?" If Tatteh were at home, he'd place a heavy hand on my shoulder and ask glumly:

"Where were you for so long, my little jewel?"

Just as I neared the house, and was looking for an excuse to give Tatteh, a young fellow with a blue shaven face carrying a locked little suitcase, stood examining the houses like a stranger.

"Tell me, kid," he called out to me, "Where around here does Duvid-Froykeh's Frimmet live?"

"What d'ya need her for?" I shot back, taking his measure from head to toe.

"What's it your business why I need Duvid-Froykeh's Frimmet?"

"Its my business 'cause she's my mother."

"Izzat so?" The shaven face grinned. "Then I'm your brother."

This young fellow must be crazy! "What d'ya you mean, you're my brother?"

"Yeh, I'm your brother Yoyneh, from Lodz. You didn't hear about me?"

Oy vey'z mir! Didn't I hear? Why, his photograph stood on our dresser! How do you like that? I didn't even recognize him!

"Mameshi!" I ran into the house and didn't even hear Yoyneh calling after me. "Mameshi, Yoyneh's here from Lodz!"

I met Mammeh, stopped in her tracks, in the courtyard, reddened and flustered. She probably thought I'd gone crazy, but she grabbed a dishrag, quickly wiped her hands, hurriedly lowered the apron that was hitched up into her belt, and rushed out with arms outstretched:

"My darling child, Yoyneh! I wasn't even expecting you! Oy vey'z mir! What a welcome guest!"

She embraced him, wiped her nose, turned to one side, then to the other, looking out over the courtyard to see if anyone saw her. After all, it was her Yoyneh, the youngest son of her first husband!

Yoyneh was slim, had an Adam's apple that bobbed around like a little mouse and had deep, sunken holes in his cheeks.

"Yoyneshi . . . ?" Mammeh's voice broke, "Why do you look so worn out?

"From working, Mammeh."

"Do they treat you well at least? Are they satisfied with you?"

"Why shouldn't they be satisfied?"

Mammeh wiped her eyes with her apron. Yoyneh had already set down his suitcase. Now it could be seen that his overcoat was too short in the sleeves, the jacket showing through, but his shoes shone as if lacquered. Yoyneh also wore a beautiful necktie with silver stripes and a mother-of-pearl tie tack.

But, where was Yitta?

"Yitta, where are you? Yitta?" Mammeh called out in a loud voice.

Yitta came down from the stalls on the balcony, her dress lowered, her elbows covered and her hair barely gathered together. Her face was red and she hardly smiled. Only her eyes sparkled, big and warm.

"Welcome to your guest, Auntie." Yitta showed off a full mouth of white, gleaming teeth.

"Thank you. It's my son, Yoyneh. Don't you know him?"

"How should I know him?" Yitta answered glancing sideways at Yoyneh.

Yoyneh stood straight, his Adam's apple bobbed as if he had swallowed something. Yitta's mouth was wide but alert.

"Its Yitta." Mammeh said. "Your Uncle's daughter."

Yoyneh shuffled his feet, big city style. His thin figure turned around on a pair of elevated heels. Yitta made a double chin, drew in her big bosom and stretched out a short, work-weary hand to Yoyneh.

That's how they met, Tatteh's youngest daughter and Mammeh's youngest son.

Chapter 10

If Yitta brought back from Warsaw the glut of laden sideboards and
the carefree attitude of the wealthy, Yoyneh came home from Lodz with
poverty hidden in his small, darting eyes and with a dark greenish film
of dust that settled on his face from the plush sofas at which he worked.

During the time that Yitta stood red-faced at the pots of the
wealthy, Yoyneh had to bow and scrape before the customers, flatter
them, convince them . . . and cheat them.

Maybe that's why Yoyneh was so thin and agile. When he spoke,
it seemed that half his mouth was closed. He spoke slowly, in a sing-
song, his lips pursed and often threw in a pretentious Polish phrase.
From time to time, he even talked this way to his own mother saying:
"*Proshen laskava pani.* . . . Please, my esteemed lady . . ."

It was obvious that Yoyneh was a big-city type. His cane was
light, his hat sat rakishily on one side of his head, and his jacket was
fitted at the waist. Yoyneh didn't walk, he danced, a hop and a step,
a skip and a step.

Yitta watched him from the side. She was peeling large crooked
parsnips and she made flirtatious signs, wagging her double chin and
laughing. When Yoyneh wasn't listening, she said indirectly:

"How well turned out he is, that Yoyneh . . ."

Mammeh smiled, sniffled, shaking her head in parental pride.

"He's handsome like gold, may no Evil Eye befall him! Eh Yitta?"

"May I have such a year . . . !" Yitta cut the parsnips into four
long pieces and dropped them into the pot of water.

Because of Yoyneh, another iron bed was added to our household.
Mammeh borrowed it and Yitta dragged it home. It was put in the
same spot where Hodel's trunk had once stood. I was told that from
now on, I would sleep in this bed with Yoyneh.

Yitta covered the bed with one of her own quilts, smoothed the
edges and tucked in the corners, measuring and patting down every
wrinkle and fold with her big hands. Then she stepped back and looked
her handiwork over with a satisfied look on her face.

"The Tsar himself could sleep in such a bed!" It was truly fit for a tsar!

The freshness gleamed not only from this bed but also from Tatteh and Mammeh's beds. The whole house sparkled. We'd never before seen such a clear, blue-tinged light on the windowpanes, or such white curtains hanging over the cupboard where the dishes were kept. When Seder night came, you couldn't recognize the house, the few belongings, or the people.

In honor of the holiday, Mammeh wore her restyled wig for the first time. It had a black curl in front that looked like a bird. Her blue eyes, opened wide, looking as if they'd been intentionally polished to resemble blue diamonds. Her soft, full double chin, which she'd lost after coming back from Warsaw, could now be seen again. The black silk blouse with white lace at the sleeves, the jabot at her throat, and the braided gold brooch, all gave Mammeh great charm and beauty.

But the holiday look wasn't as clearly seen on Tatteh. He couldn't afford to have a new kapoteh made, so he wore the cheap, old-fashioned satin one that Yitta had brushed off and ironed.

He had his hair trimmed in honor of the Pesach holiday but his face was weary and ragged from the wind.

With heavy ashen gaze, he looked at his daughter, then at Mammeh's son. Sometimes he rested his quiet gaze on me, looking me over from head to foot and sighing deeply.

I felt that Tatteh was upset because he couldn't have anything new made for me in honor of the holiday. He was also bothered about his new kittl with the blue silk collar and the strips around the sleeves that he put on over the old-fashioned kapoteh.

Tatteh didn't buy this kittl with his own money. Yitta brought it, a present from Warsaw.

Tatteh knew that his children were poor, that they toiled for strangers, so what was the use of bringing him presents? He could buy his own kittl. But Yitta smiled happily.

"Wear it in good health, Tatteh!" she wished him with all her heart, and looked with devoted, tearful eyes at how nice her father looked in the new kittl she'd brought him.

Yitta herself came to the Seder table glowing. Her face was red, her ears were red, and her hands were red too. She kept them hidden under the table. If for instance, her blouse would have been black and not red, her hands would have looked like pieces of fire.

Yitta's black head of hair was freshly washed and combed, with curls and tendrils, and it gleamed with blue shadows. She was perfumed and her step rustled. It must be that Yitta was wearing a silk petticoat.

Why shouldn't she indulge herself? She'd brought a trunk full of things with her from Warsaw. Yoyneh sat nearby and Yitta managed to pass in front of him often. She was always in his range of vision even though he came to the Seder table not dressed festively and not properly barbered either. He sat down, slim and light, his Adam's apple bobbing up and down in his throat, with two dark caverns on either side of his face, and wearing his worn-out jacket. That's how he sat down.

Tatteh recited the Haggadah story out loud and I even louder. Yoyneh growled and turned the pages stiffly, with one finger.

"Yoyneh," Mammeh called out. "You're growling into the Hagudeh just like that bear."

"Which bear is that?"

Mammeh told the story about a Jew who wanted to teach a bear how to daven. So he took a prayer book and put poppy seed cookies between the pages. Where there was a cookie, the bear grabbed and ate it. Where there was no cookie, the bear growled. In this way, the Jew taught the bear to daven.

Yoyneh's Adam's apple bobbed with laughter. Tatteh didn't hear any of this. I had already heard this story about the bear many times. Yitta smiled broadly. She looked at Yoyneh from the other end of the table and couldn't say anything, so she made do by making a face, like a fish gasping for air.

Mammeh also read the Haggadah story. Oh, Mammeh really knew that story! Sharp and clear, with Zaydeh's melody mingling with her own sighs, the words fell from her mouth like warm, shiny pearls. She kept up with Tatteh and followed his reading step by step. I knew that somewhere around this time, Tatteh would start swaying to and fro, raise his voice and at that point, Mammeh would cut in from the side in a cold and strange voice, warning him:

"Nu . . . ? Oy . . . !"

I always waited uneasily for this moment, for Tatteh to stop and begin swaying. I prayed for this moment to pass quickly, so that we could be rid of it. Year after year, the same thing happened. Tatteh forgot what had taken place the year before and Mammeh couldn't break the habit of warning him.

Tatteh began to sway. The collar of his new kitl threw off a rich blue glow. The candles trembled reflecting silvery lace in the red wine. Tatteh's voice became more powerful. Suddenly, and louder than usual, he blundered right into:

"*Al akhehs makeh v'makeh.* How much more do we have to be plagued . . ."

Mammeh's sharp voice cut in immediately: "Nu! Oy Luzeh! It says: 'al akhehs kameh v'kameh. . . . How manifold and miraculous . . ."

Tatteh became transfixed in the middle of swaying like a weary pendulum. He raised his uncomprehending face, looked at his wife's pointing finger, and in a sunken voice, he muttered:

"Yeh, yeh . . . kameh v'kameh. . . . How manifold and miraculous . . ."

For a heavy moment it was quiet. Then Tatteh began reciting again, quicker and louder than before but soon he stumbled again:

"minayen shekhol kameh v'kameh, How can one show every miracle." He began again, twisting and turning, swaying his head. Mammeh pointed her finger again:

"Nu! Luzeh! It says: minayen shekhol makeh v'makeh. . . . How can one show every plague . . ."

I couldn't look at her face. If I were as old as Yoyneh, I'd have told her not to point. Let it be as it was. Tatteh knew the right phrase. He probably just didn't see it.

Yoyneh didn't answer to any of this. While Mammeh was sawing away in that cold and alien voice of hers, the caverns in Yoyneh's cheeks smoothed out. He smirked to one side. Suddenly I saw that Yoyneh had a gold tooth, a big, arrogant looking one. It was as if the other teeth had moved away and nothing more was visible than just this one gold tooth.

I can't say for sure but at that moment, it seemed to have shoved itself front and center when Tatteh made his mistake. With that, I took a dislike to my brother immediately. I thought Yoyneh was even more sinful than me for not burning the khamets earlier today.

Not only did I dislike him but it seemed to me now that Yitta also couldn't look him straight in the face.

I saw her big black eyes dart around uneasily, now at Tatteh, now at Mammeh, and a moment longer at Yoyneh's gold tooth. Soon they came to rest on me, and I felt Yitta's inflamed cheek and the warmth of her body next to me.

"Mendelshi?" she bent down to my Haggadah. "Where are we? Show me!"

I showed her the place where Tatteh had made his mistake. She stared long and hard. Now, I felt that Yoyneh had bought himself another enemy.

Yitta stayed silent. She served the meal and set down Yoyneh's dishes last. No one in the house noticed anything unusual. I was the only one who could understand her. She was my sister; we were both from the same father. Nothing less than I hated Yoyneh all through the holiday but it seemed that Yitta couldn't hold out that long.

ꞏ⸲ꞏ

The two Seder nights came to an end. Yoyneh put on a new suit and a new necktie, small and delicate as a summer bird. During the day, Yoyneh spoke louder, whistled tunes, and danced around by himself.

"*Können sie tanzen?*" Do you know how to dance?" he once asked Yitta pretentiously in German, showing off his gold tooth.

"Why wouldn't I know?" Yitta smiled into her double chin.

"By all means, let's see *vos sie können*, what you can do." He continued in his affected German and stretched out both arms.

Yitta didn't say yes, she didn't say no, and Yoyneh didn't ask. Silently and with pursed lips he enfolded Yitta's ample figure in his outstretched, half-bent arms.

He circled around the house with her several times, whistling to the beat. Even though Yitta, may no evil befall her, had a fair amount of flesh on her, Yoyneh said that when it came to dancing, she was as light as a feather.

"Everybody says that." Yitta straightened her blouse that had ridden up during the dancing.

Yoyneh was now smiling, not only with the one gold tooth but with his whole mouth and with his sunken cheeks too.

Yoyneh's smile obviously pleased her. It seemed she had forgotten what had happened at the Seder. After that, Yoyneh began whispering to her and borrowing her scented soap, and Yitta began handing him bigger platefuls of food at the table.

During Pesach and on the intermediate days of the holiday, it was the custom to go by carriage to the Kopter Woods where eligible sons came with their families from near and far to look over the brides being arranged for them and to conclude engagement agreements.

Yitta decked herself out in a stiff and flowered dress, freshly washed with scented soap, pulled a pair of smooth chamois gloves onto her work-weary hands and went out. She didn't say where she went but she came home late that night.

She came into the house a little too fast, quickly changed out of the stiff, flowered dress and tossed the chamois gloves onto the bed. She didn't eat but set herself to washing the dishes left over from the midday meal.

Mammeh asked Yitta where she'd been so late. Yitta answered that she'd gone to visit Aunt Nemmi. Well why not? Aunt Nemmi was Tatteh's sister. Why shouldn't she visit her?

Still, it was a bit surprising to me that Yitta's face was so blotchy. Why was she moving around the kitchen so restlessly and why did she answer Mammeh's questions so curtly?

Yoyneh came back very late that night. It was hard to know how Yoyneh looked when he came back because the lamp in the kitchen had already been turned off for a long time. Yitta locked the door every night before going to sleep. So didn't she do that this evening?

I was already in bed waiting for my brother. Mammeh was sitting on her bed half-undressed, dozing, one minute asleep, the next minute awake, trying to recite the bedtime prayer. Tatteh's heavy breathing could be heard.

That's when Yoyneh walked in. Half dancing, nimble, and with his collar turned up. Mammeh sensed his arrival immediately and woke up from her dreamy state.

"Yoyneh?" she asked clearly.

"Yeh, Mammeh, its me."

"Where're you coming from so late?"

"From Aunt Miriam's."

"Did you eat?"

"Yeh, Mammeh."

Mammeh bent her head to a side again. The house was dark, half-light and half-shadows playing. A big round stain spread out like an overturned bowl on Yoyneh's head.

"Go to bed, Yoyneh." Mammeh staggered to her feet and shook out the featherbed. She crept out of her slippers, left her clothing on a stool and threw herself heavily into bed in her underclothes. That's the kind of habit my mother had. She didn't as much go to bed, as she threw herself into it.

"When you go to bed," Mammeh said, taking off her underclothes under the featherbed, "lock the door. It seems Yitta forgot to do that."

"Good, Mammeh, I'll lock it."

Mammeh fell asleep at once. Yoyneh wandered around a while. I didn't hear him lock the door. He went to the dresser where the lamp was still burning low and with one blow, he snuffed it out.

The smell of kerosene was soon felt. My throat tightened in sickly sweet nausea.

"Are'ya sleeping already, Mendl?" Yoyneh picked up the featherbed that I had warmed up so thoroughly.

"Almost, what's up?"

"Nothing. Go to sleep, it's already late."

Yoyneh threw himself into bed with me just like Mammeh. The bed shook all over.

"Ah . . . ah . . . ah . . . !" He breathed expansively. "May beds never become extinct!"

He turned his face toward the room. I snuggled into his back, the way I used to do when I slept in one bed with Tatteh.

The odor of Tatteh's body was familiar to me. It smelled of hay and fresh air.

Yoyneh's body was thin and bony and it smelled of scented soap mixed with sweat. It was hard to warm myself against him.

I turned my face toward the wall but Yoyneh turned around also and tried to snuggle up against me.

We slept. That is to say, Yoyneh didn't fall asleep so easily. He kept turning over, back and forth and the bed didn't stop creaking.

I listened as long as I could until my ears stopped hearing anything. I don't know whether I slept long or woke up after first dozing but suddenly I felt cold in the shoulders.

It seemed I wasn't covered so I tugged at the cover until I began to feel a warm emptiness beside me. Where was Yoyneh?

I opened my eyes. Tatteh was snoring. The house was pitch black.

You couldn't see the room. Maybe that's why the silence seemed so noisy. It rang in my head and in my ears. And maybe it really wasn't so quiet? When I listened carefully with both ears, it seemed to me that a piece of paper was rustling. I couldn't figure out where this rustling was coming from, but it wasn't coming from far away. Then I noticed that there was talking and that a muffled, unyielding voice came as if from the other side of the shutters.

Suddenly, there was a rattling in the wardrobe. I know that when a wardrobe rattles in a dark house it's a sign that a dead person is wandering around.

Maybe it was Moysheh?

I wasn't afraid. I loved Moysheh and he loved me too. But just the same, my skin turned to gooseflesh. I pulled the cover over my head and waited with bated breath for Yoyneh to come back but the cover was short and when I pulled it over my head, my feet were uncovered. The wardrobe rattled again. There was talking behind the shutters. . . . No, it wasn't behind the shutters. It was nearby, clearly talking.

Tatteh's snoring turned into whistling, then into wheezing. Mammeh's sleeping couldn't be heard at all.

Yoyneh still hadn't come back. Could he have gone outside? Soon it seemed to me that I could hear Yitta's voice. I'd swear it was her voice! I remembered Hodel. Many times, she'd wake up in the middle of the night and start talking. Mammeh used to say that she, Hodel, didn't allow her ragged trunk to get any sleep.

But who wasn't letting Yitta sleep?

That same minute I heard a deafening slam like a shoe hitting the floor. It came from the corner where Tatteh's and Mammeh's beds stood.

"A tomcat! A tomcat!" I heard Mammeh's excited voice. There was another slam again.

Could a cat have gotten into the house? It must be that Yoyneh had let a cat in when he came home late that night. Mammeh threw her shoe at the cat, but go find such a creature when its pitch black?

"Mammeh," I yelled, "I think the cat's at the window."

"Go to sleep!" Mammeh's voice interrupted me, and suddenly even though it was so dark, I saw her standing by my bed, tall and pale. I felt her breath on my face and her hands fluttering over my bed.

"Why aren't you sleeping?" Her voice was heavy.

"Yoyneh woke me up." I answered.

She sighed. Now she seemed even taller and paler. I thought that she was going back to her own bed but I heard someone locking the door in the kitchen. Mammeh sat down heavily on the edge of my bed.

"Yoyneh?"

"Its me, Mammeh."

"Where were you?"

"I forgot to lock the door."

Mammeh stood up. Yoyneh quickly dived into bed with me but this time I didn't move closer to him. From afar, I felt the sharp smell of sweat mixed with apples. Yoyneh kicked the cover.

Chapter 11

The next day was the last day of the Pesach holiday. Yitta got up early. Her face had a puffy, unslept look. She was preoccupied and tidied the house in silence. Her full figure was plainly visible and she didn't look at all pretty now. Yoyneh went around the house acting like a stranger. He dressed carefully, whistled under his breath, and left with his usual two-step, saying he was going to shul.

Mammeh also got up earlier than usual looking drawn and worried. Her black eyes reflecting from the roof opposite, looked green in the cold sunlight. She was silent. Everything was silent.

Yitta took a long time cleaning up and it showed. The house looked better than it had yesterday but the result was sadness. The sun on the neighboring rooftop hardly reached the upper windowpanes and the house stayed in shadow. It didn't look festive. It looked like any ordinary, midweek winter twilight.

Tatteh and I went off to the davening. Today, because of the holiday, there was to be an especially impressive service in the study house. It was the custom that the prayer leaders would alternate during the last days of the holiday.

The khazn from the shul came with his singers to the study house and the prayer leader from the study house went to the shul. Moshkeh Soup Kitchen would be making the effort to sing his military marches and lively Polish dances. It was roomy but cold in the shul. The beautifully carved western wall with the harps and clarinets, flutes, and trumpets, that usually looked as if they were accompanying the old khazn, today lay like sheep struck dumb before a rain.

It was so crowded in the study house that you couldn't even throw a pin down to the ground. Half the crowd was from the shul itself and the whole study house crowd came too. Jews also came from the smaller prayer rooms—everyone came to hear the khazn and his choir.

The khazn, an old Litvak, davened the morning service and the additional service, the taste of which lay on everyone's lips well into

the summer. The davening lasted half the day but the crowd went home
in good spirits, renewed.

Everyone hummed, sang, and trilled along, accenting with a finger
or tapping a foot to the beat, but nobody could sing as well as the
old Litvak khazn.

The house was still silent when we came home from the davening.
It was tidy, shiny, everything was in order but it felt cold and strange.
At mealtime, the plates clattered loud and empty. The Pesach cutlery
looked grey, not at all a holiday look. Tatteh told of the wonders of
today's khazn but nobody paid any attention.

"What happened here at home? What's going on?"

Tatteh's unsuspecting gaze roamed over everyone's face. He wondered to himself: "Its a holiday, everything's prepared, thank God, so
why's everybody so sad? A boat with chicken shit had sunk?" Yitta
was not at the table. She served the food quickly and disappeared back
into the kitchen even faster.

"What's the matter with Yitta? Why doesn't she sit at the table?
Why not?"

"I'll sit down soon," Yitta answered. "There's still a lot to do
in the kitchen."

Yoyneh's face was freshly shaved but still green, greener than
before and wrinkled. His Adam's apple had gotten sharper overnight
and it was bobbing in his throat like a mouse.

Yoyneh ate with his eyes lowered. Between the delicacies served,
he broke off bits of matsoh and chewed them like someone who was
already full.

Mammeh looked at him sideways, not openly. He must have felt
her strained look because he yanked his head up, turning this way and
that, as if his stiff collar was choking him.

That's not how things looked at last year's holiday table. That's
not how we made the blessings; that wasn't how we ended. I remember that Tatteh hummed a carefree, familiar melody, Mammeh quietly
accompanying him with her clear, pearly voice. Now, Yoyneh took his
light walking stick, adjusted his cravat, and went out right after eating.

"With a walking stick on the holiday?" Tatteh called out after
him in surprise.

But Yoyneh was already outside. Through the window I saw him
twirling the stick in the air as he danced himself out into the courtyard.

Yitta washed the dishes angry and stubborn, rubbing all her
strength into the holiday pots.

The house smelled of eggs and onions, borsht and fried little egg
cakes. Tatteh didn't think about it for long. With drooping eyelids and
an air of sated weariness, he lay down fully clothed under the quilt. His

big, unruly beard that all through Pesach looked so rich and dignified, now wrenched itself vigorously up toward the beams. In a few minutes the house was full of Tatteh's heavy breathing.

Mammeh was uneasy. I already recognized that she had something to say or something to hide. I watched how she took a trifle from the dresser and immediately put it back again. One minute she opened a drawer and the next she closed it. She opened the window and exclaimed:

"It's so stuffy!" She didn't stop looking at me. "Mendl," her hand fluttered over the table, "why don't you go out for a walk?"

"Where should I go?"

"I have to tell you where to go? Don't you have any friends?"

"I have. Why shouldn't I have?"

"So go visit them for a while. A boy like you should be playing games with nuts on Pesach."

"I don't have any nuts."

"Take a look! He doesn't have any nuts. Too bad! Here! Here's some nuts!"

Mammeh took out a big paper bag and poured out a pocketful of nuts. My pocket bulged. When did Mammeh ever give me so many nuts? As if that wasn't enough, I got an extra two macaroons and a piece of candied orange peel too.

"Nu, go! Go!" She put both hands on my shoulders.

"I don't have where to go," I said. "I'll wait 'til Tatteh wakes up and we'll go to Aunt Nemmi's."

"You won't be late for Aunt Nemmi's." Mammeh said angrily. "Such a beautiful day outside and you just sit here!"

Mammeh's heart must have been heavy or she wouldn't talk to me this way. In the worst days, in the coldest winter evenings when there was nothing to make a fire with, Mammeh never talked to me like this. So something must be bothering her a lot.

It could be that's why I didn't feel like leaving. I didn't want to leave her all alone. But in the end, she got the better of me. She just pushed me outside. Yitta didn't say anything. She scrubbed the pots harder, angrier, more stubbornly.

I went out the door. I understood that Mammeh just wanted to get rid of me now.

So out of spite, I put myself between the open window and the door. Inside the house they probably didn't even see that I was standing there.

On the roof across the way, doves were parading with quivering double chins just like wealthy people. From time to time, one of the doves would lift a wing, fly around the roof, and come back.

All at once, their heads began to quiver. They looked into each other's eyes and as if by the tsar's decree, fluttered their feathers in unison, and with a slap in the air, rose up looking like individual fluffs of snow made golden by the sun.

I was caught up in the flight of the doves. They were twirling in one spot, up and down but they kept together like a really devoted family. If one of them got separated for a moment, it came back to the group right away, trembling and happy. Not like at our house, where in honor of Pesach, the most beautiful holiday in the whole world, our joy was ruined.

Of course it was ruined! Just now, actually as I stood staring dreamily at the doves, I heard Yitta's hot and choking voice through the open window:

"Auntie dear," Yitta said, "I should only live and be well . . . !"

"Don't swear, Yitta," My mother's deep, heavy voice carried to my ear. "I only want to hear the truth."

"The whole truth, dear Auntie! It was like this: We met in the Kopter Woods, he and I. Nothing happened. We walked. . . . We talked about Warsaw, about Lodz, afterwards when it got dark, he wanted . . ."

What he wanted I couldn't hear. My mother's head suddenly appeared at the open window and an angry scream cut into my ear.

"Why're you standing there, you clay dummy? Go somewhere else, for heaven's sake!

The open window closed forcefully. The doves circled the roof. My mother's voice burned into me and threw me out of the courtyard. Not knowing whether she was chasing me, or she was still at home, I looked around. No one was following me but I ran anyway. I wanted to find somebody; get a hold of somebody; I wanted to play a game with the nuts. I wanted to talk. I wanted to do something . . . !

I don't know how it happened, but all of a sudden, I found myself at the house where Moysheh, it should happen to nobody, had died, and from which we had long ago moved away.

It seemed to me that I should now be able to see Yuzheh, the barrel maker's daughter. I had to see her. I had something to tell her. My face was on fire and I was hot right down to my fingertips.

I knew that Yuzheh no longer lived here; still, I looked into the window of our old home. Flowerpots stood on the windowsill; probably goyim lived here now. It seemed weird that goyim should be living in our house. The door opened and a blonde shikseh appeared with a piece of yellow challah in her hand.

It was too much for me. I couldn't look at the shikseh holding the piece of challah so openly, so freely. After all, it's Pesach! Bread was forbidden. The shikseh bent her head to a side, took the challah away from her mouth and looked at me.

"Who do you want?"

"Yuzheh."

"My name isn't Yuzheh. My name's Stasha. What's your name?"

"Mendl."

"You wanna play?".

"Yeh, but get rid of the challah. It's khumets."

"It's Easter for us today, and we eat challah.

"And for us it's Pesach and we're not allowed to eat leavened bread.

"And my mother told me that you *dzidkehs*, you Yids, use our blood to make your matsohs."

"Your Mameshi is a goyeh."

"And you're a *dzidek*! Dirty Jew!"

"And you're a shikseh!"

"*Parkhu*!" She threw out in Polish. "Scabhead!"

"*Sama parkhu*!" I answered in Polish. "You're a scabhead yourself!"

Meanwhile the shikseh moved closer to the door of her house. I also moved. We eyed each other like two dogs. I knew my way into this house; after all, it used to be our house. I knew how to get up into the attic. I remembered that a Russian soldier once came to visit Yuzheh in that attic. He clunked his heavy boots on the stairs so that the beams of the house shook.

I wanted to tell Stasha that we should both go up to the attic together but she was already at the door with her hand on the knob.

"*Vinosh shen, zhidzheh*! Get out, you dirty Jew!" She kicked me in the side and pulled open the door.

I don't know, probably I didn't see too well but in front of my eyes seemed to glitter the black, woolly head of Yuzheh, the barrel maker's daughter.

"Yuzheh," I yelled, and tried to push my way into our old kitchen. But from inside the house I heard a sharp echo in Polish.

"*Mama*! *Zhid khetzeh zabitsh*! The Yid wants to kill!"

I didn't see the shikseh's mother. I didn't see Yuzheh either. I started running from the courtyard out into the street, out to the garden, wherever my legs carried me.

I stopped only at the old garden. No one was chasing me.

The waning rays of sunshine glinted on the trees. Gilded-looking brides, clattering loudly on their high heels, were strolling with their intended bridegrooms.

If I could have said, no, not said, but yelled out: "Stop making such a racket with your high heels!" a heavy stone would have fallen from my heart.

I waited a long time until I stopped panting. I didn't take stock of what had happened to me earlier. I felt that I must somehow be at fault but against whom I didn't know.

I went home fearfully. I felt that I'd something to answer for.

Yitta was no longer in the house. Tatteh had already gotten up from his nap and was waiting for me.

"Where were you?" He asked as soon as I crossed the threshold. "Where?"

"At the old garden."

"How come at the old garden? What d'ya have to do there? What?"

"I was playing a game with the nuts."

"With nuts of all things? A big boy like you playing with nuts?"

"I told him to go." Mammeh answered for me.

"Into the old garden with those good-for-nothings there?"

"There were no good-for-nothings there." I tried to throw in a word.

"That you were there at all is enough."

My face began to burn all over again. Tatteh never talked to me like this. Why did I deserve this? Why?

"If you'd listen to me," Mammeh's words broke into my thoughts. "You wouldn't take him to visit Aunt Nemmi today."

Why not?"

"Don't you see how he's dressed?"

"Never mind, he's not in rags, God forbid."

I didn't want to visit Aunt Nemmi today either. I felt different today than usual. I was now filled with an overwhelming laziness. I yearned for warmth.

True, if we didn't go to visit Aunt Nemmi today, we'd have to wait a whole half-year, that is until the second days of Succoth. I would have been happy with that, as long as I didn't have to show my embarrassed, burning face there.

But Tatteh was stubborn.

"What d'ya mean, he won't go. What will Nemmi say?"

"Go yourself."

"No, I won't go alone."

So Tatteh and I went this time too.

If your face isn't burning and a heavy stone isn't lying on your heart, then it's not so bad to visit Aunt Nemmi. She was different from all my other aunts and her style of life was also different. She lived in a walled, two-storey apartment house with a wide, iron staircase. Dr. Pzhilensky lived in the same house and also the goyish teacher too.

When you stepped on the iron staircase, a strange hollow echo raced through the cool, dark house. The door to Aunt Nemmi's was tall and brown with brass handles. These brass handles must be the reason why Mammeh didn't like Tatteh's sister and almost never went to wish her "Git yontef, a Good Holiday."

"I also had brass handles once," Mammeh didn't stop reminding us. "So did I crow about it like Aunt Nemmi?"

I don't know whether at Mammeh's door with the brass handles you also had to press a buzzer before you could go in but here at Aunt Nemmi's, you had to wait a while. First of all, you were asked who's there, after which the door opened and you were allowed to go in.

Tatteh when he went to visit his only well-off sister, hummed a melody along the way that every half-year had a different tone and different gestures.

When he got to the door, he blew his nose first, then he cleared his throat, and after that he slowly pressed the buzzer. When they opened the door, he walked in like he belonged there, as if to say:

"I'm not a rich man its true, but I'm a real brother to you and just as good as you, my dear sister."

He really is just as good as Aunt Nemmi. They used to run around together, barely dressed and barefoot in the village of New Mill, and they ate rye bread with cottage cheese together. They used to stare at the far-off, sun-drenched fields together, and they bathed in the same river together. Now my father lived in one room with a kitchen while Aunt Nemmi lived in lots of rooms. My father could only leave a hundred copper coins for Mammeh to make Shabbes with, while at Aunt Nemmi's, they would spend three and four rubles.

Aunt Nemmi was tall and dark, with arched black eyebrows just like a scholarly Jew. I don't like her eyes. They're light, weird, and sad. I also don't like the way she talks, not openly but secretively. She sifts the words slowly through thin lips and in a sing-song voice.

"Lu-ze-eh," she says, "Git yontef. Git yu'eh! Good Holiday, Good Year! So, how are you . . . ? Izzat so . . . ? Well . . . Blessed be His Beloved Name! And how's Frimmet . . . ? Well . . . Blessed be His Beloved Name! And this is really your Mendl?"

While she was drawling out the "blessed be His Beloved Name," her eyes had a habit of half closing as if overjoyed. Her face quivered, rebbetsin style.

Her dark figure, her pointy chin, her height, all this fit in with the big clean rooms where the human voice echoed in every corner.

It seemed to me that only these walls and only these dark tables and dressers could produce such a person as Aunt Nemmi. Somewhere else, under a low beam, between warm walls for instance, she wouldn't be able to find a place for herself.

The only wonder was how her husband, Uncle Ben-Tsion fit into these rooms.

He was short, round, and fat. God gave him little legs, not like a man at all. His hands were small, soft, and puffy, only his beard was white while his belly was busy being rude, just like a rich man's belly.

Uncle Ben-Tsion didn't wear high boots but black polished gaiters with stiff rubber sides. He also liked black, pressed trousers with a crease right down the middle. When it came to the kapoteh, Uncle Ben-Tsion thought about it for a long time, discussed it with his wife, Aunt Nemmi, and together they decided that the kapoteh should be chopped off, shortened, that is to say, made modern yet remaining just a little bit pious. Uncle Ben-Tsion didn't have the gumption for a hat, so he wore an eight-sided silk skullcap in the house but in the street he wore a black, cloth cap with a narrow visor. Not only that, but the band around the visor was made of silk that the lace maker had to braid three times.

Uncle Ben-Tsion waddled like a duck on his short little feet and took tiny steps like a woman. Jews who met him were the first to say good morning to him, but when he met goyim he doffed his cap first. Uncle Ben-Tsion was a respected person in town. He knew all the goings on—when someone was getting married, when a woman was going to give birth, when husband and wife were about to divorce, and when someone died. Uncle Ben-Tsion knew it all.

Not for nothing was he the community leader and record keeper. Who for instance, would you see going into City Hall so self-confidently? Why, Ben-Tsion! Who would you meet every Monday and Thursday, that is to say often, running into the provincial government office, or to see the military officer? Uncle Ben-Tsion! And who was buddy-buddy in the street with the rabbi, if not Uncle Ben-Tsion?

It was an honor for me and for my father that Ben-Tsion the community secretary was my uncle and my father's brother-in-law. It was also an honor for me that Uncle Ben-Tsion davened in shul at the eastern wall, actually, not far from the rabbi and that after the davening he walked home with the khazn, with Royzeh Royveleh Beckerman and with a lot of other respectable people in town.

Tatteh and I davened in the study house and we went home together with Mottl Shtroy or little Moysheleh the Capmaker, so it was really a pleasure before the Torah was read on the holidays or on the first day of the month, when Uncle Ben-Tsion suddenly appeared in the study house.

We knew that Ben-Tsion didn't come to the study house just like that. He's probably bringing news of world events. So everyone pricked up his ears. Prayer shawls were lowered from men's heads, small boys were hoisted up onto the windowsills and tables.

Uncle Ben-Tsion's stout belly pushed itself up to the lectern. His white cleanly combed beard looked self-importantly down on the sober faces of the listeners. Khi'el-Sanneh, the old beadle, banged powerfully and smartly on the table:

"Sha-a! Quiet!"

It got as quiet as the inside of an ear. I was standing on a table. Why not? It's my Uncle Ben-Tsion, after all!

He looked around slowly on all four sides, and even slower, he delivered himself of the world news he'd brought.

"*Makhriz umodeyeh midi'ehs harav umidi'ehs hakol. . . .* I'm announcing and informing you on behalf of the rabbi and the community. . . ." In a cracking voice he called out that enrolling children in the free Talmud Torah could be done everyday from twelve noon until evening except for Fridays and Shabbes.

Never mind, so it's not such big world news. Everyone began taking their young boys down from the tables. Someone at the eastern wall quickly pulled his tallis back over his head and hummed into his open prayer book.

"Neh, some impressive piece of news! Wouldn't you know . . . ?"

But no matter what, Uncle Ben-Tsion still did have something to say. Jews listened. Poor mothers, unfortunate widows, deserted wives, poor things, would now know when to enroll their children in the Talmud Torah.

Now on the second days of the Pesach holiday, I sat in the same Uncle Ben-Tsion's tall, dark rooms. Aunt Nemmi sat next to Tatteh, she knew that her brother was a little hard of hearing but Uncle Ben-Tsion didn't know anything of the sort, or else he didn't want to know. He sat apart, having stuffed his tub-like body into a soft upholstered armchair, his feet dangling like little blocks of wood. He sat in his eight-sided silk skullcap cracking nuts and dunking fruit pits into a glass of mead. He looked me over while peeling oranges. What exactly did Uncle Ben-Tsion see in me? Why was he smacking his lips after each taste of mead and more to the point, why did he turn up his nose?

I had a pretty good idea why Uncle Ben-Tsion was sneering so disdainfully. This Pesach, Tatteh wasn't able to have anything new made for me. I came here in my everyday kapoteh. Mammeh was right.

How could you come to visit Ben-Tsion's house wearing such worn-out clothing? I was ashamed in front of my uncle and aunt, ashamed in front of these beautiful rich rooms but most important, I was ashamed in front of their Mendl.

Yeh, they also had a Mendl. We were both named after the same grandfather but this Mendl was older, better looking and altogether more substantial. He looked like his mother, Aunt Nemmi.

He also had a small, narrow mouth and when he spoke, the corners curled up just like hers. It seemed to me that he always had mannerisms, that he thought a lot of himself, and that was why he scowled and was so cold and disdainful.

This Mendl had reason to think highly of himself. He wore a white shirt and a cravat, his pants were long and covered his spats. He didn't study at a cheder but went to a secular school. He was able to go about free and easy in his airy, clean rooms. He could have pie in the sky anytime. He didn't have a sister or brother; he was a one-and-only child.

But all this was nothing. There were many handsome and rich Mendls who lived in roomy and pleasant homes in town. But none of those Mendls had a singing voice like this Mendl.

They say in town that Ben-Tsion's Mendl is developing an instrument that will make the world sit up and take notice! The whole city says that Ben-Tsion's Mendl could read and write fluently. Ben-Tsion's Mendl knew whole chapters of the bible by heart, so how could I not feel poor and inferior next to such a Mendl who could make old Jews run from the study house to the shul just to hear him sing?

I also ran. He was the first in the choir and he also accompanied the old Litvak khazn. His voice rose up to the hollow blue beam of the shul like a woman's voice. When Mendl sometimes sang high, it seemed that all the flutes and clarinets, all the trumpets and violins engraved on the eastern wall were singing and echoing too.

Now I was their guest. Mendl looked at me like at a stranger. He knew me. I came here every six months; still, it seemed that he didn't recognize me. His small mouth sneered and he didn't say even one word to me. I would have liked to talk to him, but how could you talk to him if he didn't even know you?

His mother asked him: "Mendlshi, sing something for your Uncle Luzeh."

Mendl widened a pair of big light eyes just like his mother's and shrugged his shoulder. You could assume that what he meant to say was:

"Maybe you know for whom I'm expected to sing?"

My father's big, freshly washed holiday beard smiled.

"Nu, really," said the beard, "sing something, Mendl. I listen to you sometimes in shul but not always can you push your way inside and not always can I hear . . ."

Mendl tightened his little mouth even more and his eyelids closed, half-dreamily. I held my breath. He really was getting ready to sing. A big warm smile lay on Tatteh's beard. Aunt Nemmi's eyes also closed half dreamily, just like her son Mendl. Only Uncle Ben-Tsion gave a satisfied slurp from his glass of mead and folded his hands over his belly.

But Mendl didn't sing. He walked out slowly and stiffly into another room.

Tatteh's beard darkened and the smile disappeared. I let out my breath. Aunt Nemmi's eyes followed her son with furrowed brow.

Several minutes later however, Mendl's voice was heard singing from the other room. Tatteh's mouth rounded, listening. Aunt Nemmi's face wrinkled into laugh lines.

"Dear God in heaven, don't ruin it for me!" Her head quivered quietly. "He sings like a bird in the forest, may no evil befall him."

I myself had no idea how a person can sing like a bird in the forest. But Mendl's singing voice went into my heart like pure honey. I can't compare him to anything. I only know that not for nothing does he think highly of himself. In his place I wouldn't be any different.

It was already good and dark in the house now. Everyone sat as if they were sick and afraid to move because of their aches and pains. The glasses of mead lay forgotten in shadow. Mendl's singing lay before our feet like an atonement for our sins. I heard clearly how this melody beat its wings.

The singing was wonderful. Uncle Ben-Tsion's young man was wonderful. I left, full from the mead and the candied orange peels, but hungry and depressed from Mendl's singing just the same.

Tatteh spoke to me but I couldn't answer him.

What am I compared to this Mendl? Not a particle, not a whiff, not even a bit of a garment was Tatteh able to have made for me for the holiday. That other Mendl was dressed clean like a lord. His voice was also clean and noble sounding, while I run around in stranger's courtyards. I had to deal with the likes of Yuzheh and Hodel. I was coarsened. It would suit me right fine if suddenly someone would come and tell me the news that this other Mendl had gotten sick and that it was necessary to cut the singing voice out of his throat. Then I'd be able to like him. He could then become my only, my best friend. Then I'd be able to tell him all about the doves on our roof, about Yuzheh the barrel maker's daughter, about Yitta and about Yoyneh. I'd have lots of things to tell him but now I couldn't do anything.

We went straight to the study house from Aunt Nemmi's. Moshkeh the Khazn blared out his military marches so dryly and heavily today that my temples throbbed violently. I begged for it to end, for it to become really late so that I could go to bed and cry into my pillow. I'd have cried a lot.

Tatteh didn't pay any attention to me at home. He told about the wonders of his sister Nemmi, about the refreshments that were served us, and about their Mendl with his beautiful singing voice.

I watched how Mammeh's forehead creased. It seemed to me that she hardly listened to Tatteh. I'd have sworn that his talk didn't please her.

"Nu, enough already!" She waved her hand impatiently. "We've already heard all about their good fortune."

I was thankful to my mother with my whole heart. She was such a wonderful person, my mother. She was doing this for me, taking on my complaint.

Tatteh got quiet. Everything in the house suddenly got quiet. Yitta was getting the table ready, her blotchy face angry and distant. Mammeh looked upset, aggravated, and she wasn't dressed festively.

"Where's that son of yours?" Tatteh asked her before we sat down to the table.

"He won't be here today." Mammeh answered abruptly. Yitta went back quickly to the kitchen. The corners of Tatteh's eyes narrowed.

"What d'ya mean? We're ready to make kiddesh."

"You can do it without him."

"I don't understand."

"What don't you understand? He's not here, and that's that. He's invited to Miriam's. He's invited there."

"Well, if that's so . . ."

We sat down without Yoyneh. Yitta again didn't sit with us. We ate silently, with difficulty.

Yoyneh didn't come back to sleep and he didn't come back the following day either.

Yitta went around with cheeks that always looked blotchy. She busied herself only with cleaning, washing, and polishing.

Right after the holiday, when we put away the holiday dishes and brought the everyday ones back out, Mammeh went out taking Yoyneh's peeling suitcase with her. Yitta, worn out, sat staring out the window into the darkness.

Tatteh had gone off to see his partner, Mottl Shtroy. Everything in the house was grey. I didn't see Mammeh come back, nor Yoyneh, nor

Tatteh. I rattled around the deserted house like an orphan. It seemed to me that I'd never see Mammeh back here again, even though she did come back late at night without Yoyneh and without his suitcase, and I was left to sleep alone in the iron cot.

Chapter 12

I found out later that Yoyneh left that night right after the holiday. He just ran off, didn't even say goodbye to anybody. Nobody in the house asked about him, it was as if they were ashamed of him. Yitta stayed with us a while longer growing thinner, sadder, and more listless. The warm sparkle that she had brought from Warsaw no longer glowed in her dark eyes.

Nobody noticed how poorly she was doing. Mammeh was silent. I looked but couldn't do anything. Tatteh didn't even notice what was happening to his daughter. Six days of the week he spent out in the open, between heaven and earth, among piles of hay and peasant carts. He could only see his daughter on Shabbes, but it was too short a day for him to notice anything. Besides, Tatteh was still preoccupied with the taste of his sister Nemmi's hospitality and her son's singing.

The time didn't pass without Tatteh remembering Aunt Nemmi's house and her talented son Mendl. At the Friday evening meal or noon on Shabbes, when it was time to sing zmirehs and I tried to harmonize with him, he made a face as if he had swallowed something bad tasting and sighed:

"Where can you find someone like Nemmi's Mendl?"

"No matter what, he always brings up Nemmi's Mendl!" Mammeh threw in, embittered.

She didn't like hearing about her rich sister-in-law, and she didn't like hearing Aunt Nemmi's son praised. She couldn't stand anything having to do with those tidy, well-fed houses.

"You'd better worry about your own Mendl," she said resentfully, "he's also the son of a father. Believe me, if God would help, our Mendl would also know how to sing."

"Silly woman!" Tatteh smiled quietly. "Why're you getting so angry? Why? Who told you that our Mendl isn't the son of a father? But singing is a gift from God."

"A gift, a shmift!" Mammeh frowned. "We've seen such gifts! When they grow up, these gifts of yours, they become moneylenders and good-for-nothings. What do you think that great, big brother-in-law of yours is, if not a good-for-nothing?"

"Who? Ben-Tsion?"

"Yes, Ben-Tsion . . . Ben-Tsion . . ."

"What's the matter with you, woman? He's the Secretary of the Community!" Tatteh was literally stunned.

"Ovah! Some impressive livelihood! I also know how to write and I don't have such an attitude about myself."

"Nu, leave me alone already." Tatteh waved his hand in scorn. "You don't even know what you're talking about."

"I know! Don't you worry! I know! I should have such good years as Mordkheh-Mendl is a thousand times more capable than all of your Ben-Tsion!"

"A year on my enemies, what kind of capable Mordkheh-Mendl is!" Tatteh shook his head scornfully.

"I'm telling you that Mordkheh-Mendl will stir up all Poland."

"He'll stir up the bedbugs, not Poland!"

"You'll see!"

"For twenty years already I'm seeing, since poor Channa became his wife."

"Channa is a thousand times dearer to me than Nemmi!"

I also liked Aunt Channa better. A full sister of Tatteh and Aunt Nemmi, she was poor, very poor in fact. She had the same dark skin and the same quiet dreaminess as in Tatteh's eyes. She spoke slowly just like her sister Nemmi, but without Nemmi's sing-song and without her arrogant airs.

We didn't go to Aunt Channa as guests. She lived outside of town in a small wooden hut with dusty windowpanes and a green-shingled roof. Her rooms weren't big or tidy. Altogether, one room with a low-slung black beam, a sloped and pitted earthen floor and two unmade beds with faded red coverlets. It had a large old-fashioned clay oven on top of which lay a few pieces of wood drying and where hungry, dirty children in outgrown shirts were warming themselves.

Tall and bent over before her time, Aunt Channa's thin hunched body was always wrapped in an old, torn, grey shawl, her head in a woolen kerchief whose color had long ago faded. In her house you ate potatoes—in the morning, potatoes; in the afternoon, potatoes; in the evening, potatoes. When you wanted to go out from Aunt Channa's house, a mountain of snow, covering half the threshold up to the window, barred the way. So we waited, looked at the frosted windows with hungry eyes until last year's stork came back to the other side of the poplar tree to announce the news that you could now go outside. The beloved summer was finally here.

At that time, Aunt Channa smelled of cows, of the milk that she brought into town, of newly flowering grain and also the smell of warm rain that landed on the balcony through the shingled roof that was full of holes.

She came to us when dawn still lay on the windowpanes. Quietly and a little reserved, she crept in with a dry "good morning," and sat down on Mammeh's bed.

Aunt Channa felt close to Mammeh, just like a real sister. She poured out her bitter heart to Mammeh, and told her about her miserable luck—that there wasn't a penny in the house, that they didn't see a piece of meat from one Shabbes to the next and sometimes not even that, the poor children were naked and barefoot, the rent money was owing for three quarters of the year—It could happen, God forbid, that they might have to go begging.

"Channa, have faith! Don't commit a sin," Mammeh consoled her."I believe in your Mordkheh-Mendl. He'll stir up all of Poland yet! And then you'll say, 'I told you so.' "

Aunt Channa also had faith in her husband even though she didn't have enough food to get through the day. Everyone except my father believed in Uncle Mordkheh-Mendl.

Wasn't he someone worth believing in? Such a clever head! Such a go-getter! Who could be compared to him?

It didn't matter that he was a pauper in seven shreds and had to borrow a coin for cigarettes, but he had big plans, ambitious ones. His brain was constantly on the go, as if on ball bearings.

Uncle Mordkheh-Mendl wasn't one of those Jews who prays on Rosh Hashanah and Yom Kippur for nothing more than a bit of livelihood and good health for wife and child. He said that such people were poor Jews with small concerns and even smaller worries. He, Mordkheh-Mendl would not place himself before the Master-of-the-Universe and pray only for a bit of livelihood. And when you actually had that bit of livelihood—then what? So you got another bowl of groats and another goose leg.

The main thing was that a person had to amount to something. You had to . . . ! The whole world had to buzz, kin and kindred had to know, that a Mordkheh-Mendl existed!

For instance, why should he, Mordkheh-Mendl, not be able to say that the Kopter Woods and all its farms, were his? How is it that Arn Shtaynberg was more entitled than he was? He could study better? He gave better sermons? And why shouldn't he, Mordkheh-Mendl, actually be the one to build a train to Bialozheg? And why shouldn't the entire great estate of Farleh—the mills, the brickworks, the sawmills, why shouldn't all that belong to Mordkheh-Mendel? Is Itsheleh Beckerman smarter than he is? Day and night, Mordkheh-Mendl traveled around visiting noblemen. He measured out fields, cut down trees, but in the earthen hut out on the highway there was nothing to live from.

So he fell on a plan, a huge one. The town didn't have a glassworks. How could such a town, with so many Jews, may no evil befall them, and with even more goyim, l'havdil, live without a glassworks? So he, Mordkheh-Mendl would build a glassworks. The glassware produced here would go to the very ends of the earth!

He'd rake in money! He'd become rich!

So he began traveling again to the noblemen. Day and night he made his reckonings. The house was stiff with cold. The dirty, ragged children fought each other for a better place on top of the oven. Everybody in the house lived in hope. Today or tomorrow, if there were a glassworks, there would also be enough room on top of the oven.

So the day actually came when Uncle Mordkheh-Mendl and two noblemen went off to the registrar to write out the conditions of sale. Meanwhile, lumber was made ready and they began building. With luck, the glassworks grew. It had roofs, fences, and kilns and an arrogant looking chimney that stretched right up to the sky.

The whole town came running to look at this amazing sight! They craned their necks, examined the walls and wagged their tongues.

"Neh! Can'ya believe this?"

But Mordkheh-Mendl didn't become a partner in the glassworks. Somebody barred his way. Somebody tricked him.

So he began banging on the doors of lawyers, judges, and officials. He knew all the paragraphs and all the points of the law by heart. He was certain that they had swindled him and that he must win the trial. But he was left with nothing more than the paragraphs and the points. The glassworks did actually send glassware to the four corners of the earth but they did it without Mordkheh-Mendl.

His thick, black beard didn't get any grayer over this matter, God forbid! Just the opposite; it seems, it got even darker and silkier. His big lively eyes sparkled, reminding you of foaming beer. His mouth with the white, pearly teeth got even more stubbornly set and wrinkled sharply at the corners.

Uncle Mordkheh-Mendl didn't waste any time. Never mind! You can live without a glassworks, too. But shouldn't such a town have a distillery? Who says that you could become rich only from glassware?

And if you sell liquor, isn't that enough? He'd already chosen the spot. There was even a commission and they agreed. The only thing missing was to actually build it.

"Channa, my wife," trilled Mordkheh-Mendl one summer morning in our house, "get yourself ready. We're going to live in big rooms. Money will swim in through doors and windows. We'll get drunk just like the goyim. Never mind! Mordkheh-Mendl is still alive and kicking!"

He ran around the house like a whirlwind, absent-minded, buttons undone, with the peak of his cap turned up and hands flailing.

"What's Ben-Tsion, the Community Secretary to me?" he boasted arrogantly. "Who's this Ben-Tsion, Community Secretary anyway?"

Mammeh's gaze followed the agitated Mordkheh-Mendl with a big smile on her face. She had faith in him. She had prophesied that her brother-in-law would yet stir up all of Poland. Now what she had foretold was coming true. Aunt Channa's thin cheeks flamed. She was proud of her handsome, talkative husband.

Only Tatteh sat quiet, staring at the table. The conceit, the boasting of his brother-in-law didn't impress him. He'd already heard such talk, not for the first and not for the last time, but if Ben-Tsion the Community Secretary was now also a nobody, according to Mordkheh-Mendl, this aggravated Tatteh.

Slowly, he lifted his gaze from the table, raised his eyebrows and oh so quietly and scornfully said:

"Okh un vey! Look who's talking about Ben-Tsion!"

"Luzeh!" Mordkheh-Mendl stopped in the middle of the room.

"You can pickle your Ben-Tsion in vinegar, even though he's the Community Secretary, and as far as business is concerned, you have as much an idea as a cow looking into scripture. All you know is hay, so go smell your fill of hay!"

"At least my hay smells good," Tatteh shot back, "but from all your big deals you don't even get a good whiff."

He looked at Mammeh with a triumphant grin. He probably wanted to see if his sharp comeback pleased her.

But it didn't appeal to her, it didn't appeal to anybody. Still, Tatteh wasn't altogether wrong. Mordkheh-Mendl really did have the idea to stir up all of Poland. He meant well but in town it was said that Mordkheh-Mendl would rot away in jail because of all his exploits.

Actually, the distillery deal was just about finalized. Today or tomorrow, they were supposed to write out the conditions of sale. Mordkheh-Mendl poured himself a stiff drink of whisky and ate a goose gizzard. Aunt Chana didn't close an eye all night, and the children didn't fight over who was to get a better place on top of the oven.

But as luck would have it, the nobleman, the partner, laid himself down hale and hearty one night and never got up again.

Mordkheh-Mendl would already be living in big rooms by now; he'd already be traveling in his very own carriage, harnessed with two horses. Ben-Tsion the Community Secretary would no longer have his nose in the air. My father would no longer ridicule. . . . But God didn't want it so. They hauled Mordkheh-Mendl off to the police and to the investigative judge for him to explain why Pan Dombrowski had died so suddenly.

Mordkheh-Mendl was still living in that run-down hovel out by the high road. Winds howled without stop and it rained through the shingled roof. Carts traveled to the markets and fairs in far off cities. There, through the dark nights stood Aunt Channa surrounded by fields and wind. She stared out after the traveling carts and pleaded with the Almighty for her sharp-witted Mordkheh-Mendl, her beautiful chanter of the kiddush, to be helped as well.

Mordkheh-Mendl no longer boasted. After the fiasco with the distillery, his black, silky beard got greyer, the glowing, restless eyes looked out with a dull, extinguished expression, but he still had enough faith and ambition to make it big again.

Maybe Aunt Channa, in the dark nights beside the empty highway, had succeeded in her prayers for help for her husband.

Mordkheh-Mendl decided to look at an estate. A new whim! A Jew like him, who all his life lived in a wooden hut, ate grits with rye bread, never had a new suit of clothes made since his wedding, how could he even dream of an estate?

Still, this estate, the Vaysufkeh, interested him.

One summer dawn Aunt Channa sat down on Mammeh's bed. A blue ray of sunlight fell on her messy yellow wig. In a restrained and secretive voice, breathing more than actually talking, she said that Fleischer the German intended to buy up the Vaysufkeh and to take Mordkheh-Mendl as a partner.

"Never mind," she said. "You know that Mordkheh-Mendl hasn't got any money of his own to speak of, but where's it written that you have to have money for an estate? Second of all, Fleischer the German is putting up the money. Mordkheh-Mendl just has to put up the brains."

Aunt Channa breathed all this into Mammeh's half-asleep face even more quietly than the shuffling of a fly. Still, Tatteh who was a little hard of hearing and was standing at the window in tallis and tfiln, turned to face his sister with such a sneering grin that it made Aunt Channa's cheeks flame.

Mammeh lay in bed, her face round and smooth. Lately, she had become more beautiful, even got back the double chin she had brought from Warsaw, together with her rich woman's arrogance that showed up when she wrinkled her nose. When she put on her white jabot and the lace at the sleeves, raised her head up to take stock of a stranger with a pair of long drawn out glances, you could have put a whole estate into her hands.

That's why she now listened to Aunt Channa so carefully. She saw how Aunt Channa reddened when Tatteh turned his scornful smile upon her, so she wrinkled her brow and sneering even more, called out loudly:

"Don't listen to him Channa! All he can do is smile, that brother of yours. He thinks there's nothing better in the whole world than to deal in hay. So I'm telling you that with God's help, you'll soon become a landowner."

"From your mouth to God's ear," Aunt Channa sighed softly.

Meanwhile, the days and the weeks didn't stand still. Just now, the deal was on, then again, it was off. The noblewoman selling the estate, wanted lots of gold; then Fleischer the German had second thoughts. Mordkheh-Mendl also wanted to take precautions.

So he ran around, didn't eat or sleep, sat days and weeks in the mortgage office. Never mind. That wouldn't matter already but who would be the guarantor if, God forbid, it would end the same way as the glassworks and the distillery. Heaven preserve us!

"Have faith!" Mammeh said encouragingly, "my heart tells me that Mordkheh-Mendl won't go away empty-handed from this deal."

You hardly saw Mordkheh-Mendl anywhere. He didn't spend nights at home. He ran out to the high road, traveled on trains, wore out his feet in the mansions of the noblemen and had no time even to run to the bathhouse before Shabbes.

But early one morning, he stumbled hungry and sleepless, his beard all messed up, into our house.

Mammeh quickly made him something to eat. She put in front of him a four-pound loaf of fresh bread, prepared a big pot of coffee, and ran out to get butter and cheese. While he ate, she leaned both elbows on the table and impatiently looked into his brown, overworked face.

"So what's new, Mordkheh-Mendl?" she asked warmly.

"It's going," he sipped his coffee, "But we still need some breaks."

"Just stay calm," Mammeh said to him as if he were her own husband. "Don't get hot."

"Being hot's got nothing to do with it. There's another misfortune: This Fleischer, this German, is a thief among thieves. They say that Jews are swindlers, but I'm telling you this German goes one better than all the Jews put together. Anyhow, you know that I haven't got any money, not even a penny. I only have ideas, know-how. So this thievish Fleischer wants to confuse me so much that I can't ever be resurrected again. For instance, he wants me to become his manager, his servant, and he'll be the master. For instance, he wants . . ."

Uncle Mordkheh-Mendl left his half-drunk mug of coffee. He warmed up and started explaining to Mammeh, clear and to the point how this German, Fleischer, wanted to trick him, lead him into the muck, and make an end of him for all eternity!

Mammeh stared mouth wide open, right into his burning eyes with a helpless smile on her pretty mouth.

Did she understand what Mordkheh-Mendl was talking about? Maybe she did but I think that she only saw his disheveled appearance, the wide arcs he made with his hands in the air, the burning eyes and most importantly, the big Polish estate that he was describing to her so glowingly.

It happened out of the blue. In the middle of an ordinary Wednesday, the whole town started buzzing:

"Mordkheh-Mendl bought the Vaysufkeh!"

"Mordkheh-Mendl?" People wrinkled their noses. "Who's this Mordkheh-Mendl?"

"Who d'ya think? Luzeh's brother-in-law!"

"Who's this Luzeh?"

"Luzeh Shonash, the hay dealer."

"His brother-in-law bought the Vaysufkeh?"

"His brother-in-law!"

"May a bad dream land on the heads of all my enemies! He's a poor man, a pauper!"

"You see?"

They asked a neighbor. The neighbor asked another. A buzzing and a chattering went from house to house, from husband to wife, from goy to Jew. Mammeh came running from Aunt Miriam's, gasping:

"Luzeh, did you hear?"

But Tatteh wasn't home yet. He was late. So Mammeh ran to the neighbors looking for someone to tell her the truth. Everybody had heard but nobody knew for sure.

Mammeh wanted to run right out to the high road, to that hovel with the earthen floor where Mordkheh-Mendl lived. She had to know right now, this minute! But at the last minute she stopped and thought it over.

No! She was insulted. She should've been the first to be told!

Tatteh came in later. He also came in not like he usually did but distracted, his beard full of hay dust and his cap crooked. Nothing else but someone bought the Vaysufkeh. But it couldn't be Mordkheh-Mendl.

"Did you hear, Luzeh?"

"Its really true?"

"What do you mean, is it true? The whole town's buzzing with it!"

Nu, yeh, he'd heard too. He was at the study house for the afternoon and evening prayers, but nobody did any praying. It was buzzing like a beehive! People ran toward him wishing him Mazeltov! "Neh! Go know?"

"So what did I say, Luzeh?" Mammeh's whole body was shaking.

"Say? Who can be so smart?"

"But Mordkheh-Mendl is clever! Eh?"

"Yeh, clever, not clever. But for an estate you need money."

"Done! He's got the money too! What then, like you? Hay today, hay tomorrow?"

"So what did you want, an estate too?"

"What's the matter? You think it wouldn't suit me?"

"If that's all that matters to you . . ." Tatteh shrugged his shoulder, "we can buy an estate too."

"Joking too, to all my troubles!"

Mammeh went into the kitchen angry. Tatteh stared after her with quiet, questioning eyes.

Mammeh didn't speak all evening. She was silent, her brow furrowed as she served him his supper.

Flies dozed on the beam. The clock ticked without stop: "Hay today, hay tomorrow." The clock balances were almost leaning on the dresser, so Tatteh slowly pulled them up. The works inside the clock sighed, just like Mammeh's heart.

After supper, Mammeh sat down at the open window staring out into the night. A cloying heat came from the opposite wall outside. Up on the balcony, someone was crawling around among the stalls. The clock struck one hour dull and fast, then another hour. Mammeh continued sitting by the window. I'd have sworn that she was now seeing the brass door handles that she'd had with her first husband, the old-time healer. She's probably comparing that life with the one she's got now. Maybe she's jealous of Aunt Channa with the new estate sitting among the grain fields, the linden trees and with such a beautiful deep sky overhead.

Mammeh . . . my mother . . . Not until death itself would she forget those brass door handles.

Chapter 13

It was really true that Mordkheh-Mendl, pauper of paupers, had become a landowner all by himself and not in partnership with Fleischer the German.

How could that be? No way Jews could grasp this! Did he rob a church or something? Maybe he did?

"So, what's with this Fleischer? Did Mordkheh-Mendl push him out?"

"Probably."

"What d'ya mean? The German just let himself be pushed out?"

"See for yourself."

It was a puzzling question. The whole town was buzzing. It didn't make sense not only to strangers but even to the members of the family who couldn't understand what was happening. People went running out along the highway in the middle of the week to see the estate with their own eyes. Maybe it was a dream, a delusion?

But to spite the enemies—it was no delusion. The whole Vaysufkeh, the woods, the meadows, the fowl, and the animals, all this now belonged to Mordkheh-Mendl.

Nobody from our house was in a hurry to run out there. Mammeh was insulted because Mordkheh-Mendl's family didn't come in person to tell her the news. Tatteh still didn't want to believe it even though everybody was now wishing him Mazeltov. Everybody started calling him "Reb Luzeh, the landowner's brother-in-law," but Tatteh wasn't in any hurry to take a look. What's the matter? He'd never seen an estate before? What, he didn't know the Vaysufkeh? Didn't he know it?

So he kept putting it off from one Shabbes to the next, from one Sunday to the next, until a messenger showed up, a tall goy with a whip who came in and asked if "Pan Merchant" was at home.

"What's the matter, little father? What d'ya need Pan Merchant for?"

The goy said that the landowner of the Vaysufkeh had sent him to invite Pan Merchant and his wife and children to the estate.

"Pan Landowner?" Father squinted his eyes. "Which Pan Landowner is that?"

"The new . . . what d'ya call it?"

"You don't know what your new landowner is called?"

"I do know," the peasant waved his hand, "Is he called Mendl or something?"

"Did he buy the Vaysufkeh?" Tatteh was mocking the goy.

"Himself."

"Neh! Some impressive landowner, as I live! You haven't made a mistake, little father?"

No, he hadn't made a mistake.

"I don't have a clue who this landowner of yours is."

"Eh, Pan Merchant, you're making fun of me! Who doesn't know him? Mendl! The swarthy Mendl!"

"Oh him! So say so right off!"

I'd never seen Tatteh so mocking. Who was he making fun of? The peasant? Mordkheh-Mendl? Why was he playing so dumb?

"What's the matter? Why're you sneering?" Mammeh mixed in. "You don't like it that your brother-in-law is doing so well?"

"How d'ya know its true?" Tatteh answered in a harsh, unpleasant voice.

"So don't go. Who's asking you?"

Mammeh's face was red. She was stacking the dishes busily, loudly putting them away but not in the right place. Tatteh's sneering attitude toward Mordkheh-Mendl offended her.

I also had complaints to my father in my heart. Did he begrudge Mordkheh-Mendl his estate? My father would begrudge anybody? This was something new and painful to me. I thought to myself that Tatteh had never had brass handles on his doors, so why did he begrudge them? Why?

We all went out to the new landowner anyway, Yitta too.

The Vaysufkeh was on the same high road as the wooden hut in which Mordkheh-Mendl once lived.

Now we took a really good look at the hut.

It was black, crooked, and slanted. The yellow, split clay with which the small window was chinked was sealed for the winter. Two dirty children in outgrown undershirts, bellies sticking out, were sitting on the threshold with empty tin bowls, scraping away at the bits of groats they found at the bottom.

Strange children! Blonde, goyish. Just recently, it was Mordkheh-Mendl's children sitting on this same threshold. They'd also scraped away at their empty tin bowls and didn't have what to scrape out of them. Now they had their own estate. Look how God arranges the world! Way off, past the Russian cemetery, lay the estate.

We, the closest members of the family, were going to visit Uncle Mordkheh-Mendl for the first time.

It was Shabbes.

The odd cart was going to and from town and the peasants stared at us Shabbes guests because we looked so well rested. Some of them knew Tatteh and tipped the peaks of their caps to him and greeted him in Polish:

"*Nyekh bedzheh pokhvaloni.* Christ be blest!"

"*Na vyeki vyekuv*! For ever and ever!" Tatteh replied

The sun was bright and high over the fields. Behind a poplar tree surrounded in shadow sat a bent figure folding his leggings. A second figure was sleeping in the grass with the sun on his backside. A peasant woman with two empty baskets beside her was kneeling before a shrine of the Holy Mother hanging blackened and faceless from one of the poplar trees. The damp, grey fence of the Russian cemetery appeared suddenly. It was cool here, strange. The crosses were scary.

"Over there," Tatteh stretched out a hand to the fields, "that's the Vaysufkeh."

From far away, darkness, a hint of a forest or a park. From time to time, a white spot glittered in the dark. "That's the courtyard," said Tatteh, "and that thing over there, the white . . . that's the palace."

A palace . . . ! The word throbbed in my temples.

I'd never seen a palace before. I only knew that storybooks told about lords and emperors who lived in palaces. But that my own uncle Mordkheh-Mendl, the Jew with the flapping kapoteh should also live in a palace, that didn't even begin to make sense to me.

Mammeh, it seemed, also didn't believe it.

"Mordkheh-Mendl really lives in that palace? She asked guardedly and held her hand to her forehead.

"Probably. If he's the landowner, then it's fitting for him to live in a palace," Tatteh answered grinning into his beard.

Never mind, Tatteh can make fun of it as much as he likes but we're still coming to visit an estate with a palace.

Is this how a palace looks? Storybooks even told that palaces had to be made of gold and crystal. But for Mordkheh-Mendl such a palace like this was good enough. I saw a bright, walled, white house with tall and shiny windows. The roof was covered with red, baked tiles with the edges turned up a little like the brim of a hat.

Formally shaped linden trees stood tall and proud like sentries around the white house. The fir trees of biblical times must have looked just like these trees.

But that's nothing. The main thing was the path that led up to the white house. It was broad and straight, with hard little white stones strewn along the entire length. This was called "gravel" and it crunched under the feet like tamped down, frozen snow.

Tatteh strode nimbly and easily over this crunching gravel. He was used to such roads. Mammeh walked stiffly, her head a little stuck-up. Hard to know whether it was arrogance or a kind of wonder or whether she was simply not used to walking on the paths of the nobility. My half-sister Yitta shuffled along carefully, at a distance. She put one foot forward and took two steps back.

They had already seen us from inside the beautiful white house. Suddenly, a large, many-paned door was flung wide open.

There, on the tall stone stairs stood my uncle Mordkheh-Mendl himself, arms stretched out, wearing an unbuttoned brocade robe.

He appeared taller and more substantial, with his unruly black beard. He no longer spoke in that dull voice that always reminded you of cold rooms and damp walls. He came towards us warmly and said loudly:

"Git Shabbes! Look who's here! Shulem aleykhem! Welcome to my guests!" He stuck out a round, rich man's belly, Uncle Ben-Tsion style.

When did Mordkheh-Mendl learn to walk in such a polite and stately manner? Go figure! Even Aunt Channa, this tiny old woman who all her life had shuffled along the walls with a bit of kerchief over her head, even she now came down the stone stairs calmly, with delicate little steps, half skipping, Aunt Nemmi style.

Aunt Channa was dressed in a shiny black wig with a curl in the front. The silk dress with the puffed sleeves rustled just like the stones on the path to the palace. She let herself be heard from:

"Gangway kids, its me! Channa the landowner's coming!"

It seemed to me that Mammeh's face narrowed. I didn't like this kind of face; she went closer with mincing little steps and with her soft Warsaw double chin. She figured that she'd be welcomed in style, that everybody would be so happy to see her.

Now here was Aunt Channa parading herself off like a rich woman wearing a black silk dress with a braided gold brooch at her throat.

How'd she get all this so fast? How'd she even know how to carry it off?

Mammeh's double chin shrunk. She frowned for a minute. Nobody else saw it but my eyes are open. Nobody knows Mammeh's little twitches like I do.

But it was misleading. Aunt Channa was the same quiet, good woman who used to come into our place every morning and sit on Mammeh's bed like a real sister.

She wasn't acting the rich woman at all and not with those sedate and delicate little steps that reminded you of Aunt Nemmi. That only seemed so at first glance.

Just the opposite! As soon as she came down the stone steps, she immediately went back to her ordinary poor person's walk. Her face shining, she ran to Mammeh and fell all over her, kissing her again and again.

"Frimmetshi," she actually sobbed for joy, "May you be well, dear heart. What do you say? Ha? Mordkheh-Mendl . . . !"

"But I always told you so," Mammeh wiped her right eye.

"You should live my dear sister-in-law. First we owe God, then you."

"May you grow older in riches and in honor, surrounded by all this!" Mammeh wiped her other eye.

"Amen, dear God in Heaven! May the Master-of-the-Universe bring you luck and great wealth, exactly what you wish for yourself. You always said," here Aunt Channa's voice shook with tears, "that Mordkheh-Mendl would stir up all of Poland."

"I know him better than you do, Channa, even though he's your husband," Mammeh answered off-handedly.

Uncle Mordkheh-Mendl was walking with Tatteh, his arm around him friendly style. It seemed that the two brothers-in-law had now forgotten their differences. There was no longer a bad smell from Mordkheh-Mendl's business ventures. These businesses now smelled like Tatteh's hay. Hearing his name called, Mordkheh-Mendl left my father standing and swept over to the women.

"Let's at least kiss, dear Frimmet," he opened his arms. "You should live and be well, you clever sister-in-law of mine!"

My mother's face dimpled. Mordkheh-Mendl grinned showing off a full face of shiny white teeth. Even though Tatteh was there and everyone was looking, my uncle wasn't put off at all. He took Mammeh by the arm and paraded her in front as if he was leading her out to dance.

Mammeh laughed a high, full-bodied laugh. Aunt Channa gave a half-smile, pious style, embarrassed. Tatteh's teeth looked sharp beneath his mustache.

According to the dainty little steps that Mammeh took alongside Uncle Mordkheh-Mendl and the face she proudly held up to the sun, you knew that she really did once have brass handles at her doors.

Tatteh walked behind with his sister Channa. Yitta and I brought up the rear surrounded by our cousins and off we went.

Burekh, Mordkheh-Mendl's oldest son, was a dark youth like his father, with sharp and pointed eyebrows. Little sisters with tousled heads of black hair walked with their little brothers wearing long flannel jackets.

Mordkheh-Mendl's beautiful daughter Rayzl also walked. She was blonde and pale, this rosy-cheeked Rayzl, with a blue vein on her forehead. Her face was broad and flat like a plate. She didn't take after anyone, not my uncle and not my aunt. Her beauty lay in her braid of soft and shiny blond hair like golden white corn stalks.

Rayzl and I were the same age. It seems that in honor of the new estate they had forgotten to buy her shoes, so she was skipping along barefoot on the rough gravel, wincing from time to time.

Rayzl talked just like her mother, slowly, from the heart, with quiet humility that probably came from the earthen floor on which Mordkheh-Mendl and his whole household had lived for so many years.

Now everyone was standing on the broad stone steps leading into the white palace with the gleaming panels in the doors. Rayzl's younger sister and brother were the first inside. Yitta and Burekh were already inside as well. Only Rayzl and I stayed outside. She said to me:

"Mendl d'ya like flowers?"

"What d'ya mean?" I answered. "I don't like, and I don't not like . . ." Rayzl took my hand and said:

"Come on, I'll show you something."

She led me to the other side of the palace through old poplar trees and tall and proud linden trees, far down onto a damp dark path that was cut straight just like the avenues of our new city park. Here a park also opened up, cool and shaded, with curved paths and several half-broken wooden benches on which time had settled with rich greenish antiquity.

Rayzl led me further, to the very end of the garden. There, bent over, was an old arbor of braided birch branches through which the checkered sun peeked through from time to time.

Here, around this arbor, Rayzl showed me garden beds in rows, with little sticks poking up from the ground and new growth sprouting.

"These are 'ostrozhne,' flowers," said Rayzl, "careful, don't step on them. See those red ones there? Those are roses. They're just little buds now, but later on they'll grow big and beautiful. Look, violets are growing here," and she showed me up close at our feet, deep satiny dots. "Look how blue they are. Have you ever seen such flowers? And those over there? And see those others, over at the side? Those little goblets are called tulips."

This Rayzl who speaks so slowly as if she were bashful, listed the names of all the flowers. How does she know all this? Who told her?

Barefoot, light, and expert, she went among the garden beds one foot over the other, a leap and a spring.

"We have a gardener of our own," she said. He served the old landowner, then later the landowner's wife who sold the estate to her father. This gardener works with the flowers. He says that these flowers are his grandchildren. If not for the flowers, what use would be his whole life?

Rayzl told me all about him, looking at me dreamily, with moist blue eyes. She made me feel ashamed of my city ways and my lack of knowledge.

Aunt Nemmi's Mendl can sing, Mordkheh-Mendl's Rayzl loves flowers, but what've I got? In our house there aren't any flowers. There never were any. An earthen pot with long, thick, dusty leaves, curled and dried up on the brink of old age stood on our windowsill. Tatteh would cut off onions from these dusty leaves to treat his sick leg. These were the only flowers that I saw and knew about.

Besides, what does a young boy like me need flowers for? What do you have from them? I don't see that Jewish boys are missing anything by not having flowers. Rayzl was a girl after all. All her life, she'd lived near a highway, between heaven and poplar trees, Her know-how and her love of flowers must come from that.

Rayzl told me a lot more about flowers. She showed me those that she planted and raised herself. I didn't listen to her any more. I wanted to be inside the mansion already and see what was going on there. A voice was heard from afar:

"Rayzl! Rayzl!"

"I'm coming, Mammeh," Rayzl answered, puckering up her face, and taking me by the hand.

"Look," she pointed, "down there's an orchard where apples, pears, and cherries grow. Everything good grows there. And you know what? It's all ours! "Of course, I knew. If it hadn't been theirs, I wouldn't be able to walk so free and easy all over this whole estate, poking into every corner.

Everything belonged to Mordkheh-Mendl, even the flowers that the gardener cared for like he did his own grandchildren, these belonged to my uncle too. The best sign was that we all came to look and take pride in Mordkheh-Mendel's wealth. Aunt Nemmi and Uncle Ben-Tsion also came, by foot too, poor things. Such a distance!

Everyone was sitting inside the white palace, reclining on soft and broad, old-fashioned sofas with high backs. Uncle Ben-Tsion was wheezing heavily, wiping the grey drops of sweat from his forehead and meanwhile, taking a good look around.

There was a lot to see and even more to talk about. Such rooms! Such a household! None of us had ever seen anything like it before! Except maybe Tatteh, who was a frequent visitor in the courtyards of the landowners.

"It's salons, not rooms," he said, "salons with dark ceilings, big and airy."

Big rooms with clocks that didn't work but just stood there under glass domes on tall, darkly carved enamel tiled stoves. Big rooms with stag horns spread out above the doors and stuffed birds with large glass eyes that look down surprised and confused.

Standing here on an old fashioned, carved brown cupboard was an eagle (Tatteh said it was an eagle) with a curved hard black beak like an iron hatchet.

This eagle was bent over, its claws digging into the cupboard, wings spread, taking up half a wall. Any minute now it would rise up, dash into the window with full force, break open the panes, and . . . off into the world!

Uncle Ben-Tsion was drying his bald and sweaty head with a white handkerchief. He couldn't stop wondering:

"It's really an eagle? D'ya know for sure that it's an eagle?"

"What then, it's, a rooster?" Tatteh bragged. "If you're told it's an eagle, then it's an eagle."

My father felt at home in these rooms, like he belonged here. He didn't sit humbled, not paying attention like he did when he was a guest at the home of his well-off sister Nemmi. Tatteh felt like he had a stake here because he was something of a regular visitor at the courtyards of the landowners, He'd already seen many of the treasures of the nobility. So what was the big deal about an eagle?

He really did know! He gave advice. He showed authority.

Now they showed us the tables, brownish-red, with oval-shaped, molded and curved legs, braided and pinched at the back. There were broken-down commodes with half-split drawers and worn-out and tarnished gilded handles at the keyholes.

We were shown into a four-cornered salon, with three tall polished windows facing the sun. The beams were white; the floor yellow like wax and pieced together from separate small boxes; "parquet" it was called. The walls were pale blue with narrow strips of gilt molding under the rafters.

On the walls hung worn out and faded tapestries, dating all the way back to King Sobietski's times, showing skinny hunting dogs, ladies in fancy ball gowns, men in white stockings and powdered wigs braided at the back. What an outlandish crowd! They must be masquerading.

The whole family stood gaping in wonder! What kind of people were these? Why were they making such fools of themselves?

It seemed to me that Uncle Ben-Tsion was something of a worldly man. He was a familiar sight at City Hall, he often went to the provincial government office; still, he didn't begin to understand the meaning of these tapestries.

But my father knew. He said that these were a kind of portrait from olden times. He said that the lords had these tapestries made the same for instance, as the photographs of today, and the reason that they were dressed up so outlandishly was a sign that they were at a ball. They called this Carnival. That was a time, Tatteh said, when rich people and their wives put on masquerades.

I understood Tatteh perfectly. This carnival was to them for instance like Purim was to us Jews. Probably they also had a Humen harusheh, Haman the Oppressor.

But Mammeh turned up her nose.

"It's not a carnival," she said. "It's nothing of the kind." She had once read a book where it said that in Napoleon's time everyone dressed like this. She said that even the poorest people wore powdered wigs and had dogs.

"Never mind," Uncle Mordkheh-Mendl interrupted. "I'll tear it down anyway, this thing of beauty! Better take a look at the beds standing here."

They were truly beautiful beds, different than those of the other houses in town. They were reddish-brown, low and wide, with a darkly gilded sheen in the corners.

"Would'ya believe me?" Aunt Channa said to my mother, "Its hard for me to fall asleep in such a bed."

"You'll get used to it," Mammeh answered with the offhand air of a rich woman, as if she herself had slept in just such a bed all her life.

"With my first husband, may he be separated from the living," she added immediately, "there wasn't much that was missing for me to have these same kind of beds. When you came to visit me and you saw the brass handles . . ."

Mammeh kept on talking but I didn't listen anymore. I looked around to see if there were brass handles here too.

Of course there were, on the tall white doors, heads hanging down. Tarnished, they didn't gleam. According to my mother's description, brass handles should gleam.

"We have to fix things up," Aunt Channa apologized, "there's lots to do. We have to put in a pile of money." Aunt Channa was talking about lots of money. She said it so calmly, so easily, as if she was certain that today or tomorrow, Mordkheh-Mendl would bring her a great fortune.

And maybe . . . you can believe anything from Mordkheh-Mendl!

Uncle Ben-Tsion was in a constant sweat, not taking away the white handkerchief from his bald and reddened pate. Aunt Nemmi, half blinking, slowly drawled out of her thin pedigreed lips:

"Mordkheh-Mendl . . . ?"

"Eh?"

"You were supposed to tell us how you came to this estate. How did'ya?" But it seemed Mordkheh-Mendl didn't even hear, he wasn't listening.

"Come," he said, standing up from the soft and deep sofa, and waving his hand broadly: "Lets go outside. Y'aint seen nuthin yet! This Vaysufkeh is some piece of land! It's filled with gold!"

He combed his silky beard with his fingers, just like King Ahashverus in the Purim story. He threw open the glass door and led the guests out to admire the great estate he bought.

There really was what to see, that is to say, what the old landowner had once owned. During the tenure of the last landowner's wife there was probably still what to see, but today there wasn't much left. According to the extent of the holdings, it should have been as beautiful outside as inside the house.

Everyone knew that an estate had stalls full of horses, cows and oxen. There should also be pigs and little piglets, roosters, chickens, turkeys, and ducks wandering around in the yard.

Tatteh said there should also be a few peacocks with their rich tails opened out, each feather of which contained a sun and a moon. These peacocks should be shrieking at passersby:

"It's an estate. It's an estate. It's an estate . . . !"

So, never mind, not all landowners had peacocks and Mordkheh-Mendl would never raise pigs, but why were there no more than two scraggly horses on spindly legs in the stalls? And why didn't you see anything more than a pair of cows wasted away to skin and bones, poor things? One of them, a barren white one with a yellow patch under one eye. The second one was a black milk cow with a white spot on its rear.

According to the size of the stall, there must have been cows upon cows here once. The empty feedbags were still hanging on the opposite wall and the dividers separating the feedbags were also still there.

The smell of warm cow dung had long ago seeped through the holes in the roof and through the two doors that were hanging loosely on their hinges. Two horses and two calves were left.

Out came the milk cow with her moist black nostrils pointed at the guests. She turned her face away from Ben-Tsion's white, broad beard and looked at my father in wonder as if she knew him.

It seemed to me that she was looking for a familiar face. Now she was looking at me with her large tearful eyes as if she was begging me to chase away the small pesty flies that had found a resting place in the corners of her eyes.

I tried waving my hand in front of the cow's face but she bent her head away, not happy. It seemed to me she was saying:

"No more, you don't understand. It's not what'ya see.

At one time, with the landowner's wife, there were a lot of sisters of mine. Whole families of ours lived here, grandmothers, mothers, and children. We didn't stand in the stalls together with the angry horses, but in a separate cowshed, bigger than the stall you see here.

We jostled each other when we went out to pasture, that's how crowded it was. Our udders overflowed; we could have flooded the world with our milk.

It's different today. Bad times! The old landowner died in some strange place far away from here and debts were left, so the land-owner's wife slowly began to sell off one cow after another, one horse after another.

There were sheep here too, big, round, well-fed ones. They sheared the wool and took it to the fairs and markets. When there was nothing left to sell, they put the estate up for auction.

Customers came, lots of them, Jews and goyim, Fleischer the German also came, that same common tinsmith who crawled on roofs and smeared them with thick red paint. He wanted to become the landowner of the Vaysufkeh. So they bargained, dealt back and forth, yelled and argued. The old Pani cried, said goodbye to the farmhands, paid off what was owed and let everyone go. She took practically nothing with her, only a bouquet of flowers.

The estate was left not to Fleischer but to that one over there, the one with the black beard, the one who's called, Mordkheh-Mendl."

This was the story told by a grizzled old peasant with a small pipe in his mouth. He was walking between Mammeh and me. He was the one who talked like this, not God forbid, the cow.

Over there strode Mordkheh-Mendl in his flowing Shabbes robe.
He waved his hands left and right. He had amazingly large hands now
and when he waved them, it seemed that he was embracing the whole
wide, empty tract together with the woods and the sky.

He told us how he got the estate. Landowners, he said, beat him to
the price. He couldn't close an eye for whole nights; his head withered.
What if it all came to nothing? What if the landowners bargained the
Vaysufkeh away from him? What then? Maybe this . . . and maybe
that . . . Until he finally decided to go into partnership with Fleischer
the German.

But Fleischer was no stillborn babe! He wasn't born yesterday!
This common little tinsmith, Fleischer, wanted to be the landowner
of the Vaysufkeh without Mordkheh-Mendl! So what did Mordkheh-
Mendl do . . . ?

What Mordkheh-Mendl did I didn't hear anymore. Rayzl came
over to me with red and blue flowers she picked especially for me and
said that I should take them back to town with me and put them into
a flowerpot with water.

Mordkheh-Mendl was still telling exactly what it was he'd done.
When I came closer, I heard Uncle Ben-Tsion interrupt:

"Nu, so what became of Fleischer?"

But Mordkheh-Mendl was so busy explaining the workings of
the estate that he didn't hear what Uncle Ben-Tsion was asking, and
he led us all out of the courtyard waving his hand broadly over the
entire area.

"Look at these fields," he said. "Look at this earth. Gold is
buried here! These hicks, these landowning boors, do they have any
idea what's here?"

By all means, we should make the effort and go on a little further
and he'd really show us something.

We all took the trouble. Spread out before us were empty, neglected
fields overgrown with nettles and with signs of lupines from years past.
There'd been no sowing or reaping here for a very long time. Tatteh
said that he didn't remember the time when any grain grew here at all.

So what kind of treasures lay in this earth? Where was the gold
that Mordkheh-Mendl boasted about?

Our feet walked on soft, slippery mud. A yellowish dampness rose
up from the field. Where'd this moisture come from? It seemed it was
from the swamps. Mordkheh-Mendl rolled up his beard.

"God forbid! This slippery moisture actually is the real gold that the
landowners before me didn't have enough sense to do anything about."

It turned out that the earth here was one large mass of clay. Mordkheh-Mendl showed us a four-squared, deeply cut pit in which stood puddles of dirty water but the walls and the corners shone with rich, dark-brown clay.

"This is no ordinary clay," said Uncle Mordkheh-Mendl. "It's oil! It's meat! It's bread and butter!

From this clay we'll make bricks, tiles for the roof, earthenware pots, jugs, crocks for sour milk, and . . . what not?" He would build a chimney here, he said, and hire goyim as potters. Work would be done here that the world had never yet seen!

He bent down to the pit and pulled out a dirty handful of this "golden" clay.

"Take a good look," he said, "This is clay? It's diamonds, not clay!"

He showed off his dirty hands right in everybody's faces. Aunt Nemmi pinched her nostrils with two fingers, Uncle Ben-Tsion touched it with the tip of his little finger, while my father looked wryly on from the side. Only my mother smelled the clay with a full face.

The "golden" clay didn't appeal to me either. In town, in our old home where Moysheh died, a pit was once dug and out of it was tossed the same kind of clay as Uncle Mordkheh-Mendl was now showing us.

Simkheleh the Bricklayer, who'd once fixed our oven, had slapped on just this same kind of clay. So why was Uncle Mordkheh-Mendl making such a big deal over it?

He showed us a lot of other things too that Shabbes. He showed us the forest that stood in a dreamy blue mist a little way off.

"This forest also belongs to the Vaysufkeh," he said.

He led us into the garden, to the pond covered with a greenish-yellow scum that was generations old.

"This'll be taken away," he said. He'd make a pool for fish, with carp and bream swimming in it.

He showed us the orchard with fruit. That is to say, without the fruit because this year it wasn't successful. With God's help, he would make it succeed!

He showed us everything, even the empty kennel.

Later, toward evening, they served us cold sorrel borscht and rye bread lavishly spread with butter.

A restful coolness spread out over the broad, flaming sky, over the blue forest and over the fields. It smelled of hay. The crickets sawed away in the garden grass and frogs could be heard croaking hoarsely in the moldy pond.

We sat outside. The sky got dark over the whole horizon. It was
more than the eye could take in. Now at last, we saw how many millions of stars there were in the sky.

Rayzl whispered to me and pointed to that star up there, the
biggest one. It seemed to her that it was so big, it was such a big
diamond that any minute it would break away and fall at her feet.
Rayzl is a foolish girl but still, it was better to sit here with her than
in our small narrow yard that smelled of pigs.

After Havdoleh, Mordkheh-Mendl sent us back to town in a
carriage.

It was crowded and we had to sit on top of each other but we
made the best of it. The night lay warm and rich on all sides. It smelled
of camomile, mint, and almonds.

Uncle Ben-Tsion spread himself out, practically over the entire
carriage.

"Ay, it's a pleasure here," he said expansively, spreading out his
belly. "If God would help me so I could thumb my nose at the whole
community too . . ." He didn't finish. Out of a corner was heard Aunt
Nemmi's drawling voice:

"Ben-Tsi-on . . . Ben-Tsi-on . . ."

It must be that he knew what his wife was about to tell him
because he gave a sigh and let it be known that Mordkheh-Mendl was
really quite a capable person. "If a person can come to such a big estate
without a penny, its really no small thing, eh, Luzeh?"

"Yeh, it's no small thing," Tatteh answered into the darkness,
"but I don't think much of it."

"What d'ya mean, you don't think much of it? Weren't you at
the Vaysufkeh just now?"

"I was."

"You saw?"

"I saw."

"Nu?"

"It's got no substance. The transaction doesn't appeal to me."

"Why not?"

" 'Cause it doesn't appeal to me."

So, too bad, it didn't appeal to him. But Mordkheh-Mendl accom-
plished it anyhow.

It didn't take too much longer and on the damp clay fields of the
Vaysufkeh suddenly a tall round chimney shot up right to the sky. It
could be seen all the way into town.

People craned their necks and pointed to the sky like stargazers: "See over there? Mordkheh-Mendl . . ."

Thick fat curls of white and black smoke curled out of that chimney, like rolled up cotton batting. The smoke rose up over the house, the garden, the orchard, and over the flowers that had so thrilled Rayzl.

Peasants coming into the city told how the smoke settled on the tops of the poplar trees. The storks were confused, looking around for some other resting place where the smoke couldn't reach them.

Near the white mansion Mordkheh-Mendl put up a round, bulging red building out of which rose the chimney. The pots that Mordkheh-Mendl fired in the hot brick ovens came from here.

The landowner's gravel road that led to the palace was now littered. Scattered pots, glazed and unglazed with broken ears, with holes in the bottom, were rolling around on what had once been gravel. On the broad, stone stairs where Mordkheh-Mendl had stood so proudly that Shabbes, in the rooms with the soft upholstered armchairs, on the clear tall windows, earthenware pots, crocks for sour milk, large peasant bowls. and double pots in which the goyim carried food to their men in the fields, lay scattered everywhere.

Mordkheh-Mendl competed vigorously because in order to get rich, you had to have the work go on day and night.

Goyim with faces lined like parchment, sleeves rolled up, arms thickly veined, eyes bright, sat bent over a wooden machine that looked like a spool from which you unroll yarn. With one foot they let the spool unroll round and round and with their hands, with their ten bare fingers, they kept a firm hold on the clay forms.

The wheel turned quickly without breath. The raw piece of clay the potter threw onto the wheel turned with it, pulling out and drawing in. Living creatures seemed to grow under their fingers. The potter patted and caressed the clay, wiped it, cleaned it, until the moment came when the vessel was finished and he cut it away from the wheel with a thin string, just like you cut off an infant from its mother's navel.

It seemed that Mordkheh-Mendl was actually getting rich from these pots. Another horse and another ladder-sided wagon for hauling were added to the Vaysufkeh. Aunt Channa, with her son Burekh and her daughter Rayzl, drove the wagons full with pots to sell at the market every Thursday morning.

In the wider world, where Mordkheh-Mendl now busied himself, you couldn't send these pots. To tell the truth, he tried once to load up a wagon and send it off to Lublin but what arrived there were shards, not pots. Carcasses they shoveled out of the wagon!

So he decided that the merchandise wouldn't be sent off to remote places but would be sold here in the local market.

All week long they looked forward to Thursday. Before dawn, when fields and people were still fast asleep, they began loading up the wagon and went off to the city without even having anything to eat. The pots, jugs, and crocks were displayed at the market, one next to the other like children from one mother. Prospective customers tapped their fingers on the earthenware to see if they were cracked, they bargained over a penny, they went away ten times and came back once to buy a single pot or a jug for two copper coins.

Standing here among the pots at the market, Aunt Channa didn't look like the gleaming landowner anymore, the one who came out to greet us on the stone steps in a black silk dress with a braided gold brooch at her throat.

Now, she was our old Aunt Channa again, wrapped in a shawl with a kerchief over her head. The sun baked her face, rain and wind chapped her skin—her hands and nose were black, her brow was wrinkled.

Rayzl, who never forgot to bring her tulips and roses into the city, her fair skin was now also burned. When she looked into the glazed shards, it seemed as if two laughing pots were looking at each other's noses.

Aunt Channa took back more pots from Thursday's market than she had brought. When they unloaded the wagon, half the merchandise was broken. It burst, it crumbled, and was strewn all over.

Aunt Channa's face burst together with her earthenware. Mordkheh-Mendl's silky black beard began to show big white streaks. He now had time to come to see us in the blue dawn, not boasting anymore, no longer ridiculing Uncle Ben-Tsion the Community Scribe. He caught Tatteh in the middle of davening and whispered something to him. He woke up Mammeh who got up at once, covered herself up with the coverlet and in a half-asleep voice, drawled:

"What's new, Mordkheh-Mendl?"

"Glory be to the One Above! Pretty good, but there's nothin doing with the pots."

"How come?"

"Too many shards, too many discards. We need a brickyard. The city is beginning to build—Mendl Danziger is building, Yidl the Gaiter Maker has already bought a site, Beckerman's street with the empty lots is already parceled out. Whoever's got an extra penny is bargaining for a piece of land and getting ready to build. Brickyards are practically nowhere to be found so we've got to bring bricks from far away but its not worth it. But if I, Mordkheh-Mendl, put up a brickyard at the Vaysufkeh . . ."

"Of course! Of course!" Mammeh nodded in agreement. "You're right."

"What d'ya mean, I'm right?" Mordkheh-Mendl rocked himself sideways. "It's as clear as day!" He was only missing some ready cash and that's why he came here, actually to Luzeh, that is, for him to endorse checks into the free loan office. Ben-Tsion had already endorsed. He didn't say a single word . . . Ben-Tsion.

Tatteh drew out the words of the prayers quietly. From under his tallis, he stole a sidelong look at his brother-in-law, Mordkheh-Mendl.

Tatteh heard everything but somehow, he didn't quite understand. "Eh?"

"Y'understand," Mordkheh-Mendl bent his beard quickly to Tatteh's tallis. "I don't need a lot, just a small thing, believe me."

"But what d'ya mean by endorsing?" Tatteh had never endorsed a check. And what was his endorsement worth anyway? In sum, he couldn't even write. Didn't Mordkheh-Mendl know that?

Yeh, he knew, but that was just a small detail. He'd learn. Frimmet would show him how and Luzeh would copy it.

A grin spread over Father's mustache, a nice, easy grin:

"What a fool y'are! What value can my endorsement have if I'm a pauper in seven shreds?"

"Then you've got nothing to be afraid of!"

"I don't hold with this!"

So Mordkheh-Mendl turned to Mammeh for help.

"Frimmet," he said, "you're certainly no fool. On the contrary, make him understand what he's putting in here. He'll save me and he won't do himself any harm."

Mammeh made a sign to him to say no more, Leave it alone. She'd handle it. In the evening after supper, when Tatteh was already sitting on the bed pulling off his boots, Mammeh called out:

"Luzeh . . ."

"Eh?"

"I think you should endorse."

"What should I do?"

"Endorse for Mordkheh-Mendl. I don't see why not. You won't, God forbid, suffer because of it."

One boot didn't want to come off easily. Tatteh gritted his teeth into the left corner of his mouth and bent over. There, into the point of the boot, he answered:

"Please Frimmet, I'm asking you, maybe you won't make such a fool of yourself?"

"But he's your brother-in-law!"

"And if he's my brother-in-law, so what? He's the landowner! So what does he want from me?"

"But we could save him!"

"So you save him! Who's not letting you?"

"I wish my endorsement were worth something, I wouldn't say another word. As you can see, Ben-Tsion also endorsed."

"That's what Mordkheh-Mendl says."

"He wouldn't lie."

"God forbid! Only twice a year."

Tatteh lifted the featherbed, fluffed it up and turned over to the wall.

"Call it a night, Frimmet," he said, "you'll think about it tomorrow."

In the morning, Aunt Channa, black, scrawny, with thin veined arms came running. She fell in at the same time as the crowing of the rooster.

"Brother," she said, "see for yourself, it's a golden business. We only need a few hundred rubles to put into it. "A moment later, she added: "You know what? Why don't you become a partner?"

"I don't want to become a landowner. I don't want it."

"But you're a brother! My children, poor things, haven't suffered enough hunger already?"

"And my children are well fed?" Tatteh shot back angrily.

"But you make a living, thank God."

"My children toil for strangers," Tatteh answered, more hot and bothered, "They're servants. My children are servants!"

"But what do I want from you? I want money?"

"I can't write."

"I'll do the writing," Mammeh mixed in, "and you'll copy it."

"I've got time."

And Tatteh had plenty of time, one week, two weeks . . . Mordkheh-Mendl and Aunt Channa came often to see us. Mammeh risked herself for their sake many times. She argued with Tatteh, told him that he was a peasant and that he wasn't a respectable person, but Tatteh didn't endorse.

One grey and foggy, a consumptive day, the wind had blown at the window shutters all night and in the morning, not even the doves on the roof were warm.

On that day we didn't go to cheder. It was a "Galuvkeh," a Russian holiday, the tsar's birthday.

In the morning, the khazn sang the Russian anthem "God Save The Tsar." Ben-Tsion's son Mendl, in a white collar and pressed black trousers, stood with the khazn on the platform where the Torah was read and trilled and embellished the song. A municipal councilor in a black three-cornered, high fur cap with silver edges, came from City Hall and stood on the platform together with the rabbi and the khazn. Everyone stared at the official, at this goy in the shul, as if he were the tsar himself.

Later in the day, Russian music played in the Central Market and Jews kept their businesses closed, so it occurred to me to go out to the Vaysufkeh.

Fallen, dried leaves were already spinning around in the ditches on both sides of the high road. The wind carried and scattered the leaves over the cut fields and it also whistled through the bare branches of the poplar trees. The alder trees in the Russian cemetery answered with an echoing lament. The high road was littered but empty of carts and people.

If not for the fact that today was the tsar's birthday and I didn't have what to do with myself, it would never have occurred to me to go to the Vaysufkeh.

I was sorry about it half way there. I would have turned back but a stooped old woman, a goyeh with a gnarled cane, came toward me from behind the Russian cemetery and stopped me.

"Where are you off to in such a driving wind, young man?"

"To my uncle, Mordkheh-Mendl."

"Who's your uncle Mordkheh-Mendl?"

"The landowner," I answered proudly, yelling right into the old woman's withered face.

"Heh, heh," the old woman showed two big yellow teeth, "so that's your uncle, the Jewish landowner there?"

"Yeh, the Jewish landowner."

"So there's no point in your going, young man. There's no longer a Jewish landowner at the Vaysufkeh. 'Nima'! No More!"

It seems this little old woman was crazy. She looked at me with two small round eyes like an owl.

I left this crazy woman and went on. Now I really wanted to get there even if the wind was tearing at me.

The tall red chimney of the pottery works seemed to me higher and redder than before. No smoke was coming out of it but that was probably because today was the Tsar's birthday. Nobody worked on a holiday.

A crow screeched down from the top of a tree while a second one rose up from a pile of rubbish flapping its wings. A flock of crows from the Russian cemetery suddenly screeched over my head. They were flying toward the Vaysufkeh. They must be flying to a wedding.

When I finally got closer, I saw a person coming toward me on the empty road and behind that person, a cow. Today was not a market day, so they were probably leading the cow to the slaughterhouse.

I also saw a horse and wagon. The closer I got, the bigger the person, the cow, the horse and the wagon got. I would have sworn that the cow was Mordkheh-Mendl's. She had a patch between the eyes. It seemed to me that the person walking in front of the cow was Aunt Chana . . . It really was Aunt Chana!

She was leading the animal by a rope. I saw everything clearly now. The horse and wagon was the same one that used to take the pots to market every Thursday morning.

But it wasn't Mordkheh-Mendl's son Burekh driving the wagon now, but a goy.

The wagon wasn't loaded with pots but with puffed up, red bedding. A table with its four legs to the sky was sticking out of the bedding. It wasn't one of those fancy reddish-brown tables from the palace. This one was plain and white.

A tub rattled between the wheels of the wagon. On top of the bedding sat Rayzl, nodding from side to side as if she was dreaming. She had picked flowers.

The wagon scraped along. Mordkheh-Mendl's oldest son, Burekh, walked behind the wagon, l'havdil, like after a cart carrying a corpse. A younger brother and sister sat facing the Vaysufkeh. The rest couldn't be seen. Mordkheh-Mendl also couldn't be seen.

The wind was racing through the poplar trees. From the other side of the mansion the flock of crows came winging back. They circled the horse and wagon with unrestrained shrieking.

What did all this mean? Were they moving out of the Vaysufkeh?

I stopped. No one saw me. The cow looked at me with large watery eyes. Aunt Channa looked but didn't recognize me. Rayzl, with flowers in her hand, looked down from the bedding but she also didn't recognize me.

"Good morning, Aunt," I yelled and ran right up to the cow.

Aunt Channa woke up: "Mendl?"

"Yeh, its me, good morning!"

"Good morning, good year! Where are you off to in such a wind?"

"To the Vaysufkeh."

"You don't need to go there anymore . . ." Aunt Chana shook
her head and slowly closed her eyes.

The chill from her blackened face went right through my bones.
It seemed to me that it was not Aunt Channa talking but the cow,
which was shaking its foolish head.

"Finished! There's no more Vaysufkeh!"

Aunt Channa tugged at the rope attached to the cow. The cow
plodded along disagreeably, leaving telltale signs behind her on the high
road. It mooed, turned its head back toward the white palace, to the
stall that didn't come along with it.

It was all the same to the horse with the spindly legs. It pulled
the wagon into town resignedly. It probably thought today was Thursday and that they were carrying the pots to market. But the flock of
crows wouldn't scatter, and they screeched out into the grey emptiness,
the same as that little old woman, the goyeh with the gnarled cane:

"No more a Jewish landowner in the Vaysufkeh! 'Nima'! No more!"

Chapter 14

So the dream of a white palace, of beautiful flowers, and golden treasures came to nothing. Just like we couldn't figure out how Mordkheh-Mendl got the estate in the first place, we couldn't figure out how he lost it either.

It was said in town that the Vaysufkeh had never really belonged to Mordkheh-Mendl. As a matter of fact, not a single lump of clay belonged to him. They said that he forced his way in through swindle, that he deceived Fleischer the German with phony checks and that at first, Fleischer didn't catch on. Later, when Mordkheh-Mendl was already settled on the estate, when he'd already put the chimney up and began bringing pots to market, Fleischer beat his head in shock.

Lawyers were consulted and a series of trials began. Money was no object and it cost Fleischer in the thousands. He moved worlds until in the end he got a piece of paper that said that until the issue was settled, Mordkheh-Mendl had to leave the Vaysufkeh together with his whole household.

So Aunt Channa, her children, and the one calf that she managed to save, moved again into a crooked wooden hut with an earthen floor. No tapestries on the walls, instead strips of blue lime; no clear white windows but four small and dusty panes; no low wide beds with gilt decorations but plain peasant ones without headboards that had been bought quickly at the market in Skarczew.

Mordkheh-Mendl wasn't seen in town anymore. The Days of Awe arrived, grey and full of anxiety. Worry and spiritual stocktaking hung over the Jewish houses. Mordkheh-Mendl didn't come to the davening.

Day and night he stood at the dusty window of the wooden hut staring out at the highway that led to the Vaysufkeh. His beard got grey and neglected and his eyes red-rimmed. His beautiful, healthy white teeth began to turn yellow and crumble.

Finally the shofar was blown and Jews finished celebrating the cycle of Torah reading. Mordkheh-Mendl continued to stare out the window watching the carts traveling back and forth to the Vaysufkeh bringing lumber for building and carrying pots and bricks away. Something was going on there but without Mordkheh-Mendl.

One morning before davening, he was standing at the window, his son Burekh had already left for town to look for work, the smaller children were still asleep, and Aunt Channa had gone outside to milk the cow.

No one knew how it happened, but all of a sudden Mordkheh-Mendl lurched forward, his hands slammed into the windowpane, the glass shattered, and his hands were covered with blood.

His daughter Rayzl was peeling potatoes into a large earthenware bowl. When she heard the sudden breaking of glass, she sprang up letting the knife and the potato fall and screamed:

"Tatteh, what're you doing?"

In that same minute her father's head fell back as if slaughtered, his bloodied hands flailed the air, and he bent over at an angle like a tree trying to hold itself upright on a sawed off trunk. As big as he was, Mordkheh-Mendl's head slammed into the edge of the table, he slumped to the ground and a stream of black blood spurted out of both nostrils.

Aunt Channa was outside milking the scrawny cow.

She didn't know if it got scared at Rayzl's scream for help or whether by instinct it felt something wasn't right, but when the unfortunate Mordkheh-Mendl hit the edge of the table, the calf suddenly tossed its tail right into Aunt Channa's face.

She told us later that she got this slap because she'd left her husband unattended.

Aunt Channa's eye got bloodshot immediately and her face smeared with mud. The little pail of milk spilled over at her feet.

When that happened, she sprang up from her stool and ran. Actually, she had no idea where or why she was running but she felt wounded right to the heart and had to come to the rescue. She found Rayzl standing at the open door with a scream frozen on her round mouth. Had Rayzl, God forbid, become paralyzed? Vey'z mir!

"Rayzl! Rayzl!"

But Rayzl couldn't bring out even one word. She could only make a sign with her hand toward the inside of the house.

Aunt Channa ran inside. It was dark in there. Did the sun just go down or what? What happened here? What? Why are the children screaming?

Aunt Channa began looking around and saw that her Mordkheh-Mendl lay with his head pressed against the edge of the table.

"Mordkheh-Mendl! Mordkheh-Mendl!" She began shaking his shoulder, but at the first shake, Mordkheh-Mendl's head leaned over to a side and laid itself out on the earthen floor without even making a sound.

Only now did Aunt Channa see the blood—blood on his face, on his hands, on his beard.

She waved her hands frantically. It seemed that she wanted to catch some air but her legs gave out from under her and Aunt Channa, smeared face, bloodshot eye and all, fell on top of her husband shrieking and wailing.

But what could Mordkheh-Mendl do now if he himself lay like a lump of clay just like the broken shards of his pots?

In town they said that an artery had burst in Mordkheh-Mendl's head. People were bothered that such a pauper wanted nothing less than to become a landowner.

It was stupid talk by enemies, by those who begrudged him. This kind of talk made my father's face darken and sink.

After the unmerciful death of his brother-in-law, Tatteh's head hung lower, right down to his lapels. For some time afterward Mammeh went around the house with a handkerchief of grated horseradish pressed to her forehead. The mood was heavy in our house. It chased you. Yitta had already gone back to Warsaw. Aunt Channa no longer came to see us, not her and not her children.

Tatteh stayed silent for days and weeks. It seemed to me that his dreamy eyes became even more absent-minded. Mammeh couldn't hide her suffering anymore:

"Such an educated person!" she sighed on more than one occasion: "Such a dear man! All he asked for was an endorsement. What would have happened if you'd given your brother-in-law an endorsement . . . the world would have gone under?"

Tatteh was in the middle of eating his supper. He chewed slowly, without taste or enjoyment. Mammeh spoke quietly as if she was talking to herself but Tatteh heard. He raised his head from the food. A deep crease lay between his eyes like a worm down his forehead. His eyes roamed over the table as if he were looking for something but couldn't see it. He didn't speak. The spoon moved out of his hand and slid as if l by itself, down into the plate.

"Luzeh!" Mammeh stood up quickly. "Nu, stop it! Why aren't you eating? Why not? What did I say?"

But Tatteh wouldn't eat his supper anymore. The plate of beans and noodles was coated with a cold, thick skin. Mammeh cried, Tatteh recited the blessing, looking heavily into the dark windowpanes.

There was no more talk of Mordkheh-Mendl. The days got foggy, consumptive feeling. On the opposite roof, the doves hid in their dovecote. At night it rained, pouring from the eaves. It made holes in your heart. It tore pieces out of your skull. In the middle of the night, a long, drawn-out yawn cut into the dark like the whistle of a train far off in the wide world.

It was Mammeh, yawning, not able to sleep, lying awake thinking.

During the day, she still went around with handkerchiefs of grated horseradish pressed to her forehead. She didn't make a fire in the grate and she didn't make the beds.

No one came to visit us. Tatteh was busy in far-off villages somewhere, so why should Mammeh make a fire? For whom should she make the beds?

So it was cold in the house. Nobody lived in the kitchen anymore. The cot stood empty, deserted. A greenish sadness drifted down from the walls. The clock ticked too loudly. The sun didn't come near the window; it was clearly offended by us.

Mammeh began to complain:

"What kind of a place is this to live in? Its worse than a cellar!" If she'd known that the wind would howl like this, she'd never have set foot here! At night she couldn't sleep. She kept feeling that any minute the door would open and Mordkheh-Mendl would come in with his silky black beard and his mouth full of beautiful teeth. Such a go-getter! Such an educated person!

Mammeh was talking to herself; Tatteh wasn't here. She didn't talk like this in front of him. She was telling me this out of her bitter, dark heart.

I felt that life was very hard for Mammeh. She hadn't gotten any letters from her children. She didn't know what had happened with Tsippeleh's wedding. She couldn't just go off to Warsaw. She couldn't just tear herself away what with the unfortunate Mordkheh-Mendl so quickly torn from this world! While here in this place, the wind howled and it stank of pigs everywhere.

This was true, the whole courtyard, the walls and the doors were smeared from the pigs.

Shikorskeleh the goy, the owner of the hut we lived in, had become partners with a slaughterer and together they opened up a pig shop that faced out to the street. A stale, rancid odor caught you right in the throat.

I was afraid of the cold white hunks of pig fat that hung in their window. I was afraid of the long dried out pieces of stuffed derma and the axe on the sign together with the ox head. But the main thing, I was afraid of the dog, a mongrel with a vicious mug, and jowls that hung down at the corners of its mouth. It sat in front of the store sniffing at the hems of Jewish kapotehs, gnashing its teeth and guarding the dead hunks of pig meat.

We had to get out of here! The days had become grayer and shorter now too, just like all over the world.

But where can you move to at such a time? People will think we're crazy . . . moving every Monday and Thursday!

Since Mammeh had begun to hate this place, we'd have to move for sure. She actually went out looking and began asking around. No one knew anything about this in the house, not even me. But I figured it out. The way she looked over the walls, the way she measured the length of the beds with a piece of string, all this bore witness that today or tomorrow, a cart would come and we'd load up our things.

And that's exactly what happened. One grey and foggy day right after Tatteh left, Menasheh the Gabber came with his white cart and began moving out our dressers and beds.

Menasheh the Gabber had a youth who helped him, a squawker with the visor of his cap turned around backward. Mammeh told me to stay home. She herself also helped and bit by bit, we loaded the bits of broken down furniture and went off to the avenue and onto the other side of the jail where Mammeh had rented the new place.

Along the way, Jews stood leaning on walking sticks behind them, wondering why on such a foggy day, someone would take it into their heads to move. Women storekeepers came outside wearing warm, padded kaftans, shrugging their shoulders and yelling from one threshold to another: "What lunacy! Who picks such a day to move?"

Menasheh the Gabber's wagon creaked. It leaned to one side as if it didn't want to haul these few bits of household goods on such a gloomy day. But we managed the move. No more pig meat, no more damp walls, no more grated horseradish on Mammeh's forehead.

The alley where Menasheh the Gabber brought us was narrow and quiet, a dead end. The alley was closed off by a tall wooden fence, over which could be seen the branches of linden and chestnut trees. This alley had no other buildings. From one side rose the yellow brick fence of the jail, from the other side an old shabby hut, a refuge for swallows and cats.

The jail stood tall and spread out. Over the thick barred windows hung tin roofs, like knapsacks on the backs of soldiers.

Here behind the long yellow wall, a sentry marched back and forth with a rifle, like a pendulum that can't make a single step more or less.

You weren't allowed to walk by this sentry or to stop in front of him, and you weren't allowed to look at him either. He also didn't look at anyone. He couldn't see anything more than the sheet metal roofs with the barred windows and the neighboring hut that no one ever went into or came out of.

The hut was yellowed and the windows were dark. There was one stone step overgrown with tufts of grass at the sides that led to a peeled brown door without a handle. A covered black hole bore witness that inside it must be cold and dark and that spider webs hung in the corners.

People said that a Russian captain had once lived in this hut. He was supposed to have had a young wife with golden hair and black eyes but she fell in love with a Polish aristocrat and ran off with him. The captain took it so much to heart that he actually hung himself, right here in this hut! To this day no one remembers if he was taken away from here and given a proper burial.

Still, my mother wasn't afraid and she rented this new place.

A low opened gate in a white, limed picket fence led into a big and roomy courtyard where on one side rose a long building with a lot of thick-set windows. Our new home was among these many windows.

It was nice and bright and it had a small kitchen similar to those we'd had till now. We could've driven around the whole place in a coach with rubber wheels.

It was four-cornered, tall with high beams and two large, clear windows that looked out onto an orchard. In my eyes it looked like those spacious rooms that Mordkheh-Mendl had at the Vaysufkeh.

Everything was fresh and new, and the floor was also painted red. Mammeh said that the floor was painted especially for her sake and that in no other house was it painted red.

It was just too bad that now, after the holiday of Succoth, the branches of the trees behind the clear washed windowpanes were already peeled and bare. Signs of white lime that had been painted at Pesach time still clung to some of the trees. Others, the fruit trees, were wrapped in bunches of straw as if in warm kerchiefs.

At night there was frost. In the morning the windowpanes were already misted over. Winter was coming.

But the winter wouldn't last forever. Summer would eventually come and then the windows would be opened wide and today's bare trees would bloom again.

I knew that here in the summertime it would be more beautiful than anywhere else in the city, more beautiful even than in the new civic garden where they didn't allow boys in long kapotehs.

That's why I felt that Mammeh was smart to choose this new place.

Such a small thing, a big courtyard! You could ride around in it. You could put up three more tenants and it would still be a roomy courtyard. Besides this, at the very end of the courtyard was a garden with an orchard closed in by a tall and thin picket fence. Flowers, cherries, currants, and apples grew there.

The owner of the building, a grey goyeh who lived on Lublin Street, kept a special person for the garden, a stooped old man bent over like a drooping shrub.

This old man went around with big shears and a tin can full of water. He plucked and cut, sowed and weeded. He also believed, just like the gardener at the Vaysufkeh, that the flowers were his grandchildren.

It was too bad that Mordkheh-Mendl's daughter, Rayzl, wasn't here. She'd have known the real names of these flowers. She would have been very happy here after being driven out of the Vaysufkeh.

Yankl, my new friend who also lived in this courtyard, said that in the summertime everyone slept outside, right there by the garden fence, even the Polish Prison Guard with his Russian wife and their blonde little shikseh daughter, Janinkeh.

ـجۇ

I became friends with Yankl right on the very first day. He helped unload the wagon and yelled to Menasheh the Gabber as if he was his equal.

Yankl was my age but smaller than me and thinner, with a face full of freckles that covered his eyes, his nose, his ears, and even his lips. He was completely covered in freckles like a burned onion roll sprinkled with cumin.

Yankl told me that he had been to Warsaw once. There, he said, he rode on a boat until they came to a bridge, not some rickety wooden affair but an iron one, a steel one with a roof and iron rods crisscrossed together like for instance, Scotch tartan. Yankl said that in Warsaw he met a Jew who owned his own carousel with maybe a hundred barrel organs and too many parrots to count, two white bears, and other weird colored birds that the world hadn't even seen yet.

This Jew had a shiny leather visor on his cap and davened every day.

Yankl wanted to stay with him in Warsaw and he, the carousel owner, wanted it too. He would have given Yankl a barrel organ, two parrots, and a little white mouse so that he could go around doing tricks in the courtyards. But his father, Yarmeh the Wagon Driver wouldn't let him. He walloped him with a leather belt, trussed him up, and brought him back home.

You could believe this from Yankl's father. This father had a pair of shoulders that could haul a horse and wagon on them. When Yankl's father spoke, his voice came not from his mouth but as if from some kind of bellows. He really didn't have so much a voice as a kind of roar that seemed to come from his big, blond mustache and his wild yellow beard.

Yankl's father owned no more than one pair of horses that he'd had for many years. He claimed they were the apples of his eye. He talked to these horses as if they were human and paid more attention to them than to his own wife and children.

"Today," he said, "the chestnut one, may no evil eye befall him, he stuffed himself."

And when he looked at the other horse, the white mare, his yellow beard smiled and his big round eyes winked to his wife.

"Good health to her bones! She needs a stallion like life itself. She needs . . ."

The white mare was truly a strange horse. Sway-backed, she had a long, yellowed and dirty half-eaten tail that bore witness to the fact that she was no longer in her girlhood. Still, she had a nice long chin and small laughing eyes.

Yarmeh had no end of trouble from this mare. An unquenched fire raged in her. She couldn't be calm anywhere. She kicked, she broke her horseshoes, she stood on her two front legs and whinnied in the middle of the night, such a wild, frantic laughter as if she was out of her mind.

Together with this piece of efficiency stood Yarmeh the wagon driver's second wage earner, the chestnut stallion, but he was full of years and it seemed, sated with mares. He could work more than two younger horses. He was patient and could take the heat and the cold. He could even do without feed as long as he was left to think his own thoughts quietly somewhere.

This stallion had sense. It wasn't bothered by the wild whinnying of it's agitated neighbor. It didn't bother him when the white mare laid her moist chin on his old neck. She fondled and patted him with her long appealing chin. She whinnied right into his foolish, absent-minded mug but he just stood there like some stranger.

Yarmeh the Wagon Driver sometimes grabbed his whip in anger and beat the chestnut horse sharply on the legs.

"My man," he grumbled, "why are you standing there like some clay dummy? Why? A blight take you! Master-of-the-Universe!"

But this "man" of his wasn't even bothered by the whip either. He had his own affairs in mind. His heart was unmoved, not by Yarmeh's anger and not by the screams of the yearning mare.

So Yarmeh the Wagon Driver had to appeal to others. As it happened, there was a goy living in the Mariatzkeh district, a moldy old goy who limped on one foot and saw out of one eye only. This goy had a stallion that did nothing more than gorge and guzzle and busy itself with strange horses of the feminine gender.

My friend Yankl once told me that this goy was going to bring his stallion here and that I should stick around. I'd really see something!

It was Shabbes morning; the wind was blowing. Mammeh was supposed to go to Aunt Miriam's but she was in the middle of reading a storybook and couldn't tear herself away. Tatteh was asleep with the featherbed pulled over his head. I had already finished davening the morning prayer said upon rising, and I was waiting for Yankl to give me the sign to come outside.

Trees rustled unpleasantly outside the window. A latch on the shutters didn't stop creaking and banging into the wall. The sky was covered with a yellowish-grey color. It started snowing.

But this didn't bother the goy and he brought his stallion anyway. Yarmeh the Wagon Driver had already gotten up from sleep and finished davening. He went out into the courtyard in a checked jacket, smacked the stallion on the rump, making it shiver and stamp its feet anxiously.

Whinnying was suddenly heard from the stall. The black, well-fed stallion raised its neck arrogantly, its ears began twitching and it answered back with a thick masculine neighing.

Yankl and I had sneaked into the stall earlier and we were hiding in a corner. There was a warm smell of horse manure in the stall. It was dark but if you looked hard, you could see everything.

The white mare whinnied again, looked around with her clever laughing eyes, stared at us for a minute as if she wanted something from us.

But now the limping goy led in his bachelor. The mare was no longer whinnying but shrieking and panting. She stood up on her front legs and began kicking, banging into the boards and tearing at the chain with which she was tethered.

The black stallion didn't stay quiet either. He tossed his head and white steam poured from his nostrils.

I moved closer to Yankl. I was afraid that the stallion would trample us and make mincemeat from us. Yankl stared, cross-eyed. He didn't hear me. He didn't even see me. I felt him shaking all over.

It got very hot in the stall. Both horses began to neigh, whinny, and laugh all at the same time.

The limping goy let go of his bachelor. The mare suddenly sank down lower and widened herself out. The stallion stretched himself out, got bigger and longer. Suddenly, he leapt up on his front legs, boarded the sacrifice, and burrowed his teeth into the neck of the mare.

A rattling of chains began, a pulling of boards, of manure rising out of the cribs of hay, steam rose up from the horses' hides, and a wheezing. You couldn't catch your breath.

Something must have happened to me. My head spun and I got faint. I couldn't feel my heart beating. My hands got heavy and I went limp. Did Yankl lead me out, or what? I sat a long time in the courtyard in the wind, and I didn't know and didn't see what happened later.

I didn't see Yankl for several days. The white mare stopped its neighing and for a time, it no longer kicked or broke its horseshoes.

But when it began to shriek again, the lame goy came back a second time with his stallion, but this time I didn't want to go into the stall anymore.

The white mare and the mournful chestnut horse made two short trips to Warsaw with Yarmeh the Wagon Driver. There in the middle of the courtyard stood Yarmeh's omnibus loaded with passengers that his two wage earners would pull.

The omnibus was tall and scrawny, just like Yarmeh himself. The roof was patched and banged together from old pieces of sheet metal that hung down on both sides. It bulged in the middle, had a door and a window cut into it that was dark and shabby from wind and rain. It was chinked with rags and boarded over.

Yarmeh the Wagon Driver said that from this little window he was able to see the whole wide world. He saw piles of hay, peasants' huts, cows in the meadow, and wooden bridges thrown over narrow streams. Through here he saw small towns and even smaller Jews, fires blazing in the villages, crosses on the churches and cemeteries, l'havdil, non-Jewish ones too.

Friday evening, summer as in winter, an hour before candle-lighting time, Yarmeh the Wagon Driver came back from Warsaw, dirty, grey, covered in dust just like his horses. He drove right into the middle of the courtyard and threw off the whole week of wandering about in strange inns and eating out of strange bowls.

After every such trip, Yarmeh the Wagon Driver looked thinner and older. He came back with misted, tired eyes and the horses came back with sunken ribs.

Still, even though he was sweaty and every bone in his body ached, he leaped down quickly, took off the heavy pack and yelled into the courtyard:

"Yankl, where are you? Where? Nu, finish! Unhitch the horses. A blight take you! Give them something to drink. And throw down a bit of fodder for them. Move yourself, you bastard!"

Yarmeh the Wagon Driver's wife came outside with Yankl. She was a woman of about forty, round and freshly washed in honor of Shabbes. She came toward her husband smiling broadly:

"Look who's here! Yarmeh, why so late today?"

"Who says it's late?"

"It seems to me that it's later today than last week."

"You're imagining it. It's not any later."

She helped him drag out of the omnibus the bit of food for the road that Yarmeh brought back with him from Warsaw—some figs and dates and a long dried-out wurst with a moldy white skin. She climbed into the omnibus with her hot smooth flesh, clean and warm. Yarmeh forgot that he was hungry, that it was almost time for candle lighting and that he hadn't gotten washed yet. He moved closer and leering, he asked: "How're you doing, Golda?"

"Thanks for asking. And you?"

"Not bad."

"Did'ya at least have a good trip?"

"Not bad. But the mare should croak."

"What now?"

"Some picky eater! A black life I have!"

"Just like all females . . ." Yarmeh's wife answered and her whole body shook with laughter.

"Heh, heh," Yarmeh laughed back and just as he was, he laid a big hand on her amply endowed blouse. "I should have such a year as some piece you are . . . !"

"Stop, you lunatic!" She moved off, "Go inside and get washed."

Yankl stayed outside. He was Yarmeh the Wagon Driver's oldest son by his first wife. Yankl unhitched the horses, gave them water to drink, threw down some fodder for them, and at the same time he told me that tonight his father would sleep in the same bed with his aunt who was also his stepmother. They slept together every Friday night.

I helped Yankl wash down the omnibus. Yankl taught me how.
He told me he would teach me to be a wagon driver too. When I'd
know the trade, we'd save up some money and buy our own omnibus
and a horse. We'd also become wagon drivers and drive off to Warsaw
with passengers. Once there, he said, he would show me the boat that
he rode on and introduce me to the Jew who owned the barrel organ
and the white bears.

Meanwhile, I poured a tub of water onto the muddied wheels
and then another one. Yankl wiped the thatched roof with a big bunch
of straw. I crawled on top and rubbed the patched sheet metal roof
until it gleamed. After that we both crawled into the balled up straw
of the omnibus that smelled of warm and sweaty Jewish and goyish
passengers. Yankl talked again about his aunt who slept with his father
and about beautiful, far-off Warsaw.

·ઙ

That was the way it was in the new place. To tell the truth, Tatteh
had a grudge against Mammeh. Not, God forbid, because of the place
itself but because he didn't even know that Mammeh had intended to
move out of the old one.

He came home in the evening as usual. He could see through
the window that it was dark inside and that the door was locked. He
knocked and called out:

"Frimmet! Frimmet!"

Frimmet didn't open the door. While it bothered him, it wasn't
a surprise. Many times, he didn't find Mammeh at home and lots of
times he was forced to knock but today, while he was standing and
knocking, a neighbor's door opened and an old woman stuck her head
out and asked:

"Pan Merchant?"

"Yeh, its me, Pani Martsinova. D'ya know where my wife went?"

"She moved out."

"Wha-a-t?"

"Moved out this morning."

May my enemies . . . !"

"Yeh, Pan Merchant. There, behind the jail."

"What d'ya mean behind the jail?"

"Do I know? Pani Frimmet told me to say that she's moving
there, where Yarmeh the Wagon Driver lives"

Tatteh later told the whole family about this. He spoke disapprovingly, with resentment. He came to the new place angry and distant.

Hunger lay on the tip of his nose. The cold of the fields, where all day long he had wandered homeless, lay on his mustache and in his wrinkled beard.

Almost everything was already arranged in the new house. Menasheh the Gabber, with Yarmeh the Wagon Driver's son Yankl, helped. I also lent a shoulder. I shoved a piece of wood where needed and broke the glass lampshade, but we got it all done.

When Tatteh came in, Mammeh ran toward him disheveled, elbows dirty:

"Nu, Luzeh, what do you say? Eh? Take a look at this place. It's a kingdom, not a house!"

"But why?"

"I couldn't take it any longer. I was choking there."

"You could've said something."

"I myself didn't quite know. And the other thing . . . do I know?" Maybe you wouldn't want. . . . Anyway . . . it's done! Finished! Let it be with mazel, with good luck!"

Mammeh spoke quickly, busying herself around Tatteh like someone who knows she's done wrong. Tatteh stood by the door, the tip of his tongue moving from one corner of his mouth to the other, a sign that this change was not such a bad one. "But why didn't they wait for him? And who put all these things together? Who?"

"It's already put together."

"The beds, too?"

"You can see."

"Yeh, I see. But maybe, something got broken?"

"God forbid."

"And who put together the wardrobe."

"The same person."

"Who is this putter-together?"

"Menasheh the Gabber."

"Neh . . . Menasheh the Gabber! But he could've made a mess of the wardrobe. He could've . . ."

"Nobody made a mess. It's standing perfectly fine. Nu, go get out of those clothes already! Go get washed! I've cooked liver for you. I've cooked . . ."

But Tatteh didn't get out of his clothes so fast. First, he carefully examined the beds and sat down on all sides. Afterwards he began examining the wardrobe, opened and closed its doors, twisted and turned his head, scowled and again tried the doors.

"Why's it opening and closing so rough? It's creaking. My wardrobe doesn't creak."

"So tomorrow, God willing, you'll fix it. Go! Get washed already. Go!"

On the table lay a big round loaf of bread with dill and dusted with a lot of flour. It was Shmiel Shmaryeh's bread. This was Tatteh's greatest temptation.

So Tatteh stopped finding fault. He cut off small and square pieces of bread, dunked them into the brown liver gravy, but he didn't stop looking at the wardrobe that some Menasheh the Gabber had put together without his knowing or approving.

Chapter 15

It seemed to me that everyone was satisfied with this place, Mammeh, Tatteh, and me especially. And to tell you the truth, where was it as warm and dry as right here?

When summer comes, said Yankl, we won't be able to find a place for all the apples, pears, cherries, and currants that grow here. Take my friend Yankl, who else could tell such interesting stories about Warsaw like he could? Where'd I have such a good friend like Yankl?

And yet, after a while, Mammeh suddenly started scowling again. This place behind the jail didn't satisfy her either. You couldn't say, God forbid, that she'd anything against the place itself, just the opposite. It was dry and bright. Mammeh was on good terms with the neighbors, both with Yarmeh the Wagon Driver's wife, with Yittaleh the Flour Dealer and even with the Senior Prison Guard's family. Nothing else but the entrance to the house and the alley behind the jail began bothering her. Never mind. During the day it was manageable but when evening came, Mammeh said, such a gloomy feeling would come over her that there was nowhere to turn.

Mammeh didn't say clearly why it's so gloomy in the evenings but I figured it out all by myself.

Yankl had told me a story earlier that really was out of the ordinary. It wasn't so much out of the ordinary as it was just plain scary.

For instance, between the yellow wall of the jail and the abandoned hut where the Russian captain had hung himself, it was so dark and oppressive at night that you could actually feel it with your hands. Not any street in the city, not even in Shul Alley, was there so much gloom as right here. It seemed it came from the sentry's booth that was used as a resting place for jail guards during the day, but at night was a haven for ghosts and demons.

This booth was abandoned at night because the jail had to be guarded, so at night you could hear hoarse sighing and moaning coming from there. Sometimes screams and laughter were also heard and sometimes you could actually hear gasping and choking.

No sooner had we moved in then I realized that all the yelling and sighing came from the barred windows of the jail and I knew that in jail people were held in chains and had to be whipped at night and made to suffer. Such vicious people like Shtshepkeh and Sherman, who had slaughtered whole families of Jews and burned down a dozen of the landowners' estates, they wouldn't just be held in prison for no good reason.

Later on I found out that they really were being held for no good reason. Maybe they were really suffering but we didn't hear anything about it on the outside.

The screaming and moaning heard in the darkness actually came from the wooden hut. My friend Yankl explained it to me:

"Here, right on this spot," he told me quietly, "is the place to meet lanky Yuzhkeh the Prostitute." He described her to me. She was pockmarked, wore her hair short with bangs on the forehead just like the shkotzim who haul sand.

The soldiers already knew where they could find this lanky Yuzhkeh so they came and went, cracked sunflower seeds, spit at her, and bargained with her.

She sat at the threshold of the hut like a hen on top of a warm egg, also cracking sunflower seeds, spitting the hulls back out at the soldiers, right into their Russian faces, and asking:

"So how much can you pay, my dear fellow countryman?"

Probably, the fellow countryman promised a small amount. At this Yuzhkeh would stand up tall in the booth and in a hoarse and nasal voice, yell out:

"Go to your mother in pig land, you damned Russky!"

It was dark. We didn't see what happened there later but after such screaming, it suddenly got quiet.

Gasping and rattling could be heard from the booth; throats wheezing and noses sniffling. The whole alley together with the walled hut of the captain, the linden trees, the prison windows, everything was panting, breathing, sweating with great dread. So, it was too bad for the person who needed to go by here at such a time. Vile talk and curses like the barking of abandoned dogs began coming from behind the stones.

Sometimes a stone hit the fence across the way, and sometimes it hit a person's head.

"*Doh kholeri tshenshkay!* God dammit!" Yuzhkeh's hoarse voice cut like a dull saw and a deep Russian voice joined her:

"*Sukin sin*! *Mat tvoy*! Son of a bitch! Go fuck your mother!"

So we avoided going through this alley at night. We'd rather sit in the dark than go out to the store for a drop of kerosene.

In the morning we found hulls of sunflower seeds, pieces of old sausage, and empty liquor bottles littered around. Snow fell every night and in the morning there were signs of deep grooves around the hut as if someone had been rolled in the snow.

Every morning Yankl ran out to take a look. He was looking for something in the grooves. His face looked deadened and his mouth dribbled.

I was afraid of Yankl on those mornings. I couldn't look at him. A bad smell came from him.

One time Yankl told me that he had talked to lanky Yuzhkeh the day before. She offered him sunflower seeds, chucked him under the chin, and told him to bring a gildn and she'd go with him into the hut. He said he had to save up the gildn. Then he'd steal out of bed at night and come to the hut.

I didn't understand Yankl clearly:

"What d'ya mean? Aren't you afraid?"

"Who should I be afraid of?"

"How should I know? The soldiers, lanky Yuzhkeh . . ."

"You're an ox!" He answered, waving his hand so that I felt very low and inferior next to him.

After all, what was I next to someone like Yankl who had already been to Warsaw? Who'd already spoken to Yuzhkeh. He was already grown up while I ran away from the likes of Hodel. Lots of times, I wanted to tell Yankl the whole story but after Yankl had spoken to lanky Yuzhkeh, I knew that he would just make fun of me.

So it was probably no wonder that Mammeh took a dislike to this nice, bright place. Tatteh didn't pay attention to any of this. The hut was pointed out to him, he was told about lanky Yuzhkeh and about the soldiers, but he himself didn't see any of it. If it happened that he had to pass by the alley at night and they'd yell at him from the booth, it never got to his deaf ears.

That was one thing. Second of all, Tatteh had Mammeh at home all the time in this new place. She didn't run out anymore, not to Aunt Miriam, not to Bubbeh Rakhl. Tatteh didn't have to warm up the left-over meal by himself and he didn't have to sit at the table alone like he did in the other places where we'd lived. He didn't always have to look at the empty four walls and at the sad flame of the kerosene lamp.

In the old place Tatteh seldom laughed. He had complaints to Mammeh about why she always left him alone and why it's cold in the house. He told Mammeh that it chased him out of the house when she wasn't there.

But here in this place behind the jail, Mammeh was afraid to go out at night. Aunt Miriam sent to ask why she didn't see her anymore. Bubbeh Rakhl took the trouble to come to us to find out.

So, Mammeh complained to Bubbeh that she'd made a mistake with this place. The jail was not outside, she said, but right here inside. She discussed this quietly with Bubbeh and winked at me.

She also discussed it quietly with Tatteh but he couldn't get worked up over it.

"I dunno what you want," he scowled, "do we need a better place?"

"Why, you like it so much here?"

"Its dry, its warm, what else d'ya want? What?"

"And I'm telling you, Luzeh, we should move out. It's in the sticks, it's a jail."

"But you picked it yourself! Who's to blame? Who?"

"If I'd known it would be like this . . ."

"Always you never know how it's going be."

Mammeh didn't answer. She pursed her lips. She was angry.

Father recited the blessing quietly, absent-mindedly. He was over-worked and worn out. The beds were made up. Tatteh stopped in the middle of the blessing and his head leaned to a side, then he jerked himself up, grabbed the thread of the blessing and started again.

It was still early. The hand of the clock moved to eight.

Mammeh would've left already to visit Aunt Miriam. She knew that the neighbors would be gathering there now. People would be having conversations and the children would be playing bingo. Yitskhak the Teacher, who taught in the homes of the wealthy, would also come. It would be cozy, warm, and bright.

But outside was that damned dark alley. It lay like a wall, like a bridge that separated one world from another.

Tatteh was dozing. Mammeh couldn't be expected to go to sleep together with the hens! So she grabbed something to wrap around herself and we went to see the Senior Prison Guard and his family who lived next door.

ح§

This Senior Guard was a Polish goy who liked to speak Russian. He had yellow whiskers and a lined face.

Also, he wasn't someone from behind the stove; he wasn't born yesterday. He'd been all over, heard all kinds of stories and he was very talkative. So he talked. He talked about the Uprising, about the Russian Socialist Labour Bund, about the Turkish war, but mainly he liked to talk about that murderer Shtshepkeh who sat in prison in chains.

The Guard said that they shaved off half of Shtshepkeh's head and half his mustache in prison. This Shtshepkeh was so tall that he wouldn't be able to get through this door.

At one time, continued the Guard, Shtshepkeh was a stonecutter and a carver of gravestones. He made monuments for the non-Jewish cemetery. He could etch birds in the air. No one knew why but he suddenly got friendly with a zhidek, that Yid Sherman, and from then on he became a cutthroat.

Sherman sat in the same prison too. He had a yellow beard and they cut half of it off as well and they also shaved half his head and half his mustache.

Both murderers were going to be sent off to Siberia in the summer, to serve at hard labor.

The Guard knew that in Siberia they'd practically be attached to their wheelbarrows. They'd eat and sleep with wheelbarrows, stand and go everywhere with wheelbarrows and even when they died they'd be buried together with their wheelbarrows.

The Guard told us that this same Shtshepkeh had a wife and two children; the children had blue eyes and blond hair and when his wife and children came to visit him in prison, Shtepshkeh would melt into tears.

I couldn't get bored day or night listening to this Guard. He explained it all so clearly, it was as if he laid it out on saucers. My mother could also tell stories but how could she compare to him?

And second of all, it was warmer and cozier here than in our house. Flower vases stood on the windowsills; in a corner of the wall above the one bed hung a dark picture of the Holy Mother.

The Guard's wife sat here now, tall and blond. She wore thick braids wound around her head and she always looked newly washed, smelling of soap and freshly laundered clothes.

She was a Russian and she came from far away. She had already lived here in Poland for a long time and she'd learned Polish but she spoke it haltingly.

She could also tell stories. She spoke often of her home in a village somewhere near the River Don. This river was so blue, she said, that it was bluer than the sky and bluer than the bluest eye. There was a church there, she said, with a domed roof and golden crosses and this church was also blue. There was a priest there, young with a black beard and he wanted to marry her.

She could have been a Pani Priest. She could be living there now in a church residence, with everyone deferring to her. But she didn't want that.

This Pole, this Senior Prison Guard, who had served in the Russian Army, he was better for her, he appealed to her more, so she picked him.

She said that where she came from, Jews lived in their own part of town. They did here too, but it was different here. There they didn't wear long kapotehs or earlocks, and they didn't speak Yiddish either.

There was no end to what this Guard or his wife could talk about.

The hours flew by. The hands of the clock sighed and fell down from one wheel to the other. Inside the clock something began rasping. Twelve old strokes rang out quickly, a sign that it was time to say goodbye and go home to sleep.

When we got home, the wick of the flame was shrinking. Shadows crawled up the walls like unraveled sacks. Tatteh was leaning his head on the edge of the table, his whole overworked body fast asleep.

Everything all around looked empty and black. It looked like all our things had moved out so that Tatteh could have more room and could be seen better.

Mammeh breathed heavily.

"Okh, how sad! How sad!"

Her voice hung over Tatteh's sleeping head, like a demand.

Chapter 16

How was it that my mother, who had lived with her first husband, the old-time healer, in spacious rooms with brass handles on the doors, ended up with Tatteh, a village Jew from New Mill? All he knew about was hay, ate sour milk and sour cream from big earthenware bowls, liked to bathe in rivers, and sleep in the forest under an evergreen tree. How did one come to the other?

This is the story that was told. Before they married, neither Tatteh nor Mammeh knew how many children the other had from their first marriage. When the engagement agreement was signed, they forgot to name the orphans. It was said that there were children but that they were all grown up and didn't need help from their mother or their father anymore.

So the wedding was held and a meal prepared for a minyan of Jews, the minimum requirement. After that Mammeh packed her belongings into a trunk, left her bit of jewelry with Aunt Miriam and went off to the village of New Mill where Tatteh lived after the death of his first wife. When Mammeh got there she saw a big, dark house with an earthen floor and a lot of earthenware pots scattered in the corners. Two broken windowpanes were stuffed with cushions and four grown girls, dark, dirty, wearing flannel shifts, were hiding behind the headboards, looking with surprised eyes at this new wife that their father had brought from town.

When Mammeh saw this, her young face shriveled up like a dried fig. She didn't take off her kerchief or her coat but just as she was, she asked:

"This is the farm you said you had?"

"Yeh, this is the farm," Tatteh answered.

"And who are these girls? Who are they?"

"My daughters."

"All four of them?"

"All four, may they be well."

181

"But you said only two."

"So . . . ? There's no limit to what you can say."

Mammeh choked on it. She couldn't say a word, what would talking help anyway? She would have fainted on the spot if she hadn't been so ashamed.

She opened the door and said:

"No, Reb Luzeh! This isn't what we agreed on. Keep your children in good health but I won't be your wife!"

"What do'ya mean? What about *khipeh-v'kidishn*, what about the marriage ceremony?"

"We'll get a divorce, Reb Luzeh."

And Mammeh took her trunk of belongings and went back to town to Aunt Miriam, her younger sister.

"Dear Miriam, what did you want from me? Why'd you talk me into this match? Why he's a pauper! Four girls in the house like oak trees! What am I supposed to do with four girls? What?"

Aunt Miriam knew that Tatteh had four girls in the house. She also knew that Reb Luzeh from the village of New Mill was a pauper of paupers. His farm, which was part of the dowry, consisted of no more than the one room hut with the earthen floor and the earthenware pots for sour milk.

But Mammeh was a widow. Reb Luzeh didn't demand any money from her and she too was left with children from her first husband, may he be separated from the living, so what's the big deal about her pedigree? Why's she carrying on like this? Why?

Why shouldn't she cry? Mammeh answered, if from such spacious rooms that she had with her first husband, she'd now have to go and live in a dark hut with an earthen floor.

It broke Aunt Miriam's heart too, and everyone who heard about it felt sorry for the beautiful, young Frimmet. But it was already done. How would wailing help?

So everyone pitched in. Aunt Miriam and Itsheh the Bull's wife Rayzeleh, and Tatteh's sister Aunt Nemmi, the one with the refined lips—they all explained to Mammeh that a person's luck depended on God. You never knew, it could end up that because of Mammeh, Tatteh would become well-to-do and also be able to provide his wife with spacious rooms that had brass handles on the doors.

So what could Mammeh do? She wouldn't just go and make a fool of herself, so even though she wept and wailed, in the end she let herself be talked into it. But she wouldn't go out to the village of New Mill anymore. Let him come into town. Anyway, she said, her husband was a pauper, so what difference did it make? He could just as easily be a pauper in town.

That was how Tatteh said goodbye to the earthenware pots, the meadows, the forest, and came into town—he and his four dark, unkempt daughters. Four such girls couldn't just sit on their father's back forever. You had to think about a future for them.

So bit by bit, Mammeh began to look after them.

Yitta, the youngest, was a cook in the houses of wealthy Jews in Warsaw. One holiday, she came home to visit her father bringing gifts.

Channa-Sureh, the oldest, was tall and dark, with strong, broad hands. Mammeh married her off to a butcher in a small town. Channa-Sureh had nothing to complain about. She had it good. Her husband Wolf was short, with a dark, drawn face. He loved his wife. With time, she brought three daughters and four sons into the world, may they all be well. All of them dark with green eyes and brown, hairy bodies, silent like their mother.

Once in a blue moon Channa-Sureh would come into town. She came to shop for a trousseau for one of her daughters and at the same time came to see her father whom she visited in silence.

Tatteh and his eldest daughter were both tall and broad like old, rooted poplar trees. They sat across from each other, looked into each other's eyes and . . . stayed silent. From time to time, a word was let drop between them:

"How ya do'in, Tatteh?"

"How should we be?"

"What's new?"

"Just so . . . How's Wolf?"

"Not bad."

"And the children?"

"Thank God!"

Enough! They took a look at each other, she said no more and left—for a year, for two years, for five years. But Tatteh had parental pride in his oldest daughter. She was well off, had the biggest butcher shop in town, married off all her children well, celebrated births and circumcisions and invited her father to all her celebrations.

Tatteh would come back from there well fed and well rested.

He told of the festive meals that were prepared, about his grandchildren, may no Evil Eye. . . . They were growing up respectable. He talked a lot about his son-in-law Wolf, who even though he was small in build and had a thin, little beard, could still get the better of an unruly young bull all by himself and who managed to get along with the peasants in the surrounding villages even though they were big anti-Semites.

Channa-Sureh was the only married daughter.

After her came Bayleh, also tall, broad-shouldered, with long, thin hands and a wide chin.

Bayleh didn't have her sister Channa-Sureh's calm, easy-going ways.

Bayleh spoke curtly and sharply. She blushed over every little thing. She looked at the world with quick, darting eyes. Strangers might think she was mean, but actually Bayleh would have given away her last shirt. She was well known to everyone, strangers and intimates alike, for her generosity. It was said that you couldn't find such an efficient housewife anywhere, even if you searched for one with torches.

She had one fault, but it was a bad one. She couldn't sit still; she had no staying power. You could chop her to bits and pieces but she couldn't stay in one place for long. She was always carried away by something. She wanted only to run, to go off to Warsaw or Lodz, even to some small town, as long as she didn't have to stay in one place.

Sometimes she took it into her head to drop into an inn to warm up. If the place and the people pleased her, she took a job there and stayed a while.

She'd milk the cows, cook up large cast-iron pots of food for Jewish travelers and passersby who dropped in. She prepared pots of bran and potato mash for the cows. She could spin cloth, knit, mend, fix; she could even hold conversations with the sons of the landowners who rode by on their plumed horses.

Bayleh knew how to do everything; but she could do nothing for herself, she couldn't hurry up her own luck. The years passed, Bayleh began to get bigger, and a marriage didn't happen.

Except once, it almost came to marriage. It happened at an inn. A Jewish traveler, dark, healthy-looking, with a pair of coal black eyes and a pack on his back came in. In conversation this Jew let drop the fact that his wife, it shouldn't happen to anybody, had died in childbirth.

Bayleh served him a big bowl of grits and gave him milk to drink straight from the cow. One word led to another and she began asking him, for instance, what does a Jew like himself do for a livelihood? Did such a Jew have children? Where did such a Jew live?

He told her that he had no children, that he lived on the other side of the Pilica River, and as far as his livelihood was concerned, may no evil befall him, he lacked for nothing. Nothing that is, except that God wanted him to remain a widower.

Bayleh listened in silence but her cheeks were on fire.

This Jew stayed overnight at the inn. Bayleh slept in a cubicle in the house where the hens dozed on a high ledge. The door to this room didn't have a latch. So what? What was there to steal here? What?

Bayleh lay in bed thinking about the dark Jew. She wanted to fall asleep, she had to get up at dawn to milk the cows and get the meals ready for the travelers, but this Jew's coal-black eyes didn't let her fall asleep.

The hens way up on the ledge were about ready to wake up when Bayleh felt that something was tickling her face. She would have sworn that a hen had slid down and was scratching her with its foot or fluttering a wing across her face.

"A-sho! A-sho!" Bayleh screamed at the hens.

But suddenly she felt this was no chicken! It was very dark in the cubicle but Bayleh thought she saw a pair of big, wide-open eyes staring at her.

Her chest tightened and a hot shudder went through her body. She already knew who had come in and she whispered: "Reb Jew, what's going on?"

"What should be going on?"

"Reb Jew, what're you doing here?"

"What should I be doing? Nothing. My wife, it should happen to no one, went and died on me."

"So you come crawling to strangers?"

"God forbid! Who says so? Its just that . . ."

And his hands flamed even hotter than his eyes.

Beyleh again whispered: "Reb Jew, are you gonna get out of here?"

"Why? Do I want, God forbid, to do you any harm, Bayleshi?"

"You're calling me 'Bayleshi,' yet! What kind of 'Bayleshi' am I to you?"

"When you like someone, you make the name more intimate."

"Since when do you like me?"

"What d'ya mean since when? From the first minute."

"And Reb Jew, you'll set up a wedding canopy?"

Why not? We can have a wedding canopy too."

"When?"

"We can do it sometime."

All of a sudden, there was turmoil in the cubicle. The hens woke up from their dreaming, flapped their wings in the dark and leaped onto the human heads. Bayleh gave a start, slapped a pair of overfed cheeks, opened the wooden door and shrieked out into the night:

"You lecher! A black life to you! Nothing less you wanted?"

Lamps were quickly lit all over the inn. Jews in feathered caps hastily poured dippers of water over their fingernails; barefoot women in sleeping caps and flannel shifts pinched their cheeks.

"Vey'z mir! Such a Jew . . . Who ever heard of such a thing?"

Children began crying from the commotion. A dog started barking. And the swarthy Jew with the blazing, black eyes disappeared in the middle of the night, leaving his pack behind.

Bayleh sent this pack home to her father with Yarmeh the Wagon Driver. Let Tatteh have something extra to wear when he went out wintertime to the villages.

Yarmeh the Wagon Driver told this whole story from beginning to end. Bayleh herself told him to, so that everyone at home would know that she, Bayleh, even though she never spent the day in the same place where she spent the night, still, she wouldn't shame her father in his old age.

And she didn't. When the right time came, she got married, *kdas moyshe v'yisroyel*, "according to the laws of Moses and of Israel." She picked out her future husband all by herself.

He was also a widower but not dark, and he didn't have the blazing eyes of the other one. He was a strong person with a big blond beard just like the Russian Tsar Alexander III.

Bayleh's husband wasn't as rich as the tsar, and he didn't have an imperial name either. His name was Wolf, just like Tatteh's first son-in-law. But he had his own horse and wagon and he could shoe horses, fix wagon wheels, and put his shoulder to a loaded wagon when an ox got tired. He and his first wife had once owned a piece of field with a little garden, but after he became a widower, may it happen to no one, he neglected the garden. He didn't have a head for the carrots and turnips that were planted there. The pigs took over and they fouled it up, so never mind, he'd move into town. He had a horse and wagon; he was a blacksmith. With God's help, this would be his livelihood.

Bayleh lived with her husband outside of town, all the way out on the outskirts of Skaryczew. Winds howled, wagons rumbled by on their way to town, and the drivers screamed under her window. Bayleh cooked big pots of grits for them. She prepared tsholnt and stuffed derma for them for Shabbes. Her husband Wolf drove his horse and wagon to all the fairs and markets. If there were no trips in the offing, he would shoe horses. They eked out a living and every year in the middle of the night the shriek of a newborn that Bayleh brought into the world would be heard.

The more children, the less of a livelihood they had. So Bayleh leased an alcove and began baking poppy seed rolls to sell to the young wagon drivers. She never complained; she wanted it this way.

Sometimes, when Bayleh came to wish us "git yontef," Good Holiday, and Mammeh asked her,

"What's new? How're things with you?"

Bayleh would let fall a word, as happens sometimes at night when the children are asleep. She remembered the swarthy Jew with the blazing eyes. She saw him as if he were standing right in front of her. She herself didn't know what to think, but after such a night her heart was heavy, the grits didn't turn out right, the young wagon drivers made faces at the poppy seed rolls, and she'd get into an argument with the roomer who lived in the alcove.

Chapter 17

That's what the fidgety and bustling Bayleh did. When she prepared food for celebrations of births and circumcisions, they didn't eat fish, or reshinkeh, that large, flat, decorated cookie specially made for such occasions. Instead, they made do with boiled chickpeas, meager little fish, and cheap meat. From time to time, Tatteh would send Bayleh two gildn for the children, a loaf of white bread, fish for Shabbes, and matsoh for Pesach. Bayleh thanked her father by bringing her children, freshly washed and combed, to visit us on Shabbes afternoons and telling them to kiss their Zaydeh on the hand.

But with the third daughter, things weren't the same. Toybeh was altogether different. She was taller than them, broader in the shoulders, and heavier. She carried herself straight, with her face open to sun and wind. Toybeh looked like one of those rich daughters who eat chunks of chicken in their soup and busy themselves embroidering little tfiln bags for their intended bridegrooms.

Toybeh's eyes were large and expectant, as if she looked at everything and everyone in wonder. During the day they were blue, but at night they turned black. Her hair was also black, curly, and tousled. On sunny days it had a bluish cast.

When Toybeh walked, the windowpanes rattled and the floor creaked. Though she worked in a respectable, well-to-do household, where she washed dishes, scraped carrots, and peeled potatoes, her hands were slender and refined, with long clean fingers. Toybeh would come to visit us on Shabbes afternoon. She enjoyed listening to Mammeh's stories about Warsaw and she also liked to remember Mammeh's son Moysheh, who was torn from this world before his time. She'd listen to the very end of the story about the brass door handles and the spacious rooms that Mammeh had once lived in.

Toybeh was patient and took everything with a smile.

She also had stories to tell about the village of New Mill, where she was born, and about her mother who could carry two loads of potatoes on her back. She talked about the little water mill where her father had once been the miller. In that little mill, Toybeh said, ghosts hid themselves at night. Many times she'd heard the mill wheel suddenly begin turning by itself in the middle of the night. Tatteh would run out to take a look, but he never saw anything. He only heard a kind of whistling and running.

Toybeh told how once during the holiday of Shevuoth, the millstone began turning so energetically that Tatteh had to wake up the manager, who lived there with his wife and child.

A lamp was lit, the manager crossed himself, and they went inside the millhouse. As soon as they went in, they suddenly heard hurrying and scurrying. The manager was a big, strong goy, and he began running around until he fell on someone, a farmhand, and then onto his own wife. She was young and beautiful, his wife, so why she went into the mill in the middle of the night nobody knew, but as soon as her husband saw her, he grabbed her by the hair, threw her to the ground, grabbed her again, and threw her against the stones.

The stones turned, the water rushed, and the miller's wife was caught in the turning stones. The stones snapped and broke, slammed and spurted blood. The mill and all the flour were covered in blood.

Afterward, the manager was sent to Siberia in shackles, and Tatteh didn't want to work there anymore.

But that was a long time ago. Toybeh was a young girl then, and she remembered that she'd run off into the forest and was gone a day and a night. Her mother went out looking for her and found her lying in a faint behind a tree.

When Toybeh was in a good mood, she could tell lots more stories. She remembered that when she was in that same forest, she had to put up with wolves that went out onto the high roads on winter nights and attacked horses and people. She told of stingy peasants who all their lives fought over a few acres of land, slaughtered one of their own mothers, and in the end rotted away in prison.

Toybeh could tell what kind of day it would be tomorrow—whether it would rain or the wind would blow or the sun would shine—by watching how the birds flew and how the smoke rose from the chimneys.

I liked Toybeh better than my other sisters. I spent days and nights hearing about Toybeh's cornfields, her forest, and her river.

I thought that if Toybeh could write all this down, you could make a book out of it. It would be a thousand times better than the storybooks Mammeh read aloud to acquaintances and neighbors on Shabbes after the meal.

When Toybeh's mother died and her children scattered, Toybeh was forced to leave the little village of New Mill and its fields and become a servant in the home of respectable rich people in town, where the doors were kept bolted day and night and people spoke to each other with their noses in the air.

Mammeh saw to it that Toybeh, the prettiest of Tatteh's daughters, should become a servant in a beautiful, well-to-do household.

The Jew in whose house Toybeh toiled wasn't old, not even forty yet. He had a pale, dark face and a small black beard that made him look like a scholar, and he wore a satin cap on weekdays. He walked daintily, with measured steps, in his squeaky little boots.

Toybeh's mistress was a strong, youthful woman, lazy and plump. She moved about her cheerful and neat rooms with two or three double chins quivering. She would say to Toybeh:

"Toybeshi, unlace my corset."

"Toybeshi, run down and get two, three oranges . . ."

Toybeshi ran, Toybeshi pulled off the shoes, laced and unlaced the corset, peeled the potatoes, lit the ovens, and still Toybeh kept the charm of her beautiful and gentle hands.

Maybe it was especially because of those hands that something very strange and sad happened to Toybeh.

This Jew, Toybeh's master with the pale, dark face, who wore a silk cap even on weekdays, didn't pay any attention to his servant girl like you would to a real person. This refined Jew never came into the kitchen where Toybeh scrubbed away her years. What did he have to do there? But once, in a very blue moon, when his wife happened not to be at home, he came in suddenly for no particular reason.

"Madame isn't here?" he asked quickly, not looking at Toybeh.

"No, Madame isn't here."

"So . . . not here . . . What was it I wanted to say? Yes . . . Toybeh, please be so good as to . . ."

He didn't say anything more about what Toybeh should be good enough to do. A refined person he was. He couldn't speak loudly.

But Toybeh felt that when he came into the kitchen once in a very blue moon, his eyes never stopped staring at her slender, beautiful hands.

Toybeh had great respect for this refined, silky employer of hers. When she brushed off his shortened little kapoteh and polished his soft little boots in the morning, she felt that his refinement and wealth also enveloped her.

Toybeh had it good in that house. She already had her own chest of linens, lace underwear, embroidered pillow cases, even her own savings book lying among her clean linen.

But lately, Toybeh had stopped coming to see us every Shabbes.

"What's the matter, Toybeh? Why don't we see you anymore?"

She didn't have time, answered Toybeh. Last week, she was with a friend, the week before she had been to an oyfruf where the bridegroom was called up to the reading of the Torah.

"You don't look so hot to me, Toybeh."

"Me? Eh? I don't look good . . . ?"

I also thought that Toybeh was paler than usual, even though she looked more beautiful and refined than ever. After that, a few more weeks went by, and still Toybeh didn't come.

"How come we don't see Toybeh anymore?" Tatteh asked Mammeh one Shabbes after his nap, sitting on his bed and yawning.

"Probably she can't come."

Toybeh couldn't come because her mistress, may it happen to no one, had gotten sick, and Dr. Fiddler had been called for.

"Dr. Fiddler . . ." Mammeh asked fearfully: "Is that how bad, God forbid, things are?"

"Yeh, very bad, Auntie."

"And how're things today?"

"Better, thank the Lord."

"What was the matter with her?"

"An inflammation of the lungs, may it happen to no one."

A sweaty, tired pallor lay on Toybeh's face today. It was no longer the refined paleness of several weeks ago.

She talked about nothing special. It seemed that her eyes that were blue in the daytime and black at night had no color at all today.

They looked over Mammeh's head, over to the dresser where the photograph of Mammeh's daughter, Tsippeh, hung, the one who was engaged to a broom maker in Warsaw.

"Tsippeh writes something?" asked Toybeh.

"Yes, she writes."

"When, with luck, will the wedding be?"

"Pretty soon, but I wouldn't swear to it."

"The bridegroom's a broom maker?"

"Yes, a broom maker." Mammeh replied slowly, strangely. It seemed that she didn't realize what she was saying because she was looking at Toybeh strangely.

Toybeh's face reddened, but that must have been from the sun. The little bit of sky that could be seen through our window burned together with Toybeh's face.

Toybeh sat today for a longer time than on any other Shabbes. Hunks of shadow crawled down from the rafters and a smell of herring and stale challah hung in the air. Tatteh sat by himself at the table. He banged the handle of the knife into the table, swaying slowly from side to side, and hummed a long, drawn-out *eskeyni seudoso*, a Havdoleh prayer chant, before beginning to eat.

"There's stars in the sky already?"

Toybeh looked up into the window. "No, not yet."

"Can you take the time to sit like this, Toybeh?" Mammeh asked.

"I'm really going now."

Toybeh stood up slowly. Mammeh stared into the darkness like someone with bad eyesight.

"Git Shabbes!" Toybeh said goodbye, and this time she forgot to give me a kiss.

"Git Shabbes, good year! Don't be a stranger!"

A dark, heavy silence hung in the house. Behind the kitchen a cricket began clicking, pointedly and stubbornly.

"Luzeh!" Mammeh cut into the silence. "Luzeh!" Her voice rose deafeningly like when you're trying to wake someone up.

But Tatteh kept on beating with the upturned knife on the table.

"He's a little bit deaf," Mammeh said to herself and began to blend her kosher "God of Abraham" sing-song into Tatteh's *bney hilkheh* Havdoleh melody.

We didn't see Toybeh again for some time. Mammeh was supposed to go to the wealthy house to ask about Toybeh, whether, God forbid, she wasn't ill herself, but somehow she never managed it.

࿐

One Shabbes after the meal, when shadows of big, fluffy clouds lay on the window sill, Tatteh had lain down under the featherbed and was fast sleep.

Mammeh had just taken down that beautiful storybook, *A Son of Two Mothers*, from the bookcase where the sacred books were kept, wiped the gold spectacles she had brought back from Warsaw, and got herself ready to read the wonderful story about the scheming Rudolph and the innocent, fair Caroline.

Here, in this house, Mammeh read a lot of books, not so much for herself as for the neighbor women who gathered at our house like hens roosting in the evening.

A week earlier, Mammeh had left off at the point where the innocent Caroline vanished mysteriously from the castle of her father, the millionaire Count.

Now Mammeh turned to the page whose corner she had creased and waited for her listeners to come. I waited with great eagerness and impatience because I wanted to hear the end of the story but also because I enjoyed hearing my mother read aloud.

She pronounced each word so clearly that even a child could understand her. She read with her own lilt, a mixture of a Yiddish version of the Bible and the singsong of prayer. When the treacherous Rudolph was torturing the delicate and fair Caroline, Mammeh fluttered her hands and screamed out. Rivkeleh, Mayer the Soldier's wife, a young woman who came with challah and a flask of warm tea, often couldn't contain herself.

"Frimmetl," she begged, "stop a minute! Vey'z mir! Okh, the poor thing, it shouldn't happen! It's really tugging at my heart strings!"

And when the refined Caroline went strolling with her beloved duke, and the moon shone and birds sang—Mammeh told this with such refinement and self-restraint that we all felt that we ourselves were strolling with the godlike duke and that the moon was shining and the birds were singing just for us.

But on this Shabbes we weren't meant to learn the fate of the innocent Caroline. Why Mammeh's listeners didn't come, only God knows. Did they all agree to stay away? Or what? Maybe they were offended?

Mammeh couldn't understand it. Meanwhile, she began reading to herself, paging forward and then back, taking off her glasses then putting them back on again. It didn't work.

While Mammeh couldn't find a place for herself, the door to our house suddenly burst open and a small, squat woman with red cheeks threw herself in—not one of the regular listeners.

It was Rayzl, Itsheh the Bull's mother, a distant relative of Mammeh's. She came by about once every six weeks or so.

She was so short that when she sat on a stool her feet dangled in the air. Mammeh always shoved a footstool toward her so she wouldn't look so foolish with her feet bobbing up and down.

Itsheh the Bull's Rayzl loved to drink a glass of lemon tea with us, unburden herself, and grumble that her children were humiliating her. She cursed her daughters-in-law and sons-in-law and always complained to my mother that Mammeh wasn't trying to arrange a suitable match for her.

"I'm all alone like a stone," Itsheh the Bull's Rayzl sipped the boiling tea and complained. "How long is long enough to be without a husband? How long?"

"But Rayzelshi," Mammeh kept back a smile, "it seems to me, may no evil eye . . . this would be a fourth one already."

"So what? Am I that old?"

No. Itsheh the Bull's Rayzl wasn't that old. It was just that she had ruddy, smiling cheeks, thin, sugary lips, and lots of little creases on the soft folds of her neck. She walked with a roll, thrusting herself forward. Winter and summer she had big complaints for the Master-of-the-Universe because He had arranged it so that she was either too hot or too cold most of the time.

Rayzl didn't think much of the fair Caroline or that deceitful Rudolph.

"Bubbeh-maysehs! Grandmother's tales!" she scoffed. "Here's a coin for all of your Rudolph with his . . . what do you call her? Carolina! Shmarolina! Is any of it true?"

But this time, ruddy Rayzl fell into our house blazing and confused. "Frimmet!"

Mammeh quickly put away the storybook and stood up with a look of wonder on her face.

"Git Shabbes, Rayzl!"

"Ar'ya alone?" was how Rayzl answered Mammeh's "Good Shabbes."

"What do you mean, alone?" Mammeh remained standing, her nose taut, a sign that she was scared.

Rayzl's small eyes immediately fastened on me. She made a sign to Mammeh. I looked at both of them, not understanding the silent conversation they were having with their eyes.

"Mendl," Mammeh said, "go outside for a minute."

"What for?"

"If you're told to, then go!"

I didn't feel like it. I didn't want to.

"Go outside for a minute! Go!"

Rayzl bobbed her small foolish head as she closed the door behind me. I stood on the other side, humiliated and mad. A black year must have sent this stupid Rayzl! Who'd have sent for her? Who?

She brought a secret with her, and if it's a secret, can't I hear it?

I knew that Mammeh sent me out of the house whenever there were secrets to tell, so naturally I wouldn't go. I'd just stand behind the kitchen door and listen.

I pressed my face and ear against the closed door, looked through the keyhole, but I couldn't see anything and I couldn't hear anything either.

It must be a really big secret if they were whispering. It must also be a very important one, because the door was suddenly wrenched open with a cry and I saw that Mammeh had hurriedly thrown her winter coat over herself.

In those minutes of secret talk, Mammeh's face had gotten drawn and scared. Rayzl's narrow, sugary lips trembled as if in fever. Tatteh heard nothing; he lay with nostrils turned up to the rafters.

Mammeh couldn't even button up her coat properly in her hurry and her kerchief wouldn't stay put on her disarranged wig. She ran around the house with half steps, one minute taking a look at sleeping Tatteh and the next minute just as suddenly looking at me in confusion. She must've had something in mind. She was trying to remember something but couldn't.

"Mendl," she said quickly and sharply, "don't leave the house. When Tatteh wakes up, there's a pot of pear soup on the shelf. I'll be back soon."

Someone, God forbid, must have passed away! Mammeh ran out as if shot from a cannon. Itsheh the Bull's Rayzl fluttered out after her on her short little legs.

Nothing but wind and emptiness were left behind in the house. A gloomy fear enveloped me.

I knew I shouldn't leave the house unattended but it seemed to me that if I stayed here I'd die, so I didn't listen to Mammeh. Let what will, be! I had to find out what kind of secret Rayzl had brought and where Mammeh was rushing.

I grabbed my coat, didn't even bother buttoning it up, and ran outside. At the German church I hid myself in one of its corners. It seemed to me that Mammeh turned around and stared to see if I was following her.

On Warsaw Street I hid again, this time inside an entranceway.

Mammeh and Rayzl went into Shul Alley and I followed. The alley was narrow and winding, like a hoop. It was dark and crowded.

The white shul with its round, blue windows, leaned over the low study house that bulged out into the street a little.

The other houses all leaned against each other as if a windstorm had bent them over, and afterward they couldn't straighten up.

Something must have happened!

The whole town, women and men, had given up their Shabbes nap and had come running here to this misfortune. Pushing and shoving and a mass of people craning their necks, standing on tiptoe looking over everyone's heads.

Every few minutes, new people and new women's caps arrived. I didn't know where Mammeh and Rayzl had got to; they were tangled up among the beards and the wigs.

I pushed myself through the cold masculine kapotehs and warm women's skirts, through the legs and elbows of strangers. I wanted to get to that spot where everyone was craning their heads. Nobody paid any attention to me.

It seemed that nobody knew who I was, otherwise they wouldn't have let fall such heavy, disconnected words:

"Yeh, Luzeh, the Hay Dealer . . ."

"Naturally, if you've got a stepmother . . . !"

"How's it the stepmother's fault?"

"Who's to blame then, Uncle Nobody?"

"If you're not decent, not even your own mother can help."

They were pieces of hail, not talk. They were talking about my father and about my mother. So that meant that this whole racket, this pushing, shoving, and muttering, had to do with us, with our house.

As I was pushing myself through the kapotehs and skirts, suddenly above everyone's heads there rose a long drawn-out whistle, a kind of cry and wail mixed together:

"Dear God in Heaven, send me death! Just send me death!"

The crowd moved in confusion. The shriek let up for a moment, faded, then it echoed again:

"Merciful Father, what did'ya want from me?"

People turned their faces away. One old woman in a cap and with a sunken mouth screamed:

"Men! Get out of here! Men!"

Shoes and boots began shuffling backwards. It got roomier. Suddenly I found myself right out in front. Right there, where everyone was straining their heads.

Now I noticed that around me where the crowd was pushing, the snow was red. The sun hadn't set yet, the windowpanes of the shul were blue, so why was the snow red?

Someone moved aside again and right in front of me, in front of my face, I saw a long blotch of a person writhing in the snow.

It wasn't a person at all! It wasn't a blotch at all! It was Toybeh! Our Toybeh!

She was lying in the red snow, torn in two, swollen, both legs naked and sticking up like logs. From between her legs, or maybe it was from her belly, blood flowed. Toybeh saw me. I didn't know whether she knew who I was. Her face was red and puffy. She looked at me with round, rolling eyes like a calf's.

All of a sudden she raised her swollen face, stretched out her naked legs into the bloodied snow, and shrieked out in a singsong:

"People, have pity! Gimme poison!!"

I saw Mammeh coming forward right then, her mouth wide open. I didn't know if she'd already started screaming or she was about to

scream. I also didn't know where she'd been until now but the crowd
of women began to move aside. It got very quiet. Over everyone's head
a restrained echo drifted:

"Frimmet!"

"Duvid-Froykeh's Frimmet!"

"The stepmother!"

Mammeh pushed through the crowd, her face dark, fallen.

The kerchief lay around her shoulders. She bent down to Toybeh.
It seemed she didn't see me. I couldn't hear whether she said something
to Toybeh or whether Toybeh said something to her, but it was as if
there was no one else there, just Mammeh and Toybeh.

From the bathhouse alley that led to the canal, a long peasant
sleigh came into sight.

On just this kind of sleigh they had, it shouldn't happen to anybody, taken my brother Moysheh away to the hospital. It seemed to
me it was the very same sleigh with the same fur-wrapped goy.

"*Nabok dzhidki!* Make way, you Yids!" the goy yelled out in
Polish and rode his horse right into the kapotehs and skirts.

"*Yak yedzhi'esh chamyeh!* Look how you're driving, you jerk!"
a young woman answered back in Polish wrenching her face away
from the horse's head

"*Nabok! Ni'eh statsh tutay, P'shah matsh!* Make way! Don't stand
here! Son of a bitch!"

"*Sam p'sha matsh!* Son of a bitch yourself!"

"Sha, sha!" voices answered. "She hasn't got who to quarrel with
any more. Not any more!"

The crowd moved aside. The sleigh stayed where it was, not far
from the spot where Toybeh lay.

The fur-wrapped goy together with another goy crawled out of
the sleigh. One of them bent down to Toybeh and grumbled in Polish:

"*P'shakrev! Ni'eh mogla toh zatshekatsh!* Dammit! You couldn't
wait!"

"*Ni'eh mi'ala tshasuh.* She didn't have time," someone answered
from the crowd.

"*Ni'eh gadatsh tam!* Shut up!" the goy exclaimed angrily.

Mammeh stood next to him. She said something to him and he
quietly shook his head.

After that the two goyim picked Toybeh up from the snow. Her
face was now white, her eyes closed. She didn't cry out. They covered
her up and placed straw around her. The crowd muttered. Rough bits
of sighs and half cries reached me:

"The bastard?"

"Dead . . ."
"A boy?"
"A girl?"

A strange policeman, arrived from one of the other streets and sat down at the foot of the sleigh the same way my mother had when they took Moyshe to the hospital.

Now Mammeh shuffled along the iron railings of the shul fence all by herself without Itsheh the Bull's Rayzl. It seemed to me that Mammeh wasn't walking so much as being pushed.

The sleigh began to move. Clumps of red snow stuck to the runners and a black, heavy cloud hung over the shul like dried blood.

Chapter 18

Toybeh was taken to the goyish hospital, that same hospital behind which I almost froze to death one wintry evening and had to be taken to Bubbeh's house.

Sick people were brought to this hospital through a red gate. Jews said that they never came back out through the same gate they went in by, but were carried out dead through a black gate that led into Khozhenitz Street.

During the week, the long hospital windows looked out on the street in guarded silence. Sometimes, a little old goyeh would arrive with a basket of food and wait half a day until it was taken inside for her; sometimes a peasant woman banged her head into the wall behind the fence wailing loudly; and sometimes a goy, a father of children, begged to be allowed in to see his sick wife.

But on Sundays or on any other goyish holiday, the white, silent windows were filled with sick shiksehs. They talked to the Russian soldiers on the street below through winks and hand gestures. The soldiers craned their necks up to the windows and spat the husks of sunflower seeds out of the corners of their mouths.

The girls cursed and mocked the soldiers in mime, made a fig with their fingers, stuck out their tongues, and if it suited any of them, she would turn around and uncover a big, white, rear end right into the windowpanes. The soldiers in the street answered with broad, beefy laughter and began to yell back three-story high Russian obscenities. They didn't just talk. They also showed their backsides and other disgusting soldierly parts.

So Jews avoided the goyish hospital on Sundays. Jews altogether didn't like this hospital because they said that they kill and slaughter in there, and they don't even bother making excuses. The Jews were afraid, not so much of the sick shiksehs and the black gate, but also because of Dr. Kozhitsky who had the heart of a Tatar, and no matter what, he would always say, cut!

201

Jews said that this Dr. Kozhitsky was a slaughterer, a belly-cutter.

So it hurt me a lot that they took Toybeh to that hospital, to that belly-cutter Kozhitsky.

Toybeh of her own free will would never have allowed herself to be taken there, to that Angel-of-Death Kozhitsky. Now, since such a terrible misfortune had happened to her, she had to lie there and wait for Kozhitsky to cut her up and send her out through the black gate.

Who knows if they haven't already taken her away?

Toybeh wasn't seen through the windows, not on Sundays, not ever. Nobody shouted up to her, nobody talked to her, nobody brought a basket of food for her, nobody came to see her, and nobody even asked about her.

From that Shabbes on, Mammeh went around with a dark face. She stopped talking altogether, stopped visiting the neighbors, and didn't finish the sad story about the innocent Caroline.

It was as if Mammeh was afraid to look at Tatteh but from time to time, she glanced at him sideways. A frightened wonder lay in that look, a kind of dreadful terror for what was to come.

"Doesn't he know anything, that Luzeh?" Her look asked, as she waited for Tatteh to wake up from his absent-minded state of not being here.

It seemed that he'd actually not heard yet, or else he was sleeping heavier than usual and snoring louder than at any other time.

When he came home tired and stiff in the evening, Mammeh hurried to serve him supper. She didn't sit with him at the table, nor did she ask him how things went in the village that day.

Mostly she busied herself in the kitchen, washed the pots and rinsed them several times over until Tatteh began nodding off heavily. Only then did she clear the table and shake him by the shoulder:

"Luzeh, go lie down! Go . . ."

But for how long can you not know? Probably a rustling of some kind must have cut through his deafness while measuring the piles of hay with his hands or poking around among the wagons at the market. Maybe some mean person, an enemy, had yelled the terrible news into his ear? Maybe the wind in the fields brought him regards from his daughter lying in the goyish hospital?

He didn't tell us. But once he came home as night was falling, not slowly and plodding as usual, like those people who deal with fields and peasants. This time, he all but fell in.

He was absent-minded, his beard was disheveled as if he'd been sleeping on it, his mouth was open, round. Nothing else but this terrible news went into his mouth and he couldn't close it! The pouch in which he carried cheese fell off him, together with his pack. The same one his daughter Bayleh had once sent home to him with Yarmeh the Wagon Driver. The plush cap was pushed over to one side of his head in confusion.

At the same time, Mammeh happened to be sitting by the kerosene lamp mending a shirt. When the door opened and Tatteh's long shadow fell into the house, Mammeh sensed at once that it was the terrible news that had brought him home in this way. She grabbed her finger to her mouth, sucked at it and stood up quickly with the shirt in her hand.

The whites of Tatteh's big blue eyes were shot through with red veins. Mammeh stood in front of him, bent over, blinking as if she was the one to blame and not Toybeh.

"Frimmet," Tatteh groaned heavily. "Come here a minute . . ."

"What happened, Luzeh?"

"Just come here a minute."

He led her into the kitchen. The shirt that Mammeh had been in the middle of mending, trailed after her, one sleeve dragging like the upturned hand of a person who had fainted away.

They half-closed the door. I didn't have the heart to follow them into the kitchen, so I leaned against the half-open door and lifted my face but no talk reached me. I only heard a drawn-out gasping. It felt like huge pieces of dough were being kneaded and thrown onto the floor. Suddenly, I heard a sound as if a breeze was rustling through paper.

"Sha, Luzeh, don't say anything."

"I shouldn't say anything? I shouldn't talk?" Tatteh stewed, his voice tight. It seemed to me he was trying to catch his breath and that I should rush in and try to revive him.

I risked my life, opened the door a bit wider and looked inside.

Tatteh was standing in the middle of the kitchen, hands hanging down helplessly at his sides. His hands had never seemed so big. Mammeh was busying herself with him like you do with a sick person. She pulled the pack off his shoulder with shaking hands. He didn't stop her. His head kept drooping lower to the ground. Nothing else but Tatteh must really be sick! Mammeh was actually taking him under the arm and leading him calmly into the room. She sat him down at the table where he stayed sitting stiff and cold as if he'd been molded out of glass. Mammeh quickly brought in a can of water and a bowl from the kitchen.

"Here, Luzeh, wash yourself already!" She spoke to him quietly as if she had tears in her throat. "I cooked liver and potatoes."

But Tatteh it seemed, didn't hear or didn't understand what was wanted of him.

"Nu, wash yourself already, the food's getting spoiled."

Tatteh's hands were shaking. The can of water slopped over the bowl. Mammeh brought in the blackened liver and the fried potatoes from the kitchen. A warm, sweet smell drifted over the room. Tatteh tried to eat, chewing slowly, his eyes fastened on the flame of the lamp.

But all at once, his spoon stuck in the potatoes. Mammeh again picked up the shirt to mend it, but meanwhile she didn't take her eyes off Tatteh. She fussed around him like a hen:

"What's the matter with you, Luzeh? Why aren't you eating?" Why not?" But Tatteh couldn't eat a thing anymore. The upright spoon bent to a side and fell away like a sawed off sapling.

Tatteh's head also fell over to one side.

It seemed to me that everything in the house now listed to one side, even the flame of the lamp had shrunk. A greenish, wrinkled skin spread over the blackened liver.

⇛

From that evening on, I never saw Tatteh any different than with his head bent. The more his head drooped, the higher his shoulders went up.

He spoke more quietly than before, ate even more slowly than before, and walked quieter too.

We neither saw nor talked about Toybeh the whole time. In our house it was as if she was forgotten. My friend Yankl, Yarmeh the Wagon Driver's son took me into the warm straw of his father's omnibus and in a feverish voice that came not from his throat but from his whole body, he breathed right into my face:

"You saw it yourself? With your own two eyes?"

"Yeh, with my own eyes."

"In the snow, you said?"

"In the snow."

"How'd it look?"

I didn't know what to answer. Actually, I didn't want to answer him at all. Why'd he need to know how it looked? What's it his business? Why's he mixing into our Toybeh's affairs?

He promised me that his father would take me along in the omnibus all the way to the inn but never mind the trip, this time I just wanted him to leave me alone.

And so that was the end of Toybeh. Her name hung on the walls of our house, lay in the tired, sad eyes of my father, in the tightly sealed lips of my mother and in my own fevered and distracted imagination but we didn't talk about Toybeh, not my father, not my mother, not Yankel, not anybody.

Chapter 19

We got through the winter bit by bit. The nights got shorter and the dawns warmer and redder. Windows were opened in the well-to-do houses and the windowpanes were polished. It smelled of warm water and aired bed linens.

Even in Simmeh-Yoysef's cheder we felt that summer was coming. He started translating the Megillah with us—Haman's ten sons were already squirming like herring on the gallows; Mordechai the Saint, was lording it about in the kingly palace, doing good deeds for Jews; and Queen Esther slept with King Ahashverus every night.

At that time, my friend Yankl was getting ready for something. Every evening he disappeared somewhere, stayed for a long time, and only came back when everyone in the house was asleep and the bread cabinet was already locked up.

It seemed to me that Yankl was planning to run away. He was sick and tired of his stepmother pinching him, sick of his father the Wagon Driver, and he wanted to take off. Otherwise, he wouldn't be so secretive with me or so withdrawn.

Yankl, would be a big loss to me. Who'd I have except him? But when the week of Purim came and the streets were full with Purim pastries, Yankl took me aside and told me his secret—that right after Shabbes, they were going to perform the biblical play, The Selling of Joseph, in Yossl Tsallels' wedding hall and that he, Yankl, was going to play the lead role of Yoysef hatsadik, Joseph the Saint!

Nothing less than the saintly Joseph himself! How did he know how Joseph the Saint looked? Did he even have a coat of many colors? Even so, how did Yankl, Yarmeh the Wagon Driver's son, come to play Joseph the Saint?

Yankl told me not to bother my head over it because Sheyveh the Seamstress had sewn a coat of many colors for him. She herself would also be acting in the play. She would play Mammeh Rukhl, Mother Rachel, and Notteleh the Tinsmith would play Yankev avini, Jacob our Father. Hershl the Hound and Blond Velvl would play Reuven and Shimen. The scene would be a tomb he said. They would show the Land of Israel, Pharaoh's Egypt with the Philistines, and Moyshe Rabeynu, Moses our Teacher, the biblical Moses.

So I see that Yankl is not just an ordinary fool but an ignorant boor too. How did the Philistines get into this story? And what was Moysheh Rabeynu doing here? For starters, when Yankev avini, our Father Jacob went off to Egypt, Moyshe Rabeynu wasn't even born yet!

Yankl answered, that's how it's written in the book, and they were putting on the play, The Selling of Joseph according to that book.

Yankl said no one could come in for free. You'd have to buy a ticket and it would be stamped when you came in. The ticket would cost twenty groshn.

So what could I do? I couldn't save up twenty groshn so fast before Shabbes. If Yankl would have told me this in the middle of winter, I'd have saved a groshn here, a groshn there and I could've had enough already for two tickets. But now?

Mammeh had also heard about the play they were going to perform in Yossl Tsallels' wedding hall.

She had once read about it in a storybook and she had seen the play put on by the Brody Singers right after she married her first husband. At that time, you also had to buy tickets. Who today could act it as well as the Brody Singers? She didn't believe that anything could come of it because what would a Joseph the Saint be worth if he was going to be played by the likes of Yankl? When the Brody Singers played it, said my mother, Joseph the Saint had a silky, black beard and you couldn't even see his face. And this Yankl of yours is all covered in freckles, she said.

Nu, okay, so she's right. But I never saw the Brody Singers. For me, Yankl would be good enough.

"Never mind," said Mammeh, "If you're so set on it, I'll go with you."

I didn't sleep the whole week. In my imagination I saw the tomb that Yankl had described, with Sheyveh the Seamstress and Yankl himself. But where would he actually find a black, silky beard like my mother had seen on the saintly Joseph of the Brody Singers?

Shabbes at the davening it occurred to me that Yankl shouldn't be the one to play the saintly Joseph but that it should be Uncle Ben-Tsion's son, Mendl. Joseph the Saint probably had to sing and who else had such a beautiful singing voice like Mendl? But he would probably consider it beneath his dignity to act alongside the likes of Notteleh the Tinsmith and Sheyveh the Seamstress.

But what's to think about if tonight they're already performing the piece? It's just a shame that Shabbes was taking so long to end. The dark red sun just didn't want to sink below our windowsill.

Tatteh took longer today to eat his Shaleshudehs meal than usual. He didn't bang his knife into the table but held it upright by the handle with the blade pointed toward the setting sun. It seemed to me that his "*bney hikhleh*" Havdoleh prayer wept right out of the knife.

Mammeh also dragged out her "God of Abraham" melody. She added new words of praise and repeated some lines twice. Everything took longer than usual. Even the stars took longer to come out today. Tatteh lingered in the middle of making Havdoleh. Mammeh couldn't find her kerchief. It was a miracle that Mottl Shtroy came by to talk to my father because my mother finally started hurrying and at last with luck, we left the house.

The building where Yosel Tsallels' hall was located, where they were acting the play this evening was a round one, standing between the wide Voyel Market and the street leading to the hospital. On Fridays before candle lighting, everyone went through here to Piyarsky River to bathe, and through here every year, summer after summer, they carried the sacrifices away that this same river claimed.

The hall itself was roomy, with red walls and tall windows; it lit up part of the Market and an even bigger part of Hospital Street. Up front, at the western wall, stood a broad red plush upholstered armchair worn and greasy from all the bridal sittings. The brides and grooms were accompanied from here to their bedding. From here too, groups of butchers and tanners, carrying a Holy Scroll would lead a procession to the Shul. Sometimes, during times of trouble, meetings of rabbis and important people in town took place here, and from here Yossl Tsallels himself, a klezmer musician with a refined black beard, let his fiddle be heard with his renditions of lively dances, as well as his own special pieces.

Now Yossl Tsallels had rented out his hall on Purim for the play, The Selling of Joseph.

A good part of the Market and half of Hospital Street were packed with people. The sky was black over the rooftops. Young men beat sticks in the air and threatened to knock the guts out of people while girls with unruly heads of hair attacked the young men. A Jew in a shortened kapoteh, hem flapping in all directions, ran around boasting:

"If you don't have a ticket, then *kibini materi*! Go fuck your mother! You won't get in."

So screaming and yelling began: "That's all he wants, just tickets . . . ?"

"That Moysheleh, that apostate! A black ticket I'll give him . . . !"

Mammeh and I stood off to a side. It wasn't fitting that she should push herself forward and she didn't have the strength for it either, but when Moysheleh the apostate, kapoteh flapping, flew by in front of us, my mother stopped him:

"Young man, excuse me. Young man!"

"What? What d'ya want?"

"I've got tickets."

"So what? So you've got tickets."

"What do you mean, so what? I paid for them."

He thought it over a minute, then looked at my mother.

"Seems to me . . . Frimmetl?"

"Yes."

"And this is your son?"

"Yes."

"He also has a ticket?"

"Of course."

"*Kömmen sie,*" he said in the formal, German style. "Come."

He led us through Hospital Street into a beer tavern where goyim were sitting with big beer mugs of leftover foam. We went into a dark, narrow courtyard that smelled from a cow. He led us up narrow, grey stairs, and said, again formally:

"You may enter here."

We went into a blue, whitewashed kitchen where a fat woman was stirring a big pot with a wooden spoon. A blond Jew, his beard wet, sat by a tallow candle studying a sacred text. The woman followed us showing the way:

"Here, here."

We came to Yossl Tsallels' hall where we were enveloped by the smell of sweat mixed with rock candy and orange peelings. The crowd was standing on long wooden benches, girls with their arms around the shoulders of young men. A bearded Jew rubbed his itching back against a wall. Women were gasping and eating pieces of squashed strudel from out of their opened kerchiefs.

The play hadn't started yet. Over where the plush armchair with the red footstool for the brides usually stood, it now looked like a goyish window during their holidays. A large, bright lamp wrapped in red silky paper hung over the tomb that was banged together from boards and smeared with lime.

Two crooked young stags, with the faces of crying cats held up the golden ornamental crown of the Torah between their front legs. At their hind legs was written, black on white:

"*Pey, nun.* Here lies . . . Mammeh Rukhl, Mother Rachel."

I imagined how beautiful this would be when soon we'd see Yankev avini, Our Father Jacob, with his sons, how they'd sell their brother Joseph to the Ishmaelites, how they'd smear his coat of many colors with blood and then come to tell their father that a wild animal had devoured his son Joseph.

While I was imagining all this, a tall Jew with a long, blond beard that looked like hemp, wearing a white kitl with an ornamental silver collar came forward beside the tomb. This Jew held a tall, twisted staff—it had to be the same one that Moysheh Rabeynu split the Red Sea with, and the one with which he got water from a stone. A murmur went through the crowd.

"Yankev avini! Our Father Jacob!"

Benches began scraping, chins were placed on the shoulders of strangers. Someone complained because mouths were chomping loudly.

So he was told that if he didn't like it, he didn't have to look.

So somebody else answered back that whoever has big eyes, may they fall out!

Yankev avini, our Father Jacob remained standing at Mammeh Rukhl's, Mother Rachel's gravestone, waiting for it to get quiet, but the longer he stayed silent, staring out from beneath his yellow brows, the harder people began pushing and complaining. Finally, Yankev avini banged his Moysheh Rabeynu staff into the floor and roared out like a lion:

"Be quiet! A black year take you!"

And it really did get quiet. Yankev avini picked up his staff and began declaiming:

"Listen people—women and Jews. We're now going to perform for you.

Of Joseph and his brothers there's news.

With sweet words and glorious song

we sing on Purim, goblet in hand

In every town, in every land."

Yankev avini didn't just talk this ballad but he sung it, half-nasally and with a little shriek. When he finally finished, he clapped his hands and called out:

"Come in, come in, my children."

And they started trooping in—Reuven and Shimen, Yehudeh and Issachar. They walked in stiffly as if they'd swallowed sticks. Naftali fell in as if someone had kicked him from behind. Then Leyvi ran in, a young man who looked like a corpse, with long red hands that he didn't know what to do with.

How handsomely Yankev's children had decked themselves out!

Reuven was dressed in a black, silk kapoteh with a gartl, a belt around his midsection like a Hassid. He wore slippers with white stockings and looked like an important rabbinical judge! The only thing missing from this get-up was a shtrayml, the wide, holiday fur hat.

Shimen had thrown a wagon driver's jacket over himself, turned inside out, with the padded cotton lining on the outside. He was sweating. Yehudeh looked like a hangman because what sensible person would wear a red shirt? Where'd he even get a red shirt? But Issachar looked like a newly minted son-in-law enjoying free room and board, with his soft, turned over collar and tie. According to my understanding, this is how Benjamin should've been dressed but he was fitted out in a tight bodice and lace-up shoes.

They placed themselves around the tomb, blinking their eyes. It was impossible to recognize who they were with such smeared and screwed up faces.

Yoysef Hatsadik, the saintly Joseph himself came our running!

Not just in the Bible but even here he was altogether different from his other brothers.

I knew that this was my friend Yankl, he with the freckles all over his face. Still, he looked very handsome.

He was wearing a velvet cap like a rabbinical student and had small, shiny black and curly side curls.

I can't understand where Yankl got side curls! First of all, he never had side curls and second, his hair was bristly and yolk-yellow.

But actually, what difference did it make since he was so handsome? His loose, silk shirt with the neck open like on a girl, suited his face but it wasn't good that they let him go barefoot. His staff also was a mistake. It wasn't crooked at the top like Yankev avini's staff should be. It was just a common stick, not at all like one from the Land of Israel.

So, never mind! The main thing was that they were all here, all the sons, and the play could now really start.

Yankev avini, Our Father Jacob looked his sons over and said to them:

"Sons of Israel, listen to me,
The Lord's might is without measure, without toll
Who can recall
What I suffered at Laban the Aramean's hand
Go now my children, tend to the cattle
And so that I won't fall into melancholy
I'll stay here with Yosef and study Toyreh."

The sons filed out slowly, one behind the other, only Yoysef Hatsadik, Joseph the Saint stayed. When only the two were left, Yankev avini, our Father Jacob, stood himself on a stool and began to chant sadly:
"Run quickly, run at once
Run to the children
And see if they're tending the cattle."
Yoysef Hatsadik bowed to his father Yankev, and replied:
"Father, father, I'll do as you command
I'll run to my brothers and bring them in hand."
Our Father Jacob turned down the bright lamp. Joseph the Saint ran out to his brothers and the tomb of Mammeh Rukhl, Mother Rachel, darkened.
No one knew if the play had ended or what had happened. The crowd again began pushing and complaining:
"Where'd he go, this Yoysef Hatsadik?"
"What's taking him so long? What?"
"As I live and breathe, you could send him for the Angel-of-Death!"
It didn't take long and the brothers came back. They placed their staffs in front of themselves self-confidently. Yoysef Hatsadik, Joseph the Saint seemed small and frightened. Not for nothing! He had good reason, unfortunately, to look like this.
Because now one of his brothers stood out front, and lowering his brow, he said angrily:
"Brother Yoysef, brother Yoysef,
What is your command, what is your desire?
Why did our father Yankev send you here?"
Joseph sat down on a plush footstool, the same one on which the brides rested their slippered white feet. Swaying like a young Talmud student, he answered:
"Brothers, brothers, listen to what I tell:
I had a dream, so listen well
We sat and studied our lessons on one hand
And bound the sheaves standing on the land.
We left this place
and my sheaf was still standing
So God said to me: I will make you shine
And that's why your sheaves bow down to mine."
When the brothers heard this, Shimen stepped forward in his wagon driver's windbreaker and responded in a coarse and angry voice:
"Now you listen to us!
Leave off with your dreams, enough!
What use is all this to you?

We have to make an end of you."

The whole crowd, me included, held our breaths. We saw right
away that the end was coming for poor Joseph. He himself, Yoysef
Hatsadik, Joseph the Saint, got up from the footstool, knelt down and
with arms raised to his brothers, began to intone:

"Therefore, the angel will weep to see one brother
Lay a murderous hand on the other."

But Shimen was a bad person. He gave a hard bang with his tall
staff, and like a king, he commanded:

"Brothers, brothers, do what you must
Strip off his silk shirt and make of him dust
Run brothers, dig a pit
And hurl him right into it."

Joseph raised his arms to the heavens and pleaded with God to
close the mouths of these snakes and scorpions so they wouldn't, God
forbid, do him any harm.

But the brothers grabbed him, this Yoysef Hatsadik, this saintly
Joseph, and threw him into the lion's pit behind Mammeh Rukhl's,
Mother Rachel's grave and then they sat themselves down to eat and
drink.

While they were eating and drinking, the other Ishmaelites came
in. There were seven of them, tall, with blond beards and big red noses,
their heads wrapped in white towels.

Shimen again stood up, bowed down to the Ishmaelite buyers
and let himself be heard from:

"You lords from far off lands
We want to sell Yoysef into your hands
As you love your lives and the world—
Pay us twenty pieces
of silver for him."

The Ishmaelites didn't bargain and they paid up the twenty pieces
of silver right off.

Yoysef probably heard all this in the lion's pit because he began
to belt out from there with great weeping and wailing:

"Mother, mother, hear my moan
What can I do? I'm here on my own.
Run, search, make an effort, plead!
So my brothers should leave me alone."

The tomb began to shake. I got cold. Probably, the whole crowd
also got cold.

A white figure came out from behind the stone, dressed in a
long shirt with a tulle veil over its face like a bride when she's veiled
before the wedding.

The figure trembled like a leaf. Everyone knew that this was Sheyveh the Seamstress, the same one who could sing songs about love, about orphans and also the song, *A Rose in the Middle of the Road.*

The hall got so quiet you could even hear a fly winging by. Sheyveh herself now seemed taller than usual. She leaned a hand on the tomb and began singing in a broken voice:

"Yoysef, my dear, Yoysef my own.

I hear your lament; I hear your moan

Alas and alack, Vey'z mir!

Why don't the murderers leave you here?"

The sons of Yankev avini, our Father Jacob, began shuffling out slowly, one behind the other like geese. Mammeh Rukhl, Mother Rachel, came face to face with the Ishmaelites. She stretched out her arms and in a maternal lament, began pleading:

"Dear people, alas and alack

Have pity on Yoysef, my child

Listen to my plea! Hear my lament!

He's your brother, your very own kin!"

But the Ishmaelites didn't understand any Yiddish, and so the brothers went home to tell their father Jacob that a wild animal had devoured his son Joseph. The buyers had paid twenty pieces of silver so how could they have any pity on poor Mammeh Rukhl?

She sang and she pleaded, but meanwhile, the brothers tied up Yoysef and dragged him off just like you drag a sheep.

Nobody knew exactly how it happened, but in the middle of all this, as soon as Sheyveh the Seamstress began to lower herself back into the tomb, there was a sudden commotion in the hall. People stomped their feet, pushed and shoved their way to the door, and way up, where women's wigs were tangled up with men's caps, a woman's shriek was heard:

"Save me! Vey'z mir!"

I was covered in a cold sweat. Such screams I had only heard before from Toybeh when she lay in the snow.

It seemed that Mammeh was also covered in the same kind of sweat because she began pushing forward, more than anyone else. She widened the passage with her elbows.

"Let me," she pleaded: "I don't feel good! Let me through!"

The crowd made way for my mother. Everyone stared at her just like they did when Toybeh lay in a heap in Shul Street.

True, this time it wasn't Toybeh, but it reminded us of that dark Shabbes when Toybeh was rushed off to the hospital.

Here too, a girl had just delivered. Women pinched their cheeks, and the men made jokes. Mammeh and I went home quickly. Mammeh

was silent. During the night she got up from bed a few times to make
sure the door was locked.

The next day she sighed all the time, had to put grated horseradish
on her forehead and was very sorry that she had let herself be talked
into going to see the play, The Selling of Joseph.

"It wasn't worth it," she said. "Was it the same as the one the
Brody Singers put on?"

The whole town buzzed about the girl who had delivered in Yossl
Tsallels' hall. Our Toybeh's name was remembered. Women spat and
said that this new girl, the whore, would come to the same black end
as Toybeh. Didn't everybody know that Dr. Kozhitsky had hacked her
to pieces and that she'd ended up croaking under his hands?

This kind of talk reached our house too. Tatteh didn't hear it but
this kind of talk bent Mammeh over double like an overloaded bush.

Chapter 20

Purim morning my father didn't go off to any of the villages. After eating, he put on his Shabbes kapoteh and his cloth cap, took his walking stick, and went out into the street looking like a regular businessman. Mammeh picked a feather off his shoulder, told him for the sake of heaven, to come home in time and went back to her kneading and baking.

The house smelled of oil and cinnamon. The big, three-cornered Purim pastries came out of the oven brown like oranges. Tatteh had bought real, blood-red oranges in the street and also half a dozen twisted and decorated Polish letters of the alphabet made from sugar and cornstarch. He put a bottle of sparkling wine from the Land of Israel on the table, a packet of raisins, and several large Turkish nuts that nobody on this earth was strong enough to crack.

The night of the Purim feast, everything was clean and bright. The painted, red floor that my mother had already wiped up several times today, shone like the wine in the bottle from the Land of Israel.

The bright lamp and the two silver-plated candelabras enveloped the house in rich warmth. Tatteh's beard, clean and combed, took up the whole head of the table. If not for his tired eyes that had become even dreamier since Toybeh's tragedy, you'd think that Tatteh had become successful all of a sudden.

What if it was really true?

Mameh had invited Yossl the Glazier's Gitteleh to the feast, the little old widow, poor thing, who summer and winter wore a big black skirt and was never without her torn bit of parasol. Mammeh said that this parasol served Gitteleh better than Gitteleh's own two feet. Besides, Mammeh said, Gitteleh was a bit of a scholar in her own right. She could study a section of the khimesh with Rashi's commentaries and even a blat Gemorah, a page of the Talmud. She was only a poor woman but Mammeh considered it an honor that Gitteleh let herself be invited to our feast.

215

So now she was sitting in her big, black skirt with a red bow on her head that bobbed up and down like an angry rooster. Her scrawny, wrinkled little face shook as well. Her lips, thin and dried out, seemed to be growing right into her mouth. She was so small, this Gitteleh that she took up no more than half a seat. It seemed that she was also deaf. Only her little black eyes were open and lively.

Mammeh's face was flushed. Her soft jabot looked rich on her black, taffeta blouse. She warmly welcomed the masked celebrators who quickly went in and out of every house singing: "Good Purim Angel."

Mammeh cut off a piece of fruit cake, picked out one of the best Purim pastries from the cupboard, added a sugared Polish letter that Tatteh had just bought, and took all this next door to our goyish neighbor, the Senior Prison Guard who unfortunately, didn't begin to know anything about Purim celebrations.

Tatteh put an orange on a plate, decorated it with a sprig of raisins, added two Turkish nuts on the side and a piece of fruitcake. He covered it all with a white cloth and giving me the only bottle of wine, told me to take all this to Uncle Ben-Tsion as a Purim gift.

Mameh was offended:

"How many bottles of wine have you got, that you're sending them this?"

"What should I do, not send?"

"Ben-Tsion can manage without your wine."

"Don't worry," Tatteh said off-handedly, "Ben-Tsion will send back a better bottle."

It bothered me too. I had waited the whole time for this bottle to be opened, we should be enjoying it already and he was sending it off to Uncle Ben-Tsion the Community Scribe. He didn't have enough wine of his own?

But if Tatteh decides to send it, I can't say that I don't want to deliver it. So heartsick, I went off to deliver it to Tatteh's brother-in-law.

Out in the street, lots of boys were carrying round, covered plates. Jews with beards were also out. Coming toward them were masqueraders with smeared faces and red, bulging noses.

Our door was open to them, but at Uncle Ben-Tsion's house, the door was locked and even though I wasn't disguised, I had to yell into the house that I was Luzeh the Hay Dealer's son and that I was bringing a Purim gift. The servant girl peeked out through a crack and asked me again who I was. She wanted to know what I'd brought, and whom did I want?

"I want Uncle Ben-Tsion." Didn't she know that, the stupid girl?

Only then did she open the door and led me into the big room.

It wasn't dark at Aunt Nemmi's now the way it'd been during the previous intermediate days of the Succoth and Pesach holidays.

The table stood in the middle of the room now and was covered with a white cloth. Two bright lamps were burning, one hanging from the beam, the other one on the table. A heavy engraved candelabra of real silver with candles bigger and thicker than ours was also standing. Bowls of oranges, dates, and all kinds of sweets dazzled and glittered on the tablecloth as well as bottles of wine, more than you could count, so why'd they need our one and only bottle?

Uncle Ben-Tsion sat at the head of the table in an upholstered chair, wearing a new, eight-sided, silk skullcap. His beard seemed whiter than at any other time of the year. He sat sprawled out and satisfied. His son Mendl, in a stiff white collar and black tie, also sat as expansively as his father. His face was clear but flushed, his hands were clean and white but he pursed his lips as if something was bothering him.

He didn't even look at me. After all, he wouldn't just look at any boy bringing Purim gifts.

Aunt Nemmi's black silk dress with the puffed sleeves rustled and changed color with the creases and wrinkles. A braided, gold brooch that looked like a coiled snake gleamed at her throat. Her pious, dark face with the sharp eyebrows smiled:

"So . . ." she drawled, "a Purim gift. . . . Blessed be the One Above! And how's your father? Izzat so . . . ? Blessed be His Dear Name! And your mother, may she live? Izzat so . . . ? Nu, indeed . . ."

I stood in the middle of the room. I didn't know whether I was ashamed or frightened by these strange people sitting around the table. I felt my skin burning. I wanted to run away from this place. I didn't feel good here.

Aunt Nemmi took two small oranges, some figs, two or three shelled almonds and put them on the same plate that I had brought; then as I was getting ready to leave, she handed me a large, dusty bottle of wine off the table, and pressed a coin into my hand.

I sensed that it was a twenty-kopek piece. I was happy enough, but even happier that I'd survived this Purim gift experience and I noticed that these strange people didn't take their eyes off me. I hurried home. I still had to deliver the Purim gifts to Zaydeh and to Aunt Miriam today but most important was the delivery to Aunt Miriam because from there I wouldn't have to hurry home and I could spend the night with them. Aunt Miriam herself, with her small, warm hands would take off my coat, sit me down at the table, and she wouldn't let me go home.

At her house, Purim was more festive than anywhere else. Chaiml, Aunt Miriam's only son, would be dancing in the center of the room

like a bear. He would show off how a monkey totes water, how a
rooster crows, how a cat stalks a mouse. Layeh, Aunt Miriam's youngest daughter, would recite Polish verses and sing a song about beautiful
Wanda who didn't want to marry a German and ended up drowning
herself in the Vistula River.

Because of all this and because Aunt Miriam's fruitcake was
tastier than any other in the whole city, I would much rather be there.

When I came back from Uncle Ben-Tsion's house, they were
already waiting for me. The candles were halfway burned down, Yossl
the Glazier's Gitteleh was dozing. I put Aunt Nemmi's Purim gift on
the table and quietly told my mother that I was given a twenty-kopek
coin. Mammeh frowned:

"You didn't need to take it." She said and glanced sideways,
watching Tatteh carefully remove the covering on his sister's Purim gift.

"Take a look what a beautiful Purim gift Nemmi sent me!" he
said proudly.

He raised the bottle of wine to the light and examined it from
top to bottom, then slowly put it back on the table, handling it as
carefully as if he was dealing with a sick child.

"Expensive wine," he pursed his lips, "It must cost a lot of money."

"What do you think," scoffed Mammeh, "rich people don't know
how to spend money?"

"And I'm telling you," Tatteh again picked up the bottle and held
it up to the light, "this is expensive wine."

"So go pickle it!"

Tatteh began preparing a new plate of Purim gifts. He picked out
two small figs, a half spoiled orange, and a piece of fruitcake. I was
sure that I'd have to take this to Mottl Shtroy, my father's partner.

Mammeh wrapped the scarf warmly around my neck and asked:
"Did you see anything nice there, at Aunt Nemmi's?"

"Very nice."

"A lot of guests there?"

"A lot."

"What did she say to you, your aunt?"

"I should give you regards."

"And that jewel of theirs, Mendl, did you see him too?"

"Yeh, he was wearing a white collar and a tie."

"She decked him out in a white collar? What is he, a girl? Or
what?"

The Purim gift for Mottl Shtroy was ready. Mammeh went with
me into the kitchen and warned me to come right back, for heaven's
sake. I still had to go to Aunt Miriam.

"Of course! What then? Don't I know?"

I was all set to go but at that very minute, the door opened from the outside and a head, all wrapped-up, stuck itself in.

The kitchen was dark and it was hard to recognize whose head it was. According to all the signs, it seemed to be that of a very poor woman. She stayed in the doorway as if she was asking for alms.

I couldn't leave because this person blocked the door. Mammeh didn't ask her what she wanted but moved back slowly a few steps, closer to the window and from there, heaving a sigh, she asked in a quiet, restrained voice:

"Toybeh?"

I got hot and bothered. It wouldn't have taken much for me to drop the whole plate of Purim gifts right onto the floor. Only now did I recognize Toybeh's face from under the wrapped-up head. Sometimes, her face was brown and beautiful, but now it was dark and shrunken. Toybeh, it seemed, had gotten taller, you could hardly see her eyes and they weren't blue-green anymore. Two round, coal-black wheels stared out from under her bit of shawl. Even her figure was different; she was bent over, misshapen.

Maybe Toybeh wasn't feeling good?

My mother also didn't feel good. She acted as if her hands and her feet weren't her own. She didn't know whether to go into the other room or to stay here.

Her eyes darted into all the corners as if looking for something. Finally, they came to rest on the kitchen stool. She shoved it with her foot toward the doorway where Toybeh stood, while she herself held on to the table with both hands. She stayed this way with her face to the window.

Toybeh didn't sit down but stared fixedly at the stool that had been shoved toward her. I wanted to tell her to go to it, to rest herself, but Toybeh opened the door again to go out.

Hearing this, Mammeh turned round quickly and ran to the door.

"Where are you going?" she asked with a heavy heart. "Come inside."

Mammeh didn't know what to do with her hands. She wanted to take hold of Toybeh but managed only to touch the doorframe.

Yossl the Glazier's Gitteleh shuffled in slowly from the other room. She looked around the darkened kitchen, short-sighted, and asked in a drawn-out sing-song:

"Fr-i-mm-et?"

"What's the matter, Gittelshi?" Mammeh turned away from the door distracted. "Did you want something?"

"No, dear child, what could I want? I'll go now. But who's that standing by the door? Who is it?"

Mammeh didn't answer. She placed herself broadside, as if she wanted to protect Toybeh from Gitteleh's small, busybody eyes.

Tatteh must have overheard something or maybe he needed something from the kitchen because he came in quickly, angry and upset. First off, he saw me.

"You didn't go yet?" He scowled, pointing his beard at me.

I wanted to tell him that . . . but his face suddenly flattened out, he pointed his eyebrows to the door where Toybeh was still standing. He was silent but suddenly I heard a voice that was not the voice of my father:

"Out'a my house, you big Yuzhkeh!"

Together with this strange voice, I saw a pair of raised fists rushing toward the door.

"You dare to come into my house? Get out'a here!"

That very same minute, my mother slid between Tatteh's raised up fists and the huddled, broken Toybeh.

"Luzeh!" she raised her hands and said loudly: "Don't you dare! Do you hear?"

"Out'a my house, right now! Her bones shouldn't be found here ever again!"

"Luzeh, I won't allow it. . . . She's your own child!"

"She's a dog, not my child. A big Yuzhkeh! Hasn't she blackened my face enough already?"

Toybeh drooped even lower. She looked like someone had slowly sawed her in half. The door opened as if by itself and Yossl the Glazier's Gitteleh shuffled out with little, old-womanish steps. Toybeh sidled out and Tatteh wanted to lock the door behind her, but Mammeh got in the way and grabbed the key out of the lock.

"Gimme the key!" Tatteh stood with an open mouth full of white teeth.

"I won't give it to you!"

"Gimme the key, I'm telling you!"

"Luzeh, stop it!" Mammeh straightened up at once. "Stop it, I'm telling you. Otherwise, I'll leave right now and you won't know where my bones went to."

Tatteh's white teeth closed. He went back into the house with his hands hanging down, deadened. Along the way, he said something terrible about Toybeh. It wasn't so much a word as a knife stabbing my sides. Mammeh shuddered as if a sharp pain had stabbed her in the shoulder.

"Mendl," she said to me, "run outside. Go tell her to wait."

It was cold outside. Toybeh sat, round and huddled on the threshold of the vestibule. I sat down beside her.

"Toybeh, Mammeh said you should wait." I felt Toybeh's hand on my face. "Maybe you're hungry, eh?"

"No, I'm not hungry," she answered in a dry, hollow voice.

"I've got Purim gifts here, Toybeh. Maybe you want some?"

"No, Mendelshi, thanks very much."

"I've got an orange. Here, eat it."

"You don't need to, Mendl. Take it away."

The wind was blowing, the sky was black; a dog began barking in the Senior Prison Guard's house.

I didn't deliver the Purim gifts to Mottl Shtroy and I didn't go to Aunt Miriam that Purim either. I sat outside with Toybeh until the door opened quietly and I heard Mammeh's voice: "Mendl?"

"Yeh, Mammeh."

"Where are you?"

"Here, with Toybeh."

Mammeh came out and bent down toward her. "Toybeh, come inside, he's already sleeping."

"Thank you, Aunt," Toybeh muttered, "I'll wait out here."

"Don't talk nonsense, you silly fool. Come inside. I'll make up a bed for you in the kitchen."

"Thank you very much."

"You'll thank me later. Nu, come already. You're probably hungry?"

"No, I'm not hungry."

"Nu, stand up already. It's cold."

Toybeh remained sitting. The Guard's dog began barking again.

"Come, Toybeh." I patted my sister's knee. "You'll eat something. It's Purim, after all! Come on!"

Toybeh was crying. I felt her tears on my hand. Afterward, when she was in the kitchen already and Mammeh was helping her take off her shawl and kerchief, she fell on Mammeh's hands, as if wanting to kiss them.

"Stop it." Mammeh waved her hands in confusion. "You'll kiss me later. Here, have something to eat . . ."

The door to the room where Tatteh was sleeping was closed. Mammeh turned up the lamp. Toybeh's once beautiful face now looked green and shrivelled, the cheekbones sharp.

There was nothing left of her except the blue-black hair that even now, combed with a white part in the middle, looked just like those of the pious and well-to-do women.

≈§

Toybeh stayed in our house. Tatteh's head drooped even further into
his hunched and pointed shoulders. It seemed to me that even his
hearing had gotten worse.

Mammeh had Toybeh's trunk brought to us from the wealthy,
respectable house where she'd been a servant. Toybeh didn't open it.
She didn't even want to know what was inside. She went about mute
and she looked scrawny. At dawn, even before the peasant came to
rap on the window and call my father, Toybeh was already up and
had made the fire. No one heard her chop wood or strike a match. It
was as if the fire had made itself and the food she cooked for Tatteh
had made itself as well.

Once, Tatteh got up before Toybeh did. He went into the kitchen
with his tallis folded over his shoulder.

Toybeh was blowing into the stove. A pot of water stood on
the grate and a bowl of peeled potatoes was nearby. Tatteh burst out:
"No way! You slut! I won't eat your swinish food!"

The food stayed untouched. Gray steam evaporated on the windowpanes. A fly crawled along the rim of the plate. Tatteh left without
eating. Toybeh stayed seated on her cot, crying.

She cried a lot since coming back from the hospital. Mammeh
spent most of the time at Aunt Miriam's place, or at Bubbeh Rakhel's.
Toybeh cleaned and polished the house all by herself. She cooked, she
made Shabbehs ready . . . and she cried.

But she wouldn't stay in the room while Tatteh was eating. She
just sat on the threshold of the house. Only when Tatteh finished making the blessing and went to lie down did Toybeh come back, clear the
table, and eat alone, all by herself.

Since Toybeh came back, every Shabbes was a sad one. Tatteh
sang zmirehs sadly and Mammeh read her Yiddish version of the Bible
in an even sadder voice. Toybeh herself didn't sit at the table. She spent
her Shabbes days on her iron cot in the kitchen.

Toybeh wouldn't sit at the table even at the Seder on Pesach.
She prepared the whole Pesach in our house, recreated the slave cities
of Pithom and Ramses but Mammeh had to serve the dishes to the
table. Mammeh also had to take Toybeh's four cups of wine out to
her in the kitchen.

When it came time to recite: shfoykh hamoskho, "Pour out Thy
wrath . . ." Tatteh spit it out this year like it was blood. Toybeh
wouldn't open the door for it, Mammeh had to do it herself.

Toybeh stared into the open, dark doorway, wide-eyed. It seemed to me that only now did her eyes get back their original double color— blue and green. She stood as if she hoped that the open door would bring her deliverance, but when the door closed again and deliverance didn't come, Toybeh cried. Mammeh cried too. Only Tatteh kept on reciting the Haggadah.

But if you didn't know that Tatteh's voice was a little too quiet, like it is for most deaf people, you could think that he was also choking back the tears.

Chapter 21

The reddish-white flowers of the chestnut trees opened up after Pesach like the branches of a candelabra. White and blue stalks of lilac hung like colored birds over the limed, picket fence.

Yarmeh the Wagon Driver's omnibus and the shutters on the windows of our big and disorderly courtyard were bathed in sunlight and greenery. We came home from cheder when the roofs were still glowing golden and masses of brown, hairy, may bugs swarmed in the air, smelling of honey.

Yankl and I had new friends that summer, boys with strange names from the other courtyards. They came over in the evenings to listen to the wonderful tales that Yankl told.

I had no idea that this Yankl with the freckled face, whose stepmother called him ganef, thief, had such a treasure of stories. Not for nothing was he picked to play Yoysef Hatsadik, the biblical Joseph the Saint!

Not only our new friends and Yaninkeh, the Senior Prison Guard's daughter, heard Yankl's stories, but even my sister Toybeh, who could have had a child of her own by now, she also sat and listened.

Yankl told stories about calves and goats that never existed but were disguised as ghosts and demons, about a wandering Jew who traveled on foot over seas and oceans and never even got the hem of his kapoteh wet! One story Yankl told was about a robber, a murderer, who had a golden belt and a golden sword.

This murderer took seven daughters of princes as his concubines. He killed off their fathers and made himself emperor over the whole world. These seven concubines bore him seven times seven children each, both male and female. These seven times seven children also bore seven times seven children each until the whole world was full of the robber's children and children's children. Yankl said that even our fathers, our mothers, and our grandparents all came from that robber. Otherwise there wouldn't be a world.

Yankl told his stories half in Yiddish, half in Polish, so that
Yaninkeh the Senior Guard's daughter would understand it too.

She had grown up over the winter and she now had dimples in
her cheeks and rosy, milky skin.

Probably, it didn't dawn on anybody else, but it did seem to me
that Yankl told these stories not so much for my sake or for the sake
of our new friend's, but only for Yaninkeh.

She sat at Yankl's feet looking up at him with thoughtful eyes.
When Yankl finished a story, she jiggled his knee, and pleaded:

"Tell one more story, Yankl. Yaninkeh begs you. Tell!"

A few times, I saw how Yankl and Yaninkeh sat on the wagon
shaft of his father's omnibus eating out of a paper bag. Yankl told
me once that Yaninkeh begged him to become a goy, that is to say,
not right away but later, when he'd be all grown up. Her father had
told her that he would make a prison guard out of Yankl, they would
marry and live on the avenue where all the goyim lived.

He told me this in great secrecy. He said that he wouldn't convert
to Christianity. He didn't want to become a goy. He didn't like goyim
and he was afraid of them but he'd marry Yaninkeh anyway.

My blood froze. It seemed to me that already tomorrow he'd go
off, commit a sin, and convert.

So I told him that if, God forbid, he did convert, he'd not only
lose this world but the world to come as well. He'd have to endure the
suffering of dead sinners in their graves. I told him that the punishment
in the world to come was so great it couldn't be borne. He'd be roasted
and burned with glowing tongs. They would pull the hairs out of his
head one by one, and the nails from his fingers. They'd first burn out
one eye, then the other, and when you were already good and blind,
they'd make you able to see again so that they could burn your eyes
out all over again. And do you know what else? In the next world a
demon went around with a pair of shears and every day it snipped off
a little bit more of the circumcision of apostates.

Yankl was covered in sweat when I told him this.

"How d'ya know all this?" he asked in one breath. "You were
standing there?"

"What d'ya mean, how do I know? Who doesn't know that?"

It seemed that my talk went right to Yankl's head. He began
avoiding Yaninkeh and no longer came out in the evenings to tell his
stories. It seemed to me that he was also avoiding me.

When the week of the goyish Shevuoth holiday came, my mother
came home one day and told us that she had seen Yankl at the church
during a procession. He stood there without a cap on his head watching
the crucifixes and the little shikseh girls in white veils carrying effigies

of their Matka Boska, Mother of God. Yaninkeh also walked in the procession. She carried a red velvet cushion and wore a wreath of blue flowers on her head.

I was very sad to hear this piece of news. If Yankl was standing bareheaded watching the procession, it's a sign that he was going to convert. Maybe he had already done it?

I wanted to ask him. I waited for him at our door every evening but who'd seen him? He'd disappeared and didn't show himself.

I finally got to see him when our own Shevuoth holiday came. He was sitting once more with Yaninkeh on the wagon shaft of his father's omnibus.

I felt right away that he hadn't converted yet. First of all, he was speaking in Yiddish, second, if he'd have converted already, God forbid, he wouldn't be sitting here like this, so free and easy cracking sunflower seeds out of a paper bag.

I asked Yankl where he'd been? Why hadn't I seen him or Yaninkeh? The Senior Guard's daughter explained that during the procession, when Christians pray in church, she wasn't allowed to be friendly with me or with Yankl. It was a sin, she said.

But when the procession was over, she came back to us and on the eve of Shevuoth, we all went off to the pond to gather reeds.

Yaninkeh waded into the pond with bared knees. Her skin was brown and covered with fine golden hairs. Yankl didn't go in but lay on the grass, watching silently as Yaninkeh and I yanked at the reeds. When we came out with a big bunch, Yankl's eyes were smoky. He wouldn't look us in the face. Yaninkeh stood there laughing, her dress hiked up, the fine golden hairs on her skin showing, but she soon stopped laughing. It seemed to me that her eyes got smoky too. She quickly pulled down her dress and asked Yankl if he was mad at her.

He didn't answer but had an angry look on his face. In that minute, it seemed to me that Yankl didn't have freckles anymore but real holes in his face.

He took the bundle of reeds from us and carried it home himself, silent the whole way. Yaninkeh complained quietly to me that I'd told her to pull the reeds without Yankl.

But I hadn't told her that. Yankl just didn't want to go into the water.

I was sorry that I'd gone with them. Probably, I was the real reason Yankl was so quiet and mad.

But when we came home and smelled the aroma of butter cake in the courtyard, Yankl began to come to himself.

The reeds were quickly spread out and then hung up in all the houses, including the Senior Guard's house.

Yarmeh Wagon Driver's wife brought her baking to show us how well it had turned out and my mother showed off her cheesecakes to the Senior Guard's wife. Mammeh promised her that tomorrow, God willing, she'd tell her the story of Shevuoth.

My mother liked to show off her learning and the next day she told the whole story.

It was already evening. The sky was cool and streaked with reddish clouds. Both my mother and the Russian goyeh sat outside on the stoop. Mammeh explained in Polish who Ruth and Boaz were. How the goyeh Ruth, said to Naomi: "Your God is my God, and your people are my people." How Ruth came to Boaz in the field to gather stalks of corn, and how later, King David played his harp and sang like a bird.

Yankl, even though he could tell the most beautiful stories himself, now also sat and listened. Yaninkeh leaned her chin on Mammeh's knee and looked up at her with wide, blue eyes.

I looked at Yankl. His eyes were as blue as Yaninkeh's now. It seemed to me that Yankl was not Yankl but Boaz, and that Yaninkeh was not Yaninkeh, but Ruth. There was no field and no stalks of corn growing in our courtyard. Here, Ruth couldn't come to Boaz.

It was after all, only Yankl, but if he could play the saintly Joseph, why couldn't he be Boaz too?

On the second day of Shevuoth, I sat with Yankl in the courtyard looking out at the orchard where the sun hung over one of the trees like a big, lit up circle.

Yankl was mad at everybody in his house. He told me that in the morning he was late for the davening and his father, in front of everybody at the study house, delivered him such a whack that he, Yankl, was almost soaked in blood. He said he wouldn't forgive his father. He'd get even with him and he'd run off with Yaninkeh just like Boaz and Ruth.

I got all hot and bothered. Only yesterday, I myself had compared Yankl and Yaninkeh to Boaz and Ruth and now, take a look! He was saying the same thing himself!

"But Boaz didn't convert."

"How d'ya know that?"

"What d'ya mean, how'd I know? It says so in the toyreh."

"Did I say I'd convert?"

"What're you gonna do?"

"Yaninkeh will convert."

"What'll the Senior Guard say?"

"Does he have to know?"

I don't know why, but in that minute I was reminded of the sad story about Rudolph the deceiver and the fair Caroline who had been stolen out of her father's palace in the middle of the night.

I knew that apprentice boys and seamstress girls fell in love. Shabbes evenings they would go out strolling on the main road. I also heard songs about love but I couldn't imagine what love looked like exactly.

Now, while Yankl was talking so quietly and bitterly, it became clear to me that Yankl and Yaninkeh were in love.

True, I didn't see them strolling along the high road on Shabbes but I did meet them once behind the orchard fence. When they saw me, they broke apart at once and ran off. A dog came running from somewhere and took off after them. Another time, I saw Yaninkeh holding a cookie between her teeth and Yankl was nibbling at it from her mouth. That must be what's called being in love.

Yaninkeh came out, her flaxen hair lit up from the sun setting behind the orchard. She came toward us but thought better of it, stopped still a while, and went back into the house. Yankl looked at me sideways. After being silent awhile, he asked:

"You're not going anywhere?"

"No, I'm not going anywhere. Why? What's up?"

"Nothing. Just . . . But you see . . ." His voice got hoarser. "Yaninkeh and I decided to go pick stalks of corn today."

"What d'ya mean, stalks of corn? How did stalks of corn get here?"

"I told her," Yankl mumbled, barely breathing, "that she'd be Ruth and I'd be Boaz. I'll stand in the field and she'll come for the stalks of corn."

"Where d'ya have a field here? Where've you got stalks of corn here?"

"Its only a kind of game. We'll turn my father's omnibus into a field and the straw that's lying inside will become stalks of corn. Now d'ya get it?"

I got it, but I didn't like the field. The stalks in the omnibus smelled of sweat and altogether, what kind of crazy idea was this?

"We'll play make believe. What d'ya care?"

"I don't care but I also want to play."

"So what can you be? You're not Ruth and you're not Boaz."

Well yeh, Yankl was right. But what would I do with myself?

"Hide somewhere." Yankl began talking hurriedly, "here, behind the boards. When Yaninkeh and I are already inside the omnibus, you go sit on the wagon shaft and if somebody comes, cough."

Yankl's eyes looked at me with greenish fire, the same kind of eyes he had when the lame goy brought his stallion to his father's mare.

"You know what else?" Yankl grabbed my arm, "I'll give you my penknife."

I didn't want his penknife. I sensed that this Ruth and this Boaz were not a pair. It was altogether a pretty weird idea but I liked Yankl a lot and I didn't have the strength to say no to him. Besides, I was also in a fever. If I could have given a clear accounting of myself, I'd probably have said that I wanted to have a love affair with Yaninkeh too.

In the end, I hid myself behind the half-rotten boards. From there I saw Yankl crawl into his father's omnibus. The red mark of the sun followed at his feet.

Yankl gave a long whistle into the empty courtyard. It took a little while, then Yaninkeh came out of her house and crawled into the omnibus too, but not easily. Her dress tore and the uncovered piece of flesh was not brown like her legs but white like cheese.

When both of them were inside, I came out from behind the boards and sat down on the wagon shaft as Yankl had told me.

A dog came in from the street. It seemed to me it was the same dog that had followed Yankl and Yaninkeh earlier. He crawled along the wall of the courtyard, sniffing, then stopped in the middle of the courtyard and began chasing his tail.

I guarded Boaz and Ruth. Inside the omnibus it was quiet. The dog retreated a few steps and then began staring at me. He stared so long until he decided I didn't please him and he started barking.

My skin crawled. No sound came from the omnibus. It seemed to me that the dog was calling to someone to come and take a look.

The Guard's door opened and Yaninkeh's mother came out and l looked quickly around the courtyard. The dog became even more daring and began jumping toward the wagon shaft where I sat swallowed up in hellish fire.

I don't know whether I actually saw the Russian goyeh coming toward the omnibus or whether I only sensed it, but I tore myself away from the wagon shaft shrieking:

"Yankl, somebody's coming!"

The frightened voice of Yaninkeh's mother followed me:

"Stop . . . Stop . . . ! Where's Yaninkeh?"

But that didn't have such an effect on me as the dog. He chased me with such barking and such power that the back of my head began to ache.

I don't know how it happened but all of a sudden, I felt the dog's teeth stab the fleshy part of my thigh.

I fell face forward into the gutter. I must have screamed. I don't
know who picked me up. I didn't see anything. I only felt the steam
from mouths and in my ears echoed dully a hard, grim voice in Polish:
Merzavi'ets, sukin sin. Doh kriminalu! "You lowlife! Son of a bitch!
To prison with you!"

✑

Early the next morning, they called Itsheh the Healer to me. He stuck
his black, leather visor between my legs and poked around, squeezing
with his puffy, old fingers.

Mammeh stood at the bedside, cheeks on fire. Toybeh stared at
me from the foot of the bed.

Short of breath, Mammeh asked Itsheh the Healer if the dog wasn't,
God forbid, crazy. What should she do and where should she run?

Itsheh the Healer shoved his leather visor up his head, and
answered angrily:

"Don't run!" He screamed tightly, "if you'll run you'll get a stone
in your belly. Here," he said, "I'm writing you out a prescription for
a special kind of water. Make compresses for him every six hours. If
he doesn't get any better, call me, and we'll put a couple of leeches
on him."

"Why leeches?" Mammeh scowled. "My Beyrl, may he be separated from the living, never advised putting on leeches."

"And that's exactly why he died, that Beyrl of yours," answered
Itsheh the Healer, not to Mammeh but to Toybeh.

It seemed to me that he didn't talk to Mammeh at all, but to
Toybeh. Even though my leg was burning, I still noticed how he looked
at Toybeh with his big white beard.

"What's your name?" he asked and unexpectedly grabbed her
by the chin.

"Toybeh," my sister answered, scared.

"Who do you belong to?"

"I'm a member of the family . . ." Toybeh slowly tried to move
away from him, but this old man's puffy fingers suddenly dropped
down from her chin onto her big round breast.

She almost choked. Even though Itsheh the Healer was a respectable Jew and had a reputation in town as a big expert, still our Toybeh
had the nerve to throw off his hands and say angrily:

"I'm not sick. You don't need to examine me."

"Don't you have any respect for an elderly Jew?" Itsheh the Healer
was taken aback, his handsome beard awry.

"The elderly Jew shouldn't go crawling where he doesn't belong!"
Toybeh turned away, her face to the window and she didn't even answer
when the old healer said, "Good Day."

Compresses were put on my leg. Toybeh sat on my bed patting
my face with her warm hands. Tatteh didn't know how it happened or
why the dog had even bitten me. As soon as he came home, he bent
over my bed, felt my forehead, thanked God that I didn't have a fever
but thought that a piece of onion put on the wound couldn't hurt.

"No matter what, he's always got his onions!" Mammeh said
scornfully, furrowing her brow.

Itsheh the Healer wasn't called to me anymore, and my leg healed
without his leeches.

In our house, nobody talked about what had happened. My mother
didn't go anymore to visit the family of the Senior Guard. I heard that
Dr. Pzhilensky was called to Yaninkeh. She had a fever and her father
was looking for Yankl. He wanted to have him jailed.

But Yankl had taken off. Toybeh said that Yankl was a crazy dog,
a good-for-nothing, a thief! Why, he'd bitten Yaninkeh! What'd he want
from the little shikseh? What? I didn't know why he had bitten her
either. He really must be a crazy dog. Not for nothing did he disappear.

Mammeh came home once and said that Yarmeh the Wagon
Driver had found him, that great sage Yankl. He had probably hidden
himself at a goyeh's house near the Zamlineh part of town. She had
given him unkosher kielbasa sausage to eat, bought him a dark blue-
colored cap with a leather visor, and had talked him into converting.
Yarmeh the Wagon Driver found out and went there, gave his son two
fiery whacks, tore the boots and the dark blue cap off him, trussed him
up like a sheep, bound and tethered, and packed him off to Warsaw.

Who knows if I'll see Yankl ever again? Especially since my mother
was actually talking about moving out of here again.

Chapter 22

My leg healed. Nothing was left of the dog's bite but a reddish-blue, wrinkled scab that faded day by day.

Tatteh came home one evening, sweaty, overworked and asked for a basin of soap and water. He threw off his vest and undershirt and standing hairy and sweaty over the basin, he said that after Shabbes, God willing, we were all going to go out to a village.

Mammeh looked at him in surprise. She thought that he was probably drunk because first of all, what was all this washing up with soap in a basin of cold water on an ordinary Wednesday? And second of all, what was with this going out to villages?

Tatteh buried his bearded face in a big towel. He paced around the house, grunting, gritting his teeth and explained that he was washing up because he had just this minute come back from a long trip where he had to put up with heat and dust that was hard to take. So that was one thing. Second of all, he said that he'd made a business deal, a big one and because of it, we were going to go out to a village.

Mammeh didn't understand. Toybeh and I also didn't understand. Tatteh had never before made any big business deals, and never before did we have to go out to any villages.

So Tatteh explained that he, and his partner Mottl Shtroy, had rented the meadows in Leniveh, about seven miles from here for the whole summer. They were going to mow the hay and take off the gleanings. It'd last until the holidays, we should all live and be well. Mottl Shtroy had to stay here in town but he, Tatteh would go out to Leniveh. He had figured out that why should he have to go seven miles there and seven miles back every day when he could take himself out of here altogether—and be done with it!

Mammeh listened, wincing. Toybeh watched from the open door to the kitchen. Everybody was quiet, then Mammeh asked arrogantly:

"And where is it, this Lineveh of yours?"

"Its in a good area, its got everything—a forest, river, cheese, butter, eggs, and its dirt cheap."

"And where would we live, in this Lineveh of yours?" Mameh asked with her aristocratic attitude.

"We'll live, do'ntcha worry!"

Mammeh wasn't satisfied; she was frowning too much.

"This Lineveh must be out in the sticks."

"What kind of out in the sticks? It's right by the road and there's a town less than a mile away."

"For the whole summer?" Mammeh asked fearfully.

"What d'ya think, just for a day? And another thing, you'll be out in the fresh air."

"Never mind fresh air! What can you learn from peasants?"

"What d'ya want then?" Tatteh said, already getting angry, "that I should run seven miles there and seven miles back every day?"

"Who tells you to run? Go with a horse and cart."

Tatteh didn't answer. He ate the leftover grits without taste. He was good and aggravated.

My heart also ached. Summers in town were hot and there was nowhere to turn for relief and even if Tatteh drove out and came back every day, was this place suitable for people?

Why shouldn't we move out to Leniveh? Tatteh said that there was a forest and a river, and that we'd mow the hay. It would be a different kind of life altogether. And anyway, Yankl wasn't here anymore. You couldn't even look at the doorway where the Senior Guard lived. Blonde Yaninkeh didn't pay attention to me anymore. Simmeh-Yoysef's cheder was crowded and dark. Simmeh-Yoysef himself spent the whole day in bed groaning. So why wasn't it worthwhile for Mammeh to go out to Leniveh?

Toybeh also wanted to go. She already knew what a village was like but she didn't dare say anything while Tatteh was at home but you could see in her eyes that she would pack up and leave in a minute.

"Nu, what about you, Mendl?" Tatteh turned his beard to me, "To you its also out in the sticks?"

"No," I said, "I wanna go."

"Him he asks!" Mammeh interjected. "So that he won't have to go to cheder!"

"The rabbi doesn't teach us anything anyway." I said, getting bolder, "he lies in bed all day."

"So go! Who's stopping you?" Mammeh shook her head angrily. "I also have where to go. Warsaw is anytime as nice as Leniveh."

"Again with Warsaw!"

"Yes, again Warsaw. It seems to me, I have a child in Warsaw, no?"

"And Mendl's not your child?" Tatteh shoved his beard forward.

"But why to Lineveh? Why? At least, if it was to Garbatkeh . . ."

"Garbatkeh is for rich people, for the summer colonists. Luzeh the hay dealer hasn't got enough money for any Garbatkehs."

Enough. With this Tatteh finished. Mammeh went around mad. Toybeh straightened out Tatteh's bed and served the food to the table. Tatteh said nothing.

I stopped going to cheder altogether. Dr. Fiddler had to be called to Simmeh-Yoysef; they said he needed a lot of pity now.

The other boys and I roamed around idly among the peasant carts, poking sacks of wheat and cracking nuts that came from the Land of Israel. Nobody at home knew whether we were staying here or going. Shabbes after eating, Tatteh took a nap and afterwards he went off to see his partner. Toybeh sat in the courtyard. Mammeh also wanted to go out but Bubbeh Rakhl came to visit.

Mammeh didn't need more. She burst out with complaints, wailing that he, that is Tatteh, wanted to send her off somewhere out in the sticks for the whole summer. He had no pity on her young years! He was a murderer, not a husband! This was enough reason for her to end it all!

Bubbeh Rakhl had never gotten along with my father, that is to say, they never, God forbid, actually quarreled but both Bubbeh Rakhl and Tatteh had complaints against each other. More than once, Tatteh said that all the bad that Mammeh had in her came from her mother but Bubbeh felt that after having brass door handles with her first husband, her daughter had been deceived by my father, her second husband. Now, with Mammeh complaining so bitterly to Bubbeh Rakhl, it was pretty clear that Bubbeh would also tell her not to go.

But in the end, I was altogether wrong about her.

"You should thank God," Bubbeh answered after Mammeh finished, "You should thank God that you have such a chance."

My mother was confused. "You too, Mammeh?"

"What d'ya mean, me too? Who'd say no?"

"But to such a hick place?"

"To say it's a hick place in the summertime? What've you got here? What? And another thing," Bubbeh turned to face me, "Take a look at the boy, how pale he is and you yourself—d'ya look any better?"

"I don't want to go to any villages!"

"What d'ya mean, you don't want to? It's always the way a person wants? And another thing, what's it going to cost you? What?"

Mammeh was angry but she kept quiet. Bubbeh talked a lot more. She praised Tatteh and said that her own husband, that is to say, Zaydeh, would never have made an effort for his wife to get any fresh air. As she was leaving, she told Mammeh that she should, for the sake of heaven, not do anything else. In the evening after Havdoleh, Tatteh asked:

"Nu Frimmet, what's left?"

"I'll think it over some more. It's not a burning issue yet."

On Sunday, we still didn't know what she'd decided, but all day she rummaged around among the linen. She sewed and she darned. Toybeh stood over a washtub, red-faced and busy, doing the laundry. Mammeh took down two dusty bottles of blueberry syrup from the cupboard and asked Toybeh:

"What do you think, should I take this?"

"Better take it. Summertime there's all kinds of sicknesses going round."

On Wednesday morning, after having spent a few nights lying on uncovered red linen, a peasant cart and horse came to our house, and a young goy, as tall as a tree, came in with his whip raised and asked in Polish:

"*Yadzhehs, tshi ni'eh yadzhehs?* Are we going or not?"

"Yadzhehs, yadzhehs," Tatteh answered gleefully. He shook his head at Toybeh and said:

"Nu, start taking things out."

It was the first time since Toybeh came back from the hospital that Tatteh had spoken directly to her.

So we loaded up the red featherbed, took the noodle board and the rolling pin. Mammeh put the two bottles of blueberry syrup into a tub and dishes and bowls were tucked into the bedding. We said goodbye to the big courtyard, the orchard, and to Yarmeh the Wagon Driver's omnibus.

Tatteh still had to make a stop to see his partner, Mottl Shtroy and he told us to wait for him at the city gate. Mammeh didn't want to get on the cart right away. She wasn't going to let herself be tossed around on a cart through the whole city. She'd also meet us at the city gate.

So, never mind. Meanwhile, Toybeh and I sat ourselves on the cart, Toybeh on top of the soft bedding with her back to the young goy and me in the front near the horse.

The air in the courtyard was blue, the rooftops glistened with dew, and the weak sun trembled among the trees in the orchard. A sheet hung over the window of the Senior Guard's place, Yaninkeh was probably sleeping. Yankl wasn't here, either. I didn't have anyone to say goodbye to. I was going off to a village and I should've felt good but I dunno why, I just didn't feel right.

Yarmeh the Wagon Driver and his wife came out to say goodbye to us. He wiped his hand on a bundle of straw and told me to go in good health and be a decent person, not like that bastard of his, Yankl.

Yarmeh's wife kissed Mammeh and wished us good luck on the trip and we should meet only at celebrations.

The cart moved off. The streets were cool and half-empty, store-fronts locked and iron bars still in place. A boy from Simmeh-Yoysef's cheder ran out of his house and yelled up to me:

"Mendl, where're you going?"

"To Leniveh." I stood up so that he'd see all of me. "To get some fresh air."

He looked foolish to me now. If I'd had a choice and if his mother would've given him food for the trip, I'd have made my father take him along to Leniveh too.

The city fell away behind us, only the goyish hospital could still be seen with the clump of trees that looked like a single tree.

The sun, now thick, was already hanging over the cross on the Bernardine Church. The shadows around the poplar trees on the road fell away into the fields. It was bright everywhere.

Tatteh was already waiting at the city gate but Mammeh wasn't there yet. Tatteh looked the cart over from all sides, felt the bedding, tested the rope again and told me to take off my coat. He said it was going to be a hot day and I'd roast.

We waited for some time until Mammeh finally showed up, short-winded and overheated. She said she'd have come sooner but she had to find a parasol.

At last, we were on our way. Mammeh sat in the middle under her opened parasol that cast a pale green sheen, making her look like a mushroom.

Wooden houses with straw roofs were scattered here and there in the fields and they also looked like mushrooms. Grain was sprouting greenish in the light. The Jewish cemetery came into sight. There among the trees lay our Moysheh.

Mammeh closed the parasol and stared. She looked back a few times until the fence got smaller and melted away in the heat.

A wooden bridge over a river came into view. Barefoot peasant women in rolled-up flannel shifts were beating pieces of laundry with wooden sticks. Our horse and wagon stopped. The peasant unhitched the horse and led him to the stream to be watered.

We also got down from the cart. Mammeh had brought warm tea, bread and butter, hard-boiled eggs, even whisky. We sat down by the water under the only tree and began eating.

Tatteh took small sips of whisky while the peasant threw his head back and swallowed smartly, right down to the bottom of the glass. Mammeh dunked a piece of roll into the glass of tea and Toybeh and I drank half a glassful of tea each. We continued on our way satisfied and full.

It was midday. Tired spotted cows wandered slowly through the meadows. A peasant raised his hand to shade his brow and stared at the big, white sun that was burning our shoulders.

The road was empty. Nobody was going to the city today because it was just an ordinary day. An old woman walked along carrying a bundle and a sweaty, blond Jew was goading a stubborn, yellow spotted calf.

Our horse stopped again.

"Yanishev," said Tatteh climbing down from the cart. Four bare and peeling wooden poles held up a small vestibule that led into an inn. A lanky Jew with a greenish-grey beard came out onto the balcony of the inn:

"Shulem aleykhem!"

"Aleykhem shulem!"

"How're you?"

It's Lozeh the Innkeeper. He helped us down from the rumpled bedding and yelled into the dark doorway:

"Sureh! Sureh!"

Out came a tall, thin girl with frightened, blue eyes. She blinked as if she had just come out of the darkness. When she saw who was climbing down from the cart, she clapped her hands:

"Vey'z mir!" and ran back into the dark doorway.

They knew my father well here at this inn so because of him they were happy to see us too. They treated us like family. Sureh, lanky Lozeh's daughter who earlier had come out barefoot, now bustled around in a red blouse and high heeled, laced-up shoes. She put in front of us borsht laced with sour cream, a big loaf of rye bread with caraway seeds, butter that she herself had churned, some cheese and asked us if we wanted some warm milk straight from the cow, or maybe some cottage cheese?

"So, you say you're going to Leniveh?" Lanky Lozeh asked slowly.

"Yeh, y'already know that."

"Did'ya pay a lot for the meadows?"

"Enough."

"And what d'ya think? There'll be a profit?"

"I think that God forbid, we won't lose."

"Izzat so? So what else is new?"

"The same."

Lozeh rolled a cigarette from a wad of tobacco. After a few minutes of silence, he asked again:

"D'ya get any letters from your Laybkeh?"

"He doesn't write much."

"When's he coming home, with luck?"

"For the holidays I think, we should all live and be well."

"He at least made some money in the Russian army?"

"How should I know?"

"I know him, your Laybkeh." Lozeh smoked his cigarette. "I've heard he's a good craftsman."

"Yeh, he could be a master craftsman already if not for the Russian army."

"We'll probably see him if he comes."

"Probably."

Tatteh made the blessing. Flies crawled around our emptied bowls. The peasant had already removed the feedbag hanging from the horse's ears. A big, yeasty shadow settled around the inn.

Mammeh was the first to get up. She opened her parasol and went out arrogantly like some rich woman.

The whole time that lanky Lozeh was talking to Tatteh, Mammeh didn't say anything but made an angry face, a sign that the conversation didn't appeal to her.

Only when we were again sitting on the bedding and lanky Lozeh and his daughter had gone back inside the inn after seeing us off, did Mammeh let herself be heard from: "Why'd he ask so much about Laybkeh? Why?"

"Its a worry?" Tatteh shrugged his shoulders.

"That's his daughter, that skinny thing?"

"Yeh, his one and only."

"Some bargain!"

Tatteh looked off into the distance. The horse was plodding along tired even though it had rested.

"He doesn't have a wife, that Lozeh?" Mammeh asked again.

"A widower, it shouldn't happen to anybody!" Tatteh answered, absorbed in thought, as he stretched out his arm to the distance. "There, over there is Leniveh."

"Where?" I stood up quickly.

"There behind the poplar trees."

"Is it still far to go?"

"A good half hour."

I was impatient. I kept standing up and looking. The horse steered onto a sandy road, axles creaking heavily. Several times our peasant took off his cap in front of the limed blue shrines in which the Holy Mother stood with withered flowers at her bare feet.

The sun slanted behind a stable. The more it bent to the other side of the rooftop, the more the sky was covered in melted copper. Behind the fences, dogs started barking. Cows came toward us leaving behind big manure patties in the sand. Church bells began pealing forlornly in the distance and blue ribbons of smoke rose up from the chimneys. The odor of bran mixed with warm milk fresh from the cows was in our noses.

Chapter 23

Tatteh said that he'd rented a house with two windows and a vestibule from a peasant he knew in Leniveh.

But when we came to the peasant's hut, it turned out that he wasn't even expecting us today. He said that the merchant, that is to say, Mottl Shtroy, had told him that we were actually supposed to come a week later. But never mind, since we're already here, we could stay in the barn tonight and tomorrow, said the peasant, he'd clean out the hut and we'd be able to live there for the whole summer.

Mammeh stood by silently. It was hard to know whether she was silent because she was angry or because she was so upset. She still hadn't closed her parasol even though it was now good and dark all over the village.

Tatteh was mad at the peasant.

"What d'ya mean, you weren't expecting us? I told ya clearly that we were coming today."

"No, The other merchant told me different."

A dog with a stick between its front legs was trying to get at us from its doghouse. Two blond little shkotsim in short linen pants, hiding behind a wall of the hut, peeked out at us in surprise.

The peasant's young wife with heavy, milk-laden breasts carried two stools out of the hut, wiped them off with her apron, and said in Polish:

"*Proseh, ni'ekh pantsvoh shondzheh.* Please, be so good as to sit down."

She didn't bring out a stool for me but I didn't care. Standing up you could see the stars and the whole sky better. I'd never seen such a black sky with so many millions of stars.

So what if we had to sleep in a barn one night? It seemed to me that Mammeh should be pleased since she always slept in a bed with fleas and bedbugs, so for once we'd try lying on freshly mown hay. It must be special.

Toybeh told me that there was actually no greater pleasure than burrowing your head into fresh hay. She said it was like lying among grapes and apples.

But I'm not familiar with the smell of grapes. At Aunt Nemmi's on Rosh Hashanah, when they made the blessing over grapes, we had to make do with plums. But whichever way it was, whether fresh hay really smelled like grapes or not, I slept through the night in Leniveh as if with one breath.

When I opened my eyes, little blue streaks of daylight came through the cracks. Tatteh was already gone. It seemed that I'd missed the peasant's rapping on the window.

Here I was, sitting up on the warm rumpled hay, in a tall dark building with swallows flying around above me.

I saw my mother sitting in a corner without her parasol now. She looked like a hen snuggling into its own feathers, holding a lock of her wig in her mouth.

Not far from me, Toybeh was scrambling out of the hay. Her black head was covered more with hay than with hair. She yawned widely and spread her hands out like a cross. Mammeh, all the while combing a lock of her wig, asked her:

"Did you sleep?"

"A kind of sleep."

"And you, Mendl?"

"Very good, Mammeh."

"The fleas didn't bite you?"

"What fleas? Where've you got fleas?"

Mammeh stayed quiet for a while, then answered: "You know what I'll tell you? I also don't know where the night got to."

"Look here, Auntie," said Toybeh in Polish: "*Ni'eh tak di'abel strashni, yak no maloyon*. The devil's not as black as he's painted."

"Nu, okay, but I don't wish it on my enemies to have to spend the night in a barn."

"Its not so bad," I called out.

"Everything's okay by him."

"As long as we don't have to sleep here every night . . ." said Toybeh. "The peasant is going to clean out the house today."

The peasant kept his word. He took out all his bedding, pots and bowls, leaving only the beds, the table, the stools and the holy pictures on the walls.

It went against the grain for Mammeh to have to lie in a bed and look at a red oil lamp day and night lighting up the dark, silent

face of the *Shvi'enteh Paneh*, the Holy Mother with the infant at her
breast. On the wall over the other bed where Tatteh and I slept, was
a brown wooden cross, encircled with black beads.

Many times I dreamed about this cross, that it came down from
the wall, weighed my heart down and crushed it.

Tatteh was ready to tell the peasant to take down the pictures,
but Mammeh held him back:

"Nu, stop already," she said, afraid. "I don't need anything more
now!" So because of the *Shvi'enti Paneh* and the crucifix, Tatteh had
to leave his tallis and tfilin outside.

The two blond, little shkotsim sneaked in and whispered quietly
in Polish:

"*Zid seh modli abats.* The Jew is praying for us"

"*Ah, ni'ekh seh modli,* Let him pray," answered their mother.
"When a Jew prays," she said, "it's a sign that you can believe him.
And you," she said, "*vinostah seh stond.* Get out of here!"

"*Ah ti seh modlis?* You're praying?" the two shkotsim once asked
me when no one else was around.

"Of course! What d'ya mean? All Jews have to pray."

"So why don't you wear a 'tsitseleh' like your father does?"

I told them that, with luck, one day I'd get married and then I'd
put on a tsitseleh, that is to say, a tallis. They broke out laughing and
from then on, they called me nothing else but "tsitseleh."

That didn't bother me because I knew that they were just
poor shkotsim unfortunately, and they didn't begin to know what a
tallis was. And another thing, they were decent shkotsim with
suntanned faces and blue, fearful eyes. We'd become friends right away
and besides, why should it bother me that my father wasn't known
here as Luzeh the Hay Dealer, but as Pan Merchant, and that my
mother sat in the fields during the mowing of the hay and read her
storybooks?

Here in the village they accepted my mother better than in the
city. Here they knew that this Pani Merchant was educated. They knew
that her first husband was a respected old-time healer, and if you had
such a person for a husband, then you yourself also knew something
about sickness.

So the wives of the peasants began coming—whoever had a pain
in the side, a cough, or was just plain yellow like wax, came to her.
Mammeh placed cupping glasses as a remedy for various ailments,
advised giving a teaspoon of Spanish Fly to this patient, or to massage
another with pig fat. The peasant wives would kiss Pani Merchant's

hand, go home, and send others to her. So Mammeh's reputation in Leniveh grew from hour to hour and so did her vanity.

Her skin got brown and her warm double chin folded over. She went around the village holding herself straight and proud; she was always presentable, always had her parasol open, and always wore the white jabot around her neck.

I had it good in Leniveh too, maybe even better than my mother did.

Dawn—the sun was still asleep when the cocks began crowing their first cock-a-doodle hymn and my father and I were already waking up. We poured ritual water over our fingernails, recited the morning prayer, and immediately went out to the fields.

White dew already lay on the meadows just as it did on the windowpanes in autumn. The greenish-yellow grain stood with sagging heads, worn and slumbering, and the sun rose over the forest like a big golden plate. Stalls opened up and lazy rested cows began wandering out to the pastures.

The dew rose slowly from the fields like froth; blue ribbons of smoke began rising from the low-set chimneys, a sign that large cast-iron pots of potatoes and borsht were already cooking.

Leniveh was not big, some twenty-odd huts thrown together, one on top of another like stuffed, wet sacks. The huts stood empty from morning to night. All the goyim worked in the fields, their sharpened blue scythes ringing out thin and far, cutting one row, then another, and the damp grasses laid themselves out obediently like living but sickly souls.

Tatteh davened in the forest, standing tall and white in tallis and tfiln, saying his prayers into the old pine tree which had probably never heard such weird chanting before. Somewhere in the depths a cuckoo bird warbled, hollowly and secretively. Young, overworked shiksehs raised their faces, leaned on their rakes a while, and counted how many times the cuckoo trilled out its hymn. According to the cuckoo's count, the shiksehs knew how many more weeks they still had to wait for a suitor to show up, how many children God would grant them, and how many more years each of them was destined to live.

At noon, when the sun was white hot on the bent shoulders of the peasants, women would come out of their huts carrying double earthenware pots of food for their men in the fields.

Toybeh also came out with a double pot. She was even browner than Mammeh, a flowered peasant kerchief wound around her head. Here in the village she looked taller and fuller than Mammeh. She was barefoot like all the peasant women, smiling broadly, her sides quivering like a young colt.

Mammeh didn't eat with us. She said it wasn't fitting for her to eat in the fields. She had to have a table, a tablecloth, a fork, and besides, she didn't like it that strange, goyish eyes were staring right into her mouth. Never mind. So she ate in the house.

But if she'd have asked me, I'd have told her that as long as I'm living, I've never tasted food so good as right here in the field among these peasants and shiksehs.

They laid down their scythes and rakes, sat themselves down at the edge of the grain fields or in the woods under a tree. The burning sun looked down into the pots, the forest rustled in the depths, and every minute there was a different bird and a different kind of warbling. The sweaty toilers ate, mouths chomping quietly and seriously.

Tatteh, brown and barefoot just like the peasants, with his beautiful, grey-black beard, sat in a buttoned vest with the farm hands and the shiksehs. The peasants crossed themselves while Tatteh recited the blessing.

Mammeh came to the field when the sun was already moving away from the middle of the sky. She was always too late to see the dew on the grass, hear the call of the cuckoo, or smell the satisfying odor of burning wood rising in ribbons out of the chimneys.

Mammeh came with her parasol, sat down in the shade at the edge of the woods, and began reading her storybook.

I don't know why Mammeh needed her storybooks now. Reading was good in the wintertime when the windowpanes were covered with ice and the kitchen was warm.

By all means, let her see how Pietrek, Yanek, and I spent a day in the fields.

I rolled around in the high grass, crawled on top of the piles of hay, helped gather it together, and one peasant actually gave me a scythe and taught me how to use it. The scythe was too long for me; it was too heavy at the tip. But I worked anyway and ended up stabbing myself in the foot. A row of grasses fell down, spattered with blood.

At the same time, Mammeh jumped up from reading and screamed that she didn't need any Lenivehs and what did he, Tatteh, want from her young years! From being a well-to-do woman with brass handles on the doors, she had now become a peasant woman in Leniveh! And now to add to all her troubles, I'd gone and hurt my leg, nothing less than the same leg that was bitten by a dog on the holiday of Shevuoth.

Tatteh carefully explained to her that Leniveh wasn't to blame at all. I myself had crawled where I wasn't supposed to go and that she should stop screaming because the goyim were staring and poking fun.

And really, what was the whole commotion all about if nothing hurt me? For a little while, I hopped about on one foot like a tethered horse, but as soon as I was able to walk straight, I jumped onto a straw-colored horse and without a saddle, rode all the way home together with Pietrek and Yanek.

No, my mother wasn't right. It was much better here in Leniveh, in the sticks than in Konskewola with the brass handles on all the doors.

But for all that, when Shabbes came, there was sadness and a yearning in the heart.

Friday at dawn, before even Tatteh and I got up, Toybeh was already running to the neighboring village to buy a pound of little fishes, a piece of veal, and two or three small challahs. But you couldn't make tsholnt here. Even though Toybeh was a great housekeeper and could cook the produce of the fields, still the food here didn't have the flavor and the smell of Shabbes.

The Shabbes table with the white tablecloth and the two silver-plated candlesticks were missing, as was the yellow sand on the floor and even old Pavlova who lit the stove in the kitchen for Shabbes. Here in Leniveh, Friday evening fell later than it did in town. Here you didn't hear the storekeepers banging their shops closed, here you didn't see late-coming Jews hurrying by, their beards freshly washed and their side curls still wet.

Friday evening was just like any other day in the week, the church bells pealed, the goyim came home with rakes and scythes on their shoulders singing their songs, the cows lowed as usual, the same as any other evening in the year. Even the sun, that on Friday evening before candle lighting was so fiery over the shul, went down here pale, as if it was cold.

We, the only Jews in Leniveh, were also cold, even though the smell of peppered fish and roasted veal settled in our mouths. Under the oil lamp, the *Shvi'enti Paneh* the Holy Mother, smelled of Shabbes cooking, but we didn't make Shabbes in the house.

Sweaty and brown from spending the whole week in the sun, we washed ourselves at the peasant's pump and then clean and dressed after six days of living like the goyim, we went out to the freshly mown meadow to make Shabbes. On one side, the grain swayed peacefully; on the other side, the forest lay in deep-blue calm. Our Shabbes table was a piece of field between the forest and the growing rye.

Here Mammeh spread out an old tablecloth, placed the thin, small-town candles into four hollowed out potatoes and made the blessing over them, not like at home standing up, but sitting on the ground with her feet tucked under her.

It could be that here in this bare field surrounded by a black, star-studded sky, Mammeh's candle lighting meant more than it did in our old home.

Tatteh's welcoming the Shabbes also had to be done differently here. Tatteh, belted for prayer, stood up expansively, facing the dark forest and sang into it the *l'khu neraneneh* and the *lekho doydi* Shabbes melodies.

Here my father was not just Reb Luzeh with the city ways and absent-minded, grey eyes that never demanded anything more than what was destined, nor was he the hay dealer who lived on the horse and wagon, and he wasn't even "Pan Merchant," who barefoot and wearing a pair of linen pants, helped out by working in the fields.

Here Tatteh was one of God's Jews, one of those who together with Moysheh Rabeynu went out from ancient Egypt and stood at Mount Sinai. I developed great respect for my father. I sang and davened along with him even if it was in a disorganized way and even though my village friends, Pietrek and Yanek, snickered. Still, I now felt bigger and stronger than they.

I noticed that Toybeh also had great respect for Tatteh now.

He acted different to her here. He was no longer angry, he no longer yelled, and he ate the food she made for him. Many times, he stared at her warmly and long. Toybeh also was different. She gave off the smell of fresh air and sunshine all the time.

"Tatteshi," she said when he stood overworked in the middle of the field, "Tatteshi, I brought you something to eat."

Tatteshi left everything and went with his daughter to the edge of the forest. He looked her over, her strong, brown legs, her whole figure. After eating the meal on Shabbes, when he was resting at the edge of the forest and quietly finishing reciting a chapter of the Mishnah, he asked Mammeh:

"What d'ya say to Toybeh?"

Mammeh didn't raise her spectacles from her storybook but sniffed into it.

"What should I say?"

"A girl straight like a tree, may no evil befall . . ." A little while later, he added: "If a bit of a proper match would happen . . ."

"Here in Leniveh, you want a match to happen and a proper one yet too?"

"Its the same everywhere, Frimmet."

"But there are only shkotsim here in Leniveh."

Tatteh didn't answer, he recited another sacred verse, and after several minutes, again said: "Its a pity to me, this girl . . ."

"Who told her to . . . ?" Mammeh quietly answered.

Toybeh came out of the forest now, dressed in her Shabbes clothes, well rested and with a flowered kerchief thrown over one shoulder, beautiful, blooming—but sad.

She had no one here in the village. The shkotsim eyed her from under their visors but she avoided them. All week she toiled in the house and slept heavily, breathing healthy and deep. Only on Shabbes when she had nothing to do, she tossed and turned in her bed and sometimes she even talked in her sleep. After eating, she wandered around in the forest or among the grain fields. It seemed like she was looking or waiting for someone.

Maybe, she'd actually met somebody?

Chapter 24

It was the beginning of the week and Toybeh was cooking supper. The work in the fields was in full swing and a light breeze was rustling, hardly noticeable. A small white cloud could be seen far off in the distance behind the last hut. You'd hardly have noticed it if you didn't raise your head and look carefully.

The peasants, squinting up to the sky, said that we should hurry up because a storm was coming. They started working faster, a sweaty smell pouring from their overheated bodies. Little by little, the white cloud filled with blueness, and hardly noticeable to the eye, it began moving closer to the huts. The sun dipped a few times behind a big, wide shadow as if under a cool sheet.

Uneasy sounds came from the forest. Birds started circling over the grain in confusion and a horse whinnied. A peasant woman, sleeves rolled up, came out of her hut and began quickly gathering the bit of laundry drying on the fence.

The darkening blue under which the sun had disappeared, settled on the stacks of hay. Dust from the dirt road tumbled in the air together with the falling leaves. The peasants grabbed their rakes and scythes, left the cut grasses lying where they fell and rushed off to the nearby church, or else they went straight home.

At the first rustle Mammeh ran home with her parasol open. Tatteh and I stayed in the field figuring that it would pass.

All at once, from one end of the sky to the other, there was a stab of hot-blue lightning and a minute later the first thunderclap, thick and round, burst from the forest.

There was no point in waiting. We grabbed what we could and started running. A second thunderclap, sharp and pointed, followed. It seemed to me that it was not far from us. A stale smell of sulphur settled in the air.

I ran, reciting prayers all the while. Not far from our hut, it suddenly began to pour, beating at us slantwise as if with taut whips.

Toybeh came running toward us with a sack, quickly threw it over my head, grabbed me by the arm and dragged me into the house. Tatteh came in a few minutes later, drenched, his beard sopping wet, his shirt clinging to his body.

Crosses stood in the neighbor's windows. The wind suddenly gusted at the blacksmith's fence, raising it like a big piece of kindling wood and hurled it away. Nobody went out to straighten it. It was as if the whole village had all at once died out.

Suddenly, a living soul appeared. All alone, under the downpour, he ran head down and fell into our vestibule. Nothing less but he must have fallen from the sky together with the rain! This person was barefoot, thin, wearing a long, drenched kapoteh that shone like black sheet metal. Over his shoulder was thrown a pair of boots that were full of water. He was rumpled and looked like an old boot himself.

"*Ni'ekh bedzeh pokhvaloni.* Christ be blessed," he said in peasant Polish.

"*Na vi'eki vi'ekuv,* Forever and ever," Tatteh answered in the same peasant Polish.

"*Ah skond toh?* Where is this?" The one who fell in raised a skinny, bony face. We all stared at him. Tatteh quietly asked:

"It seems to me . . . a Jew?"

"A Jew. What else?" The other said straightening himself out, and shaking the rain off like a dog when it comes out of the water.

"Shulem aleykhem, Jew," Tatteh said and stretched out his hand.

"Aleykhem shulem. Go know that Jews live here!"

"Where are you from?"

"From Bzhozowa."

"Where is it, this Bzhozowa?"

"Some four viorsts from here."

"You aren't something of a klezmer musician?"

"God forbid, how do I come to klezmer music?"

Tatteh smiled. He'd always thought of klezmer musicians as fools and lazy good-for-nothings. "Nu, come in. Take off your kapoteh. You're soaked through."

"Who'd have expected this? I went out in the morning and it was a heat wave."

He threw the boots off his shoulder and the water poured right out of them like out of a watering can. He took off the kapoteh that looked like sheet metal with some difficulty, and he was left standing in an old, ragged, unbuttoned vest.

"What kind of a Jew are you?"

"A shoemaker."

"A shoemaker yet! How does a shoemaker get here in such a storm?"

"This isn't my first time here. I go traveling through the villages fixing shoes, but go be a prophet and know that a Jew lives here! Believe me, I'm very happy!"

This shoemaker had a sparse little beard and thin veined hands. He spoke like a Litvak, smiled and coughed.

Toybeh turned on the lamp and warm shadows settled over the house. Mammeh sat, face furrowed, glanced at the stranger sideways, as if she couldn't believe that someone had come in and that what he said was real.

The thunder quieted down. The shoemaker dried himself off. Actually, he should have left already by now, but Mammeh told him to stay and eat supper with us.

He told us at the table that he wasn't from around here. He was from Brisk (Brest-Litovsk); he was still a bachelor and he didn't have a mother. He had nobody here in Poland but he had a father who was the head of a yeshivah, in Leipzig Germany.

"Is that so? How come a head of a yeshivah has a son who's a shoemaker?"

He didn't know himself. But at home there were, may no evil befall . . . a lot of children, boys and girls and no livelihood, so his stepmother apprenticed him to a shoemaker.

Mammeh's face was no longer furrowed and she no longer looked at him so coolly. She listened attentively now. "What's your father's name?" she asked warmly.

"Yankev-Yitskhok."

"If he's in Germany, then he must know German, your father, no?" she asked further.

"Probably. What then, he wouldn't know German?"

"And what's your name?"

"Wolf."

Listen to that! Wolf yet! My father has two sons-in-law and both of them are named Wolf. One is a butcher; the second one fixes wagon wheels, and shoes horses too. But this one here, this stranger, this shoemaker with the Litvak accent, with the little smile on one side of his mouth, he was also called Wolf?

This was a surprise to me.

It seemed that Mammeh didn't care for his name. So the following morning she began referring to him as "the little shoemaker," and that's how he was known forever afterward.

The little shoemaker didn't go home that night. They fixed up a cubicle for him where a crock of cabbage was pickling and where the hens had their roosts. Before going to sleep, he thanked us. He looked at our bare feet and asked if we didn't need shoes fixed sometimes. He was a good craftsman, he said, he'd even worked in Warsaw once.

That night, Toybeh tossed and turned in her bed. Several times, Mammeh called out:

"Luzeh, are you sleeping?"

But Tatteh was tired and snoring loudly. It seemed to me that Tatteh was the only one sleeping that night.

I was also tossing and turning. I thought that the little shoemaker bedded down in the cubicle must be a lamed vovnik, one of the hidden righteous men for whose sake the world continues to exist. He looked like one of them, thunder and lightening had brought him here, and his father was the head of a yeshivah. What kind of shoemaker had a father who was the head of a yeshivah? And anyway, we were all so uncomfortable now. Toybeh tossed and turned in her bed all the time—all this just couldn't be happening for no reason.

In the morning when Tatteh had already poured the ritual water over his fingernails and Mammeh's face peeked out sleepily from under the covers, the little shoemaker was ready to go on his way.

Standing in the house with yesterday's boots thrown over his shoulder, he thanked them again for supper and also for the bed for the night. He had added a pair of Mammeh's shoes to the boots thrown over his shoulder. She had given them to him to fix the day before.

Toybeh's face was stuck into the pots. She was standing now, not in her short, red flannel shift but in a long dress, not barefoot but in the lace-up shoes she wore on Shabbes. She was tall and well put together, like a narrow watering can.

The little shoemaker, well rested, talked to Mammeh first, then to Tatteh, but he kept looking into the kitchen where Toybeh was preparing food.

Actually he was looking at her shoes because just before leaving, he slowly asked:

"You bought these shoes or you had them made?"

Toybeh bent her face even more and began blowing on the grate.

"Upon my life, you need a pair of shoes." The little shoemaker bent down knowingly.

"Who's got money for that?" Toybeh answered somewhat angrily, her cheeks puffing on the grate.

"But you don't even need money. I'll make it for you without any money." Toybeh didn't answer.

The shoemaker said goodbye for the third or fourth time, and went out shoulders hunched, looking even smaller than yesterday.

An echo of the shoemaker's dry Litvak way of talking stayed in the house. Toybeh straightened herself out. Tatteh was in a hurry to get out to the field.

The shoemaker was already some way off when Mammeh suddenly broke the silence:

"Luzeh," she said, "maybe we should invite him for Shabbes?"

Tatteh didn't hear. His head was already in the field among the haystacks but since I was already dressed, I called out that I could run out and tell him to come for Shabbes.

"Don't," Tatteh suddenly raised his head, "it's not necessary."

"Why not?"

"I dunno . . . some kind of a shoemaker there . . ."

"And if he's a shoemaker, does that mean he isn't a human being? You yourself heard that his father is the head of a yeshiveh."

"Here's a three kopek coin for all of his being the head of a yeshiveh . . . somewhere off in Leipzig. Where is it anyway, this Leipzig?"

"Wherever it is, it is. But we have to invite him as a guest for Shabbes."

"For all I care . . . invite him."

"What d'ya say, Toybeh?"

"What should I say?"

It smelled of tree sap outside. The little shoemaker had already gotten as far as the big wooden cross that stood at the crossroads.

"Hey you," I called out. "Tell me . . . You!"

The boots on the shoulder turned around to the cross. The shoemaker looked at me thoughtfully, face narrowed. I told him that Mammeh asked that he come to us as a guest for Shabbes.

His bony, hard face filled out with dimples. Now I saw that he wasn't as homely as he had seemed in the house.

"As a guest, you say?"

"Yeh, as a guest."

"How old ar'ya, young man?"

"What's it your business?"

"It's my business."

"How old I am, I am. But Mammeh is inviting you."

"And what's your name?"

"What's it your business?"

"It's my business."

"My name's Mendl."

"And the other one, the girl. . . . Is she your sister?"

"Yeh, she's my sister, from the same father."

"Isn't your mother her mother?"

"No, she's her aunt."

"D'ya have other sisters?"

"What's it your business?"

He laughed deeply, not at all like a little Litvak shoemaker. He said that for Shabbes, God willing, he'd come and he asked me to give his regards to my sister, to Tatteh, and especially to Mammeh.

⁓

It was still far off to Shabbes but Toybeh was busy. She put on the heavy lace-up shoes every morning and then she took them off again. Lots of times in the evenings, Mammeh and Toybeh went out into the fields somewhere, coming back only when the peasants had already shouldered their rakes and scythes. Toybeh was silent and right after supper she went straight to bed.

All day Friday she glowed. She was busy baking big yellow challahs with saffron. She had brought back a big, flat fish from town. Before candle lighting she washed herself at the pump with scented soap, powdered herself generously with cornstarch, changed her clothes, and looked as if she should be the one to bless the candles, not Mammeh.

The shoemaker came when we had already lit the candles. He brought back Mammeh's shoes, all fixed and gleaming. He also shone. He was dressed now, not in the well-worn, greasy old visor, but in a new, black cloth cap, a kapoteh down to his ankles split in the back, and a pair of spats with patent leather points at the toes. He was no little shoemaker now, but a respectable young man, the son of a father.

That Friday evening out in the field, three Jews welcomed in the Shabbes: one, a father; the second, a young man; and me, a little Jew.

Tatteh swayed more this time than last week. The shoemaker stood still, said each word distinctly, welcoming in the Shabbes loud and clear. Every word fell clean and spare, like a shelled nut.

Mammeh listened knowingly and kept her lips closed as if she was savoring a fine taste in her mouth and didn't want it to melt too fast.

Toybeh stared off into the distance. It was hard to know whether she was listening to the loud rustling of the woods or to the Litvak rattling off the Sacred Tongue.

Kiddush was also made in the little shoemaker's Litvak manner. At the reciting of *m'ranan v'rabonan, the masters and the rabbis*, he strained on the melody in such a way that the words came out of his mouth doubled.

The next day we ate the Shabbes meal in the woods. The peasants were working in the meadows under a white-hot sun. The cows suffering from the heat and the flies, had wandered into the woods. The little shoemaker sang the zmirehs loudly and with pleasure, Tatteh humming along. Big blue flies buzzed around the tablecloth and red and black spotted ladybugs crawled all over, but nobody chased them away because we were all listening to the Litvak shoemaker's beautiful zmirehs.

After eating, when Toybeh had already cleared everything away, the Litvak again began to talk about his father who was the head of a yeshivah. He said that his father wrote him letters in Hebrew and in every letter he asked him why he hadn't become a bridegroom yet. How long was long enough to wait?

He himself knew that too but a decent match was hard to find. He was a pretty good craftsman, had even saved some money too. But shoemaking he said, was considered an unworthy craft.

"And what about serving in the Russian Army?" Mammeh asked, raising her head from her storybook.

He wasn't worried about the Russian Army, he said. He was free of military service. Enough! There was nothing more to ask, and he didn't say anything more either.

Shabbes, after Havdoleh, he asked Toybeh to allow him to measure her foot for a pair of new shoes. The holiday was coming, he said, how could she show herself in town in the shoes she was now wearing?

Toybeh stood red-faced, eyelids lowered. I was surprised that she was so embarrassed, that she said nothing to the little shoemaker. She kept silent the whole Shabbes.

"Nu, alright, take her measurements," answered Mammeh.

Toybeh stuck out her right foot and he measured it every which way. No shoemaker anywhere in the world would've taken so long. He said that such a foot with such a fine shape, he'd only seen the like on his own mother, may she be separated from the living, and that the shoes he would make for this pair of feet, the Tsarina herself would be glad to wear!

It was true. Besides davening and singing zmirehs so beautifully, this Litvak could make shoes fit for a tsarina. They were black, patent leather, with a point, stitched and carved on high, hollow heels and as light as a feather.

Toybeh really looked taller and thinner in them, her whole figure more compact. She actually wore them the next Shabbes when she went out walking with him.

They were gone for so long that the sky slowly settled over the fields. Swallows like blue arrows, flitted and dipped in the cooling air.

Echoes of the last cuts of the peasant's scythes were heard, but we still didn't see Toybeh coming back with the little shoemaker.

Mammeh closed her book and asked me if I didn't want to go out for a walk with her. We went out to the same paths through the rye that Toybeh and the little shoemaker had walked earlier.

The big yellow sun was now in our faces and worry lay on Mammeh's face with her rich woman's double chin. She stared right into the sun with blinking eyes, wiping her forehead as if she was sweating. I had the feeling that she was now very worried about Toybeh.

At last we saw them. They were coming, not from the woods, not from behind the stacks of hay, but from the path that led out to the highway.

Toybeh was looking at the points of her new patent leather shoes as she walked and chewing on a flower. The little shoemaker, small and pitiful looking, held Toybeh under the arm and was taking slow, little steps. He looked up to Toybeh like you would into a high window.

When we came toward them, the shoemaker pulled his hand away from Toybeh's arm and grinned foolishly. Toybeh straightened up, spit out the flower and in a voice that was too high, she asked: "Where're you off to, Auntie?"

"Just out for a walk," Mammeh answered, looking Toybeh sharply in the face.

"We went to the little town," Toybeh said uncertainly as if she didn't believe her own words.

"How come you went so far?"

"Its not so far," the shoemaker answered with his foolish grin. "Just a stroll, there and back."

We all came back together, the shoemaker walking with me. His cloth kapoteh, split in the back, smelled of leather and apple peelings.

He started questioning me. What was happening with me? Was I satisfied to be in Leniveh? Could I put up a haystack all by myself? Did it bother me that I didn't have any Jewish friends here?

No. Nothing bothered me. What was more than I could stand was that he talked too much. Mammeh and Toybeh were quiet. Maybe he'd also have been quiet but he just didn't know how to stop.

He looked very foolish to me now, this little Litvak shoemaker. I was surprised that Toybeh had let herself be led under the arm. What was he to her? A prospective bridegroom? A relative?

Later, he didn't talk at all. He listened intently to Tatteh's *eskeyni seudoseh* Havdoleh prayer that settled on the damp fields with a heavy sigh. There was a damp smell and a taste of salty herring in the air. Mammeh didn't recite her *God of Abraham* prayer. The forest began

to press in on us. Tatteh rushed through Havdoleh quickly and we
all went into the house, that is to say, not everybody. Toybeh stayed
outside. She sat on the threshold, hands on her knees, busy with her
own thoughts.

The house was warm as if it was already autumn. The shoemaker
was getting ready to leave. He didn't have anything to take with him
this time, no boots and no shoes, but he still acted like he was looking for something.

There was no kerosene; one tallow candle was burning on the
table. The red flame that lit up the Holy Mother flickered. A colorful butterfly flew first toward the tallow candle and then drew back.
Everybody's eyes were busy watching this stupid creature that crawled
right into the fire.

From outside we heard a loud insistent whistle, whether it was a
signal to somebody, or whether some sheygets was just letting off steam
but this sudden, unexpected whistle untied the shoemaker's tongue:

"Frimmetl," he began, shame-faced, "Have you got a minute?"

Mammeh wasn't doing anything, so of course she had time.

"Why? What's up?"

"I wanted to talk to you about something."

"With me? What about, exactly?"

"I want," the shoemaker gagged, "that Reb Luzeh should also
hear."

"Then you have to speak up."

"Well, if that's the only thing . . ."

Tatteh looked up from his prayerbook, over his metal spectacles.
The shoemaker coughed, hard and dry.

"Maybe you caught a cold?" Mammeh asked, worried.

"God forbid!" Nothing less but he wanted to say that he wasn't,
God forbid, as poor as he looked. He still had another kapoteh, brand
new. He also had two pairs of gaiters, also new. Just recently he'd had
some underwear made, and why should he deny anything? He had a
cashbook in the savings and loan society too. He wasn't a bad craftsman either, the proof—Toybeh's shoes.

"They're not ugly shoes," Mammeh agreed. She bent her face
in such a way as if she wasn't really my mother at all but the most
privileged woman in the world.

"Oh, really? Frimmetl herself says so?" The shoemaker grabbed
onto these words. "So, if we're already talking. . . ." He wanted to say
that Toybeh appealed to him and it seemed to him, that he appealed
to her too so he was ready to take her, just as she was, without a
penny dowry.

"Neh," Tatteh answered slowly, taking his face out of his prayer-book and pushing his spectacles up onto his forehead even more slowly.

"Without a penny dowry," the shoemaker bewildered, repeated again. He was even ready to agree about the trousseau.

"How old ar'ya?" Tatteh pointed his beard and at the same time, addressed the shoemaker by the intimate "di" Instead of the more formal "ir." It happened so unexpectedly that I blinked, and it seemed to me that Mammeh did too.

"What d'ya mean, how old I am? You ask an adult male how old he is?"

"And what about making a living?"

"What d'ya mean, what'll be? I am, thanks to the One Above, a craftsman."

"Yeh, you're really a craftsman, but a wife is like, lehavdil, a horse; you have to feed it regularly or it'll fall down."

The shoemaker grinned broadly. He was puzzled. "Toybeh is not, God forbid, a horse." And as far as a livelihood is concerned, he would work and with God's help, he'd be able to support a wife.

"But tell me, I ask you," Tatteh drew out every word separately, "who are you, after all? I don't even know you."

"What d'ya mean, who am I? Reb Luzeh, you should know me a little already. Ay, just because I'm a shoemaker? That's my stepmother's fault. My father, the head of a yeshiveh, wanted to make a shoykhet, a ritual slaughterer, out of me."

While he was talking, Tatteh studied him again, staring right into his skinny, bony face. Then he turned his quiet, absent-minded eyes to Mammeh:

"What do you say, Frimmet?"

"How do I know? After all, we have to ask Toybeh what she thinks too."

"Nu, of course we have to ask her." Tatteh took off his spectacles and asked the shoemaker: "Tell me, I'm asking you. Maybe you're a hothead?"

"God forbid!"

"And you'll treat her good at least?"

"What d'ya mean good? The saucer out of heaven won't be too good for her."

"As long as it's not an empty saucer."

"God forbid, Reb Luzeh! What're you saying?"

"Nu, never mind."

With this, the shoemaker left. The candle on the table flickered blue and every once in a while threatened to go out. Toybeh came in from outside and quietly began making up the beds. Tatteh-Mameh watched her from the side. Maybe that's why Toybeh made a mistake in how she laid out the cushions? Or maybe the shoemaker said something to her outside? We could see that Toybeh was restless and couldn't find a place for herself. She was just like a sick hen that goes around in pain looking for where to lay her egg.

Tatteh slowly undressed and went to bed. Mammeh lit another candle. Toybeh arranged the pots on the hearth. It didn't take long and Tatteh began to snore. Only then did Mammeh ask:

"Toybeh?"

"What is it, Auntie?"

"Did he say anything to you?"

"What was he supposed to say?"

"How do I know? You were gone so long."

"He said . . . that . . . that he wants me."

"Nu . . . ?"

"I don't know myself. He's so short."

"That's what's bothering you? What benefit do I have that your father is so tall?"

"If I were also short . . ."

"All of you are tall, may no evil befall. . . . Others would wish to be as tall but it seems to me, that he's quite a decent young man."

"Yeh, he seems to be decent. But he talks with a Litvak accent. I won't be able to understand him."

"And if I don't understand your father?"

"But my father is no Litvak."

"So he's something else. The main thing is, does he appeal to you?"

"He's so skinny. A shoemaker. . . ." Toybeh's voice came as if not from her throat. It was a strange voice, downhearted.

"Listen to me, Toybeh." Mammeh's voice was downhearted too. "God is my witness that I only want what's good for you, but not everything is the way a person wants. That he's an honorable young man, we can see. A wage earner he must also be not a bad one. He comes from a good family; his father is the head of a yeshiveh, and he himself is no boor as you heard. So my advice is . . ."

Mammeh stopped. Toybeh's shoulders fell.

"Dear Aunt . . ." she sighed and could no longer stop crying.

"Nu, enough already. What can we do?" Mammeh patted Toybeh's shoulder. "I know. In other circumstances . . ."

Toybeh cried even more. Her shoulders shook until deep into the night.

Chapter 25

In the middle of the week, grimy sweat pouring off his bony face, the little shoemaker came running again.

He came to find out what was new. He said that it so happened that he could rent a place with a little garden in a neighboring town. He wanted to buy a goat too; it wouldn't hurt to have their own milk. So if he knew for certain, he'd rent the place, get some furniture, and pay cash for the goat.

Toybeh stood with her face buried in the pots as usual, not answering. She didn't even turn around.

Mammeh heard him out to the end but after he finished, she told him that she didn't understand what the big hurry was all about. Toybeh was not, God forbid, an old maid and second, for a wedding you need to have a bit of a shirt, a shoe. . . . So her advice was that since it was before the Days of Awe that precede the High Holy Days, he should visit us in town during the intermediate days of Succoth, and we'd talk some more at that time.

The little shoemaker stopped in his tracks, dejected.

"All the way 'til Sikkes (Succoth)?"

"What's the matter? How long is it then?"

"If you want to really think about it, it's a long way off."

Actually, he didn't understand why it had to be put off for so long because he wanted Toybeh just the way she was. He didn't need her to be outfitted. With God's help, he'd even have a bit of money left over after renting the place and buying the goat and he'd have outfits made for Toybeh himself.

After supper, he complained again to Tatteh. His complaints buzzed through the house like restless flies. Tatteh didn't answer—not yes and not no but looked at Mammeh absent-mindedly, asking her advice.

"Let's ask Toybeh herself," Mammeh found a solution at last. "She also has some say in this."

But Toybeh didn't have anything to say. Sad, listless, she served the supper dishes to the table. The little shoemaker's eyes followed her every step but Toybeh stayed quiet. So Tatteh decided we should wait another week. He would see, he said, he'd find out who this Wolf really was. Maybe, he wasn't even a bachelor.

The little shoemaker grinned. Only now did we see that he had a mouth of sparse, black teeth. It could be because of those teeth that Toybeh wouldn't say whether she wanted him or not.

"He's not to my taste," she said later to Mammeh, "But if you want, Auntie . . ."

"I'm the one who wants?" Mammeh quickly replied: "Where'd you even get such an idea? But you don't have a dowry and the years don't stand still."

"I know," Toybeh frowned, "but what'll be?"

Mameh looked around the house as if she was about to tell a secret, then bent her head close to Toybeh.

"No!" Toybeh's voice trembled in fear. "No, Auntie, what will be, will be!" And that was that. The match went ahead.

Mammeh went into town, stayed overnight and bought a piece of linen, a length of material enough for two dresses, and some gauze for a veil.

She didn't stop anywhere else and she didn't talk to anybody. She left on a peasant's wagon and came back to Leniveh to prepare Toybeh's wedding.

The fields had already been harvested and looked stubbled like brushes. The storehouses were full of harvested grain. The smoke from the peasants' chimneys settled on the ground and the evenings got cool and damp. In the middle of the day one Wednesday, we saw storks flying off to warmer lands.

That's when Toybeh's wedding took place.

The day of the wedding, Mammeh spent a long time quietly talking to Toybeh. Toybeh put on a new shirt and a white lace petticoat. She also put on the white slippers that the little shoemaker had made and sent her the day of the wedding. Mammeh herself sewed up the veil with a crown of white cherries in the front and a train in the back.

When Toybeh, pale, lips dry, tried on the veil, she no longer looked like Luzeh the Hay Dealer's daughter but like the cherished, one-and-only daughter of a rabbinical judge! Mammeh herself said that Toybeh's hands, the same ones with which she'd all her life peeled potatoes and washed dishes, were on the day of her wedding, as small and white as two dainty doves.

Tatteh put on the cloth kapoteh he wore on Shabbes and the new cloth cap. Mammeh put on a fresh white jabot on her black, taffeta blouse. Toybeh in a long overcoat on top of her wedding dress, me in a pair of stiff pants, we all sat on a peasant's ladder-sided wagon and drove off into the little town.

Goyim stood at their thresholds watching. They took off their caps as we passed and shouted good wishes. My friends Yanek and Pietrek followed us part of the way. Pots were placed between the seats of the wagon. Mammeh held a big yellow sponge cake on her knees, the smell of which settled in our mouths with damp sweetness.

The sun was already setting when we came to the woods. Thin, dusty rays of the dying sun fell on the horse.

Tatteh climbed down from the cart and got ready to daven the afternoon prayer. Here and there, spots of sunlight also fell onto his Shabbes kapoteh. The peasant threw a bit of fodder down for his animal. It got darker and damper.

"Luzeh, make it faster," Mammeh called out, "Its getting to be night."

It really did get to be night. Hardly noticeable to the eye, the trees began blending into one another. It was black on every side. Toybeh was hot and took off her coat. In the dark woods and in her white dress, she looked like a corpse.

We continued on after davening, the horse plodding along in the dark. Mammeh was afraid of robbers but nothing happened and we came to the little town at the right time. Shadows grew out of the darkness, it was already good and dark. A band struck up a welcome.

"The bride's here!" A racket was heard that sounded like it was coming from underneath the wheels of the cart. A door was thrown open forcefully. Someone brought a lamp out from one of the shops and held it high over our heads.

"Here, here." They led our wagon forward in the dark, the bass from the band accompanying us.

"There, there . . ."

I felt like laughing. It seemed to me that out of spite, the trumpet joined the bass and screamed: "Not here and not there!"

They led us into a big, whitewashed room without beds or cupboards. A bright lamp hung from the beam. Girls and women, all strangers, freshly washed and combed, were busying themselves like stuffed geese.

Across the way, separated by a vestibule and with steep steps leading up to an attic, stood a door opened wide into another room, painted blue with two dark beams on the ceiling.

Here the men were gathered waiting for the bridegroom who was to come later.

Flattened noses and eyes full of wonder were pressed against the windowpanes. Toybeh tired, eyes half-closed, sat on a judge's old upholstered chair.

A small, round Jew with a clipped beard strummed angrily on the bass. A tall, untidy youth in short sleeves helped him out on a long trumpet. Over the sounds of both, a swarthy young man poured his heart out into his fiddle.

Girls and women who had scattered like ducks earlier, now danced in and out of the circle like angry turkeys.

Mammeh, distracted, with a lock of her wig messed up, was swept along with the dancers who were being offered tea and cookies. She wished weddings for all the unmarried girls, God willing, and for the married women she wished circumcisions and bar mitzvahs. Refined, like only my mother knew how, with her pursed lips and her rich woman's air, she gave everyone to understand that she'd once had her own house with brass handles on the doors.

Later, Mammeh got quiet and the dark fiddler struck up a waltz from Warsaw.

When Mammeh danced with Toybeh, the girls and women moved away to make room for them. The men came in from the other room. The flattened noses against the windowpanes became denser. All this was in order to see how the mother-in-law, no longer young herself, danced with the bride. And there really was what to see! With her head tilted to one side, her face full and satisfied, her big-city style, and her air of privilege, Mammeh led Toybeh easily, gliding on the tips of her toes, changing from one beat to another with charming feminine gestures. Her silk dress ballooned out. She turned her head, first this way, then that way, as if she was eyeing herself coquettishly in front of a mirror.

Toybeh didn't hold back either. Taller than Mammeh and with her long white train held in one hand, she allowed herself to be led and she swayed on her high heels, faster, her dark face quietly flushed, her head slightly thrown back, her mouth half-open, not laughing and not crying, but as if calling to someone.

After the waltz, the dark youth with the fiddle bowed to Mammeh. He said that he'd played in all the big cities already but he'd never seen dancing like this before.

The crowd of women pursed their lips. Smiling and shy, they looked admiringly at Mammeh.

"Can you believe it . . . ? May no Evil Eye!"

Later, they led Toybeh to the judge's upholstered chair in the middle of the room, the women and girls gathered around them. A short little Jew who had more beard than face, hoarsely called out in tune:

"Klezmer, play!"

The bass roared, the trumpet blew, and the fiddle wept in real Volyn style. He, the little Jew, stood himself on a stool and wrinkling his nose, began to talk to the bride in a controlled but expansive voice:

"Today is a day comparable to Yom Kippur. Today is your most beautiful and most bitter day, because today you stand before the Kingdom of Heaven just like a soldier stands, lehavdil, before his king. How does a soldier stand before his king? With virtuous habits, with good deeds, and with great awe! Therefore, today you must do penance and plead that you may find favor and grace in the eyes of the Almighty."

In the middle of his speech, this little Jew got short of breath. His overgrown face had an unhealthy flush. We had to wait until he breathed easier, wiped the sweat off his face and started in again:

"Today," he said, "you are a bride comparable to a tree that grows out of the earth but doesn't yet bear fruit but when the sun begins to warm the roots of the tree, the leaves begin to sprout and flower, only after that does this flowering turn into fruit. That's how you are too. Today you're still nothing, a dash of pollen, chaff in the wind but If God wills it, then your leaves will sprout and your fruit will blossom."

Toybeh's shoulders quivered quietly. Mammeh, with a handkerchief to her eyes, wept.

The little Jew made it faster with the bridegroom. The groom in a cloth kapoteh, seemed smaller than usual sitting at the head of the table, his face into the tablecloth. Around him sat Jews in heavy, ordinary clothes, with hard, rolled up beards.

The little Jew chanted the prayer for the dead, for the groom's deceased mother, the saintly one, and praised his father, the head of a yeshivah, to the skies.

"Even though," he said, "you're no more than a shoemaker, you're just as worthy to the Master-of-the-Universe as the richest man, because the Tana Reb Yoykhenen was also a shoemaker, therefore bridegroom, take an example from Reb Yoykhenen the Shoemaker, so that Zion may be redeemed. Amen."

When it came time for the ceremony, Tatteh put his big hands on Toybeh's head but there was no one to bless the skinny little shoemaker who stood shrunken and thin under the four poles of the bridal canopy, a stranger's overcoat thrown over his kitl.

He recited the marriage formula, in a dry and hungry voice. He couldn't even manage to break the glass the first time it was placed under his foot. A sickly, green color lay on his face.

The musicians struck up a Mazeltov March. Mammeh danced in from the vestibule with a big, braided challah held high. She skipped

sideways, waved the challah over everybody's heads as if she was playing and dancing with a tiny infant.

The crowd spread out. Mammeh didn't look at all like a rich or
privileged woman now but like some plain, good woman without a
double chin, an alms giver who had come to celebrate a poor bride
and groom and by doing so, earn a good deed for herself.

That's how she danced the Mitzvah dance with Toybeh too. Mammeh took one end of the white handkerchief and Toybeh the other end.
She bent her head forward and dipping as if in and out of water, they
circled each other and then straightened their heads. It looked like she
was doing it with her whole heart and not just like a stepmother. She
acted like a real mother to Toybeh.

But Tatteh danced the Mitzvah dance with his beautiful daughter
differently. He didn't look at her, didn't dip his head but bending down,
he took one end of the handkerchief and with heavy steps, slowly and
wearily, turned around several times, shuffling his feet uncertainly. He
was in a dilemma and it seemed to me that if Tatteh hadn't been too
embarrassed, he probably would've said:

"Toybeh my daughter, maybe I once made you suffer, so forgive
me. I'm a father after all. I only wanted what would be good for you,
nothing more. It was you yourself who sinned."

But he didn't say any of this; the fiddle said it all for him. It
was not to understand how this klezmer youth took it out of Tatteh's
mouth and out of my own heart.

Toybeh cried. Great damp spots appeared on her white wedding
dress. Maybe she also heard the klezmer's fiddle talking and maybe
she sensed that something wasn't quite right.

Dawn was breaking outside. A thin blueness settled on the windowsill. The girls and women were sitting sprawled, yawning loudly.
They'd already called out the wedding presents and the crowd was in
the middle of reciting the blessings when suddenly there was a commotion. The groom, may it happen to no one, had passed out.

Mammeh was the first to jump up from her stool. Picking up
the skirt of her silk dress she ran into the room where the men were
gathered. After her, pushing like sheep, came the girls and women. The
doorways opened wide and got crowded.

People were screaming over everyone's heads.

"Water! Maybe an old-time surgeon. . . . Should we run for the
surgeon?"

But nobody ran and nobody brought water, they only remarked
that at the table, the groom had smoked a lot of cigarettes. Those sitting close to him saw him turn a strange green color.

Any other person would've told what was the matter but no, he just sat there and before anything, the cigarette fell out of his mouth, he slid down from the stool and fell onto the floor face up.

Someone began shouting into his greenish face. A Jew in a shortened kapoteh pressed his temples, and tried to open his mouth but this had no effect.

It was a different kind of passing out. His upturned knees shook, his hands were spread out like a cross, his head writhed this way and that, and white foam bubbled on his lips.

"Don't!" Someone caught a stranger's hand running with water, "Can't you see this is a bad sickness? Put a key under his head."

Tatteh put the key under his head. He stood bent over his son-in-law as if wanting to make an apology. It seemed to me that from now on, Tatteh would never again be able to raise his head and look another person in the eye. Mammeh's shoulders also fell. She shuffled outside. A blue day lay on the threshold. Toybeh's wretched weeping could now be heard from the whitewashed house where they'd been dancing all night. She tore off the veil, took her beautiful black haired head into her hands and began rocking from side to side.

"What did'ya all want from me?" She called out to Tatteh, to Mammeh and to everyone gathered there: "Why do I have to be so shamed? A person who's sick unto death for a husband? I'll be a servant, I'll go wash floors, but I won't live with him . . . no, I won't!"

Toybeh didn't become a servant. Hadn't she washed enough floors for strangers? Didn't she cook and bake enough for those refined Hassidic Jews with their ivory walking sticks? She stayed in the little town.

Her husband Wolf, passed out from time to time. Toybeh put keys under his head, brought one boy with a big blond head into the world, then another, a black haired one. Then she had a daughter with eyes that during the day were blue and at night they turned green. These were Toybeh's eyes that lost their color altogether during the time she had to place keys under her husband's head.

Chapter 26

We finished the second harvesting of hay after Toybeh's wedding. The sun was already setting after only half a day and a cold, damp, yellowish, half-rotten odor seeped from the earth. The granaries and barns were full. What else was there left for us to do in Leniveh? So we packed up our bit of bedding, the pots, the bowls, and well rested and browned from the sun, we went back to town.

On the way we saw peasants already turning over the earth in preparation for the following year. Black clouds of crows flew over the plowshares and there was a smell of rotting apples, pickled cabbage, and warm bran in the air.

On our way back, lanky Lozeh stopped our cart and horse, wished Tatteh Mazeltov, asked us how our summer was, and if we made any profit. He insisted that for the sake of heaven, we should let him know when Laybl came back from serving in the Russian Army.

Over the summer, Lozeh's daughter Sureh's face had gotten clear and smooth, and she now had shapely hips. She offered us bowls of garlic borsht, fried potatoes, fat pieces of boiled beef, and vishnik, the cherry liqueur that she'd made herself.

After the refreshments, when we were already back on the wagon, Mammeh said that the girl back there at the inn looked to be a very good housekeeper and manager and that her father must have a lot of money. When Laybl comes back from military service, it might pay to have a talk with Lozeh.

Tatteh didn't answer. He looked sad. I also felt heavy-hearted. Toybeh was missing from the cart. I could still see her husband lying on the floor, foaming at the mouth.

Our horse plodded along disagreeably. Crows shrieked down from the poplar trees. We didn't stop at the bridge to let the horse drink from the stream, like we did earlier. Even here we felt the weight of the coming Days of Awe that precede the High Holy Days with their melancholy and dread.

In town Jews were already absent-minded. Lack of sleep from the Slikhehs nights, and worry about the coming days of repentance, lay on their faces.

I didn't like these days. It was a time when Tatteh would wake me up in the middle of sleep and drag me through the dark Shul Alley to Selichot, the penitential prayer service. I'd have to listen constantly to Moshkeh Khazn's cracked voice.

Everyone in the house would be going around worried. I'd have to run to the morning prayers in the study house and listen during the week to the cold shofar blowing that always reminded me of death. What would it bother anyone, I thought, if it could be summer all year round? Wouldn't it be better to recite the Slikhehs prayers when the grain was still in the fields? And wouldn't the Master-of-the-Universe like it better if a younger khazn with a sweet voice stood at the pulpit davening? Not Moshkeh the Soup Kitchen who groaned away like a dull saw. And altogether, why did Jews have to pick such bleak, sad holidays?

We arrived at our big courtyard.

No one came out to meet us. Yarmeh the Wagon Driver and his omnibus must be in Warsaw.

The orchard was damp. When we opened up the house, a smell of mice and spider webs greeted us. There were worms crawling around in every corner—black, yellow, fattened up from nothing at all.

Mammeh, together with a hired goyeh, sleeves rolled up past their elbows, feather dusters and rags in hand, cleaned and washed in preparation for the holidays. I wandered around with nothing to do; nobody went to cheder before the holidays. And besides, my teacher Simmeh-Yoysef died during the time we were in Leniveh.

Yarmeh the Wagon Driver's wife told us that the rabbi and Reb Arn the rabbinical judge, accompanied the body. Nobody knew what an honorable man Simmeh-Yoysef really was. His body was taken to the shul and the rabbi himself delivered the eulogy. The weeping and wailing carried up to the heavens. Only his pupils, those silly, good-for-nothings, didn't cry.

I probably wouldn't have cried either because Simmeh-Yoysef, that honorable man, had the habit when he was alive, of pinching the boys in the soft flesh of their seats. This honorable man had a habit of chasing us out of the cheder with a kerchief like you chase chickens, and locking the door on an ordinary Wednesday. Velveleh the goy, who'd already eaten pork, said that Simmeh-Yoysef chased us out because he wanted to go to bed with his wife. He, Velveleh, had seen it with his own eyes. Another habit he had, this Simmeh-Yoysef, was to take the food belonging to his pupils, and also to borrow money from them and not pay it back.

But no matter what, Simmeh-Yoysef was now in the True World. He had to be shown honor because he was after all, a very poor Jew.

I didn't know yet into what cheder they would enroll me. I wanted to go to Pomerantz' secular school but only wealthy boys were sent there. Aunt Nemmi's son, Mendl, went there.

Meanwhile, I did nothing. Yankl was no longer here; nobody even spoke of him. Yarmeh the Wagon Driver's wife showed herself with a swollen belly.

"She must be pregnant," said Mammeh wondering, "At her age! Can you believe it?"

The Senior Prison Guard's wife was stuck-up, with a face full of yellow spots. Mammeh wouldn't look at her, and the Russian goyeh also turned her head away. She wouldn't talk to anybody in the courtyard anymore. Her husband strode around clanking his sword and wouldn't answer anybody's "Good Morning" either.

I wanted especially to talk to him, to ask him what was happening at the jail. How were Shtshepkeh the murderer, and Shermandl the cutthroat? Had they been sent off to Siberia yet?

I also wanted to speak to the Senior Guard's daughter Yaninkeh. She had grown up over the summer. Her eyes were a deep blue and her long, flaxen hair was braided with a blue silk ribbon. She wore a navy blue dress and a black apron. Yarmeh the Wagon Driver's wife said that Yaninkeh had become a student and was already going to the gymnasium for girls.

It was impossible to get near her, and I felt that I'd never be able to approach her. What could I talk to her about? How would I manage, if I knew nothing more than a little khumash with Rashi? I'd almost forgotten that much in Leniveh. It was good that the holidays were coming. During the holidays you didn't think about anything practical.

❧

The house had gotten bright in honor of the holidays. Mammeh bought grapes and honey, and big, braided challahs that looked like birds.

A live carp slapped around in a big bowl of water. There was a smell of boiled chicken. It was just too bad that this Rosh Hashanah nobody was coming to visit, not from Warsaw and not from Lodz. Even Toybeh wasn't here anymore.

So in spite of the tidiness and all the tasty dishes that were prepared, it was still sad in our house. There were only three people at the table and we ate in silence, staring into the clear, newly washed windows as if we were looking for someone.

I cheered myself up by telling myself that it must be even sadder in Leniveh now. The fields were harvested long ago, the woods were black and wet. There, in that house, the kerosene lamp or a tallow candle would be burning, while here at least, no matter what, it was bright. The smell of the grapes and honey wafted up from the table and if you wanted, it wasn't so sad after all.

On the second day of the holiday, Tatteh brought a guest from the study house, a young soldier from Russia, with a black mustache and with round, rosy cheeks. If not for the fact that his head was closely shorn like a thief's, you could think that it was my dead brother Moysheh.

He spoke in a deep Litvak accent, with a lot of rolled r's. Sometimes, he got lost for a word and he helped himself out with Russian ones.

"*Da*," he said, "*tak totshnoh barinyeh.*Yes, that's how it is, lady."

And the "barinyeh," that is to say Mammeh, liked talking to him. She asked him where he was from, what he did and how much longer he still had left to serve in the Russian Army. Her double chin puffed up and quivered just like a rich woman.

The soldier told us he came from Kiev, that his father was *pervoy gildi kupi'etz*, a Merchant of the First Guild, that he had a sister who was a *zubnoy vratsh*, a dentist, and that his older brother was an *apteker*.

"A what?" Tatteh frowned with his whole face

"An apteker."

"What is that, exactly?"

"Apteker," the soldier explained. "Nu, someone who fills prescriptions."

"Maybe you mean an ap-tey-ker," Mammeh interjected.

"Da, da, berinyeh, apteker. Yeh, yeh, lady, a pharmacist."

"Can a Jew in Russia become a pharmacist?"

"*Kanyetchno*! Certainly!"

"Listen to that!" Tatteh was amazed. "Go know! That's not possible here in Poland!"

"Even in Warsaw," Mammeh interjected, "there's no Jew who's an *apteyker*."

"*Ni'e'uzsheli*? Really?" The soldier pulled at his mustache.

"*Da, da*," Mammeh answered also in Russian, and told the soldier that she had a bit of a connection with apteykers because her first husband had been a respected old-time healer and that she had an older son who was also learning to be a healer.

Tatteh listened carefully, staring at the soldier. The soldier talked a lot about his city, about a street called Kreshtshatik. He told us that Jews weren't allowed to live in Kiev, that they were required to have a *pravozhshitelstvoh*, a residence permit, that it cost blood and money to be allowed to live there. Tatteh, engrossed, stared right into his mouth until he finally interrupted.

"Yekaterinoslav is far from Kiev?"

"Far, certainly far."

"Izzat so?" Tatteh was taken aback. "I thought it wasn't far."

"Why d'ya need to know?"

"I have a son there, in Yekaterinoslav."

"In military service?"

"Yeh, in the Russian Army."

"A long time?"

"He should've come home already."

"When?"

"According to my reckoning, he should've been here already."

"He'll probably come after the holidays. The Russian Army lets soldiers out in October."

"*Tak totshnoh.* Yeh, that's how it is."

⌁

But the release actually came earlier, in time for Yom Kippur.

It was after minkheh, the late afternoon prayers. A tall, thin candle in a mortar filled with sand stood on the table. A chilly blue shadow had already settled on the top of the windowpanes. We'd just finished eating the soup with the noodles, the boiled chicken, and cooked apples but Tatteh only tasted each delicacy.

"The less you eat, the easier to fast."

Mammeh had already pinned the white jabot onto her black taffeta blouse. I helped her clear the table. The tall, deathlike candle burned with a yellow flame that was reflected in the mirror where it looked whiter and the mirror looked even yellower.

Tatteh was looking for the special skullcap that he wore on the Days of Awe, the one sewn with silver thread that had grown yellow over time.

Go expect that at such a moment the door would open and a stranger would come in carrying a small suitcase and dressed in a short, black overcoat with a hard, black derby hat. He looked like a doctor!

At first glance, it seemed to me that the short, black overcoat hung on him as if it didn't belong to him. The hat also didn't fit his

face. Tatteh was still searching for his skullcap. The stranger slowly put
his suitcase down, looked at Tatteh who was busying himself absent-
mindedly, and with a smile on his trimmed and pointed mustache,
called out.

"Git yontef!" Good Holiday!

Tatteh took a step backward, startled, even his voice sounded
frightened. Half-suppressing a sigh, he said quickly:

"Laybkeh?"

"It's me, Tatteh," Laybkeh took a bold step forward into the room.

Tatteh wanted to say something more but he must have been
breathless, or what? He only wiped his hand over his forehead and
sighed again:

"Laybkeh?"

Mammeh couldn't believe it either. She stood there, surprised
and apart, but when she heard Tatteh twice repeat his son's name, she
answered as if with an echo:

"Laybkeh, Welcome to our guest! Take a look! A guest!"

Without my knowing it and without my willing it, my voice rang
out too:

"Laybkeh!"

The whole house got full with Laybkeh. Tatteh's big beard got
tangled up in Laybkeh's pointed mustache.

"How d'ya like that?" his voice shook, "So unexpected. . . . How
ar'ya? Show me! Lets see what you look like."

Mammeh stood off to a side. She waited for Tatteh to let go of
his son so that she could greet him too.

I didn't know what to do either. Should I go up to him, should I
embrace him, should I kiss him? But Laybkeh quickly remembered us.

"Meemeh, Aunt," he pronounced the 'm' heavily, "how are you
Aunt?"

"Thanks for asking. And you?"

He kissed Mammeh's hand and embraced me as big as I was. He
kissed me right on the mouth leaving a smell of tobacco.

"Mendl, may no Evil Eye. . . . You've grown up! Take a look!
May you be well! You're a candidate for marriage already!"

I warmed up in Laybkeh's big hands. I felt closer to him, this
brother, a lot more than to Yoyneh when he came home for Peysekh.

"You're probably hungry," Mammeh only now remembered herself.
"Here, sit down. Eat something. Its right before *Kol Nidreh.*"

"Don't trouble yourself, Aunt. I've already eaten."

"Where could you have eaten? You just arrived!"

"I'm here a few hours already. I went to an inn first, washed up, ate, and came here all ready."

"You went to an inn? You don't have a home, or what?"

"Never mind, Aunt, its better this way."

"You probably want to change?" Tatteh asked, "so hurry up, its getting late."

"No, I don't need to change."

"You're going to Kol Nidreh looking like that?"

"Why not? This isn't nice?"

It appeared to be not to Tatteh's taste. When Laybkeh left for military service, he had worn a long kapoteh and a Jewish cap on his head. Now he had returned, darker, harder, altogether more like a German. How could Tatteh show himself in the study house with him looking like this?

Still, he went out into the street shoulder to shoulder with his son. I shuffled alongside Laybkeh's black overcoat. After all, he had come all the way from Yekaterinoslav! So let everyone see how my brother looked!

Tatteh kept stopping, first with this one, then with that one, wishing each, *gmar kh'simeh toyveh, may you be inscribed with a good name* and introducing Laybkeh:

"My son Laybkeh just came back from service in the Russian Army."

"Izzat so? Welcome to your guest! How ar'ya? What's the news from there?"

Everyone said "Shulem aleykhem" to Laybkeh. They stared into his face, and looked him over. They looked all of us over.

Even in the study house that was already full of people, they noticed Laybkeh. Among so many kitls and prayer shawls, he was the only one wearing a hard, black derby hat.

It could be that it wasn't right for Laybkeh to come into the study house in this German get-up. He should've gone instead to the shul; there he'd find many such hats.

But Tatteh couldn't deny himself such parental pride, not to show off his only son by his first wife, who'd just this minute come from Yekaterinoslav.

The quiet, sighing voice of Reb Arn the rabbinical judge, lost nothing of its shivering and fear as he began to chant with great dread and awe:

"*Al das hamakom v'al das hakal* . . . With the consent of Heaven and with the consent of this holy congregation. . . ."

The sight of Laybkeh's hard, black, derby hat didn't stop Moshkeh Khazn from making a mistake in his wailing and go off somewhere out on a limb.

Laybkeh smirked into his pointed moustache and said that in the synagogue in Yekaterinoslav, this couldn't have happened.

"*Ni'evozmozhnoh!* Impossible!" he said in Russian, "there its like being in the service. You can't grab and you can't rush. You had to pay attention to the officer, the sergeant-major, that tuning fork.

Aha," said Laybkeh, "there its *sovsi'em drugoy moleben ee sovsi'em drugayeh zhizn*. It's a completely different kind of praying, a completely different kind of life."

Laybkeh continued telling us what life was like there until the middle of the night.

Tatteh sat on the edge of the bed in his long tallis-kotn, busy with his sick leg. Mammeh sat on the other bed in a white night cap with a ruffle under her chin, and me beside Laybkeh, we all heard that in Yekaterinoslav there were a lot of *barins* and *barinyehs,* gentlemen and ladies. Jews were also *barins* there. They wore big fur coats and lambskin shtraymlekh, and they kept their shops open on Shabbes. They only davened on the holidays.

"And you also didn't daven?" Tatteh raised his head from his sick leg.

"If there was time, we davened."

Tatteh sighed heavily: "A wild land! A swinish country!"

"Its not so wild, Tatteh. People there are rich merchants. *Pervoy gildi. V'toroy gildi*—Merchants of the First Guild, Merchants of the Second Guild."

"And how'd it go with you?"

"*Khorosho*, Good." Laybkeh answered in a satisfied voice. "Commander Polka wouldn't have given me a sack of beets to make borsht otherwise. "Lyovkeh, he'd say, take a run, Lyovkeh, and bring me a bottle of liquor. He loved his glass, this commander. I was hale fellow with him, this sergeant-major. For a small coin you could do whatever you wanted with him."

"And did you eat out of the community pot?" Tatteh asked sorrowfully.

"*Kakoy tebyeh kesl*? What kind of pot?" Ivan can pig out from the community pot, but I ate in town."

"Did you at least make money in the Russian Army?"

"Who needed money? What use was money to me?"

Laybkeh was still boasting after Mammeh turned over to the wall and Tatteh finished looking after his sick leg. He was still talking after he lay down beside me on the iron cot. A smell of tar came from his body. It was the same smell that came from the little soldier who ate with us on the second day of Rosh Hashanah.

I had a hard time sleeping, what with the smell of tar still in my mouth. Laybkeh's Russian commander, the *barins* and the *barinyehs*, all of this got tangled up in my imagination with Laybkeh and with Tatteh-Mammeh.

The next day I went around with a head fragile like glass. There was a stifling, heavy smell from the dripping candles in the study house. The hunch-backed goy crawled between the tables, trimming the wax, straightening out a candle, and was deaf to the weeping and pleading of the congregation sighing into their prayer books.

Fishl the ritual slaughterer's son who was already learning the Talmud with the Commentaries, helped out at the pulpit during morning services. He chanted better than Aunt Nemmi's Mendl. It was sweeter and more pious.

But this year's davening didn't appeal to me. Moshkeh the Khazn mispronounced his Hebrew just like a goy. I yearned to go to the shul. I wanted to hear the old Litvak khazn and the main thing was that I wanted to be with Laybkeh because that's where he said he was going today.

I got there in time for the Torah scrolls to be taken out of the Ark. They were already reading from them but I didn't see Laybkeh. Pale, sweaty Jews sat outside sighing. Others went to relieve themselves against the building across the street. Young boys were eating big chunks of challah smeared with honey, but Laybkeh was nowhere to be found.

Tatteh asked me later whether I had seen Laybkeh there.

"Sure I saw him! What then, I didn't see him?"

My heart ached that I had to fool Tatteh on Yom Kippur.

I went back to shul for the closing Neilah service, but I didn't see Laybkeh this time either. I was very sorry that he wasn't there.

The rabbi himself davened, without a choir and without a melody. He only recited, but it was such a recitation that the lions and the deer, the flutes and the fiddles, the drums and the trumpets that were etched into the western wall came down and davened together with all the Jews.

Laybkeh wouldn't have been able to say that it was any nicer in that synagogue in Yekaterinoslav, where they needed an officer, a sergeant major.

But go look for him if he wasn't even there! I saw him in the house only after the holidays. Who knew if he davened at all or whether he even fasted, because he started in on the prunes. Who eats prunes on an empty stomach? And after all the eating was finished, he went at the prunes again.

It bothered me why he was eating so many prunes. Why?

Even when guests came, he still didn't stop chewing on the prunes. Our sister Bayleh came with her tall, blond husband Wolf, and Yarmeh the Wagon Driver came with his pregnant wife too. Laybkeh kissed his brother-in-law and embraced his sister who was patting him on the shoulder like you pat a pet animal. All the while, he was grabbing prunes off the table.

His brother-in-law Wolf sat with Yarmeh the Wagon Driver, both of them sprawled out. They listened in amazement to Laybkeh's descriptions of the marvels of Yekaterinoslav. They kept asking Laybkeh if he had made any money serving in the Russian Army, but Laybkeh didn't have time or maybe he just didn't want to give away the secret. What was the point of talking to such common people? Suddenly, the Senior Guard and his beautiful Russian wife came into our house.

It seemed that these goyim had forgotten that they were not on speaking terms with Mammeh. They came in uninvited, grinning and more than a little embarrassed.

"*Zdrastiyeh*, hello," they said in Russian and remained standing at the door uncertainly.

Mammeh was happier to see these offended neighbors even more than her own guests, and even more than Laybkeh.

She went toward them the way you welcome dear in-laws. She placed stools for them, and in even greater embarrassment, talked absent-mindedly to herself and not to anyone else.

"Can you believe it? I never expected it! Such welcome guests!"

"*Nitshevo*," Its nothing," the Senior Guard said, making a disapproving gesture with his arm and sat down, legs stretched out too. The Jewish guests got quiet and began moving their stools.

Laybkeh sensed that his kind of people had now come in and in the blink of an eye, he forgot his own sister, forgot Tatteh and Mammeh, and began telling his stories in Russian, not for us to understand but for the sake of the Senior Guard and his beautiful wife.

He began again about his Russian commander, how he used to call him Lyovkeh, and what a brilliant man he was. The Senior Guard also remembered his own commander and told about his *v'zvodni*, his platoon leader, and about some general whose wife had run away with her lover.

Afterwards, the Russian goyeh asked Laybkeh whether he knew the town she came from on the River Don.

"Of course I know it! What then, I don't know it? I was there on maneuvers."

"Really! Izzat so?" said the goyeh and made herself more comfortable on the stool. "So what's new from there? Did you ever see the priest from there?"

"Of course, I saw him! What then, I didn't see him? Pretty old already, that priest."

"Old, you say? How could that be?" When she left her home, this priest had a black beard.

"Oh no, *sudarinyeh*. He's already old. His beard is now white."

"Maybe its somebody else?"

"No, it's the same one, madame."

Yarmeh the Wagon Driver and the tall Wolf wanted to interrupt because they had also once served in the Russian Army, but the Senior Guard's wife and Laybkeh rattled on in Russian. Who could follow them?

Tatteh beamed with parental pride. When you give hay to Russian horses, you understand Russian so he sat, grinning widely with white teeth, and every few minutes he looked over to Mammeh.

"Eh, Frimmet, what d'ya say to Laybkeh? Did you expect this?"

Mammeh was silent. Just as earlier she had been glad to see the goyish neighbors, now she kept quiet. It wasn't her style that others should talk and she shouldn't be able to say anything. She liked to be seen and heard but others were doing the talking now; nobody even noticed her.

So the next day when Laybkeh was not in the house, she remarked several times over that Laybkeh told and retold the same stories about Yekaterinoslav as if he had just now come from the other side of the ocean. And if a Russian commander called you Lyovkeh, so what was the big deal?

"Little fool," answered Tatteh, "isn't it interesting?"

"Once, but over and over again? Here in our regiment . . . there in our regiment. . . . Eating nothing but delicacies also gets boring!"

"And I'd listen and keep listening," Tatteh answered smiling warmly into his beard.

"Gladly! Anyone who begrudges, should himself have to do without."

But Mammeh was good and aggravated. It was too cramped with Laybkeh in the house. He wasn't her son and he didn't address her as intimately as Toybeh who called her Meemeshi, Auntie. Laybkeh addressed her with the ordinary Meemeh, Aunt. He didn't get under her skin the way Toybeh had. It must be that because of that, Mammeh had complaints. He snored at night and he didn't come home in time for meals. She wasn't responsible for watching over his pots of food.

All this was put aside when a postcard arrived from Warsaw announcing that Tsippeh, Mammeh's one and only daughter by her first husband, was coming to us for the Succoth holiday.

We couldn't tell from the card whether she was coming alone or with her intended, the broom maker. Mammeh didn't know what'd happened with the prospective bridegroom.

But never mind! What had to be done was to get ready and prepare everything well.

So Mammeh got busy. She cleaned and polished all over again. With her own hands, the same ones she'd once used to squeeze brass door handles, she now washed the floor. When Tatteh left her money for the holiday, she didn't even bother to count it, but began to complain:

"How much are you leaving me?"

"How much should I leave?"

"You've forgotten that Laybkeh is also here?"

"I didn't forget anything. Actually, I left you more."

Mammeh quickly counted the copper coins and before Tatteh had time to put on his kapoteh, she threw them on the floor.

"What're you leaving me? What? What should I buy first?"

"Why're you getting so mad? How much is enough to leave you?"

"What do you mean? Don't you know that before the holidays there's always a scarcity? Your Laybkeh likes better quality food and my Tsippeleh, may she be well, is also coming for the holidays."

"Your Tsippeh," Tatteh asked dumbly, "how come?"

"Why not? Isn't she my child?"

"I'm not, God forbid, taking her away from you. By all means! Why not? But where'll you put her?"

"Where I'll put her? What do you think? She won't have where to stay at her own mother's?"

"I'm not saying no. But still, we have to figure out where to put her."

"I've already figured it out. She'll sleep in Mendl's cot."

"And where'll Mendl sleep?"

"With you."

Tatteh was silent a while, staring at the scattered coins and asked as if with mouth closed:

"And Laybkeh?"

"Laybkeh can go sleep at your sister Nemmi's."

"At Nemmi's? What's the matter? Doesn't he have a father, until 120 years?" Why shouldn't your Tsippeleh go sleep at Miriam's?"

"You're driving her away already? She hasn't even come yet and you're already driving her away?"

"I'm not driving her away but my Laybkeh is just as dear to me as your Tsippeh is to you."

"Laybkeh is a man. He can sleep wherever he wants. And my Tsippeleh is not your Toybeh!"

This gave my tall and broad-shouldered Tatteh such a jolt that he couldn't even manage to get his arm through the sleeve of his kapoteh. He didn't ask anything more. Sighing, he put on the kapoteh, took another wrapped bunch of coins out of his deep pants' pocket and leaving half of it on the table, he went out silently, heavy-hearted, bent over, his shoulders drooping.

After he left, Mammeh started cleaning faster and grimmer. She blew her nose loudly and often, hiding her face in the things she was polishing. She was crying.

Who needed this? Laybkeh himself agreed that the cot should be given to Tsippeh and that they should find a couple of stools for him in the kitchen.

Chapter 27

Tsippeh arrived in the morning just before the holiday, young, radiant, with a strange big-city racket, and a strange big-city smell. All of a sudden the whole house was full of her. She put down her baskets and little boxes, threw handkerchiefs, purses, and veils down on the bed, and ran all over the house like a dazed hen making a lot of dust. Right from the first day she had complaints because the mirror was hung too high and also when you looked into it, you saw a blue face.

Mammeh got flustered, her wig got messed up, and she didn't know what to do with herself.

"Tsippeshi," she asked, wandering around worried. "How are you? How are things going? How's your health? I heard that you were coughing, unfortunately."

"I'm good, Mammeh," Tsippeh answered quickly. "I didn't cough."

"So why do you look so bad? You don't, God forbid, have something you're aggravated about?"

"No, Mammeh, why should I be aggravated?"

"How should I know? You're all alone in Warsaw . . ." Mammeh frowned. She wanted Tsippeh not to look so good.

But Tsippeh's youthful face was radiant with shiny red cheeks, and blonde dew lay on her pretty little chin that was split in half by a dimple that seemed to smile all by itself, even when she didn't want it to. When Tsippeh opened her fresh little lips, still more dimples smiled from both sides of her face.

Toybeh who'd married the little Litvak shoemaker, had small, clear white teeth, like Tatteh, but Tsippeh's teeth were big and wide. If not for those teeth, they'd be running after her in the streets.

They followed her anyway. Her finely boned figure, her long legs and narrow, swaying hips drew young and old alike. Besides that, Tsippeh's thick head of dark brown hair, damp like chestnuts just bursting out of the shell, made her even more beautiful.

Laybkeh didn't take his small black eyes off her and he couldn't stop smiling at her, embarrassed.

Because of her, Laybkeh put on a pair of new, patent leather shoes with big, flat points, in honor of the holiday of Succoth. He shoved his black derby hat to one side of his head, washed with scented soap in the morning and doused himself with toilet water that tickled your nose. He combed his hair with a part in the middle and didn't stop picking lint off his new suit.

He spoke to Tsippeh in Russian. She knew that language; otherwise she wouldn't be a sales person of women's clothes in the biggest shop in Warsaw.

Tsippeh said that in that shop they spoke Russian or Polish and sometimes even French too. Who really spoke French Tsippeh didn't say, but probably she did too. The wives of generals, noblemen, dancers from the big theatre, and who not, shopped there.

Tsippeh told us that the Governor General of Warsaw had a mistress and that she was the most beautiful woman in the whole kingdom of Poland. Tsippeh knew her too. She knew her as well as she knew her own mother, maybe even better. Tsippeh went to all the operas and theater presentations without having to pay even a penny. She was tired out from attending so many performances already. Besides which, in Warsaw she had to get up early, go to the shop, pay attention, prepare. She was the senior salesperson after all.

That's why here, Tsippeh slept half the days away. The door of the room was shut and everyone went around on tiptoe. Tatteh had to daven in the kitchen. Laybkeh wandered around stiffly, dressed in black like some temporary guest. Mammeh cooked milk and cocoa for Tsippeh, and served her honey cake right into her bed. Tsippeh didn't wash at the big slop pail in the kitchen like the rest of us, but right there in the room in a blue basin that Mammeh borrowed every day from the Senior Prison Guard's wife.

It took a long time until Tsippeh got up and it took even longer until she got dressed. She had lots of mirrors and little combs. Assorted hairpins, hairbrushes, and little bottles lay thrown together on the table and on the windowsill. From all of them a sickening sweet smell rose up that you could taste even in your food.

Tsippeh sang Polish and Russian songs all morning. Not like Yitta who sang a song about a boy who went off to Vienna, but about someone called *Pienkneh Helena*, Beautiful Helen, and about someone else who was thought to be a priest's daughter, but it turned out she was Jewish after all. Tsippeh said this was a kind of opera called *Zhiduvka*, The Jewess, and it was playing in the big theater in

Warsaw. Tsippeh said that she also knew a singer, Battistini, and he sang more beautifully than anyone else in the whole world, not even the angels sang like this Battistini.

"*Da, Da*, Yeh, yeh," Laybkeh nodded his head in agreement, "he was in Moscow too, this Battistini."

"He's everywhere," said Tsippeh. "Its no small thing! He even sings for the tsar."

"A Jew?" inquired Mammeh respectfully, not so much because of Battistini but because of her beautiful, one and only daughter.

"Nothing else but a Jew? They'd let a Jew sing in the big theater?"

Mammeh's face narrowed. It didn't so much bother her that Battistini wasn't a Jew but more so because Tsippeh dismissed Jews out of hand.

"And did Tsippeh ever hear of Davidov?" Laybkeh moved forward. What kind of singer was Battistini anyway? But Davidov really does sing for the tsar, for Tsar *Batyushka* the Father himself!"

"And did Laybkeh actually hear Davidov?" Tsippeh asked, taken aback.

"Of course! What then, I didn't hear him? Laybkeh put one foot in front of the other, waved his hand in the air and tossed his head.

In a high-pitched voice he began to sing:

"*Volga, Volga, mat rodnaya* . . . Voga, Volga, my native land . . ."

But that one there, that Davidov, must have sung it different because Tsippeh waved her hand in contempt.

"Laybkeh should better stop . . ."

She always did this. If Laybkeh wanted to talk about his Yekaterinoslav, about his regiment or about his Russian commander, Tsippeh would wrinkle her dainty little nose, and would say, off to a side:

"We've heard that one already."

Laybkeh's mouth would fall. His derby hat would slide down onto his forehead, and in that minute you could see that Laybkeh had coarse, hairy hands and one deformed thumbnail.

Tsippeh said that men with coarse hands didn't appeal to her.

That wasn't hard to understand because she was so refined. She could purse her lips so daintily that it would be no bigger than a groshn. Not only was she so refined, but even her big hat that reminded you of a mushroom, even her draped silk clothes that rustled, and the patent leather slippers on high heels, all of this made her look charming and refined. When she put on the short jacket with the turned up collar that she called a Mary Stuart collar, Laybkeh would twirl his moustache, shuffle his foot, and ask in his Yekaterinoslav Russian:

"*Mozhet poguliat poyidyom?* Maybe we'll go for a stroll?"

"*Spasiboh*, Thank you" Tsippeh answered also in Russian, with her dainty little mouth and went off by herself.

Mammeh followed her out the door, watching. Yarmeh the Wagon Driver's wife, arms over her pregnant belly, also watched. The Senior Prison Guard's wife looked out of her window, and the new neighbor who lived in the attic above us stared out of her rooftop window and nodded her head.

"What a regal person she is! May no evil befall her . . ."

Yarmeh the Wagon Driver, well rested, entered from one side of the courtyard, and taking slow and careful steps, he asked:

"How come by herself? How come not with Laybkeh?"

"How does Laybkeh come to her?" Mammeh retorted, so arrogantly as if she owned her own ship at sea.

Even though Tsippeh was so beautiful and Laybkeh didn't measure up to her, it was still cold and strange with her in the house.

Tsippeh didn't pay any attention to me at all and she didn't bring me anything from Warsaw. She didn't bring anything for anybody. Her songs about the *Pienkneh Helena*, Beautiful Helena, and about *Zhiduvka*, The Jewess, were strange to me. I liked Yitta's song about the nice young man who went off to Vienna to see his parents.

It was as if there was nobody else in the house except Tsippeh. Mammeh didn't stop talking about her. She cooked and baked for her, scoured the pots and bowls all by herself while Tsippeh primped and admired herself in the mirror. Mammeh carried the food into the Succah all by herself, and Tsippeh never once said:

"Let me, Mammeh, I'll help you."

Even at night when the whole house was sleeping, Mammeh would get up from her bed to take a look at Tsippeh. She tried the closed door that led into the kitchen where Laybkeh slept. She would look at Tsippeh in her bed and listen to her breathing.

Tsippeh was conceited and arrogant, she knew that Laybkeh couldn't hold a candle to her. She didn't speak to Tatteh at all. When she first arrived, she didn't even ask:

"How are you, Uncle? What's new, Uncle?"

But from afar, standing over one of her open little valises, she asked into it:

"How's it going, Reb Luzeh?"

Tatteh didn't answer. Mammeh yelled at him:

"Luzeh, she's asking you something. Why don't you answer?"

But Tatteh wasn't listening. He didn't listen the entire holiday and he stayed silent.

Right after the holiday, Mammeh packed up Tsippeh's baggage. Yarmeh the Wagon Driver, who by nightfall had already harnessed the horses, wanted six gildn for the trip to Warsaw. The same trip by train cost a ruble and fifty kopeks, so Tsippeh chose the train. After all, she couldn't be expected to just lurch around all day and night with some Yarmeh the Wagon Driver! What would people in Warsaw say? Nothing less, but she was short a ruble for the train fare to Warsaw. Mammeh didn't have it. Right after Havdoleh, Tatteh drew on his kapoteh and got ready to go out, but Mammeh stood in his way:

"Luzeh," she said, "maybe you've got a ruble to give me?"

"Wha-at?"

"I need a ruble."

Tatteh didn't answer. He drew his head into his collar and quietly went out. Tsipeh's beautiful almond eyes followed him, and not at all almond-eyed, she threw after him:

"Luzeh *yolok*!

The blood rushed to my face. Yolok was an epithet that Mammeh sometimes threw at Tatteh but first of all, she was his wife, maybe she was allowed. Second, Mammeh all her life believed that she did Tatteh a favor by marrying him.

But Tsippeh who stayed here the whole week of the holiday and ate from his sweat and toil, what nerve did she have to throw out such a word?

It nagged at Mammeh that Tsippeh would be late for the train but if in that minute I could have gone up to the oh so beautiful and refined Tsippeh and slapped her right in that glib mouth of hers, I'd have added ten years to my life.

I was very pleased that Tatteh pretended not to hear and didn't give Mammeh the ruble even though Tsippeh went off by train after all.

Laybkeh gave her the extra ruble, one from Yekaterinoslav, a spanking, newly minted one. He also helped carry Tsippeh's baggage out to the waiting carriage.

We traveled through Lublin Street, Mammeh and Tsippeh sat on the high seat, Laybkeh and I on the low bench. At the train station, Laybkeh bought the ticket for Tsippeh and carried the baggage into the coach. He kept shuffling his feet and parading himself in front of Tsippeh like an officer. When the train began to move, he followed along beside it, waving his derby hat in the air and speaking in Russian:

"*Do svidaniyeh, do svidaniyeh*! Goodbye, goodbye!"

Mammeh wiped her eyes, kissed Tsippeh again and again, and warned her to keep God in her heart and not let herself get preoccupied because Tsippeh had confided to her during the holiday that the intended bridegroom, the broom maker, didn't appeal to her. He was a boor, she said, didn't know a word of Polish and couldn't mix with people.

Mammeh sighed and said that Tsippeh should have looked around first. Now when she'd been going with him for so long, it was too late. And besides, he was willing to take her as she was, without a penny dowry.

But Tsippeh argued that she didn't know yet. She had a better match in mind, an educated person, a bookkeeper, for instance . . .

That's how she left, without giving anybody anything and without saying goodbye to Tatteh.

Mammeh sighed deeply and kept sighing for many days afterward. That sighing together with the smell of Tsippeh's little boxes and bottles hung in the air at our house well into the winter.

Chapter 28

The orchard in our courtyard turned damp and black after the holidays. Zaynvl the Fruit Grower, brought home a red, wrinkled featherbed and the last cartload of winter apples. Thick and foggy evenings began falling in the middle of the day, and the leaves turned yellow on the misted windowpanes.

On such evenings Tatteh sat in his quilted jacket with a piece of chalk busy figuring out on the table the profits from Leniveh for himself and his partner, Mottl Shtroy.

Laybkeh was no longer in the house. He was supposed to go to Warsaw to look for work but he was waiting for a letter from Tsippeh. She had promised to write and to give back the spanking new Yekaterinoslav ruble, but it seemed that she'd forgotten. Laybkeh was withdrawn now and he no longer told his stories about military service. The smell of tar had already evaporated from his body when he came home one day and said that he was moving out. He was going to live on his own. He now had work with Pinkhehs the Locksmith. He'd be paid wages of six rubles a week and he'd be fed the midday meal too.

So he moved out. Shabbes after we finished eating he came back to visit, humming and tapping out the beat with his foot. He asked about Tsippeh, whether she'd written, whether she was married already, and he asked Mammeh to send his regards when she wrote to her.

Laybkeh must have seen that we weren't exactly swimming in gold in our house because he told Mammeh she could borrow some money from him if she needed.

Mammeh really did need. Not for herself, God forbid, or for anything exceptional but for me because right after the holiday, I wasn't a cheder boy anymore. Mammeh had enrolled me in a new secular school where the tuition cost a lot of money and where the Russian language and grammar were taught.

Tatteh didn't even want any of this. He said that at this new school they turned children into ignorant goyim and what's more, they taught them with heads uncovered. Laybkeh mixed in and gave an example from Yekaterinoslav, about somebody, an official rabbi, who also went to a secular school. You never know, he said, maybe someday, I'd turn out to be an official rabbi too.

Laybkeh was probably joking but in this new school they really did teach very different. When you graduated from this school you'd be able to read the sacred texts together with the musical accents. You'd be able to read the new, Hebrew newspaper, "Hatsefireh," and you could take part in discussions about Zionism.

It was altogether different from Simmeh-Yoysef's cheder. Here, there was not one dark room with sweaty benches around the walls but two big, airy rooms with lots of clear windowpanes and a wrought iron balcony facing the street. In the middle of the second room stood rows of benches one behind the other like soldiers, black, short, with holes for inkpots, and compartments where each person could store his food and writing implements.

On one wall hung an old, half-peeling, big blue map with towns and villages, lakes and oceans. On the opposite wall hung pictures of wild and domestic animals, fish and scorpions, vegetables and fruit.

At the very top, where the blond tsar hung with the blue satin sash across his chest, two other portraits hung also.

One was of a thickset person in an eight-sided silk skullcap, a grey, trimmed beard and a white jabot around his short neck. It was said that this person was Moisheh Montefiore and that he was a great lord.

I liked him because he wore the same kind of white jabot as my mother.

The second portrait was of a very different type. Here was a person without a beard, with a goyish face, sharp eyes and a black, turned up mustache.

It was a surprise to me. How did such a severe, goyish face come to this new school? But the other boys explained that this was, God forbid, no goy, but a Jew, one of the big wheels, a powerful figure. It was Baron de Hirsh himself, who wanted Jews to be redeemed from exile.

I couldn't believe it! In spite of the fact that he was such a powerful person, I couldn't stand this Baron. He stabbed too hard with that black, turned up mustache of his. A person should stare into your face all the time? And not just stare, but glare, as if he was hired to watch our every step, our every move.

We were watched enough already even without him. He, this Baron, could depend on our Rabbi Reb Duvid!

This Rabbi Reb Duvid, was a kind of Simmeh-Yoysef, but different. He was a coarse Jew in a coarse, old-fashioned smock, with a coarse, sparse beard and coarse feet, one of which was shorter than the other. Besides teaching, he owned a spice shop, had a grown daughter, and a round little strap taken from a sewing machine.

This rabbi taught us khumash with Rashi, and how to read the portion of the week with the musical accents.

Actually, it wasn't he so much that taught as the round little strap that he wound between his fingers like a coiled snake that did the teaching. This Rabbi Reb Duvid had a round, low-slung backside that he hoisted onto a bench, leaned his short leg on a low stool, and in this way he looked over the heads of all the pupils. He had small, squinting eyes and arched rabbinic type eyebrows. Still, he saw what was cooking in every pot. And if he noticed that something wasn't right, he took his backside off the stool, pretended to look the other way, and limped over to the perpetrator. Indirectly like a silent cat, he would unexpectedly wrench the cap from his head and let the leather snake fly over the whole width of the uncovered head.

"A cho-o-lera! A plague take you!" His mouth twisted to one side. "You won't stop playing games with the buttons, you bastard?"

A welt rose up immediately on the "bastard's" head that went down part of the cheek and stayed there like a swollen, bloody vein.

It was said that this Rabbi Reb Duvid was already on his third wife and that he'd bury her too. Everyone in town knew that he hated her and called her terrible names. Still, he wanted to have children by her even though he had a grown daughter by his first wife.

This Rabbi Reb Duvid came to school later than his pupils. He limped in wearing a pair of old, worn-out slippers, and a pair of old cloth pants that were twisted around like pipes. He considered himself a Talmud scholar. At Slikhehs-time, he hustled himself to the pulpit and on Shabbes he read from the Torah scroll at the Zionist shul.

It was said that this Rabbi was a fierce Misnaged, an opponent of Hassidism, that he'd have nothing to do with the Hassidic rebbes, and that he hated them. It was also said that he'd once loudly cursed out a Hassid and because of that he limped from then on. Never mind, so he was just a coarse Jew, and a rabbi who liked to flog.

He did have one virtue and because of it we forgave him, not only for his opposition to Hassidism but even for that cursed, round little strap. Nobody taught like Rabbi Reb Duvid, ever. He taught with a melody but it wasn't a Misnaged one at all, and it also wasn't from someone who liked to flog either. He took the words apart like you peel the shell off a nut, and put the kernel into our mouths so that we'd feel the real taste.

According to Rabbi Reb Duvid, the biblical Joseph was a tall, dark young man, so handsome that you couldn't look into his face for too long. He wasn't just our father Abraham's great grandson but a prince who supplied food to all of ancient Egypt, yet he himself was very modest.

Moysheh Rabeynu didn't have a white beard like you see in the portrait that hangs in Aunt Miriam's house, but was actually a young man with a head of curly hair like a sheep, tall and strong like a cedar tree, and here was the proof—Pharaoh's only daughter, the Egyptian princess, wanted him to be her husband.

It was especially nice to hear how Rabbi Reb Duvid explained *parshehs besholekh*, the chapter dealing with the Exodus from Egypt. He became a different person, no longer the one with the ordinary face, wearing a cheap, old-fashioned robe. The rabbi's voice wasn't miserly and cracked as usual anymore, but now rang out broad and self-confident, coming not just out of his mouth but from his whole body. He recited and sang out the verses, not only to us but to the whole world.

Here we left ancient Egypt together with Moysheh Rabeynu. We could hear the footsteps and the wheels of Pharaoh's chariots. The sea was split right before our eyes. We watched as the Egyptians with their horses and wagons sank into the sea, heard Moysheh Rabeynu sing *az yashir, thus he sang*, with the People of Israel while Miriam the Prophetess kept time on the tambourine.

If we could study the Book of Exodus all year we'd never get bored, especially if Rabbi Reb Duvid forgot all about his little leather strap and about the "choleras!" that he poured out over our heads. But he didn't teach us everything. Besides khumash with Rashi you still had to learn other things too.

There was another rabbi, not at all a coarse Jew, and not dressed in a coarse, old-fashioned smock, and that was Rabbi Reb Yankeleh.

During winter evenings, by the red glow of the big lamps, this particular Jew taught us *posek*, the sacred verses, and grammar. He couldn't teach this during daylight. His voice, his whole figure was so dark and shadowy that it matched the winter evenings.

He was tall and hunched over, his pale face encircled by a small, pointy black beard. Rabbi Reb Yankeleh came to school from a long way off, all the way from the gates of Scarczew. He didn't wear old, worn-out slippers like Rabbi Reb Duvid but a pair of small, shiny

Shabbes boots that squeaked like those of a rich man, and an ebony
walking stick with a white bone handle. They were left over from the
time when he had been a timber merchant. His slow, measured walk,
his white collar with the black cravat were all that was left from those
years when his rafts went floating down the Vistula River all the way
to Danzig.

Those years were now long gone. Rabbi Reb Yankeleh used to
speak loudly then, and he'd bang his ebony walking stick into the floor
when a pauper came in seeking alms. He didn't have such a pale face
and such watery, sunken eyes then as he did now.

From those long-gone forests and rafts he was left with nothing
more than the refined name of Reb Yankeleh and the even more refined
prophets, Isaiah and Ezekiel.

It was said that Rabbi Reb Yankeleh became a melamed, a teacher
of young children in his later years, not because he had to earn a livelihood and not because he had once had trouble from his children, but
because of his great devotion to the Bible.

When he started the first chapter of Isaiah with us, we saw how
this once rich and powerful Jew suddenly withdrew from the world.
It wasn't the prophet Isaiah who punished the sinning People of Israel
but our own Rabbi Reb Yankeleh. At that time, his voice got black
just like the rest of him:

"*Bonim g'dalti v'romamti! I raised children,*" he thrust his head
down, "*v'hem poshu bi, and they rose up against* me." He sighed into
the stillness as if he was complaining and lamenting his own bad luck.

When we learned Lamentations with him, he got small and
shrunken just like the prophet Jeremiah. He didn't scream out the
tragedy of the Destruction of the Holy Temple but mumbled it into
himself just like the doves mumble outside the window at dawn.

Rabbi Reb Yankeleh lived with his youngest daughter Dvoyreh,
but in a separate alcove. She had married when her father was already
poverty-stricken, so she was forced to take a young man with no
special pedigree.

Dvoyreleh polished her father's squeaky little boots and brushed
the dust off his ebony walking stick every day, and even though she
had two grown sons who were studying for their examinations at the
gymnasium, she still said to her father:

"Tatteshi, maybe you'll take something with you? A cookie? An
apple?"

My sister Bayleh who was a neighbor of Rabbi Reb Yankeleh,
told how he sat by a tallow candle for whole nights, writing. They

said he was writing a seyfer, a sacred text. All the neighbors knew about it and everyone had something different to say about him, but he himself said nothing.

He went around the schoolroom leaning on his ebony walking stick, stooped shoulders thrust forward, listening carefully to the verses of the Bible, busy with his own thoughts, and even though it seemed that he didn't know what was going on around him, he still knew who paid attention and who was busy playing games with buttons.

Then he would go quietly, not with the teaching strap like Rabbi Reb Duvid or with the "cholera" on his twisted mouth, but just like that, leaning on his stick with one hand and with his other hand on the bench, he'd ask:

"Whose son are you, young man?"

"Itsheh the Tailor's son."

"What's your mother's name?"

"Fradl."

"Then tell your mother, and let your father hear as well, that it's a waste of their efforts. Your father probably toils for a piece of bread. I understand your mother scrapes together groshn by groshn to pay for your tuition, and here you make a complete ruin of all their hard work! You think that the prophets of old just railed out into the empty world? They were as poor as your father is, and they didn't earn a living from prophecy. They wanted only to be heard. And you go and play games with buttons! So tell me yourself, by all means. Aren't you sinning by doing this?"

He was quite right, this rabbi. How could you play games with buttons while he taught Bible? Wasn't it better to listen to his chanting than to win a few more silly buttons from a friend? But Itsheh the Tailor's son and the other boys like him stayed blockheads until the shards were placed on their eyes.

They didn't understand that you could learn something even without all the slaps and curses. For them Rabbi Reb Duvid was good enough, or even Matyas the Teacher.

It must be because of those boys that Matyas the Teacher was hired at this school, because it was hard to understand how such a rabbi as Reb Yankeleh and a person like Matyas the Teacher could both teach under the same roof.

Matyas the Teacher was not a Jew and not a goy, but a Muscovite, a Russky, nothing else.

He taught us the Russian language, penmanship, and arithmetic, all of this in a hoarse, drunken voice with drunken hands and a drunken head. While teaching, he smoked one cigarette after another, had fits of coughing and he'd spit into all the corners. He had a habit of tensing his cheekbones. His wrinkled, unslept looking face looked like a piece of shrunken cloth. He didn't hold the cigarette between his lips but in the yellowed teeth that were pointed and chipped like those of a wolf.

He prowled around the school like a wolf watching for the moment when he could pounce on us and make us cringe. It was hard to understand how there could be so much anger and fury in such a dried out, skinny body.

It was said that Matyas the Teacher hadn't slept with his wife for many years. He didn't sleep at all. He played cards. His wife was a newcomer. She wore a long, yellowed fur coat left over from Poniatowski's times and she went around with her hair uncovered.

Everyone in town knew that Matyas the Teacher's wife bought her meat in the goyish butcher shops and when she brought it home she didn't even bother making it kosher. At Christmas time she put up a crèche and made the sign of the cross over herself. It was also known that Matyas the Teacher would come home at dawn from playing cards all night and would beat his wife, spit on her long, yellowed fur coat, and break everything that came to hand.

All this was known in town. People were offended and avoided the house where Matyas the Teacher lived.

Still, every mother wanted her children to go to this new school where he taught anyway. My mother made excuses first of all, by saying that when you finished your studies at this school, you'd be able to read seyfer, the sacred texts. Second, she really wanted me to learn grammar and penmanship. She'd learned penmanship too and today she could write letters for brides to their bridegrooms who were serving in the Russian Army, and also for women whose children were in America.

Mammeh said that nothing would happen to me. King Solomon himself had said that giving a child a whack from time to time wouldn't do him any harm, and that if you beat the behind it would go straight to the head.

First of all, I wasn't such a child that you could just wallop me and second of all, Matyas the Teacher never just whacked you on the backside but actually right across the head. Third, slapping wouldn't help anyway because I'd never be able to write like Mammeh.

She'd been taught by a different kind of teacher. He must have been an easy-going person, her teacher. He probably didn't have drunken hands, or else how could he teach penmanship? You had to think about how to form the letters. Sometimes thick strokes, sometimes thin, another time, either rounded or pointed.

How could I do all that if Matyas the Teacher's every step hung over my head like a slaughtering knife, making me shake in body and soul?

Suddenly he'd throw one cigarette away and light another one. We all sat with our heads bent to one side, hearts pounding, and drew the letters onto the lined blue paper. The teacher's shoes squeaked creating terror in the quietly held breath of everybody in the room. Even his shoes were drunk.

I was covered in sweat even though he couldn't really have anything against me because I rounded and twisted every single letter so that it couldn't be any better, even if my own mother herself had written them.

In the middle of it, I felt the bitter smell of cigarettes. Something was wheezing above me from out of a raw throat. I didn't even have time to look up when suddenly my head rang with an unexpected blow, and with a fist under my chin, he screamed in Russian:

"*Svolotsh!* You dirty swine!" and he went into a fit of coughing. "*Sukin sin!* Son of a bitch! That's how you write '*shtsha*'? Over there, to the blackboard! Write it again, you dog, you!"

He dragged me by the ear. My whole face burned, my temples throbbed, sparks flew in front of my eyes. My friends burrowed their heads deep into their shoulders.

Their heads were black now like charred wedges of cabbage.

The blackboard on its three spread-out, wooden legs was now no longer just an ordinary blackboard to me, but a t'hareh board for the ritual cleansing of corpses.

We were more afraid of this blackboard than of Matyas the Teacher himself. It was like a living thing and it stood in such a way that it also looked drunk. You couldn't hide anywhere. Here he stood, Matyas the Teacher, tense, feet spread apart, ready to pounce like a wolf on a lamb. Nothing would help now, even if you could write "*shtsha*" properly—the whack under the chin had to come, the teeth had to rattle.

It happened once that little Yoseleh's tooth got loosened and he later dug it out of his bloodied gums with his tongue. To me, after I had written out half a blackboard with "*shtshas,*" decorated it with little pig's tails, my left ear was wrenched. A warm rivulet of blood trickled into my throat. Matyas the Teacher had white lips so the rivulet of blood didn't bother him any. He gave me an added kick to my backside and screeched into my ear again in Russian:

"*Poshol von! Svolotsh!* Get lost! You dirty swine!"

That's how it was every day. Sometimes I was the sacrifice, sometimes it was somebody else. Only Moyshl the Tavern Keeper's son didn't feel the taste of Matyas the Teacher's drunken hands on his body.

This Moyshl even though he had a girlish face and went around with sugary lips, still, he was Matyas the Teacher's best pupil. This best pupil ate a lot, loudly smacked his wet lips, got a swollen belly from overeating, and had white, puffy hands.

But it didn't stop him from having proper penmanship or to know how much nine times nine is, or what adjectives meant.

Everyone in school hated Moyshl. First, because he really did know; second, because he didn't want to help anybody. And third, because he tattled on the rest of us.

He had only one friend at this school, a poor, skinny boy, Yukeleh. Yukeleh didn't have a father. His mother was a young, hearty woman who went begging from house to house and telling everybody that her Yukeleh was fathered by a tree.

Yukeleh didn't have to pay any tuition. He was taken into the school out of pity.

So this Moyshl the Tavern Keeper's son became fast friends with Yukeleh and treated him like a servant. He loved to pinch and tickle Yukeleh until his mouldy face got pale and swollen, but in return he'd get from Moyshl the Tavern Keeper's son, a bit of cold chicken gizzard, a small piece of goose liver, a hard-boiled egg, and sometimes Moyshl took him along to his father's tavern and let him lick the foam from the beer glasses that the young wagon drivers left behind.

Because of Moyshl the Tavern Keeper's son, we detested Yukeleh too, even though he was so skinny and had a tree for a father. They were always together.

Nobody talked to them and if one of us felt like teasing, they never answered back. They always ran away but the next day, when Matyas the Teacher came in, Moyshl would stand up and tattle on us:

"Gospodin Utshitel, Mister Utshitel, they threw stones at me yesterday . . ."

"Who threw?" Matyas the Teacher pointed his charred yellow mustache.

"Itsik threw, Mendl threw. All of them threw."

Matyas the Teacher whacked with his fist under chins, tore at ears, and wheezed out of his drunken throat:

"*Svolotsh, parshivayah! Ya tebyeh pokazhu* . . . You dirty swine! You scabhead! I'll show you . . ."

Life was bitter. Everyone prayed that Matyas the Teacher, Moyshl the Tavern Keeper's son, and the blackboard would all meet with a violent death.

But what was the use of praying if Matyas the Teacher continued to souse himself at Moyshl's father's tavern, the blackboard still stood on its spread out, drunken legs, and Moyshl tattled on us even more than usual?

Chapter 29

Our curses didn't bother Matyas the Teacher because he looked even healthier but death carried off our Rabbi Reb Yankeleh even though we all blessed him.

Sleet was blowing that day and the shutter on our window kept tearing at its chain, sighing like a sick person. Tatteh didn't go traveling anywhere, and Mammeh didn't let me go to school.

"You'll get sick, God forbid," she said. "Stay home."

But I especially wanted to go to school today. During the night, I'd woken up heavy-hearted. It seemed to me that my dead brother Moysheh was wandering around in the kitchen looking for something in the pots. I heard mice scrambling around, and I couldn't figure out if the clock was ticking or not.

I didn't tell anyone in the house what I'd imagined during the night but when Mammeh told me not to go to school, I was enveloped in dread.

I told her that I had to go today because Rabbi Reb Duved was going to call on me to explain the sedreh, the biblical portion of the week.

The sleet slapped me hard in the face and the wind pushed me backward as if it didn't want me to go to school today either.

But I got stubborn.

Last night's heaviness still lay on my chest. Even though I hurried, I was late anyway, but nobody at school said anything to me. They didn't even notice when I came in.

The school looked strange now. Not one boy was sitting in his right place. Nobody was studying. Everyone was running around and the doors stood wide open. Rabbi Reb Duvid limped quickly around on his short leg and made some motions with his hands. Matyas the Teacher was already there too. He looked shrunken; smoked cigarettes, but didn't finish the last one before starting a new one. Every minute, another boy came running, said something to Rabbi Reb Duvid and

waited, distracted. Skinny, moldy Yukeleh sobbed quietly. Could it be
that Moishl the Tavern Keeper's son had pinched him so hard?

But here came Moishl himself, and it looked like he was making
straight for me. I wasn't on speaking terms with him, so how come he
was coming over to me now? Moishl pushed himself forward with his
swollen belly, his soft girlish face white like dough, and made a face:

"D'ya know," he said, his voice tight, "that Rabbi Reb Yankeleh
died?"

"Oy vey'z mir!"

I didn't know whether it was Moishl or I who yelled it out, but
the heaviness in my chest suddenly rose up to my throat choking me.
I didn't see Yukeleh come over to us but only felt his small, moldy
hand on my shoulder.

"Rabbi Reb Yankeleh . . ." he sniveled. "Rabbi Reb Yankeleh . . ."

Rabbi Reb Yankeleh had died during the night and it was actually from heaviness on the chest. They said it went to his throat and
choked him.

"Is everybody here?" Suddenly, we heard the cracked voice of
Rabbi Reb Duvid.

"Everybody's here."

"Be quiet! Stand up!"

Matyas the Teacher, his head sunken, stood looking at our feet.
"Nobody's shoes are soaked?" He asked in Yiddish, in a deep voice,
not at all drunken.

"Nobody."

"We'll have to go to the funeral."

"So we'll go."

Rabbi Reb Duvid raised his hand now empty of the little leather
strap.

"Children," he called out, "your rabbi, Reb Yankeleh has died.

"Dead!" Yukeleh sobbed."

Rabbi Reb Duvid closed his eyes, wiped his forehead and quietly
shook his head. "Yes, dead!"

Matyas the Teacher asked us to go to the Scaryczew city gates.
There we were to stand in lines of three and wait until he and Reb
Duvid would arrive.

They carried out Rabbi Reb Yankeleh from his daughter's house
in the afternoon. The tall Jew with the stooped shoulders now lay in
a small, narrow coffin that swayed from the mass of moving black
caps. The rabbi's satin top hat, and Reb Arn the Rabbinical Judge's
pinched yellow shtrayml, stood out higher than the rest of them. It

was Friday. The wind that had torn at the sheet metal roofs earlier in the day, now quieted down. The sleet delayed itself over the small black coffin, probably waiting for the burial.

Shops closed hurriedly. Jews went to the next street and some even went all the way to the three trees, to accompany the procession and ask forgiveness from the corpse.

The whole school with Rabbi Reb Duvid and Matyas the Teacher at the head walked in front of the coffin, three in a row. With all our hearts and souls, we chanted into the cold, wet streets:

"*Tsedek l'fonev yihaleykh. Tsedek l'fonev yihaleykh. Righteousness goes before him. Righteousness goes before him.*"

This was the first time that I was in a cemetery ever. It seemed to me that not even the living could come back from there and I kept looking back to see if they weren't closing the cemetery gates behind us.

Here under this tree, Rabbi Reb Yankeleh, the one-time timber merchant, the master of bible studies, the devoted follower of the Enlightenment, would be laid to rest. Probably his two prophets, Isaiah and Ezekiel, would come to greet him and probably too, the prophet Jeremiah would weep at the death of such an honorable, respectable Jew.

But why are they putting such an honorable and respectable Jew into such a narrow and wet grave? Why was the gravedigger in such a hurry? Didn't this coarsened Jew know that such a deceased person should be handled with respect, just as he'd been when he was still alive?

But it was Friday. The wind waited, the rain stopped, and the rabbi and the rabbinical judge had long since left. The remaining Jews were hurrying to get back to town too. Women were already seated in the carriages. The young wagon drivers were haggling when the wind suddenly reminded itself that it was now after the funeral. It whistled among the poplar trees and the sleet whipped up. Rabbi Reb Yankeleh's daughter, his son-in-law, and their two sons were already coming back from the grave. Only Matyas the Teacher and the small, moldy Yukeleh remained standing so long until two tallow Shabbes candles appeared in the window of Zalmen the Gravedigger's hut.

⁓

For some time afterward, we still continued to hear the squeaky step of Rabbi Reb Yankeleh's little boots. Small, yellow flames flickered in the bright lamps after his death. The new little glass cups that were replaced in the lamps didn't make any difference at all, and neither did the kerosene that was now bought in a different shop than usual.

Everything looked yellowed in our eyes, the map on the wall, the portrait of Moisheh Montefiore, even Rabbi Reb Duvid had a yellowed face and puffy eyes.

Matyas the Teacher smoked and wheezed even more hoarsely than usual. He continued to slap us around and box our ears. Even Moishl the Tavern Keeper's son began to feel the taste of Matyas the Teacher's hand from time to time, and the teacher himself seemed to shrink and become a head shorter during this time.

Rabbi Reb Yankeleh's blond, young son-in-law who was a follower of the Enlightenment and also a Zionist, now taught us Bible. This son-in-law had a pale, distant face, a thin little beard and a flat voice. When he explained a biblical passage it came out cold and dry. It was said of him that he nourished us with stale challah and musty grits.

It was true. In his dry, listless voice, the speeches of the prophets seemed like tired flies buzzing around on the chilly windowpanes with their last strength. He never hit anyone or told anyone off but went among the benches with a soft, little bamboo stick that he banged on the tables.

We didn't know his name so in the first few weeks we called him Rabbi Reb Yankeleh's son-in-law but later, when someone let fall the words, "stale challah," that's how it stayed.

We didn't like him, and we didn't not like him. He'd come in with a little dance, repeatedly bang his little bamboo stick, describe several passages to us, and then with the same, dancelike steps, leave without even saying, 'good night.'

It was said that this "stale challah" was teaching us only temporarily, that we'd get another rabbi in the coming semester, someone with a sharp head who had already graduated from the gymnasium and for whom my Zaydeh had once sewn navy blue uniforms with silver buttons.

But the "stale challah" stayed with us in the new semester too, and my Zaydeh finally stopped sewing the navy blue uniforms.

It was already after Pesach and warm, blue mornings began rising over the orchard. The smell of newly washed bed linen and freshly washed floors could still be felt in the house. Who'd expect that on such a blue morning my Zaydeh would die? I always thought that Duvid Froykeh's, with his ditties and good cheer, would be the last person in town to die.

In the end he lay stretched out on the floor, long and narrow, like a dead fish.

The door to Zaydeh's small house stood wide open. Strange Jews were mingling inside and out. Vladek, the witless goy, sat at the pump in the courtyard with his two empty, watering cans shaking his unkempt beard and mumbling to himself in Polish:

"*Nima, Pana Kravtsa. Nima!* Not here! Pan Tailor's not here!"

Mammeh had left the house at dawn, disheveled, her shoes unbuttoned. Now she lay on Bubbeh's unmade bed, her face in the pillow, not sleeping and not crying, giving out only hoarse belches and hiccoughs.

Aunt Miriam, Zaydeh's other daughter, stood at her father's workbench talking into it in a thick voice like you talk to a real live person:

"Who's going to do the work now? And who's going to do the singing now?"

She kept repeating this over and over again. It looked like it was coming out of her all by itself, as if she herself wasn't even here, but in the middle of all this she seemed to remember something, waved her hands over the room and standing in one spot, she called out:

"Let me . . . ! Let me near my father!"

But how could her father help her if he's no longer in our world? He's now no longer her father or my Zaydeh, but a body, a corpse.

Two yellowed and shrunken big toes stuck out from under the black cover that was tied together with straw.

Strange women were sitting in the house praising the virtues of my Zaydeh. The pots in the kitchen stood cold and chipped, but you couldn't see this. The only thing you could see was the two big, dead toes and my Bubbeh Rakhl.

Small and shrunken, she stood over the body of her dead husband and shook her dainty head into the black covering:

"Duvid," she complained, "How could you abandon me? Duvid, who'll now make kiddesh, eh? You went out like a light! At least, if you'd have said to me: 'Rakhl, I don't feel so good,' but you go and turn yourself to the wall . . . and that's it! For that I had to spend a lifetime with you, so that in the end I shouldn't even be able to save you?"

She talked like this all day, my Bubbeh, speaking ever more quietly, mumbling. She wouldn't take anything into her mouth, not even a glass of tea. She quieted down only in the evening when the two white candles at Zaydeh's head began flickering with a yellow mist.

The night descended like the black cover on the corpse. A swarthy Jew, his beard tucked under, recited tilim, psalms. Mammeh leaned her head on the headboard of Bubbeh's bed, Aunt Miriam did the same on the other bed, her children and I were heaped together across the width of the same bed. Bubbeh Rakhl moved her trunk closer to the corpse and stayed there all night guarding the two yellowed, dead toes.

The funeral was held the following afternoon. We waited for Zaydeh's two sons, Uncle Avrum-Ayzik from Warsaw, a desperate pauper who could playfully make birds fly through the air and Uncle Luzeh from Lodz, a wealthy Jew, but he couldn't make birds fly through the air.

The uncle from Lodz arrived with a rich man's little cough and a snowy white handkerchief that he held to his nose all the time. The uncle from Warsaw wore an eight-sided cap and spectacles. He was thin and his blond beard was neatly combed. He put his head and both hands on the coffin. Uncle Luzeh from Lodz walked with slow steps and from time to time looked behind him.

The rabbi and the rabbinical judge didn't accompany my Zaydeh's coffin, shops weren't closed for the occasion and cheder boys didn't chant: "*Tsedek l'fonev yehaleykh, righteousness goes before him.*"

Nobody in town even knew who'd died except maybe the sun because it lay on the coffin, on our shoulders, and in front of the horses' steps, looking for all the world just like the Pillar of Fire when the Jews went out from ancient Egypt.

Chapter 30

After Zaydeh's death we were very sad. Rich Uncle Luzeh returned to Lodz the very same day right after the funeral. Uncle Avrum-Ayzik, the pauper, stayed and sat shiveh in Bubbeh Rakhl's little hut. Stories were told about Zaydeh all week. After the shiveh was over, Uncle Avrum-Ayzik, who was also a tailor, finished the last blue uniform that Zaydeh had started.

That same evening, he sat himself into Yarmeh the Wagon Driver's omnibus and went back to his wife and child in Warsaw.

Bubbeh was left all alone in the little white hut. Nobody did any pressing and nobody sang any songs. The only person who watched over her was Vladek, the witless goy.

So Bubbeh began to sell off and give away the inheritance that was left from Zaydeh. Uncle Avrum-Ayzik took Zaydeh's tallis and tfiln, a pair of high holiday prayer books, some wax, and a packet of needles back with him to Warsaw. My mother got the Pesach dishes and Elijah the Prophet's wine goblet. The only thing that Bubbeh Rakhl kept for herself was Zaydeh's workbench and her own little trunk. With this bit of household goods, she moved in with Aunt Miriam.

Aunt Miriam was then living in part of a big, walled house that had a long rectangular courtyard. Her part of the house, including her kitchen hung off a balcony. It was crowded, but Aunt Miriam still found room for Bubbeh's bed, her trunk, and Zaydeh's well-worn workbench.

It seemed to me that now, after Aunt Miriam had changed her living space and after Bubbeh Rakhl in her old age had to move in with one of her children, it made no sense for us to stay in Jailhouse Alley anymore, especially since Mammeh had now taken such a dislike to where we were living.

So she started asking around about a place that'd be warm and dry and where it wouldn't cost a lot of money. This time it took longer than usual but when the goyish *Shvienti Yan*, Saint John holiday came along and it got very hot, we loaded our bit of household goods onto a wagon once more, said goodbye to the neighbors and the beautiful orchard, and with luck, we took ourselves off to the same street where my Zaydeh Duvid-Froykeh's had lived out his years and died.

My heart cried when I looked at this new place where our beds and wardrobe were now carried. Tatteh, who helped with the moving this time, stood lost as if he had made a mistake and gone into a strange house where a woman was undressing.

What could Mammeh have found pleasing here? Why did she exchange the orchard and the garden for this run-down tavern? Why, the windows weren't even windows! Two dove cotes stood on the roof and a hellish heat came from the sheet metal roof. So what if we could see all of Warsaw Street with its chimneys and roofs from here when down below there was such a stench of horses' urine from the horse cabs that stood in the street?

Maybe what Mammeh found pleasing was that ours were the only windows on the roof? Maybe it was the fact that down in the street, Loony Laybl propped up the wall chewing horse dung?

There wasn't even a painted floor in this new place. Where's the kitchen? Where did the kitchen get to? There wasn't even a kitchen here but one big room like an inn, with a low beam and a sprawling, old-fashioned clay oven with two little chambers on either side from which you smelled cats.

It must be that what pleased Mammeh was the corner between the oven and the wall, what she called an alcove.

"If you want," she said, "it's not an alcove at all, but a real room where you can put two beds and a commode, hang a curtain over the entrance, and rent it out. Down below on the first floor lives the Natshalnik, the Chief of the Povyat district, and the stairs are painted red."

The Chief of the Povyat district really did live on the first floor but the stairs were only painted red up to his door.

To get to us you had to climb up through crooked and dirty steps, past the attic where stranger's laundry hung whose empty shapes scared us. You had to move along carefully and feel your way with your hands so as not to step on the cats that came up here to yowl their guts out.

Even the courtyard in this new place was not like the old one in Jailhouse Alley. Here it was crowded, hemmed in by walls and balconies that led to wooden stalls and chicken coops. The only attraction here was the round, green pump. You couldn't tell any stories in this courtyard, I thought to myself.

I won't have someone like Yankl, Yarmeh the Wagon Driver's son here. For sure, there'd be no omnibus here. Where'd I be able to find a place for myself? I was very sad at heart, so sad, that lots of times I went back to Jailhouse Alley to look at the orchard, the garden, and to stare up at our old window where goyish flowerpots now stood.

But God doesn't abandon us. After living here a short time, Mammeh got acquainted with a neighbor who was a different sort of person altogether, with a different attitude than that of our former neighbors.

"She's no gabby old biddy," Mammeh said, "but a real woman."

This woman went around with her own hair showing, didn't make the blessing over the candles, and she never went to shul. Still, my mother and some of the other neighbors said that Rayzeleh the Wine Dealer was a saintly woman and a kosher Jewish soul.

Rayzeleh was short, thickset with a puffy double chin. She hiccoughed slightly when she spoke just like wealthy women did. She ran a shop where she sold cookies and lollipops as well as wine.

Rayzeleh could speak German and write French too. She sat in her shop in a black alpaca apron tucked in top to bottom and she read books in strange languages through a pair of gold-rimmed spectacles.

Year after year, Rayzeleh traveled to the warm baths and came back gaunt looking. She kept a goyish servant in the house and even though she herself was educated and could talk even with the governor, she still called her servant girl not by the familiar "di" for you, but "Pani," Miss.

The rich women held this up to her.

"Rayzeleh," they complained, "who ever heard of such a thing! You're ruining the servants."

But Rayzeleh answered that the Master-of-the-Universe had created everybody equal but that people themselves had divided up the world in such a way that one person had it good while another had it bad. Why? Was it the unfortunate little servant girl's fault that she had to be a servant to others? And if she had to be a servant, why did she deserve that other people should humiliate her?

The rich women thought Rayzeleh was out of her mind. They ridiculed her quietly and said that she gave herself airs to make people think that she really was a somebody.

But the poverty-stricken women didn't ridicule her. They said that you'd have to go searching with torches throughout the whole world to find someone like Rayzeleh with the kind of husband she had.

It could actually be that a Jew like Rayzeleh's husband, Reb Menakhem, really had to be searched for with torches.

First of all, he was exceptionally tall, so tall he was actually bent over and on top of that, he had a hunchback.

He was the only tall, hunchbacked person in town and maybe even in the whole world. He was a Koyen, a descendant of the ancient priestly class, an angry man, a scholar, and a follower of the Enlightenment. In his later years he was forced to become a bookkeeper to some wealthy Jew who had a clean, combed beard, wore polished, squeaky little boots, but had the head of a peasant.

Just like his wife, Reb Menakhem didn't hold with blessing the candles or with davening.

"Let the boss go daven," he'd say, "he's a thief, and everybody knows that thieves are afraid of God."

When he was accused of bad mouthing his own boss, Reb Menakhem screwed up his bony face and answered:

"Did I ask him to become my boss? And secondly, the Master-of-the-Universe doesn't like him either. Three things the Master-of-the-Universe doesn't like—apostates, pigs, and wealthy people."

Reb Menakhem wore a dusty, black derby hat—a businessman's hat, a long coat with a split up the back, and a pair of unpolished gaiters. But he didn't especially like this get-up.

"A person shouldn't even be able to dress the way he wants?" he complained.

"Of course not," the respectable Jews ridiculed him. "Why shouldn't a Jew like Reb Menakhem wear a velvet cap and a silk kapoteh?"

Reb Menakhem understood the ridicule and shot back, "Why's it such a good idea to put a lot of work into a velvet cap?" He also said that satin kapotehs should be made into silk underwear for women.

"When did Jews ever wear such garments in the past?" He boiled in anger, "Just the opposite! Show me where it says in the Toyreh that the Jews of old wore satin kapotehs and velvet caps. Isn't it better and healthier to go around bareheaded, without shoes and without all these ridiculous clothes?"

"You're already wearing a long coat! What else d'ya want?"

"This long coat is good for nothing too! That's how my wife decked me out! If you ask me, I'd say, wear a cape. There's nothing better than a cape. Its open, airy, and you have where to put your hands."

"Just like Tshappeleh the Magician or Duvid-Froykeh's the Tailor," Jews smirked into their beards, and secretly murmured that Menakhem the Bookkeeper was out of his mind too.

"Tshappeleh the Magician and Duvid-Froykeh's the Tailor," Reb Menakhem said, his face reddening, "are worth much more to the

Master-of-the-Universe than you with your greasy kapotehs and your thieving ways. Tshappeleh can at least do tricks and Duvid-Froykeh's can sew up a garment, but what can you do? Why you can't even explain a passage of the khimesh with Rashi properly!"

But Reb Menakhem could. It was said of Reb Menakhem that he'd become a heretic from too much learning and that he'd also gotten interested in Zionism. Years earlier he'd become friendly with a Reb Yisroyel the Teacher who'd proposed the new school, and it was said that the only thing this school graduated was a generation of 'goyim,' that is to say, ignoramuses. Reb Menakhem and Reb Yisroyel talked about the sacred books all their lives. They carried on debates day and night and pulled at their beards while playing chess.

But since Reb Yisroyel the Teacher's death, Reb Menakhem didn't bother getting to know anyone else, except for the Litvak teacher who drew on the shank of a tobacco pipe and kept asking:

"Is there a Master-of-the-Universe or isn't there a Master-of-the-Universe?"

Was it any wonder then that my friendship with Oyzeh, the youngest son of Reb Menakhem the Bookkeeper and Rayzeleh the Wine Dealer, made such a big impression on me?

I'd heard about Oyzeh when I was still in Simmeh-Yoysef's cheder. It was said of him that he was as angry as his father, that he didn't perform the ritual washing of hands before eating and that he went around bareheaded. It was even said in town that he was a bit out of his mind too. But when I became friendly with him I realized that everything that was said of him was out and out lies.

This Oyzeh was different, not the same kind of person as Yankl, Yarmeh the Wagon Driver's son, or like any of the boys at my new school.

Oyzeh was tall, almost as tall as his father, and skinny. He had his father's bony face, his father's black, restless eyes, but he didn't have a hunchback like his father.

When I got to know him, he was already going to the Russian gymnasium, and he wore a blue uniform with silver buttons that my Zaydeh had sewn for him a while ago. The silver buttons got tarnished over time and the uniform changed color from blue to green but that didn't bother Oyzeh. He didn't like to use a comb and it didn't bother him that dandruff fell from his thick, black forelock. He also didn't like the wine and the cookies in his mother's shop. He thought the best food in the world were dry, crackling rolls fresh out of the oven.

He actually brought a lot of rolls to our courtyard and laid them out at the pump or on the steps. Then he'd sit down on top of them like a hen on top of her eggs and he'd pinch off pieces from there and put them into his mouth. He wasn't, God forbid, a glutton. He didn't suffer from hunger. But, just because . . . He said it made him think and talk better. And Oyzeh loved to talk.

On summer evenings when the dusty sun fell into our courtyard and I was already home from school, we'd meet either at the damp pump or on one of the balconies that led into the small cubicles. Oyzeh talked slowly, thinking it over first before he spoke. He actually asked more questions than he answered.

I never saw him laugh or tell a story just to get a laugh because he didn't hold with storytelling at all. He said that all storybooks were made up out of someone's head.

I didn't know whether I liked Oyzeh because I never gave it any thought, but I was now drawn to him more than I had ever been to Yankl, Yarmeh the Wagon Driver's son or to any of my friends at school. Lots of times in my sleep or even at school, Oyzeh's words pressed down on my heart like a stone. It was hard to be with Oyzeh but it was even harder not to be with him. One really hot evening, he put a hand on my shoulder and looking right into my face, he asked: "D'ya believe in God?"

I didn't know whether I got weighed down from the heat or from his question. I shivered from head to toe. What could I answer him? As long as I've lived nobody had yet asked me such a question. How can you even ask such a question?

"What d'ya mean, do I believe in God? Who doesn't believe?"

"You're afraid to say?"

"I'm not afraid to say. Why should I be afraid? But you're not allowed!"

"Who told you that you're not allowed?"

"It says so in the Toyreh."

"What d'ya think the Toyreh is?"

"Its holy."

Oyzeh moved a little away from me. Loony Laybl strolled slowly into the courtyard, the same Laybl who stood all day in the street chewing on what the horse's left behind. Oyzeh and I got very quiet, following Loony Laybl's step with our eyes until he disappeared into his father's house. Only then, did Oyzeh ask:

"D'ya know why he went crazy?"

"I dunno."

"Because he was waiting for the Messiah and he couldn't wait any more."

"Every Jew's waiting for the Messiah."

"So every Jew'll go crazy."

I began to shake. Nothing less, but Oyzeh really was out of his mind! It seemed to me that even though no one was around and no one could hear what we were talking about, still, any minute now, a hail of fiery stones would come down on us.

I was afraid to sit with Oyzeh anymore. All night I kept seeing him, mouth twisted, running through the streets with horns on his head and the beard of a goat, while I ran after him, barking. Nothing else but Oyzeh was changed into a demon and I into a dog!

The next day we met again. I didn't tell him about my dream but I paid careful attention to whether he actually had horns and a goat's beard. The next time Oyzeh asked me another question:

"Did'ya learn any khimesh?"

"I did."

"D'ya know how the world was created?"

"I know, it says so in breyshis, in Genesis."

"Well my father says that nobody knows. What it says in breyshis is just a story."

"A story?"

"Yeh, a story. My father says it's a beautiful story, but it's not true."

"An'ya believe what your father tells you?"

"My father knows all of khimesh together with Rashi, and the whole bible, even the Talmud and the Commentaries he also knows. He says that all of this was written by people."

"And what d'you say?"

"I dunno. My father learns the whole Bible with me. He says that a Jew should know all of it. He says that I don't have to believe in it, but I have to know it."

"Are you gonna put on tfiln?"

"I dunno. My father is teaching me the laws about it."

I knew that Oyzeh knew a lot more than I did but why was he asking me such strange questions. Wasn't he afraid?

"So, if your father is really so smart, let him tell me who created the world?"

"Nobody," answered Oyzeh, "it created itself."

"What d'ya mean it created itself? What thing creates itself?"

"See for yourself."

"I don't see anything."

"And if I tell you," Oyzeh got mad, "will you know?"

"Of course, I'll know."

"Nu, already . . . Nature created the world."

"Nature?" I was taken aback. "What's this nature?"

"You see how you don't understand?"

I really don't understand at all, but I'm not ready to give in so easily. "And what about Moysheh Rabeynu? And what about the Ten Commandments?"

"Nobody knows if there really was a Moysheh Rabeynu."

He grabbed my arm and pressed closer to me, hot breath coming from his mouth. His eyes had a look of something I couldn't define, but it must be that was how someone looked who was going out of his mind.

I remembered how Rabbi Reb Yankeleh, may he rest in peace, learned the whole Bible with us. His prophets Isaiah and Ezekiel really lived, and Rabbi Reb Duvid's Moysheh Rabeynu we saw right before our eyes! And altogether, how could Oyzeh say that Moysheh Rabeynu never lived if, in our house just like in lots of Jewish homes, his portrait hung on the wall? And besides all that, who was it that went to Pharaoh? Who took the Jews out of ancient Egypt? Who destroyed the Golden Calf? Enough already! The whole world was crazy but Oyzeh's father was the only sane person?

I was afraid of him. It seemed to me that his hunchback was a living thing and it looked at me with live eyes and laughed right in my face.

"Of course, all Jews are crazy! What then, they're not crazy?"

Oyzeh became an angry hunchback in my eyes too. His words tormented me. They took away from me my father and my mother, this world and the world to come. It seemed that Shabbes was not Shabbes any more, and the holidays were not holidays to me anymore.

And yet, I couldn't tear myself away from Oyzeh.

He scared me but he also drew me. Besides, sometimes he forgot all about his father's talk and became a friend just like any other friend, a boy just like any other boy. He was already a student at the gymnasium. Still, he came to our house evenings after Shabbes to play bingo and when Mammeh wasn't at home, to do impersonations.

This was one of our best games. Oyzeh would bring colored papers from his mother's shop. We spit on them to make the color run and with the dye we smeared our faces. We turned our clothes inside out and with brooms in our hands, we strode all over our sprawling house. Oyzeh was Moysheh Rabeynu, I was the People of Israel, and he was leading me now out of ancient Egypt.

"Come on," he said, "let's leave Pithom and Ramses and go to the land that flows with milk and honey. Enough of drudging for Pharaoh, enough of being slaves!" He took me by the hand and continued:

" 'Ostrozhniyeh,' Watch it, People of Israel! Here's the sea. So don't fall in. Soon it will split. Oh take a look, the waters are parting left and right. Come on! Don't be afraid."

We went into the sea. That is to say, we jumped over the noodle board that lay in the middle of the room. When we were already on the other side of the sea, dry and intact, we stood and sang the song of praise and watched as the Egyptians with all their horses and all their chariots drowned.

This game was very nice but sometimes I was overcome with a strange sense of dread.

At those moments Oyzeh had dimples in his cheeks and yellow spots in his eyes.

I threw the broom away, threw off the rags and screamed out, as if it wasn't coming out of my own mouth:

"Oyzeh, we're not allowed to make fun! Oyzeh, we'll be roasted and burned in the world to come!"

It seemed that Oyzeh was scared too because he threw the broom away immediately, turned his cap back to the right side, and stood bewildered in the center of the room, lips blue, breathing heavily.

We didn't disguise ourselves as Moysheh Rabeynu and the People of Israel every time.

Sometimes Oyzeh impersonated the rabbi, how stiffly he walked in the street with his umbrella out front, and how Ben-Tsion the Community Scribe ran after him with mincing, little steps.

He mimicked how Aunt Nemmi's son Mendl puffed himself up when singing, how his cheeks got red and his eyes popped.

I gasped with laughter. I liked it that Oyzeh wasn't afraid to make fun of the rabbi or of Ben-Tsion the Community Scribe or Mendl, the aspiring singer or even such a rich man as Royveleh Beckerman.

But what I liked best was when Oyzeh took a coverlet off the bed, wrapped himself up in it, stuck his foot out, and raised his hand up high. At such a moment, his unruly black head of hair looked like a new broom.

Oyzeh told me to stand still and to look at him. First, he cleared his throat, then in a stiff voice and with trembling chin, he began to recite in Russian:

> Prophetic Oleg now sets forth
> To avenge himself on the wily Khazars
> For their ferocious raids.
> He has condemned their villages

And fields to fire and sword.
(Adapted by SK from Daniel Dolinov)

He didn't so much recite it as sing it. His voice as he went along
got higher and clearer. Now he was no longer the Oyzeh who asked
wild questions and didn't know how to answer them. It was a differ-
ent Oyzeh that stood here now, taller, older, stranger, but handsome.
  "D'ya know what this is?"
  "I dunno."
  "It's poems, Pushkin's poems. D'ya know who Pushkin was?"
  "I dunno."
  "And Lermontov, d'ya know who he was?"
  "I don't know anything. Matyas the Teacher doesn't teach us this,
not Pushkin and not Lermontov. We're just at penmanship."
  "Wait!" Oyzeh spread out his arms. "I'll recite some Lermontov
for you."
  Again, he assumed a stance, one foot forward, shook his unruly
head and began with a kind of vanity as well as chutspah, so that his
eyes were actually flashing:

> But tell me uncle, why our men
> Let Moscow burn, yet fought again
> To drive the French away.
> I hear it was a dreadful fight
> A bitter war by day and night.
> (Translated by Eugene M. Kayden)

  Again, I didn't understand any of it. I felt that he was talking
to someone but I didn't know to whom. He was Oyzeh but he was a
stranger. He asked questions and then answered them himself.
  He argued with himself and then he'd give in.
  Only later did Oyzeh tell me that this was a story about the emperor
Napoleon who went to Moscow with his army but he couldn't defeat
Russia. Only when Napoleon's soldiers froze, was the army forced to
pull back. Oyzeh also told me that this Pushkin, who wrote poetry,
was an intimate in the tsar's court, that he wrote a story about a little
golden fish and also about somebody with the ugly name of Mazeppa.
He also wrote another story too about a prince, Eugene Onegin, and
that this Pushkin was no older than twenty-something years, and the
end was that he was shot to death with a pistol.
  Oyzeh said that he wants to be someone just like Pushkin when
he grows up.

This Pushkin didn't begin to interest me. I didn't know who he was anyway but I liked to listen to Oyzeh recite. He was near and dear to me now. He said that he would teach me all these poems. He would bring me books from someone called Tolstoy who was a Count, but that later on, this Count Tolstoy became just an ordinary peasant.

Oyzeh knew everything but I wasn't destined to know more because a black cat ran between us and for many years after that, our friendship was broken.

Chapter 31

I forgot to mention that besides the cubicles, the balconies, and the green pump, our courtyard had a small building off to one side. It had two windows and a door whose paint was peeling, and it didn't have a door handle.

The two windows were covered in dust as if blinded. It was said that a Jew had once lived there, a watchmaker. All his life he'd looked through a magnifying loupe, and while doing this, he managed to honor his wife with a male child every year. But these babies never lived long. It was said of this particular watchmaker that it was decreed in heaven, that during the vakhnakht, the vigil before a circumcision, the newly born soul should be taken away. Nobody knew if a black cat had devoured it, or whether the mother herself had choked it between her breasts. It was enough that a Hassidic rebbe had told the watchmaker to move out of this place because years earlier it had been a house of prostitution.

The watchmaker moved out and from then on the little building stayed banged shut, together with its two dusty, blinded windows.

No goy and no Jew wanted to move into the place. Bats flitted about at night and women said that these were the souls of the watchmaker's dead children, not yet circumcised according to Jewish tradition.

Some time after we moved in, the cursed little building was fixed up and the door was opened.

Carpenters and bricklayers came. They banged and they sang, they painted, and they recited portions of the Rosh Hashanah liturgy.

Everyone in the whole courtyard came running to see who was risking life and limb to move in here.

Oyzeh's father, Reb Menakhem stuck his head in and said that it was very fitting for people to live here. He, himself, would also move in here if only to spite all the good-for-nothings and fools who believed in ghosts and demons.

The workmen worked day and night while the whole courtyard waited impatiently to see who the new neighbors would be.

Maybe they'd be goyim? No, they weren't goyim.

Early one winter morning, sleeves rolled up, arms white and puffy as if from flour and milk, Khantsheh the Widow arrived, a woman not wearing a wig, with a black, coiffed lock of hair the size of a swallow right on her forehead.

Everyone in the courtyard knew Khantsheh the Widow. Her father was a half-blind Jew who sewed patches onto big Hassidic overcoats. Her mother, who was bent over like a goyeh in front of the church, liked to buy bargains off the peasants' carts, bargaining so long until the peasant lost count.

Khantsheh had lived in Warsaw for many years. Nobody knew what she did there in that Warsaw, but when she got sick and tired being there, she came back home with a big green trunk on wheels filled with tablecloths and sheets, shirts and towels, and lots of silk dresses.

Khantsheh also brought her fifteen-year-old daughter. It was said that she was no daughter but a mamzer, a bastard. This "mamzer" had fresh, rosy cheeks, a dimple in her chin, and a blue-black head of hair.

It was for Khantsheh's and her daughter's sake that they were banging away at that cursed little building, singing zmirehs, and planing the boards. A new white floor was laid, the windows were puttied, the doors were painted, and on that first evening after they moved in, the flames of two bright lamps assaulted the whole courtyard. It was unbearable. The neighbors had to cover their windows with sheets and kerchiefs because who could close an eye in all that blazing light?

Khantsheh the Widow built herself a teahouse in that cursed little building. She had a big boiler installed into the wall, with heavy brass faucets that looked like angrily lowered heads, and she put long wooden tables and benches in there. Soldiers, young wagon drivers with their brides, and all kinds of young people, who didn't have where to go to smoke on Shabbes, started coming there.

Shiny white-bellied pitchers, from which tea with lemon was poured, stood on the tables. This was guzzled along with big oil cookies and also pieces of fruitcake that Khantsheh herself baked. Along with that they cracked dried sunflower seeds and sang songs from Warsaw, Russia, Buenos Aires, and even from America too.

A new world opened up for Oyzeh and me. We stopped sitting on the green pump telling each other secrets. Oyzeh didn't ask me if I believed in God anymore, and whether there really had been a Moysheh Rabeynu or not. He didn't have time for such questions anymore. We spent long evenings standing outside the windows of the teahouse listening to the beautiful songs from far away.

I don't know whether it was like this for Oyzeh too but for me there was nothing nicer or better in the whole world than Khantsheh's teahouse.

It could be it was because of all those songs and the cheerfulness of the place or maybe it was because we just loved to look at Rukhtsheh, the widow's daughter.

I didn't say anything to Oyzeh and he did the same, but during the time that we both stood outside the half-curtained window, we quietly looked for that figure that flew in our imagination even when our eyes were closed.

"Are you cold?" Oyzeh asked.

"No, I'm not cold," and I burrowed my head into my collar.

"I'm not cold either." Oyzeh stamped his feet on the tamped down snow.

"Can'ya see her?" He asked quietly.

"Yeh, I see her." I answered, even quieter, though sometimes I didn't even see her.

"I can't see her at all." Oyzeh moved his face over the cold window looking for a wider crack to peer through.

I thought that if God would help me and I could move the curtain aside to see all of Rukhtsheh, who'd be my equal then?

Oyzeh uttered his thoughts out loud. He said that if he weren't scared, he'd strike right through the windowpane and tear down the curtain.

"Spiteful people are sitting inside," I answered. "What would it bother them if the windows weren't covered?"

But Oyzeh explained to me that it had to be this way or else the whole courtyard would go dark.

"You can see," he said, "that young guys are sitting there with girls." Why, he himself had seen a soldier embracing and kissing a girl! Soldiers were in the habit of kissing girls.

I don't know what happened to me that minute but I got hot. It must have been the heat that tore it out of me:

"Oyzeh, wouldn't you like to kiss Rukhtsheh?"

"Are'ya crazy? You think she's just anybody?"

"God forbid! Who says that? Don't I know who she is?"

"You just don't know her," Oyzeh replied, his head arrogantly in the air. "She's altogether different, not just any ordinary girl."

He said it in such a way that it seemed to me that he was already acquainted with Rukhtsheh. I don't know for how long. Maybe, he'd already spoken to her, maybe already gone out walking with her, and maybe he'd even kissed her already too?

I was heavy-hearted when I left him that evening.

It tormented me and I didn't know why. Why did he toss his head so arrogantly? Had he actually gone out with Rukhtsheh? Had he already spoken to her? And if so, why was he so guarded with me? And if he did go, why was he standing outside the window not going in?

It was a puzzle to me and an even bigger puzzle that Oyzeh had asked me to take him along to the teahouse on the following Shabbes.

I was an important person on Shabbes, a person of influence because after the Shabbes meal, Mammeh would send me to Khantsheh's for a kettle of boiling water, and then I was able to see all of Rukhtsheh.

Oyzeh's mother never sent him. First of all, because he was a student and second, because they had a goyish servant who did the cooking and baking for Shabbes.

So I told Oyzeh to come home earlier from the gymnasium the following Shabbes and I'd take him with me.

Oyzeh stashed his texts and workbooks under the stairs, stuffing his cap with the badge on it into a pocket. We went into Khantsheh's teahouse, he, bareheaded with his unruly lock of hair, and me in my Shabbes kapoteh, kettle in hand. He stood by the door and shook his forelock arrogantly. Even though my heart was pounding like a thief's, I went right over to the two brass faucets.

Rukhtsheh herself drew the water for me. Tall, a dimple in her chin, wearing a white blouse that smelled of Shabbes fruits and honey cookies, she stood a little bent over, waiting for the kettle to fill up. Girls and young men sat together at the tables, flushed and sprawling. Khantsheh the Widow, Rukhtsheh's mother, sat there with a young man too, laughing right into his face. But I didn't see any of this, except for Rukhtsheh's head of blue-black hair, and her small white hands. I also saw that during the time the boiling water was pouring into the kettle, Rukhtsheh would turn her head several times to where Oyzeh was standing by the door.

Did they wink at each other? Did they really know each other?

My eyes got hot. As if through a fog, I saw a soldier, hair cut short, get up from the table and stagger toward Rukhtsheh. He must have been drunk. Otherwise he wouldn't have staggered, and he wouldn't have had the nerve to put a hand on her waist and shove his black whiskers right into her face.

"Come on, my beauty," he grinned with a mouth full of teeth and said in Russian, "Give me your *mordotshke prelest moya*, your sweet little face, my lovely."

I was already holding the kettle of water with both hands. It was heavy, as if it was filled with sand, but even heavier was the feeling that choked me. If I weren't so scared, I'd have spilled everything over the head of that vile little soldier.

But it was worse for Oyzeh, who stood at the door, face taut and cheeks flaming. He looked taller than usual now, like he looked when he was reciting Pushkin's poems.

I don't know how it happened but all of a sudden I saw Oyzeh standing at the boiler. He was as white as the pitchers on the table and his upper lip was sweating.

"*Svolotsh*! You dirty swine!" He suddenly threw out in Russian, both hands in the air. "*Svolotsh*! *Merzavyets*! You dirty swine! You lowlife!"

The scraping of stools was heard. Someone sniffled lazily.

"*Tshtoh-oh-oh . . . ?* Wha-a-t?"

He started forward with bearlike steps toward Oyzeh and me.

Khantsheh the Widow grabbed Oyzeh from behind and quickly pushed him out. I managed to get out all by myself. Boiling water spurted from the kettle. I didn't see where I was going. Another minute and I'd fall down and be scalded to death for sure!

I didn't see Oyzeh outside. I heard strange and pointed laughter behind me and this laughter scalded me even more than the burning kettle.

All during Shabbes I was ashamed and afraid to go out. I ventured out in the evening only after Havdoleh.

When I saw Oyzeh it seemed to me that he'd shrunk.

He told me that it wouldn't have taken much for him to choke that soldier to death and that he'd do it yet, because what right did a Litvak pig have to put his hand on Rukhtsheh's waist?

Oyzeh stayed silent most of the evening. His unruly lock of hair looked like it wasn't even his. He told me that he pitied Rukhtsheh. If he'd have money, he wouldn't let anything stand in his way. He would marry her and go off with her to a faraway land. She wouldn't have to serve tea to anybody anymore. He, Oyzeh, would recite poems to her. It would be good, really good.

I understood that it would be really good but what would I do all alone? Would it be so good for me too? And anyway, what did it mean that he'd marry Rukhtsheh? Was he already *royi l'khupe*, in a position to be led to the marriage canopy? How would he earn a living? What would become of his studies at the gymnasium?

Rukhtsheh would be a loss to me too. I pitied her too. If I'd have money, I wouldn't marry her at all, it's foolish even to talk. I'd just give her money so that she could move out of the teahouse into a nicer street. Let her live there, eat and drink, and . . . good enough!

But Oyzeh told me that I was a fool and an idiot. What would she do with herself, all alone in that place?

"What should she do? She'll eat, she'll drink, and she'll have a good time."

"Just like it says in the Hagudeh." Oyzeh poked fun at me. "That's nothing. The main thing is to love her."

"Who's gonna love her?"

"Me!" And Oyzeh brought his fist to his chest.

Something was choking me again, worse even than earlier today, when the soldier tried to embrace Rukhtsheh. I felt like I wanted to slap Oyzeh.

"A week from now, next Shabbes, will'ya go for tea again?" Oyzeh asked me quietly.

"I dunno. Probably."

"So tell Rhukhtsheh that I want to see her." He spoke thoughtfully.

"You won't come with me?"

"No. Tell her that I'll wait for her Shabbes evening on Warsaw Street near the jail."

He didn't say goodbye, but left me sitting all alone on the balcony and went down with careful steps. He walked like a grown man who had big worries on his head.

❧

It was still a whole week to Shabbes. If you wanted to count how many hours and how many minutes there still was, you could go out of your mind.

Anyway, I didn't know what was happening to me. I saw Rukhtsheh and Oyzeh everywhere. I saw them in my opened khimesh, I saw them in the book of Russian grammar, on the blackboard, everywhere.

Matyas the Teacher boxed everyone's ears even harder and continued to wack with an iron fist to the chin. Rabbi Reb Duvid began teaching us Hebrew grammar—*poked, p'kodeti*, "I command, I commanded." You could break your teeth on this! Oyzeh's words kept ringing in my head:

"Tell her that I'll wait for her on Warsaw Street, near the jail. *Poked, p'kodeti*, "I command, I commanded."

Chapter 32

The next Shabbes I went for boiling water again. The teahouse floor was spread with dry sand and the two, long tables were set with gleaming, freshly washed tablecloths. It looked as if everything was now ready for the prospective in-laws to arrive.

At the head of one of the tables a young man sat quietly talking to a girl and they were staring into each other's eyes. There were no other guests here now. A half muffled laugh of pleasure could be heard from behind a red-flowered curtain that led into a dark alcove.

"Stop it already," the laughter said, "What's the matter with you? Can't you wait?"

From the voice, I figured out that this was Khantsheh the Widow. Rukhtsheh looked pale today. She drew water for me but every few minutes she turned her face anxiously toward the flowered curtain.

The water poured slowly into the kettle. I stood as if on hot coals because I had something to tell Rukhtsheh but how do I tell her? How do I start? Maybe I shouldn't even say anything at all? What am I, Oyzeh's messenger?

Rukhtsheh stared at me, examining me with blinking eyes but she wasn't really looking at me at all but at the door.

My whole body ached. I wanted to tell her that Oyzeh wouldn't be coming today. He wouldn't come anymore. He died! But in the middle of everything, I again heard from behind the curtain:

"What're you doing? Falek? Nu . . . Stop it already!"

Rukhtsheh gave a start. "What's your name?" She asked me too loudly.

"Mendl."

"Whose son are you?"

"Frimmet's. Duvid-Froykeh's."

"You live here in this courtyard?"

"Yeh."

"And that other one, the one with the forelock, he's your friend?"

"Yeh, my friend Oyzeh."

"Why didn't he come today?"

"He's a student at the gymnasium. He doesn't have time. He's studying."

`"What's he studying?"

"Poetry.

"Wha-a-t?" Rukhtsheh crinkled up her whole face in laughter.

I didn't understand what there was to laugh about and I also didn't understand why a minute later, Rukhtsheh said:

"Tell your friend I like him."

I don't know what happened to me that minute, whether the kettle got too heavy for me, or if I myself . . . but I couldn't move from the spot.

"Did' ya want something else?"

I felt that a tragedy was about to happen now. Either I'd fall down crying, or I'd bash someone's head in with the kettle.

Rukhtsheh's big warm eyes looked at me. Warmth came from her dainty white blouse too.

She bent closer to me, and in a reserved, secretive voice, she asked me again:

"Did'ya want something else?"

"Oyzeh," I stammered. "He wants to talk . . ."

I couldn't finish, choking on every word.

"He said he'd wait for you this evening near the jail."

The girl sitting at the table started laughing. Behind the flowered curtain it was too quiet. I couldn't see Ruktsheh anymore, but only felt a smooth warm hand like velvet under my chin.

"I'll come. Tell him I'll come."

I don't know how I got out. It seemed to me that someone threw the kettle out after me.

I met Oyzeh on the stairs.

"Did'ya tell her?" He practically fell on top of me.

"I told her," I answered angrily.

"Nu?"

"She'll come."

His face reddened and his eyes got swollen. He started jumping around.

"Mendl, you'll see. Mendl, you'll come with us. We'll take you with us."

But his happiness didn't make me happy. Just the opposite! Everything was on fire in me just like a boiling kettle. Suddenly, I started running up the steps and when I got near our door, I yelled down in all my anger:

"You Goy! You heretic! I won't go with you. The hell with you and your Ruktsheh!"

He ran after me.

"Mendl! Mendl, what's the matter with you?"

I hated him so much now that it wouldn't have bothered me if he would have fallen down and broken both his legs.

I hung around the house all afternoon and decided that I wouldn't go out that evening either. Anyway, I wouldn't show myself in the courtyard ever again. My feet wouldn't cross the threshold of that teahouse ever again! I'm finished with Oyzeh! Finished with Rukhtsheh! I need them like I need a hole in the head!

At Shalesudoth time, a bluish shadow fell across our window on the roof. It seemed to me that it was Oyzeh. The smell of herring hung over the house. Mammeh and a neighbor were sitting by the stove whispering to each other.

I looked up aimlessly at the sky to see whether any stars could be seen yet. No lamps needed to be turned on for my sake today because I wasn't going out anyway.

But after Havdoleh when Tatteh took the Shabbes tablecloth off and put a piece of chalk on the bare table, and Mammeh got ready to go and see Aunt Miriam, I couldn't stay in the house any more. I grabbed my coat and ran to the door.

"Where are you running to like that?" Mammeh stopped me in the middle.

"I'm not running. I'm just going down to see Oyzeh."

"Look how he doesn't have time! He won't run away, that Oyzeh of yours."

"He's waiting for me downstairs."

"So he'll wait another minute. Button yourself up all the way. Don't run. You hear?"

"Who's running?"

I actually left the house very slowly but once on the stairs, I flew down so fast that I heard our door being thrown open upstairs.

The moon was shining tonight as if for no reason. It was a full moon, and it sailed over the roofs and streets like a white torch surrounded by a distant blueness. The windowpanes were blue, the gutters were white, and the cross on the Russian Orthodox Church was blue too.

All the shops were open. Jews were going to the station by horse cab to make the eight o'clock train. I shuffled along the shops towards the jail. I totally forgot what I had decided earlier that day.

I wasn't thinking about it at all now. I only wanted to see if Oyzeh and Rukhtsheh would really meet.

From a distance, I could see a big, bluish-white spot on the sidewalk in front of the Russian Orthodox Church. Black legs cut through it from time to time. I was hidden by the small garden surrrounding the jail. I could see everything but nobody could see me.

So I saw a pair of long legs standing in this big, bluish-white spot. Nobody in town had such long legs like Oyzeh. He was standing there looking around on all sides. If I moved out a little more from behind the garden, I could even see his face. It was craned upward, and he looked like a giant bird on a hill.

For the first time since I met Oyzeh, I saw him with a little stick. He twirled it in the air, paced back and forth along the sidewalk, and craned his face even higher toward the moon.

I also craned my head. It seemed to me that Rukhtsheh would actually fall down from there.

Oyzeh didn't bother me anymore. I didn't even hate him right now, but that playful little stick of his, twirling in the air, that bothered me.

It looked like Rukhtsheh wasn't going to come. She's got nothing better to do than come here to the jail?

I had revenge on Oyzeh. He shouldn't have the chutspeh, the nerve, to say that he wanted to marry her and that after the wedding he'd recite poems to her. But my revenge didn't warm me for long. Rukhtsheh did come. There she was, crossing Warsaw Street, not walking but running.

She didn't even see me even though she went right past the jail garden. Oyzeh wasn't standing in the middle of the spot anymore, but had moved away a little and he was no longer twirling the little stick.

It seemed to me that the closer Rukhtsheh got to Oyzeh, the further he moved away, and that he was moving backward.

I followed behind Rukhtsheh who stopped in the middle of the bluish-white spot where Oyzeh had stood a few minutes earlier. He'd now moved onto the avenue and Rukhtsheh also went there.

All at once, Oyzeh turned his back on her, threw the mischievous little stick out into the street, and as if not with his own strength, he began running toward the old garden. Either he must have seen somebody or else he's just gone crazy!

I myself must have gone crazy too, or else I wouldn't have run after him, and I wouldn't have screamed after him in such turmoil:

"Oyzeh! Oyzeh!"

"Stop! Where're you running?" Rukhtsheh grabbed me by the collar and shook me like a lulev branch.

She also ran. It was dark, I couldn't see her face, I only felt the heat and rage rising out of her.

"Don't run," she said heavily. "He's a barrel of snot, your friend. You don't have to run. I know you like me."

I didn't know what to answer. I got hot in the legs from her talk. God is my witness that I myself would have run away now too.

"Come on, let's walk a little," she said and she took my arm. Now I got hot in the head too. I walked beside her and felt that I wouldn't get to go home tonight. A tragedy was going to happen for sure!

"Why'd he run off, that piece of shit?" She gritted her teeth angrily.

I didn't know why he ran off either. Maybe he saw his father, or maybe he saw somebody from the gymnasium.

"What's he afraid of, that snot nose?" Rukhtsheh still couldn't quiet herself.

I wanted to ask if Oyzeh had actually told her that he'd marry her and go off to a country far away with her. I also wanted to know whether they were in love, but Rukhtsheh stopped in the middle, let go of my arm and asked:

"How old is he, this guy?"

"He already puts on tfiln."

"And you?"

"I'll be putting them on soon too."

The moon came out from behind the jail and the whole avenue turned blue with snow.

"Let's sit down," Rukhtsheh said, and she led me to the German church. We sat down on its broad steps. Rukhtsheh put her arm around my shoulder and laid her cheek to mine.

I was scared. I didn't know what to do but I hoped that Oyzeh would pass by right now and see what was happening.

"Did'ya ever kiss a girl?" Rukhtsheh asked.

"No."

"Would'ya like to kiss me?"

I don't know if I answered her. I didn't even have time to answer because Rukhtsheh already had her warm mouth on my lips. Or maybe it was the opposite.

I don't know if I even had a thought at that minute. It was as if my head had fallen off. I only heard a quiet, hot voice:

"Slow down! Don't bite, you mamzer, you bastard you! Who taught you to kiss like that?"

Nobody taught me. I was kissing a girl for the first time in my life. Honest!

"D'ya love me?" Rukhtsheh wrapped her arms around my neck and around my face. At this minute, it was as if she didn't have two hands but hundreds. They were everywhere, those hands of hers.

"I love you."

"Will ya marry me?"

"I'll marry you."

"What'll we do after the wedding?"

"We'll go to a country far away." I was already mimicking the way Oyzeh talked. "We'll go to America and I'll recite poems to you."

"You'll wha-a-at? What're you going to do?"

"I'll work." I drew back. "I'll rent a place. You won't have to do anything, just eat and drink, and have a good time."

Rukhtsheh moved away from me like a cat, slowly and lazily.

I wanted to draw her closer, give her at least one more kiss, but in one minute a weird change came over her. She stood up quickly. When I wanted to be stronger than her, she pushed me away and in a strange voice, angry, like an old goyeh, she threw out:

"*Poshol von*, get lost, you mamzer! You bastard!"

I didn't understand. To this day, it's not clear to me. It must be that it was the cursed word, poems, that destroyed my dream about Rukhtsheh forever.

She didn't even say goodbye to me but just ran away like Oyzeh had run away from her.

I was left all alone on the avenue.

Behind me was the black, German church. In front of me, the sleeping jail, over which the moon was moving as if behind a film.

All night Rukhtsheh kissed me in my dreams. In the morning, my mother looked anxiously into my eyes and asked me why I'd been yelling in my sleep and why was I cursing Oyzeh?

I really did curse him, and not just in my dreams but awake too. I didn't want to see him ever again. The only thing that mattered to me was Rukhtsheh. I ran to the German church, maybe she'd come there. I went to get boiling water again on Shabbes but Rukhtsheh wouldn't pour it out for me anymore. She went around with her hair uncombed and her arms bare. She passed right by me and didn't even see me.

Chapter 33

A big change took place in the teahouse over the summer.

For no reason, fewer young people began coming to Khantsheh the Widow's teahouse. She didn't bake honey cakes anymore and she didn't pay attention that the pitchers and glasses should sparkle. Songs weren't sung anymore, and there weren't any freshly washed cloths covering the tables anymore.

It seemed to me that Khantsheh was on the outs with her daughter Rukhtsheh. I saw how that guy Falek with the stiffly curled whiskers didn't sit behind the flowered curtain with Khantsheh anymore, but now sat openly at the table with Rukhtsheh, looking right at her as if she was some precious jewel.

Somehow this wasn't usual. Did the hatred I felt for Oyzeh not so long ago, transfer itself now to this swarthy guy? I hated him a thousand times more than I did Oyzeh. Why he didn't even know poems, so how'd he even have the nerve to look at Rukhtsheh? He was actually eating her up with his eyes!

Khantsheh the Widow must've hated him too. She called him a freeloader and a lice-cracker right in front of me. "Why don't you go to work? May you have a black life!"

The guy grinned with a mouthful of teeth, didn't even get angry, and didn't hurl curses back. He only said that if she didn't stop, he'd make mincemeat out of her.

Everyone in the courtyard knew that Khantsheh was fighting around with Falek. They could hear the yelling and the screaming, but Mammeh felt that even though they were quarreling, the swarthy Falek would soon marry Khantsheh anyway.

Mammeh didn't tell a lie. One fine morning, Khantsheh bought a tallis with a blue silk collar from Zisheh the Scribe. The shops on Warsaw Street sold her material for bed linen and Khantsheh rented a dwelling with a kitchen in our courtyard. After all, she couldn't be expected to just go live in a teahouse after the wedding!

Avreyml the Furniture Dealer delivered two wooden beds and a mirrored oak wardrobe.

Khantsheh looked smoother and clearer now, even though she was busy and overworked.

She ordered a woolen suit of clothes and a pair of gaiters for that guy of hers, came to an agreement with Simek the Klezmer Musician, and gave out wedding invitations to the soldiers and all the young fellows and girls who were frequent visitors to the teahouse.

But suddenly, a day or two before the wedding, when Khantsheh had already baked two big, sugar cakes, and live carp were swimming around in a washtub—disaster struck!

We found out about it first thing in the morning. We had just gotten up and Tatteh was standing out front davening. A golden strip of sky lay on the windowpanes. Mammeh in her nightcap was already up, sighing quietly. She wasn't feeling too good and she just wanted to prepare something for us to eat, and go right back to bed.

It was quiet. All of a sudden, we heard a clattering on the stairs and several voices talking at once.

"Who's talking so loud first thing in the morning?" Mammeh took a step toward the door but it was flung wide open. A strange woman with a kerchief on her head burst in and in one breath yelled out:

"Frimmetl, come down. A terrible disaster happened to her!"

The woman didn't say to whom such a disaster happened. She didn't have time. She said what she had to say and ran right back down the stairs.

Mammeh started fluttering her hands in the air just like you do when you chase a goose.

"Vey'z mir! Poor thing, it shouldn't happen . . ." and began rummaging around for something to put on: "Mendl! Luzeh! Run downstairs. Go see what's happened."

Tatteh let his unsuspecting eyes wander over Mammeh's distracted face. He either didn't hear or he didn't understand. Half dressed, I began buttoning my shoes fast and pulling on my suspenders, but as if out of spite, everything fell from my hands.

Sobbing and screaming were heard from the courtyard. Somebody, God forbid, must have died! I got dressed the best way I could and slid down the railing in one leap.

The whole courtyard was full of people. Women with children were running from every balcony and every staircase. Everyone was talking at once, asking questions and pushing into the open door of the teahouse.

Khantsheh the Widow, disheveled, in a short, white shift and a pair of red slippers with pompons, was running around like someone on fire.

"People! Jews! Have pity!" She flailed her hands in the air. "They've left me one shirt, the thief, and that whore! They've made a pauper out of me! Vey'z mir! A disaster to my whole life! People! What should I do?"

She tore at her cheeks, threw open the new, mirrored oak dresser, opened the lid of her trunk and showed one and all:

"All my hard work, my bitter toil, the nights I didn't sleep, the food I didn't eat, the drinks I didn't drink! You mamzer, you bastard!" She began stomping her feet. "You vile whore! What did'ya want from your own mother? What?"

Girls and women stuck their noses into the open trunk and into the empty dresser and asked how could it have happened? Didn't she know? Or what?

How could she have known if she was getting ready for a wedding? How could it even occur to her that a daughter of hers, that whore, was having a love affair with that cur of a guy? Who could believe such fury, such a terrible decree from heaven?

Khantsheh's face was swollen from crying but she didn't have the strength to scream anymore. She bent over the empty trunk like a mourner over a corpse. Strangers ran for the police but before they could even come, Khantsheh had torn herself away from the empty trunk and began smashing the white pitchers for tea, the little teapots and the drinking glasses. She tore down the flowered curtain from the alcove showing a messy iron cot.

"Here's where she bedded down, that mamzeyrehs, that little bastard!" She grabbed the featherbed and tore it into two pieces.

The whole teahouse filled up with white feathers flying out the open window into the courtyard, settling on the pump, on the balconies, and onto the people gathered outside. When the police came, Khantsheh was lying on the floor among the feathers and the broken shards, lamenting the way you do at a grave.

Poor thing, she had what to mourn, this unfortunate Khantsheh. It was said that except for the fact that the swarthy Falek stole from her and ran off with Rukhtsheh, he also left the widow with a belly.

No sign was left of the teahouse. Khantsheh ran to the Natshalnik, the chief of the Povyat district. She even managed to get all the way up to the governor, but the pair had disappeared as if into the sea.

It was said they'd gone to Paris, but my mother found out that Falek had sold Rukhtsheh into white slavery in Buenos Aires. Still, Khantsheh wouldn't rest. She filed petitions and sent them off to Warsaw. She ran to lawyers until finally, the little building in the courtyard was closed up.

No one wanted to rent it anymore. The once clear, shining windowpanes quietly got covered in black dust again, and someone tore the knob off the door. Cats sat on the roof again. Khantsheh went off to Warsaw once more and the courtyard became a ruin again. I couldn't look into the windows of the teahouse in the evening anymore.

I didn't see or speak to Oyzeh anymore either, but I did notice that he'd grown too tall for his years. One more day and he'd end up with a hunchback just like his father! I didn't know what to do with myself. After Khantsheh's misfortune our house got good and gloomy.

Mottl Shtroy my father's partner didn't come after Shabbes to figure things out anymore. There wasn't even what to make a reckoning over. The hay from the fields had rotted. There wasn't what to buy and there wasn't who to sell it to.

Tatteh as usual, got up before dawn, spent more time on his wounded leg, took longer to recite tillim, psalms, and continued to daven out front. We ate burnt soup and soldier's bread.

Mammeh bought a small piece of cheap meat for Shabbes and instead of fish she put herring on the table.

The autumn was hard and rainy. The little windowpanes cried day and night and the rain dripped constantly from the roof.

Mammeh had dark creases around her mouth and sighed:

"How've I sinned that I have to pay for it now by spending my years in such an attic? Luzeh, how long is enough to sit here? Luzeh?"

I didn't understand my mother. First, because she herself had rented this attic and second, how could Tatteh help it if the hay in the whole area had rotted and the army had begun to buy compressed hay from Russia?

So our livelihood disappeared. Tatteh went to Mottl Shtroy to ask for an interest-free loan but Mottl Shtroy shrugged his shoulders. How could he have it to give if there wasn't any business?

Tatteh came home in the evening crushed. Pieces of black, cotton padding hung out of his quilted jacket. Mammeh had no head for fixing it. She couldn't stay in the house, there was nothing here, so what was the point in just sitting?

I was sent home from school.

Mammeh sent off a letter to that rich brother of hers in Lodz. She wrote him that I, her son, was sent home because she couldn't pay the school tuition anymore, that they were all suffering in the house from the cold and that her husband Luzeh, wasn't earning anything, so she was asking him, her brother, to take pity and help her out in her need.

An answer didn't come and the shadows in our house got longer and colder. Sleighs were already gliding in the street, their bells tinkling happily up to me to come down, but I was ashamed to show myself in the street because I didn't want to be asked why I didn't come to school anymore.

The door finally opened only on the last day of Chanukah, and the postman came in with his white, Jewish beard.

"Pani Luzerova," he spoke in three languages, Russian, Yiddish, and Polish: "*Diyengi, gelt, piyeni'ondzeh.* Money, money, money."

Mammeh got red and the pit of my stomach started to ache. Nothing else but this postman's white Jewish beard must belong to Elijah the Prophet!

The postman had brought a ticket to claim money from the post office.

Mammeh, sickly red, ran right out to get the money but it was too late. They weren't paying out any more money today. Still, she came home overjoyed, quickly made a fire in the stove, cooked borsht and potatoes that today smelled just like wine. Even the lamp burned brighter. The moon hung over the roof across the way, and the frost on our windowpanes slowly melted.

I had nothing more on my mind than the money that Mammeh would get from the post office tomorrow. I was sure that we'd now gotten rich and we'd be able to move to a better place. Mammeh also remembered about another place to rent and about getting me a pair of new boots.

Only Tatteh sat more silent at today's supper than he usually did, staring into the windowpanes.

The next morning, Mammeh ran to the post office and I waited in the house my heart banging. Several times I opened the door and went down the steps.

But that rich brother of hers in Lodz didn't send much. He explained that times were bad and that he had a daughter to marry off.

But my boots were fixed, the school tuition was paid, and Mammeh bought Tatteh a new quilted jacket.

"How come?" Tatteh rolled his tongue from one corner of his mouth to the other.

"It's a quilted jacket."

"I've already got one."

"Some jacket! Pieces of lining are falling out of it."

"Neh . . . Some idea!" And he slowly put the new jacket away, staring at it from time to time.

But he wouldn't put it on. A few days later, it still lay there, and nobody went near it.

Only on Shabbes morning, after changing his underwear and after Mammeh had already cleared out the old, torn jacket, Tatteh wandered around back and forth for a long time, until finally at last, he put on the new quilted jacket.

I also got something new. I don't mean the boots that were fixed and I also don't mean that the school tuition got paid and I don't even mean the woolen mittens. It was something I couldn't even give a name to.

Maybe it was Tatteh's quiet voice that as far back as I could remember was never so quiet as it was right now or maybe it was Mammeh's tearful eyes, but one day in the middle of the week, Tatteh helped me put on my coat and went with me to the study house, to a blond Jew with green whiskers, with whom I was going to start learning the laws about putting on tfiln . . .

Glossary and Notes

Glossary

Sources are indicated by the following symbols: (H) Hebrew-Aramaic, (P) Polish, (PY) Polish Yiddish. Unless otherwise designated, sources are Yiddish. I have translated most Yiddish words directly in the text and include the glossary for such words that require a too-lengthy explanation. I have mostly followed the YIVO/Library of Congress system of transcription of Yiddish words. The exceptions are in the cases of Polish-Yiddish dialect in people's names; their diminutives are treated similarly.

Bubbeh (PY): Grandmother.

Bubbeh-Zaydeh (PY): Grandmother-Grandfather. Grandparents.

Challah (H): Challah. Egg bread. Loaf of braided bread used for Shabbehs and holidays.

Channukah (H): Eight-day celebration commencing on the twenty-fifth day of Kislev (November–December), commemorating the victory of Judah Maccabee over the Syrian king, Antiochus, and subsequent rededication of the Temple. Called the Festival of Lights.

Cheder (H) Kheyder (Y): Literally, room. Jewish religious elementary school usually located in the home of the teacher, for boys ages three to ten.

Daven(ing):To pray, praying.

Dreydl(s) (Y): Four-sided spinning top played with by children during Channukah.

Farfl (Y): Twisted, small pieces of dried dough, boiled and fried.

Gemorah (H) Gemureh (PY): Later portion of the Talmud that comments and interprets the material in the Mishna, which is of an earlier period.

Goy(im) (H): Literally nation. Gentile(s), non-Jew(s). Also refers to Jews ignorant of Jewish traditions and observances.

Goyeh: Gentile woman.

Goyish: Pertaining to Gentile.

Gymnasium (P): State secondary school similar to North American high school.

Haggadah (H) Hagudeh (PY): Literally, the telling. The book of the Passover home service, recounts the tale of Jewish slavery in Egypt and the liberation, through narrative and song.

Halvah: A delicacy made from sesame seeds.

Havdalah (H) Havduleh (PY): Ceremony marking the conclusion of Shabbes, Festivals and the onset of the week.

Hassid(im) (H): Literally, the pious. Follower(s) of an extensive and significant religious movement (Hassidism) founded in the eighteenth century in Eastern Europe, emphasizing religious fervor, mass enthusiasm, close-knit group cohesion, and charismatic leadership. At its height, this movement embraced nearly 50 percent of the Jews of Eastern Europe.

Hatsefirah (H): Hebrew-language, pro-Zionist periodical, later a daily, published in Warsaw from the 1880s to the early 1930s.

Haman (haroshah) (H) Humen harusheh (PY): Haman the Wicked. An official in the court of the King of Persia, archenemy of the Jews whom he planned to exterminate. His plans were foiled by Mordechai and Queen Esther and he was subsequently hanged. The triumph of the Jews over their enemies is celebrated in the holiday of Purim as described in the Book of Esther.

Kaddish (H): Memorial prayer for the dead.

Kapoteh (Y): Traditional long, black coat worn by Hassidim in Eastern Europe.

Khazn(onim) (H): Trained professional singer(s) who lead(s) religious services by singing portions of the liturgy. Also referred to as a Cantor.

Khamets (H) Khumets (PY): Leavened food forbidden during the festival of Passover.

Khumash (H) Khimesh (PY): The first five books of the bible. The pentateuch.

Kiddush (H) Kiddesh (Y): Blessing over wine before and during Shabbes and Festivals.

Kittl (Y): White linen or cotton robe symbolizing purity, worn by Jewish men on Yom Kippur, at their marriage ceremony, the Pesach seder, and for burial.

Kol Nidreh (H): Literally, All Vows. Public declaration of uncertain origin chanted three times at the beginning of the Yom Kippur services cancelling all forced or harmful personal vows.

L'havdil (H): Literally to make a distinction, not to mention in the same breath. A linguistic structure that serves to distinguish, differentiate and insulate the sacred from the profane. Traditional Yiddish speakers use this term when a comparison might seem an indecent denigration of one of the items referred to.

Litvak(s) (Y): Jew(s) from Lithuania, traditionally reputed to be more reserved and scholarly than Jews from other regions. Having a reputation for being dry and humorless.

Matsoh (H): Matseh (Y): Unleavened bread eaten during Passover to commemorate the Exodus from Egypt.

Mazel (H) Mazl (Y): Luck.

Mazeltov (Y) Mazal-tov (H): Literally, good luck. Congratulations!

Mead (Y): An alcoholic drink usually drunk on Passover, made by fermenting honey, water, and hops.

Megillah (H): Scroll. Usually, the Book of Esther, read aloud in the synagogue on Purim.

Mishnah (H): Collection of oral laws compiled in the second century that forms the basis of the Talmud.

Mitzvah (H) Mitsveh (Y): Good deed.

Moysheh Rabeynu (H): Moses our Teacher. The greatest Hebrew sage and lawgiver and presumed author of the Five Books of the bible.

Okh un vey! (Y): Woe is me!

Oy vey'z mir! (Y): Contraction from vey iz mir. Woe is me!

Pan, Pani (P): Form of address equivalent to Mr. or Mrs.

Pesach (H) Passover. Peysekh (PY): The eight-day spring festival that commemorates the deliverance of the Jews from Egyptian bondage.

Purim (H) Pirim (PY): Celebrates the Feast of Lots in memory of the triumph over Haman, who had selected the fourteenth day of Adar (March) for the extermination of the Jewish People. It is a holiday noted for its gaiety, masquerades, and festive meal.

Rabbi (H): Literally—my master, my teacher. Religious leader of the Jewish community.

Rashi—Contraction of Rabbi Solomon Itzkhak ben Isaac, the great commentator of the Bible and Talmud born in Troyes, France (1040–1105) whose notes traditionally accompany the text.

Reb (Y): Mister. Used with a first name when speaking to adults.

Rebbeh (Y): Rabbi of a Hassidic sect. Teacher.

Rebbetsin (H): Wife of a rabbi.

Rosh Hashanah (H) Rosheshuneh (PY): The Jewish New Year, celebrated late summer early autumn. Together with Yom Kippur, considered the most solemn days of the Jewish year.

Seder (H) Seyder (Y): Literally, order. Home service observed on the first two nights of Passover (one night in Israel), when the Haggadah is read.

Selichoth (H) Slikhehs (Y): Penitential prayers recited on days preceding Rosh Hashoneh and during the Ten Days of Penitence.

Shabbes, Shabosim (H): The Sabbath. Starting at sundown Friday evening and ending Saturday after sunset. A day of rest and worship, and a reminder of divine justice on earth.

Shabbes Nakhmu (H): Sabbath of Consolation following Tisha B'av when the consoling prophecy of Isaiah is read.

Shalesudoth—Shalosh Seudot (H) Shalesides (PY): The third ritual meal eaten on Shabbes.

Shevuoth (H) Shevi'es (PY): Feast of Weeks, celebrated seven weeks after Passover. Commemorates the giving of the Torah to Moses on Mount Sinai.

Sheygets, Shkutsim (Y): Non-Jewish young man, usually of peasant origin. Also used humorously for troublesome Jewish boys.

Shikseh (Variant: Shiksl)—Non-Jewish girl or young woman usually of peasant origin.

Shiveh (H): Shivah: The Jewish week of mourning following the death of close kin (parent, spouse, child, sibling).

Shofar (H) Shoyfer (Y): Ram's horn, blown several times during the Rosh Hashanah service and once at the conclusion of Yom Kippur.

Sholom Aleichem (H) Shulem Aleykhem (PY): Literally, peace to you! Traditional greeting to which the response is the reverse: Aleichem sholem. Through repeated usage simply signifies hello or goodbye.

Shtrayml(ekh) (Y): Broad fur-edged hat traditionally worn by Hassidic men in Eastern Europe on Shabbes and Holy Days.

Shul (Y): Synagogue. House of Prayer.

Succah (H) Sikkeh (PY): Wooden hut or booth with thatched roof symbolizing the temporary abode of the Israelites in the desert after they left Egypt.

Succoth (H) Sikkehs (PY): The Feast of Tabernacles; eight-day harvest festival, commemorating the Jews living in make-shift dwellings during their wanderings in the desert.

Tallis(eysim) (H): Tallit. Prayer shawl worn by adult men, usually after marriage, during the morning service on Shabbehs and festivals.

Talleskutn (PY): Talles kotn (H).—Four-cornered, fringed undergarment worn by pious Jewish males.

Talmud (H): The expansion of the post-biblical body of written Jewish law and tradition.

Talmetoyreh (Y) Talmud Torah (H): Primary school providing education for poor children where they are taught Hebrew, prayers, and khumesh at community expense.

Tatteh-Mammeh (Y): Father and mother. Parents.

Tfiln (H): Phylacteries. Two leather cases with straps, containing scriptural passages, bound to forehead and left arm during weekday morning prayers. Traditionally worn by male Jews over the age of thirteen, except on Shabbehs and festivals.

Torah (H) Toyreh (PY): In the stricter sense, the five books of Moses, the foundation of Jewish law and tradition. More broadly, learning in general. Often used as a synonym for the whole complex of traditional Jewish learning.

Tsholnt (Y) Tshulnt (PY): A stew usually consisting of beans and meat, prepared on Friday and simmered overnight in a community oven for the noonday Shabbehs meal.

Vey'z mir! (Y): Contraction from vey iz mir. Woe is me! Alas!

Viorst: Russian unit of measure, approximately .66 of a mile, slightly less than a kilometer.

Yeshivah (H): Religious school for older boys, primarily for the study of Talmud.

Yomkipper (Y) Yom Kippur (H): The Day of Atonement. The holiest, most solemn day of the Jewish year. A fast day spent in prayer, atonement, and confession of sins by the individual in direct communion with God. Takes place on the 10th day of Tishrei (September–October), eight days after Rosh Hashanah.

Zaydeh (PY): Grandfather.

Zhid(ek), zhidkeh(s), zhidzheh (P): Derogatory terms for Jew(s).

Zmirehs (Y) Zmirot (H): Devotional songs sung at table on Shabbehs and festivals.

Notes

What is known about Yehoshue Perle's life is derived from the entries in the Encyclopedia Judaica; in the *leksikon fun der nayer yiddisher literatur*, (The Lexicon of New Yiddish Literature); in *Mayn Leksikon*, (My Lexicon), by Meylekh Ravitch; in the introduction to the second Yiddish edition of *Yidn fun a gants yor*, published in Buenos Aires in 1951, written by his friend and colleague, Leo Finklestein who gives us the most detailed account of his life; in the memoir by Rokhl Oyerbakh, *tseshotene perl* (Scattered Pearls), published in *di goldene keyt*, #79-80, Tel Aviv, 1972; in the yizkor book, Seyfer Radom, edited by Yitskhok Perlov and published in Tel Aviv in 1961; and in the recollections of survivors with whom I met who knew him in Radom, Warsaw and Lemberg. Despite recollections from various sources, there are gaps and sometimes outright contradictions in the information gleaned about Perle.

1. Ruth R. Wisse, *The Modern Jewish Canon* (New York: The Free Press, 2000), p. 18.

2. Celia Heller, *On the Edge of Destruction: Jews of Poland Between the Two World Wars* (New York: Schocken Books, 1980) 71–72 and 215–26.

3. Joseph Roth, *The Wandering Jew* (New York: W. W. Norton, 2001). 16.

4. Benjamin Harshav, *Language in the Time of Revolution* (Berkeley: University of California Press, 1993) 29.

5. Benjamin Harshav, *Language in the Time of Revolution* (Berkeley: University of California Press, 1993) 29.

6. Reuven Brainin, Quoted by Arthur Hertzberg and attributed to Reuven Brainin on Mendele in an article, "Speaking the Reader's Language: How a Yiddish Magazine has Stayed Alive." *New York Times Sunday Magazine*, December 20, 1992.

7. Rokhl Oyerbakh, Tseshotene Perl: vegn Yehoshu'e Perle (Scattered Pearls: About Yehoshua Perle) *Di goldene keyt*, #79–80, Tel Aviv, 1973.

8. Ruth R. Wisse, *I. L. Peretz and the Making of Modern Jewish Culture* (Washington University Press, 1991. 56, 107.

9. I. L. Peretz, "Monish." Translated by Seymour Mayne in *The Penguin Book of Modern Yiddish Verse*. Ed. Irving Howe, Ruth R. Wisse and Khone Shmeruk (New York: Viking, 1989) 14.

10. Leo Finklestein, *Hakdome* (Introduction).

11. Leo Finklestein, *Hakdome* (Introduction).

12. Leo Finklestein, *Hakdome* (Introduction).

13. Meylekh Ravitch, *Mayn Leksikon* (1945: Montreal Book Committee) 168–70.

14. Rokhl Oyerbakh, Tseshotene Perl: vegn Yehoshua Perle (Scattered Pearls: About Yehoshua Perle), *Di goldene keyt*, Tel Aviv, 1973. P. 232–41.

15. Rokhl Oyerbakh. Tseshotene Perl (Scattered Pearls).

16. Leo Finklestein. *Hakdome* (Introduction).

17. Rokhl Oyerbakh, *Tseshotene Perl* (Scattered Pearls).

18. S. Y. Agnon, "Only Yesterday," *Introduction* by Benjamin Harshav (Tel Aviv: Schocken Publishing House, 2000) xxiv.

19. Leo Finklestein, *Hakdome* (Introduction).
20. Leo Finklestein, *Hakdome* (Introduction).
21. Leo Finklestein, *Hakdome* (Introduction).

Bibliography

English

Ain, Abraham. Swislocz—Portrait of a Jewish Community in Eastern Europe. *YIVO Annual of Jewish Social Services* (Vol. IV). New York: YIVO, 1939. 86–114.

Alcalay, Reuben. *Words of the Wise—Anthology of Practical Axioms*. Jerusalem: Masada Press, 1973.

Alter, Robert. *Hebrew and Modernity*. Bloomington: Indiana University Press, 1994.

Ben-Sasson, Haim Hillel. Poland. *Encyclopedia Judaica* (Vol. 13). New York: MacMillan, 1972. 709–32.

Birnbaum, Solomon A. *Yiddish—A Survey & Grammar*. Toronto & Buffalo: University of Toronto Press, 1979.

Davidowicz, Lucy. *The Golden Tradition*. Boston: Beacon Press: 1967.

Dobroszcki, Lucien & Kirshenblatt-Gimblett, Barbara. *Image Before My Eyes*. New York: Schocken Books & YIVO, 1977.

Dubnow, Simon. *History of the Jews in Russia and Poland* (3 vols.). Philadelphia: Jewish Publications Society, 1916–1920.

Gaster, Theodor. *Customs and Folkways of Jewish Life*. New York: William Sloane Associates, 1955.

Geipel, John. *Mame Loshn: The Making of Yiddish*. London: Journeyman Press, 1982.

Glanz, Rudolph. *Eastern European Jewish Women* (Vol. 2). New York: Ktav Publishing, 1976.

Glinert, Lewis. *Hebrew in Ashkenaz*. Oxford: Oxford University Press, 1993.

Goldsmith, Emanuel S. *Modern Yiddish Culture—The Story of the Yiddish Language Movement*. New York: Shapolsky Publishers, 1987.

Greenberg, Louis. *The Jews in Russia*. New York: Shocken Books, 1976.

Gottesman, Itsik Nakhmen. *Defining the Yiddish Nation: The Yiddish Folklorists of Poland*. Detroit, MI: Wayne State University Press, 2003.

Harshav, Benjamin. *The Meaning of Yiddish*. Berkeley: University of California Press, 1990.

Heller, Celia. *On the Edge of Destruction*. New York: Shocken Books, 1980.

Heschel, Abraham Joshua. *The Earth is the Lord's*. New York: Farrar, Straus, Giroux, 1978.

Heschel, Abraham Joshua. Introduction. *Polish Jews—A Pictorial Record.* New York: Shocken Books, 1976.

Hoffman, Eva. *Shtetl: The Life and Death of a Small Town and the World of Polish Jews.* Boston: Houghton Mifflin, 1997.

Hundert, Gershon David. *Essential Papers on Hassidism, Origins to Present.* New York: New York University, 1991.

Kacyzne, Alter. *Poyln Jewish Life in the Old Country.* New York: Henry Holt, 1999

Kassow, Samuel D. *Who Will Write Our History?* Emanuel Ringelblum, The Warsaw Ghetto and the Oyneg Shabbes Archives. Bloomington: Indiana University Press, 2007.

Katz, Dovid. *Words on Fire: The Unfinished Story of Yiddish.* Cambridge: Basic Books, 2004.

Kugelmass, Jack & Boyarin, Jonathan (Eds.). *From a Ruined Garden. Memorial Book of Polish Jewry.* New York: Schocken Books, 1983.

Levin, Nora. *While Messiah Tarried Jewish Socialist Movements 1871–1917.* New York: Schocken Books, 1977.

Liptzin, Sol. *A History of Yiddish Literature.* New York: Jonathan David Publishers, 1985.

Liptzin, Sol. *Peretz—A Bilingual Edition* New York: YIVO, 1947.

Mendelsohn, Ezra. *The Jews of East Central Europe Between the World Wars.* Bloomington: Indiana University Press, 1987.

Mendelsohn, Ezra. Poland. *Encyclopedia Judaica* (Vol. 13). New York: MacMillan, 1972. 732–52.

Miron, Dan. *A Traveler Disguised: The Rise of Modern Yiddish Fiction in the 19th Century.* Syracuse, NY: Syracuse University Press, 1996.

Peretz, I. L. *My Memoirs.* New York: Citadel Press, 1964.

Pogonowski, Iwo Cyprian. *Jews in Poland: A Documentary History.* New York: Hippocrene Books, 1993.

Polonsky, Antony. *From Shtetl to Socialism, Studies from Polin.* London: The Littman Library of Jewish Civilization, 1993.

Richmond, Theo. *Konin: A Quest.* London: Random House, 1996.

Roskies, Diane K. & David G. *The Shtetl Book.* New York: Ktav Publishing, 1975.

Roth, Joseph. *The Wandering Jews.* New York: W. W. Norton, 2001.

Rubin, Ruth. *Voices of a People.* New York: Thomas Yoseloff, 1971.

Samuel, Maurice. *In Praise of Yiddish.* New York: Cowles, 1971.

Schwartz, Leo. *Memoirs of My People.* New York: Shocken Books, 1963.

Segal, Harold B. *Strangers in Our Midst: Images of the Jew in Polish Literature.* Ithaca, NY: Cornell University Press, 1996.

Shmeruk, Khone. Yiddish Literature. *Encyclopedia Judaica* (Vol. 16). New York: MacMillan, 1972. 798–833.

Shwartzbaum, Chaim. *Studies in Jewish and World Folklore.* Bloomington: Department of Folklore and Ethnomusicology, Indiana University: 1968. 417–24.

Silvain, Gerard & Minczeles, Henri. (Eds.). *Yiddishland.* Corte Madera, CA: Ginko Press, 1999.

Singer, Isaac Bashevis. *A Day of Pleasure: Stories of a Boy Growing Up in Warsaw.* New York: Farrar, Straus and Giroux, 1969.

Singer, Isaac Bashevis. *In My Father's Court* New York: New American Library, 1967.

Singer, Isaac Bashevis. Nobel Lecture. *The Jewish Almanac.* New York: Bantam Books, 1980. 435–36.

Trachtenberg, Joshua. *Jewish Magic and Superstition.* Philadelphia: Jewish Publications Society, 1939.

Trunk, Isaiah. Poland. *Encyclopedia Judaica* (Vol. 13). New York: MacMillan, 1972. 752–74.

Vishniac, Roman. *Children of a Vanished World.* Berkeley: University of California Press, 1999.

Vishniac, Roman, *Polish Jews: A Pictorial Record.* New York: Shocken Books, 1947.

Vishniac, Roman. *A Vanished World.* New York: Farrar, Straus & Giroux, 1983.

Wechsler, Robert. *Performing Without a Stage: The Art of Literary Translation.* North Haven, CT: Catbird Press, 1998.

Weinreich, Max. *History of the Yiddish Language.* Chicago: University of Chicago Press, 1980.

Weinreich, Uriel, *College Yiddish.* New York: Yiddish Scientific Institute YIVO, 1949.

Weinreich, Uriel. *Modern English–Yiddish, Yiddish–English Dictionary.* New York: YIVO, McGraw Hill, 1968.

Weinstein, Miriam. *Yiddish: A Nation of Words.* New York: Ballantine Books, 2001.

Wex, Michael. *Born to Kvetsh.* New York: St. Martin's Press, 2005.

Wisse, Ruth R. *I. L. Peretz and the Makings of Modern Yiddish Culture.* Seattle: Washington University Press, 1991.

Wisse, Ruth R. *The Modern Jewish Canon.* New York: The Free Press, 2000.

Wisse, Ruth R. *The Schlemiel as Modern Jewish Hero.* Chicago: University of Chicago, 1971.

Wisse, Ruth R. Two Jews Talking: A View of Modern Yiddish Literature. *Prooftexts* (Vol. 4[1]). Baltimore, MD: John Hopkins University Press, 1984.

Zable, Arnold. *Jewels and Ashes.* Carlton North, Australia: Scribe Publishers, 1991.

Zborowski, Mark & Herzog, Elizabeth. *Life Is With People.* New York: International Universities Press,1952.

Yiddish

Bal-Makhshoves. *Geklibene Shriftn.* Vilna, 1910.

Finklestein, Leo. *Hakdome,* Yidn fun a gants yor (2nd ed.). Buenos Aires. 1951.

Fuks, Tania. *A vanderung iber fremde gebitn.* Buenos Aires: Central Union of Polish Jews in Argentina, 1947.

Glatshteyn, Yankev. *In tokh genumen. Esseyen.* New York: Farlag fun yidish natsionalen arbeter farband, 1956.

Graubard, Pinkhes. *Bay undz yidn*, zamlung fun folklor un filologi'e. Warsaw: M. Vanvild, 1923.

Manger, Itsik. *Shriftn un proze*. Tel Aviv: I. L. Peretz Farlag, 1980

Mark, Yudel. *Groyser verterbukh fun der yidisher shprakh* (4 vol.). New York: Yiddish Dictionary Committee, 1980.

Miron, Dan. *Der imazh fun shtetl Dray literarishe shtudi'es*. Tel Aviv: I. L. Peretz Farlag, 1981.

Niborski, Yitskhak. *Verterbukh fun loshn-koydesh shtamike verter in yidish*. Paris: Medem Bibliotek, 1997.

Niger, S. *Bleter geshikhte fun der yiddisher literatur*. New York: Yidish Kultur Congres, 1959.

Niger, S. *Yidishe shrayber fun tsvantsikstn yorhundert* (Vol. II). New York: Congress for Jewish Culture, 1973.

Niger, S. & Shatzky, I. (Eds.). *Leksikon fun der nayer yidisher literatur*. New York: Congress for Jewish Culture, 1956.

Oyerbakh, Rokhl, Tseshotene perl: vegn Yehoshua Perle. *Di goldene kayt*, #79–80. Tel Aviv: 1973. 232–41.

Perlov, Yitskhok (Ed.). *Sefer Radom*. Tel Aviv: Yizkor Bukh, 1961.

Ravitch, Meylekh. *Mayn Leksikon*. Montreal: Book Committee, 1945.

Shtutskof, Nokhem. *Der oytser fun der yidisher shprakh*. New York: Yiddish Scientific Institute—YIVO, 1950.

Singer, I. J. *fun a velt vos iz nishto mer*. New York: Matones Press, 1946.

Weinreich, Max. *Oysgeklibene Shriftn*. Buenos Aires: Literatur Gezelshaft baym YIVO, 1974.

Weissenberg-Akselrod, Perl. *I. M. Weissenberg: Zayn lebn un shafn*. Montreal: Y. M. Weissenberg bukhfond, 1986.

Yehoash-Spivak. *Verterbukh*. New York: Farlag "Veker,": 1926.

Hebrew

Alcalay, Reuben. *The Complete Hebrew–English Dictionary* Tel Aviv: Masada Publishing, 1970.

Cohen, Nathan. *Seyfer, sofer v'iton* (Books, Writers and Newspapers, The Jewish Cultural Center in Warsaw, 1918–1942) Jerusalem: Magnes Press, 2003.

Einhorn, Dr. Shimon. *Mishle am b'yidish*. Tel Aviv: Dvir Company, 1954

Even-Shoshan, Avraham. *Hamilon hekhadash*. Jerusalem: Kiryat Sefer, 1969.

Miron, Dan. *Hatsad haafel betzkhoko shel sholem aleichem: al khashivuta shel retsinut beyakhas l'yidish ulesfritu* (The Dark Side of Sholem Aleichem's Laughter: Essays on the Importance of Being Earnest About Yiddish and its Literature). Jerusalem: Am Oved, 2005.

Polish

Pogonowski, Iwo Cyprian. *Polish–English, English–Polish Dictionary*. New York: Hippocrene Books. 2001.